PRAISE FOR *THE SHADOW WOMEN*

"Angela Hunt's finest work yet....In-depth research, breathtaking pacing, and superb character development...a victory for biblical fiction. This is a keeper for years to come."
— Lisa E. Samson, author of *The Church Ladies*

"From the first words, the reader can hear the music, feel the rhythm of the ancient Egyptian and Hebrew cultures. THE SHADOW WOMEN is rich in detail, enlightened with the surprise of insight."
— Janet Chester Bly, author of *Hope Lives Here*

"Hunt is a master at weaving fact and fiction....THE SHADOW WOMEN raises the bar on the genre of biblical fiction...[and] far surpasses Cecil B. DeMille's *The Ten Commandments*."
— *CCM Magazine*

"Thrums like an ancient harp playing the songs of the women who dwelled in the shadow of Moses....This is a great welcome in biblical fiction. Hunt's heart-pounding prose ignites your senses and makes you want to cheer!"
— Patricia Hickman, author of *Sandpebbles*

"Only Angela Elwell Hunt could write THE SHADOW WOMEN. Her meticulous research brought the biblical account of Moses to life with a fresh and vivid reality."
— Colleen Coble, author of *Wyoming*

"Touched my heart and challenged my faith...a masterful job.... Hunt weaves a story that wouldn't let me go despite the fact that I already know how it ends. She uses real people to bring history alive and challenges us all to dare to walk with a God 'who is not benign.'"
— Janelle Schneider, author of *Grace Happens*

"An imaginative epic....Hunt's research and superb storytelling have created a masterpiece. This poignant story breathes life into the historical figure of Moses. It is also a vivid portrayal of a holy God who is always just, but seldom safe."
— *CBA Marketplace* magazine

ANGELA ELWELL HUNT

The
SHADOW
WOMEN

WARNER
Faith™

A Division of AOL Time Warner Book Group

Scripture quotations are from *The Five Books of Moses,* by Everett Fox (New York: Schocken Books, 1995).

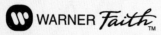

WARNER *Faith*™

A Division of AOL Time Warner Book Group

Warner Books, Inc.
1271 Avenue of the Americas, New York, NY 10020
Visit our Web site at www.twbookmark.com

Printed in the United States of America
Originally published in hardcover by Warner Books, Inc.
First Trade Printing: October 2003
10 9 8 7 6 5 4 3 2 1

The Library of Congress has cataloged the hardcover edition as follows:

Hunt, Angela Elwell
      The shadow women / Angela Elwell Hunt.
            p. cm.
      ISBN 0-446-53011-5
            1. Moses (Biblical leader)—Fiction. 2. Bible. O.T.—History of
Biblical events—Fiction. I. Title

PS3558.U46747 S48 2002
813'.54—dc21
ISBN: 0-446-69232-8 (pbk.)   2002071337

Book design by Mada Design, Inc. / NYC
Hand Lettering by Ron Zinn
Cover design by Don Puckey
Cover illustration by Robert Hunt

ACKNOWLEDGMENTS

I owe thanks to the following wonderful people:

To the novelists of ChiLibris, who allowed me to pester
them with several head-scratching questions while I was
writing.

To Susan Richardson, who volunteered to read very
rough drafts and made many astute observations.

To my secret pal, who bolsters my flagging confidence
with helpful suggestions and early morning phone calls.

To Rolf Zettersten, Leslie Peterson, and the other folks
at Warner who gave me this opportunity to revisit ancient
history.

To Mark Buchanan, whose excellent book *Your God Is
Too Safe* inspired many of the thematic issues that fueled
my thoughts.

Men stand at center stage,

Spotlighted, examined, scorned or applauded—

Yet women move in the curtained shadows,

Moving, motivating, molding

With words and whispers.

If not for shadow women there would be no play.

—Darien Haynes, Reflections

BOOK ONE

EGYPT, THE BLACK LAND

Now a new king arose over Egypt, who had not known Yosef. He said to his people: Here (this) people, the Children of Israel, is many-more and mightier (in number) than we! Come-now, let us use our wits against it, lest it become many-more, and then, if war should occur, it too be added to our enemies and make war upon us or go up away from the land!

So they set gang-captains over it, to afflict it with their burdens. It built storage-cities for Pharaoh—Pitom and Ra'amses . . .

Now Pharaoh commanded all his people, saying: Every son that is born, throw him into the Nile, but let every daughter live.

Now a man from the house of Levi went and took (to wife) a daughter of Levi. The woman became pregnant and bore a son. When she saw him—that he was goodly, she hid him for three months. And when she was no longer able to hide him, she took for him a little ark of papyrus, she loamed it with loam and with pitch, placed the child in it, and placed it in the reeds by the shore of the Nile.

EXODUS 1:8–11; 2:1–3

MIRYAM

In my seventh year, as the waters of the inundation rose to cover our fields, I noticed a subtle change in my mother. Yokheved, who usually hurried from one task to the next in thin-lipped concentration, became quiet and dreamy. She hummed the old songs as she worked the dough and cut the reeds, and at night she lit the lamp in our small hut and murmured her evening prayers with renewed fervency.

Neither my father nor my mother explained this change, and my little brother, Aharon, knew nothing of women—at three, he cared for little more than his next meal. My aunt Adah, however, who had always longed for a little girl, drew me onto her lap one afternoon and spoke of the secret my mother carried.

"Your mother, Yokheved, is going to have a baby," she whispered, the corners of her eyes crinkling. "And if the God of our fathers is faithful, this baby will grow to be a man strong enough to deliver us from this bondage."

I knew nothing of bondage then, for we children were as free as the birds who lived in the marsh, but I knew babies were dangerous. Twice in the last month Pharaoh's soldiers had come into our village and taken boy babies away from their weeping mothers. Though no one would tell me what happened to those baby boys, I knew. Once I followed the soldiers to the edge of the marsh, where their boat waited. They climbed aboard the vessel with the crying baby, but as the boat drifted into the river's current, one of them dropped the baby over the side as if it were of no more importance than dung. I heard a splash, then nothing but silence as the baby disappeared forever.

Why did my mother think the Egyptians would not come for *her* baby boy?

My eyes fell upon my brother, Aharon, whose life, everyone assured me, was a sort of miracle. The midwives who attended my brother's birth had been supposed to kill him in Pharaoh's name, but they would not. Those two old women did not look capable of killing anyone, and they often patted my head when they came to our village. But they always rejoiced more over the birth of boys than the arrival of baby girls, and their obvious preference puzzled me.

Why should boys be more celebrated than girls? Girls did all the work in the village. Girls grew into women who bore the babies and cooked the meals. Women told the stories and said the prayers. Boys grew into men who got up every morning, went away for a few hours, came back, ate dinner, and went to sleep.

So why were they so prized?

Aharon was certainly nothing special. He was like one of the dogs that lived in our village—always following, always rubbing against my leg, always sticking his nose into my things. Yet my mother doted upon him, pulling him onto her lap at night while she crooned the old songs until he had fallen asleep. . . .

I do not remember her *ever* singing to me.

"This new baby," Aunt Adah said as she fondly patted my leg, "might be the leader for which we have been praying."

This remark caught my attention. Not many of the women in our village prayed at all; a few actually presented offerings to carved statues of the Egyptian gods. But my mother prayed to an unseen God she could not even call by name.

"So you must help your mother more in the days ahead," Adah continued, "and you must keep her secret from the others as long as you can.

And the Egyptians must never, ever know that a new baby has been born in Amram's house."

I nodded, knowing that Adah would take my silence for agreement, while I wondered why things in our house had to change. I did not want another brother; I did not want to have to help my mother keep a secret. Most of all, I did not want my mother to do anything that would bring the Egyptians to our village.

But I was only a girl, and a little one at that. So no one asked what I wanted.

No one seemed to care.

MERYTAMON

On the first day of the third month of akhet, the season of flood, in the fifth year of the reign of King Ramesses II, my mother told me I would soon marry a god.

The thought made a shivering rise from my belly. Marriage itself did not frighten me—I had lived among wives of the god for all my fourteen years. Since lying in the arms of a god did not make them overanxious, I did not fear marriage to the king.

Nor did Pharaoh's divine nature alarm me—though then he was not so familiar as in later years, I had seen him laugh. Once, when he returned from a hunting trip, I saw him bleed from a cut on the arm. Though he lived among us as the incarnation of Horus, I knew a cloak of flesh solidly concealed the burning spark of divinity.

Neither did the shivering in my soul have anything to do with marriage to my father—in truth, I hoped to know him better. As king, he had countless wives and concubines, and pharaohs before him routinely married their daughters and sisters. Since the time of Narmer, the great king who united Upper and Lower Egypt, whoever married the Great Royal Wife possessed the right to sit upon the throne of the Two Kingdoms. My mother was Nefertari, bearer of the king's firstborn son, Great Royal Wife and Lady of the Two Lands. She was Isis to us, God's Wife, God's Mother, Sweet of Love and Beautiful of Face.

The trembling in my belly rose from an empty place . . . a fear that what should be was not, therefore what must be might never occur. If my fears proved true, how could I be Isis to Egypt? How could I please the god my father if I could not bear children? For despite my daily sacrifices to the gods, I had not yet begun to bleed as women should.

"Mistress, be still. I cannot apply the kohl if you jiggle on the bench."

Though Nema, my handmaid, was but a Cushite slave and a full two years younger than me, I obediently stilled my nervous knees and lifted my gaze to the adorned ceiling in my chamber. Nema dipped a smooth-tipped rod of alabaster into a jar, then clucked her tongue. I closed my eyes as the rod swept over my quivering eyelids with gentle strokes, leaving trails of ground malachite. The priests say evil may enter the body through the five orifices of the head, and the eyes are the most easily breached. Since malachite magically prevents access, I have never neglected this aspect of my toilette. I would never appear before Pharaoh with unadorned eyes.

When Nema finished, I lifted the bronze hand mirror and stared at my reflection. My deep-set eyes appeared even wider and deeper with the outlining of black kohl. The green glittered above my lashes like the summer waters of the Nile, and my lips shone with an application of red ochre mixed with oil.

"Very good." I lowered the mirror and stood. Without a word, Nema moved to a carved chest, then lifted out a garment of white linen. Ordinarily I would wear a long linen gown held up by shoulder straps, but the Beautiful Festival of Opet called for more elaborate attire.

First, Nema draped me in a fine shift that covered my body from chest to ankles, then she dressed me in a transparent pleated robe that opened below the waist and brushed the floor. The garment was similar to those worn by the priests, except the women's version gathered over the left breast and left the right exposed. A short, fringed sleeve left my forearm bare, the better to reveal my heavy gold and silver bracelets. As an added touch, one that signified my high standing, Nema fastened a golden belt around my waist.

Nearly ready, I returned to the stool at my dressing tray and gripped the carved armrests. Nema furiously brushed my clipped hair, then wiped oil on her pink palms and smoothed my hair into submission. Finally, she lifted my heavy wig from its stand.

I tightened my grip on the bench as she tugged the wig into place. I have seen pictures of former kings and their consorts and envied them their compact wigs. But Ramesses was mightier, richer, and more powerful than any king in history, and his women had to reflect his glory. So my woolen wig, like my mother's, was long, heavy, and intricately woven with gold beads. A handsome tiara of turquoise, lapis lazuli, and gold sparkled from atop the fountain of braids.

"There." Nema pressed her hands together and backed away, her head bowed in obeisance. "You look every inch a royal lady."

My stomach, which had settled under Nema's steady ministrations, lurched upward. I was not one of the king's women, not yet, but everyone seemed determined to move me from my mother's apartment to the royal harem.

Rising upon legs that felt as hollow as river reeds, I smoothed the wrinkles from the fabric at my belly. "Are the others assembling outside?"

"Wait, my lady, and I will see."

Nema turned on the ball of her bare foot, then moved silently toward the carved door and the hall beyond.

The day was an auspicious one, another holiday for the house of Pharaoh and the entire kingdom of Egypt. Twenty-four days ago, the Festival of Opet had begun at the temple of Karnak in Thebes. With my mother, my brothers, and me in attendance, along with more priests than I could count, Pharaoh had presented offerings to Amon-Re and Mut, the goddess wife of Amon, then burned incense and poured out purified water in front of the festival barques of Amon, Mut, and Khonsu, god of love and fertility. With the idols that represented the three gods, we boarded highly decorated barques that sailed upriver.

Once we reached Opet, the citizens of that city came out to pay homage to Pharaoh as he descended. As priests carried the barques of the three deities to their shrines, we of the king's family strode past sacrificial altars, musicians, and jubilant dancers. With the aromas of frankincense and roasting meat filling our nostrils, we followed Pharaoh to the temple. When he had finished offering additional sacrifices to Amon-Re and Mut, we retired to a royal residence in the city.

Today we would offer more sacrifices, my father would reenter the temple's holy place to be strengthened by Amon-Re, and the festival would draw to a close.

I, for one, was glad. Though Opet was lovely, with a grand temple built by Amenhotep III, Thebes felt like home in a way the southern city never could.

The door opened; Nema bowed again. "Your mother and sisters are assembling in the hall."

"I am ready." Though the thought of facing my father—soon to be my husband—sent a tremor scooting up the back of my neck, I stood, accepted the palm-leaf fan Nema pressed into my hand, then lifted my chin and stepped into the hallway.

The atmosphere outside my small chamber vibrated with the voices of excited women and children. Not all of Pharaoh's family had made the trip, of course, only his most favored wives and offspring above the age of ten years. Pharaoh's wife Isnofret and her daughter, Bint-Anath, stood closest to me, inclining their heads as they smiled in greeting. Bint-Anath was a year younger than me, shorter, and more rounded. Though she often seemed empty-headed, I liked her and found her mother pleasant company. But Isnofret was a lesser wife and her daughter a lesser daughter, so I affectionately squeezed my half sister's hand, then threaded my way through the crowd of royal women and children. I sought the light of my universe, Nefertari.

I found my mother at the end of the hallway, standing apart from the others in a deliberate aloofness. As Nefertari turned to survey the noisy group behind us, I saw signs of suffering in her face. Thin lines appeared around her lips, and her heavily painted eyes were half closed. As a tear leaked from one of them, I realized my mother was in agony. Again.

She regularly suffered from excruciating headaches, and thus far none of the royal physicians had been able to cure her malady. When the head pains struck, she could not bear noise or sunlight. Retiring to her chambers, she often took to her bed, pale, trembling, and unable to eat, but when duty demanded that she appear before the king, she obeyed. 'Twould be unthinkable to refuse.

"Mother." I slipped my arm about her waist. "Can nothing be done for you today?"

Wordlessly she lowered her head to mine. The weight of her ponderous wig added to my own, but I bore the burden gladly. We stood for a moment in silence, one offering sympathy, the other, pain.

She straightened as the door beside her creaked upon its leather hinges. One of the white-robed priests of Amon stood beyond it, lifting his hand in a come-forward gesture.

I released my mother and stepped back to take my place in line, then followed her through the open doorway guarded by a pair of white-robed priests. My mother would occupy the honored place at the front of the procession, for Nefertari, Beloved of Pharaoh, was a marvel, a beauty like no other. Sometimes I could not believe the gods had been good enough to fashion me in her womb. Nema often said I looked much like my mother, but I did not dare hope to equal her in beauty. When I entered his chamber, Pharaoh would see me as a pretender, a skinny shadow of the wife he loved best.

Now, like me, Nefertari wore the colors of malachite and kohl and ochre upon her chiseled features; she also wore a sheer garment of pleated linen. We were nearly the same height with a similar cast to our features, but there the resemblance ended. My body was yet young and unformed; motherhood had molded hers into soft curves. My belly was flat; hers, a gentle mound. My breasts resembled the budding fruit of a palm tree; hers recalled the round ripeness of melons.

The most striking difference in our appearance, however, lay in our headpieces—I wore a simple tiara in my wig, while the golden cobra of Egypt rested upon my mother's forehead, the symbol of Wadjet, the goddess who traditionally offered the crown of Lower Egypt to Pharaoh.

As I followed her, behind me shuffled the other children of Nefertari—my brothers Amon-hirwonmef and Prehirwonmef, and my sister, Mertatum. They were followed by Isnofret and her daughter, who were trailed by lesser wives and their children.

As we snaked through the freshly scrubbed halls of the palace, the priests' music, complete with the rattle of *sistra,* the clicking of *crotals,* and the thump of drums, heralded our approach . . . sounds that could bring only more discomfort to my suffering mother.

∽∾∽

I had been visiting the temple at Opet for years, but never before had I looked about and considered that I would soon be married to the god for whom the temple had been designed. As the son of Horus, Pharaoh was the intermediary between men and the gods, the one who made offerings and recited the prayers that ensured the sun's successful journey through the night. He alone made certain that the river known to us as Hap-Ur would rise and bless us with bounty, the crops would yield a full harvest, and our livestock would thrive and reproduce. The priests who made these offerings throughout the land merely represented him; everyone knew our lives depended upon Pharaoh.

And this man would soon become my *husband.* I would be like my mother, connected to these temples in practice and in purpose. Yet if I could not have children when the land demanded fertility . . .

In earlier dynasties, if famine descended upon the land, the king would offer his life in sacrifice for the people. Wearing the jackal mask of Anubis, a priest-executioner would present Pharaoh with a cobra in a basket. Duty required the king to offer his arm to the poisonous snake, and the resulting bite usually resulted in a relatively quick death. The priests would then bury the king's heart and lungs in order to infuse the famine-stricken earth with divine life.

Egypt had not experienced the sacrifice of a pharaoh in generations, but still the procedure troubled me. Though no precedent existed for sacrificing a barren queen, the principle remained—of what use was a royal wife who could not bear children? How could the gods bless Egypt if the one who represented Isis, the mother of all, could not give birth?

Troubling thoughts furrowed my brow as we strode out into the morning. The air was warm and burnished with sunlight that arced off the flooded Nile in starbursts. A crowd of onlookers applauded our appearance while musicians strummed lyres and dancers leaped to the rhythm of the sistra.

The facade of the temple faced the rising sun, but the building seemed dwarfed by the magnificence of six colossal statues and two obelisks built by Amenhotep III. Behind me, the undisciplined younger children gasped at the sight of the pharaoh statues, now adorned in wreaths of flowers and glittering golden robes.

We passed through the colonnade and two rows of papyrus columns, where a hypostyle hall opened into the inner temple. Reliefs on the temple wall depicted Amenhotep's birth and his royal parentage. The flower-strewn barques of the three gods who had accompanied us from Thebes rested here, and the heady scent of fresh-cut blossoms wafted toward us on the breeze.

As a double line of priests appeared from the side vestibules, we were escorted into a chamber, then to the doorway of a shrine containing the three deities to whom this temple was dedicated—Amon-Re, patron god of Thebes; Mut, the mother goddess of the sky; and Khonsu, son of Amon-Re and Mut as well as the god of fertility. As we watched, the rising sun shone through the roofless temple and gilded the three enthroned figures. Again a murmur rose from the younger children, followed by shushing sounds from their mothers.

At a signal from the priest, the younger children sank to the floor, sitting cross-legged in a silent row as a pair of bronze doors opened. As a mature woman, I stood with the king's wives at a respectful distance, for only Pharaoh could enter the shrine and approach the gods. I watched breathlessly as my father, the second to call himself Ramesses, came into the anteroom and observed us, his spellbound subjects.

I had always thought my father a handsome man, and his appearance this morning elicited awe from all of us. He wore the *hemhemet*, the ram's horn crown, a tall helmet featuring curved horns, the cobra uraeus, and the two feathers worn only by gods. His dark eyes had been painted with bold lines, and his mouth was set and serious. He wore a long white robe of spotless linen, and when he entered the shrine I saw the gleam of golden sandals on his feet.

As the all-powerful sun god, Re was the only deity to whom Pharaoh owed allegiance, but in order to ensure that local gods were not offended, the name Re was attached to others, thus allowing Pharaoh to worship them as well. But Re was everything to us—he was Khepri at dawn, Re at noon, Atum at night. He was also Horus, the horizon-dweller, who each day sailed across the sky in his Boat of Millions of Years. Re begat Geb, the earth, and Nut, the sky. The waxing and waning of the moon was the monthly restoration of his eye by the god Thoth. Re was the heavenly form of Amon, the hidden god who birthed himself, and so Amon-Re was the most powerful god in all creation. Re was the Living King, while Osiris was the Dead King. My father, therefore, was Re, or Horus, and as his daughter I carried a spark of divinity within my frame.

We of Pharaoh's household watched in silence as the king accepted offerings of frankincense from the priests, then held them up before the stone statues in the shrine. Behind him, the priests chanted in song, while sweet aromas infused the atmosphere. The streaming sun touched my skin, warming it as I watched my father make his sacrifices to the gods.

"O Amon-Re, stand up, see that which your son has done for you! Awake, hear that which Horus has done for you!"

My thoughts wandered as the priests sang and Pharaoh offered incense in a bronze censer. Many of my siblings had chosen a favorite god, just as many Egyptian cities had elected a patron deity, but I was uncertain which god I should choose. My mother followed Taweret, the protector of women in childbirth, but I had not been able to summon any adoration for the goddess depicted with a hippo's head, a crocodile's tail, a lion's claws, and a woman's breasts. Why should I follow Taweret, when she had not yet ripened my womb?

My favorite god—and my reason for favoring him was inexplicable, even to me—was Khnum, the divine potter, whose name was written in the shape of a vase. His physical form was only slightly more pleasing than Taweret's, but at least he had a human body. With the head of a flat-horned ram, his no-nonsense expression appealed to me.

Khnum, the priests said, created the other gods, the divine kings, and all mortals at his potter's wheel. Divine beings were made of gold, while mortal men were fashioned of the reddish brown mud lining the banks of Hap-Ur. Somehow it seemed logical that the creator of all other gods should be favored above all others. Or perhaps I liked him most because I knew the daughter of Pharaoh and the Great Royal Wife must have been created from gold.

My father turned, drawing my attention as his praise to the gods continued: "He has caused Thoth to turn back for you the followers of Seth. He has seized your enemy for you, so he is beheaded together with his followers; there is not one whom he has spared!"

From a golden platter, Pharaoh took several small balls of incense, then fed them to a fire in a bowl. Beside him, two lashless priests, shorn of all body hair, repeated my father's offering, chanting all the while. Behind them, several other priests lay prostrate, muttering prayers into the tiles.

"He has beaten for you him who beats you," Pharaoh chanted. "He has killed for you him who kills you. He has bound for you him who binds you."

At a side doorway another group of priests appeared, bearing a gilded litter loaded with a mound of fruit, scented meats, and drink. This food offering was presented to my father, who bent and lifted each element, symbolically offering it to the gods.

The priests, who would do this in Pharaoh's place when he had returned to Thebes, sang out their praises during the ritual: "O lord of green fields, rejoice this day! Osiris will henceforth be among you; Horus will go forth in his environs. Horus will live on that upon which you live. O Bulls of Atum! Make Horus green! Refresh Horus more than the Red Crown which is upon his head, more than the floodwaters which are upon his thighs, more than the dates which are in his fist!"

Pharaoh stepped aside as one of the chief priests came forward and faced us, the royal family. Shifting my weight, I tried to imitate my mother's regal expression. The priest was about to tell the story of Isis and Osiris, which I'd heard hundreds of times before. But the story was elemental to our family, to Egypt, so I knew it would be told again.

"Isis and Osiris were sister and brother, husband and wife," the priest began.

Though I kept my head turned in the storyteller's direction, my gaze shifted to the man who stood motionless in a stream of sunlight. My divine father.

The priest pressed his hands together and narrowed his gaze as he looked down at the smaller children. "Osiris brought civilization to Egypt, bringing towns and farms from the great chaos of flood. Osiris freed us from misery, then he left Egypt to bring civilization to the rest of the world, leaving Isis to watch over Seth, their evil brother."

The shadow of a smile played at the corner of my father's mouth, and it took every bit of willpower for me to resist turning my head to follow his gaze. Was that smile for my mother or Isnofret?

"Upon Osiris's return," the priest continued, "Seth obtained his brother's exact measurements and constructed a wooden box to fit him precisely. During a banquet for the gods, he offered the box as a gift to whomever could fit into it, but of course no one could . . . except Osiris. When he settled inside the chest, the evil Seth sealed the lid, poured molten lead over it, and had it thrown into Hap-Ur, where Osiris died. A storm then carried the box to Lebanon, where it washed up in the branches of a huge tree. Later, the king cut down the tree and found the box with Osiris's body."

Carefully, I turned my head and looked directly at my father, quite certain he hadn't been smiling at me. I was right—his gaze was not turned in my direction, but in my mother's. His small smile had faded, and a vertical line now filled the space between his brows.

I felt the familiar trembling rise in my belly. Was that look a sign of concern or displeasure?

"When Isis learned what had happened to Osiris," the priest droned on, "she had the body returned to Egypt. But before she could give her husband a proper burial, Seth stole the body and chopped it into fourteen pieces, then scattered them throughout Egypt. But Isis eventually recovered the pieces and reassembled the body. Transforming herself into a bird, she hovered over his body and brought him back to life by reciting magical words. Shortly after this, their son Horus was born, and he waged a victorious battle to avenge his father's death and punish the evildoer Seth."

Relieved smiles wreathed the faces of the younger children. Glancing back at them, I caught Bint-Anath's eye and nodded. We both knew the priest had simplified the story for the sake of the younger ones. Our tutors had subjected us to a longer, more explicit, and much more uncomfortable version of the legend.

At the tale's conclusion, our father stepped forward and surveyed his wives and offspring. "As children of a god"—his painted gaze swept over us—"you must understand one crucial thing: Life is eternal. Those who came before us now walk in the afterlife, and those whose hearts were uncluttered with evil deeds are enjoying the next world. But those whose hearts were heavy with evil have been thrown to the devourer, a monster with the body of a crocodile and the head of a hippopotamus."

I smothered a smile as one of the younger princes screwed up his face in distaste. 'Twould not be wise to laugh in the midst of a dire warning from Pharaoh.

"I do not believe any of my children will suffer such a fate," my father continued, his tone softening. "And so I send you out with this command: Keep your heart as light as the feather of ma'at, and honor the god, your father. Then all will be well with you and Egypt will be blessed."

That remark apparently completed our lesson. A pair of priests opened another set of gilded doors, and the younger children departed first. My mother and I turned toward the exit, awaiting our turn, and on an impulse I glanced back to look again at my father. I rarely saw him, save on public occasions, and last year he had spent months away from us, engaged in a military campaign against the Hittites.

He was still standing apart from the priests, his arms locked behind his back. My mother had again captured his attention, though she did not seem to realize it. I thought I saw a flicker of compassion in my father's eyes, but could not be sure. For my mother's sake, I hoped he had noticed her pain and appreciated all she had endured to come here today.

I stopped breathing when the king's gaze met mine. I felt a rush of guilt, as if I'd been caught in the worst kind of trespass, but his expression remained impassive, neither softening nor hardening. As my cheeks burned, I lowered my traitorous eyes and focused on the gleaming tiles at my feet. Did he know who I was? Did he know we were soon to be wed? Did he care?

I turned toward the door, tapping my foot against the tiles as my royal siblings filed out. I wanted to flee, to take off my heavy wig, to find a place of quiet and darkness for my mother. Then a thought occurred to me, one that might not have crossed my heart if I had not learned I would soon become part of the harem: When a king has dozens of wives and even more concubines, why should he concern himself with the feelings of one girl?

∽

Two days later, after the king had offered his final gifts, the temple attendants sang, "How glad is the temple of Amon-Re at the Beautiful Festival of Opet," while a team of bareheaded priests carried the gods to the river in portable barques. The largest barque, belonging to Amon, featured ram's-head ornaments at the bow and stern. Mut's boat had been adorned with the painted heads of two women, each wearing a vulture skin, while falcon heads jutted from the bow and stern of Khonsu's vessel. As the priestly bearers carried the sacred barques along the processional way, other priests paced along the route with swinging censers, perfuming their short journey with burning turpentine-resin.

My royal siblings and I followed the priests, trying to mask our eagerness to return home with pious expressions. I walked beside Bint-Anath, my palms pressed together and my head bowed, grateful that she seemed sufficiently awed by the ceremony to keep quiet. I was not in the mood to answer questions or share small talk. My mother was still not well, and none of my questions about marriage to Pharaoh had been answered.

The god's portable ceremonial boats bore little resemblance to the floating temples that waited at the quayside. Amon, Mut, and Khonsu would each ride in painted vessels as long as fifteen men lying end-to-end, glorious barques built from the finest firs of Lebanon and decorated with gold, silver, copper, turquoise, and lapis lazuli. The hull of Amon's barque bore images of the king performing rituals in his honor. The Great House, in which the portable boat, statue, and other divine objects were sheltered, rose from the center of the bridge. In front of this cabin, brightly colored pennants fluttered from four poles between a pair of obelisks.

Pharaoh's ceremonial barque, which was nearly as ostentatious as Amon's, waited at the docks, too, along with less ornate boats for the king's wives and children. Once the three gods and members of the royal family had safely boarded, uniformed soldiers from Pharaoh's army towed us to the main channel of Hap-Ur. Moving to the crack of overseers' whips, there the king's warriors unfastened the towing lines and freed us to ride the current back to Thebes.

As the daughter of Nefertari, the Great Royal Wife, I stood on the deck of the fifth barque and watched it cut through the heavy winter waters and leave a shining wake on the silver water. Ahead of us, the ceremonial barques of Amon-Re, Mut, and Khonsu elicited shouts of praise from the celebrants on shore, and men bowed low before the fourth vessel in which my father rode. They would bow to us, too, but only nod to the lesser wives' boats that trailed behind us.

A swarm of watercraft of every shape and size waited to accompany us, including an adorable merchant's boat in the shape of a bird. As my brothers and I drank in the sights and sounds from the railing of our ship, the fruit merchant aboard the bird-boat called out to us, attempting to entice us with jokes and silly smiles. Merrymakers tossed flowers and greenery toward our vessel while spectators poured from the temporary tents and drinking booths to catch a glimpse of the royal procession.

The scents of cooking food and manure wafted across the river as we sailed north. I gazed out at tethered oxen, gazelles, ibex, and oryx, knowing they would soon be slaughtered and grilled in the makeshift markets. While the blood-splashed butchers wrestled with heavy animal carcasses, Libyan dancers thumped their drums while dancing girls, naked to the waist, leaped and spun to the pervading rhythm. I rose on tiptoe, trying to watch the people on shore, then groaned in frustration. Pharaoh's royal guards, whose chariots kept pace with us on the black ribbon of soil between the water and the temporary festival booths, kept blocking my view.

Celebration reigned over the crowd. The people of Egypt had taken pleasure in nearly a month of eating, drinking, dancing, and shouting. They had enjoyed a splendid view of their gods and their king, and they undoubtedly realized anew that their lives and prosperity were indelibly entwined with the divine pharaoh who had escorted Amon on the journey between his two great shrines.

All was well in Egypt, and the land would prosper for another year.

While my brothers jostled for position along the railing, I crossed my arms and tried to behave like a mature woman. Three months before, the waters of Hap-Ur had been the bright green verdigris that grows on brass, but the inundation had flushed the green away. The waters beside us were gray, heavy with silt that would flood our fields and imbue them with life and fertility. Because of these dark waters our kingdom was called the Black Land, but due to these waters our land was also called Beautiful.

I turned as the wind flecked the surface of the river with wavelets and clicked the beads of my braids against each other. My mother, I noticed, did not come up to enjoy the passage but remained below deck, where she had a private compartment. Feeling that I had endured more than a fair share of my royal siblings' chatter, I descended the narrow wooden stairs and rapped on the door of the small stateroom.

Her slave, a Nubian woman called Huda, lifted a brow when she recognized me. I glanced beyond her, but could not see my mother, so something was amiss.

"May I see your mistress?" I offered the question in politeness; I fully intended to enter. Only Pharaoh himself could keep me from my mother's room if I thought she needed me.

"Is that you, Merytamon?"

The voice came from beneath a mound of fabric upon the narrow bed. Moving past Huda, I knelt at the bedside. "It is I, Mother. Are you well?"

There were no windows in the small chamber, but still the willful rays of Re found their way into the space through chinks and crevices in the deck flooring. A corner of the fabric lifted, and in the shadows I saw my mother's dark eyes shining wetly. "It is my head. The light hurts, and the sounds of the children—"

"Shall I command them to be quiet?"

She wriggled two fingers at me. "That is asking too much. They are excited about the sights of the journey."

Her eyes closed, and Huda stepped forward with a wet cloth. "Here, my lady, is another cool compress," she said, folding the cloth until it fit into the palm of her hand.

I lifted the veil as Huda placed the compress on my mother's temple. She groaned softly at the cool touch, then motioned toward the veil. Obediently, I dropped the dark fabric back into place. "Is there nothing I can do?"

As her slender hand crept out from beneath the veiling, I caught it and held it tight. "The physician will come to me," she whispered, "when we reach the palace. He has treated me many times."

I stayed with her until we reached Thebes; then I helped her off the barque and onto the dock. She grimaced as trumpeters heralded our arrival, but I signaled for one of her servants, who promptly summoned a litter. We climbed inside, and within moments we found ourselves en route to the palace.

As the Great Royal Wife, my mother had her own spacious apartments in Pharaoh's house, and I heard her sigh in relief as we crossed the threshold. Her servants scurried to bring her wine and food, but she held one hand over her eyes and staggered to her bedroom, then dropped onto her bed.

"Please, Merytamon." She closed her eyes. "Send Huda for Tanut-amon. He will know what to do."

Less than an hour had passed on the water clock when the priest appeared. I had seen Tanut-amon in my mother's apartments many times, for either she or one of her servants often had need of a physician-priest. But never had I felt compelled to remain in his presence . . . and hope that I might ask him a question.

Tanut-amon was a small man of perhaps forty-five years, a bald priest who wore a short white robe and carried a round tummy within it. Nodding at me in greeting, he did not ask my mother of her complaint, but immediately set about preparing an unguent for her headache. I watched as he removed a mortar from a leather case, then mixed dill seeds with bryony, coriander, donkey's fat, and two plants I didn't recognize. "Daughter of Pharaoh,"—he turned to me with the bowl in his hand—"apply this to the painful area and leave it upon the spot until the pain subsides."

I took the bowl, sniffed it, and made a face.

His mouth thinned. "It will help her."

"And if it does not?"

"Then we must explore other possibilities."

"What sort of possibilities?"

"Surgery." He pressed his hands together. "Your mother presents a troubling situation. The pain grows worse and persists longer each time she suffers. I fear we may have to release the bad humors built up in her head, but I cannot do that without informing Pharaoh. The king must give his permission."

With no choice but to trust him, I dipped an ivory spoon into the salve, then smoothed some of the malodorous mixture onto my mother's temple. The cool touch of the mixture seemed to relax her, and the physician nodded in satisfaction.

"You see?" He beamed at me. "Do not doubt the king's physician, daughter of Pharaoh. The healing wisdom of the gods has been given to me."

I lowered the applicator back into the bowl, then set it on a tray and glanced around the bedroom. Huda had gone to unpack my mother's clothing chests, so the priest and I were alone . . . as I had hoped we would be.

"Forgive me for doubting." I inclined my head in a sign of respect. "I know Amon has gifted you. Is not my father's health a sure sign of your skill?"

The bantam priest threw back his shoulders. "You are astute, daughter of Pharaoh."

"As are you." I mustered a smile. "And I wonder if you have healing wisdom for me? I have a question about a personal matter, and would not ask it of anyone untrustworthy or unreliable."

A ripple appeared in the flesh where his brows had been shaven away. "Are you ill?"

"Not ill—but perplexed. And if you can help, I would be indebted to you forever."

Tanut-amon pressed his palms together and inclined his head in a deep gesture. "You have but to speak, and I will give whatever aid I can."

I glanced at my mother, who appeared to sleep upon her bed. Her eyes were closed, her breathing steady.

"What I will tell you"—I spoke in a low, distinct voice—"must remain between us. No one else is to know."

"No one but Pharaoh," he countered. "We should not keep secrets from the divine king."

Running my hand over the carved pillars of my mother's bed, I considered the implication of his words. Tanut-amon obviously felt that keeping a confidence from his divine king would be akin to blasphemy, but Pharaoh must not know about my problem.

I looked the little man directly in the eye. "Did you tell Pharaoh what you ate for breakfast this morning?"

The priest laughed. "Why would I risk the king's displeasure with such trivial news?"

Nodding, I sank onto the foot of my mother's bed. "Exactly. And why would you risk his displeasure by telling him of our conversation? If he asks if I am ill, Tanut-amon, you may tell him, but if he does not ask, why bother him? Besides, since he is a god, he undoubtedly knows all things of importance without our having to speak to him."

Appreciation sparkled in the old man's eyes. "You are clever, daughter of Pharaoh. You have something of your grandfather Seti in you."

I smiled. I had been born in Seti's reign, but had few clear memories of him. What I did have was a thorough knowledge of Pharaoh's court. The most dangerous weapon in the palace was gossip, which could inflict a lethal wound even upon a member of Pharaoh's household.

But I had to trust someone, and who better than my mother's priest?

"I need your help"—I lowered my gaze from the physician's piercing eyes—"because though I have passed fourteen years, I have not begun to bleed in the way of women. And my mother says I must soon marry the king."

The priest's jaws wobbled for a moment, then he lifted his hand. "Stand, daughter."

I did.

"Turn, please. Slowly."

I obeyed, feeling a bit self-conscious as his gaze roved over my body. The sheer garment I wore concealed little from him, and after a moment he grunted softly and pointed toward the stool by the bed.

"Sit," he said, his voice gruff. "It is not unusual for some girls to mature later than others."

I smothered a hiss of exasperation as I sank to a stool. "I know this. I've grown up in a household of women, and I've read all the medical papyri."

He shot me a look of surprise.

Lifting my chin, I met his skeptical gaze straight on. "I like to read. I read everything I can get from the House of Life."

The aged priest's eyes crinkled for an instant, then he laughed, muffling the sound with his palm as he rubbed it over his mouth.

"Your mother mentioned that you are a scholar. Well, scholar, let me explain what I see in you." His hand rose in the air, tracing the straight lines of a boyish figure. "You have matured in heart and voice. You are of marriageable age, but still you possess a girl's body. So the seeds of womanhood within you must not have sprouted."

I leaned forward. "Why not?"

He hesitated, then shook his head. "I cannot be sure, but the gods may have neglected to form a womb within you."

I stared at him. How could such a thing happen? Khnum, my favorite deity, created everyone on his potter's wheel. As Pharaoh's daughter, he had created me from gold, not mud, so how could he have neglected to give a daughter of Isis something as crucial as a *womb*?

I braced my head against my trembling fingertips. "Impossible."

Tanut-amon shrugged. "I may be wrong. After all, there is no way to know for certain unless I open your belly and search—"

"No." I cut him off with a sharp glance. "I will know you are wrong when I give Pharaoh a son."

At the mention of my father's title, the priest bowed his head. "May it be so. And you must call me when you have news. I live to serve you, my lady."

He stood and bowed his way out of the chamber. At the quiet sound of the door latch, my mother's eyes opened.

"You must never tell anyone what Tanut-amon said here," she whispered, her voice heavy with portent. "A wife who cannot give Pharaoh sons is nothing, worthless. You are his daughter, but you are destined to be his wife. You must give him a son."

I lowered my head to meet her teary gaze. "How can I do that, Gentle Mother? If Khnum truly created me without a womb—"

"I will think of something." A flicker of a smile rose at the corner of her mouth, then died out, falling victim to her pain. "I will find a way to protect you, beloved, for you are my firstborn and my favorite."

∿

In view of my approaching wedding, within a week I found myself installed in my own apartment in the palace, complete with additional servants to meet my needs. These would be temporary, the captain of the Great House assured me, for Pharaoh was planning to move his household from Thebes to a new capital at the ancient site of Avaris. He had begun construction years before, but I paid little attention to such matters, for my father loved building even more than he loved women. An endless stream of architects and designers, masons and miners filtered through the palace, but I could never remember details about any of the building sites.

I was grateful for the new apartments and the resulting rise in status, but I was far more concerned about my mother's health. The headache that assailed her at Opet had passed, and Pharaoh's physicians seemed intent upon curing her condition before the next attack occurred.

She did not summon me to her chambers for a week after my move, but the servants told me that Pharaoh himself had dedicated his time to her comfort. Though his days were largely filled with meetings about the progress of the new northern city to be called Pi-Ramesses, he reserved his nights for Nefertari.

Tanut-amon and his fellow physician-priests visited her each day, guarding her health with offerings and prayers. In time, I learned the reason why: They had scheduled a surgical procedure to relieve the malevolent humors that occasionally built up in her head.

I found Tanut-amon in my mother's chamber when I hurried there after hearing the news. "Do not worry, daughter of Pharaoh." He drew me aside as my mother reclined on her couch. "We have completed this trepanning treatment many times. And often our patients are completely healed."

"Often?" A sudden chill climbed the ladder of my spine. "What will you do to her?"

The priest gave me a smile. "First, we shave the head completely. Then, while she rests comfortably upon her couch, we drill a small hole into her skull. When the skull is opened, the bad humors are free to escape, and she will be relieved of her pain. Sometimes, if the pain was severe and persistent, we insert a glass rod and move it back and forth, dislodging the stubborn humors."

The procedure sounded simple—yet still I felt the bitter taste of fear burn the back of my throat.

"If it is so easy," I asked, "why don't all Pharaoh's subjects with headache have this surgery?"

The old man's smile dipped into a frown. "There is a danger, of course. The procedure is not always successful. Opening the body is always a risk, for evil can enter as easily as it can escape. But we will guard your mother with herbs and incantations, and we will do our best to make her well."

His words did not put me at ease, but his confident manner did much to calm my fears. I thanked him for speaking honestly, then went to my mother's couch. Sensing my presence through an intuition I had learned to trust, she opened her eyes and smiled up at me. "Merytamon."

"Royal Mother." I knelt at her side. "Are you well?"

"Yes, and I am glad you have come. I wanted to speak to you before tomorrow."

I lifted my head to meet her gaze. "I wish you would not do this thing. You are not in pain now, are you?"

"I do not ever want to be in pain again. Pharaoh wants me to be free of this agony." Her lovely smile faded a little. "And your father has more important things to worry about than a sick wife. But in these last few days I have been thinking of you."

"Me?"

"Yes." She lowered her voice. "Are you aware, daughter, of the slaves in Goshen? They are a low, common people called the Hebrews."

In truth, I cared little what happened to slaves. If Khnum created mortals of mud, he surely created slaves from dung, but my mother would not be asking me these things without a reason.

I crinkled my brow as I searched my memory. Goshen lay near my father's new city, but it seemed a world away from Thebes. And there were all kinds of slaves in Egypt—Cushites, Nubians, Hittites, Midianites. . . .

I rested my arm on the edge of her bed, then propped my chin on my hand. "I do not believe I have ever seen a Hebrew."

Rising up on one elbow, Mother tapped my wrist with a hennaed fingertip. "Your father fears those he calls 'the dusty ones,' for they have grown mighty and populous in Goshen."

"Why should he fear slaves?"

"Some years ago Pharaoh had a dream," my mother whispered, pushing herself to an upright position. "He woke in the middle of the night, drenched in sweat, and called for the wise men and magicians."

"What was the dream?"

Even now, anxiety radiated from my mother's pale face like a halo around the moon. "Pharaoh stood in the Judgment Hall and saw the scales of justice, but 'twas not his heart being weighed against the feather of ma'at. Instead he saw the elders and nobles of Egypt being weighed against a suckling lamb, and the frail lamb outweighed them. At first, none of his counselors could interpret the dream, then one priest stepped forward and declared that the suckling lamb was an infant who was not of our people. One day, the counselor proclaimed, this child would throw the kingdom into chaos and defeat Egypt. Since the Hebrews were shepherds when they entered our land, your father decided that the infant had to be a male Hebrew. In order to defeat this threat, he ordered all Hebrew baby boys killed."

I sat silently, absorbing this information. In a way, it made sense—if you wanted to stop a race from reproducing, you would destroy all the females, but if you were after a particular child destined to incite a rebellion . . .

Mother stared past me, looking at nothing; then she shifted her gaze and gave me a sad smile. "Two years ago he commanded that the Hebrew midwives kill all the baby boys as they exited the womb, but the midwives claimed Hebrew females gave birth too quickly. The people continued to multiply, and now they are still as abundant as frogs."

I frowned, still not understanding her reason for telling the story. "They are in Goshen, Royal Mother. A world away from us."

She shook her head from side to side, clicking the beads in her intricately braided wig. "Listen, Merytamon. When the midwives failed your father, he called for the magicians and diviners, who looked into the future and told him that water would play a role in the child's death. So Pharaoh's second decree went out: All male Hebrew babies are to be drowned in the river. Your father is now confident that his dream will come to nothing."

I nodded and looked away, not wanting my mother to see how little this information concerned me. Slaves were slaves—Egypt could not function without them—and if the wise men were correct, my father had acted properly. I found it hard to believe that a single slave could overthrow Egypt, but no prophecy could stand if our divine Pharaoh took the appropriate action.

"Pharaoh intends to take you to wife," my mother said, abruptly changing the subject. "You will soon be wed."

I smiled, determined that she should not see my anxiety. "On the next auspicious day."

Leaning forward, she lowered her voice. "Wives who bear sons are honored; wives who do not are sent to the harem and forgotten. If you should need a son, you have but to go to Goshen, where you will find one among the Hebrews. Under the terms of Pharaoh's edict you can take any child you please, but do not let the king know what you have done. In this way, you will give him a son. You will also preserve your honor."

Stunned by her suggestion, I brought my hand to my lips, then sank to the floor. I might have attributed her words to the effects of wine, but she had not been drinking. Love glowed in her eyes, bright and focused, and something in me realized she feared she would not be able to advise me in the future . . . so she had risked dispensing this bit of treasonous advice today.

I rose back to my knees, then covered her hands with my own. "You're going to be fine, Mother. The priests know what they are doing."

"I'm not worried about the surgery. I'm worried about you, Merytamon. I love you . . . and I know what your father expects of a royal wife."

I dropped my eyes before her persistent gaze. "When the time is right, I will consider what you have said."

A masculine voice broke into our conversation: "You would do well to remember your mother's advice." Startled, I turned and saw Tanut-amon standing in the doorway. Apparently, the diminutive priest had heard every word.

My mother squeezed my hands. "Do not fear Tanut-amon. For years I have entrusted him with my confidences."

I accepted this assurance with a nod, but as I rose and made my way past the little priest, I couldn't help wondering what sort of secrets he held for my mother.

～

The next day, drawn by curiosity, love, and a foreboding I could not deny, I slipped through the halls of Pharaoh's palace and entered my mother's chambers. Dressed in a simple linen gown, my mother sat on a bed in the central reception hall. A retinue of white-robed priests surrounded her, speaking to her as she smiled and sipped wine from a goblet. When she saw me, her eyes widened for a moment, then she gave me a confident smile.

I returned her smile, then sat on a small gilded bench against the wall. She had not told me to stay away, but neither had she told me to come. I noticed, however, that I was the only one of her children in the room.

As I leaned against the wall and tried to relax, I noticed that Tanut-amon had brought several priests of Sekhmet to attend my mother. In this procedure, it would be helpful to have the lion-headed goddess of healing interceding on our behalf.

In a far corner, Huda and my mother's other maids knelt before a statue of the goddess, offering sacrifices of incense and fruit. In another corner, a blind harpist strummed a gentle melody that rippled through the air like the rising waters of Hap-Ur.

The scene had been designed to encourage peaceful sleep and rest.

My mother now lay before the physicians on her bed. She folded her hands upon her chest, then gave Tanut-amon a fluttering smile. The chief of the priests of Sekhmet offered her another drink in a golden goblet, and she lifted her head high enough to drain the cup. Before reclining again, however, she looked at me.

"Merytamon," she called, her voice slightly slurred, "you should go now."

I would have protested, but Tanut-amon turned and gestured toward the door with a no-nonsense expression on his face. I lingered, reluctant to leave my mother, but the small priest came forward and gripped my elbow.

"You will see her in a few hours." He gestured toward the half-empty water clock on a table near the door. "Come back when the clock empties, daughter of Pharaoh, and see how your mother fares."

Another priest ushered me out the doorway, but not before I glanced back to see that they had begun to drill into my mother's head.

By the time the water clock emptied, my mother was sleeping. Upon entering her chamber, I moved to the headrest at the end of the bed and looked at her scalp. The flesh over my mother's skull had been opened just above her right temple, and through the mouthlike opening I could see that a hole had been drilled into white bone.

I looked away as my stomach lurched upward, then fixed my gaze upon Tanut-amon. "Why is she still sleeping? She was awake when I left."

The priest spread his hands. "Perhaps she is tired. Come tomorrow, daughter of Pharaoh, and let your mother greet you with a smile."

I did return on the morrow, and the day after that. By the third day my mother had awakened, but as I watched Huda spoon beef broth into her mouth, a terrifying realization washed over me—my mother had changed. Perhaps permanently.

Again, I sought the priest, and found him in the vestibule. "She does not speak." I gestured helplessly toward the main chamber where my mother rested. "She does not seem to know me."

A muscle quivered at the man's jaw. "She does not know me, either, or her maid. I fear we may have opened her skull for too long—it is as if her *ba* has flown away and escaped us."

I looked again at the blank-eyed woman who sat in the chair. The priests had taught me that mortals had six parts, including the heart, the seat of intellect and emotion; the *ba*, or eternal soul; and the *ka*, the force that animated our bodies. My mother's ka was obviously still intact, for she ate and breathed and, with urging, walked. But some powerful part of her personality had departed.

How could the gods allow this? I stood in silence, feeling as if there were dozens of divine hands on my heart, maliciously twisting the life from it.

"Who can understand the mysteries of the gods?" Tanut-amon's eyes brimmed with tears as he watched my mother. "The ba flies out every night and returns to the tomb where the body is buried, so it may be that Nefertari's ba will return to us as well. Until then, we will care for her."

Like a powerful undertow threatening to pull me under, childhood fears of abandonment surfaced and swirled in my heart. My mother had never neglected me, but the space I longed to fill with a father's love had gaped with emptiness.

Was I to lose the only parent I had truly known?

I opened my mouth, ready to murmur polite words of consolation, but could not speak over the painful knot of sorrow in my throat.

Apparently understanding, Tanut-amon clucked in quiet sympathy. Something in me hoped he would draw me into a comforting embrace, but I knew he could not risk his life by doing so.

I pressed my hands to my face and wept for several minutes, then palmed my tears from my cheeks. When I looked at the priest again, a weight of sadness lay upon his thin face.

I reached out and squeezed his shoulder, for the priest seemed to be suffering as much as I was. We would mourn Nefertari together, but neither of us could afford to shed many tears now.

On the morrow, I had learned, I would marry my father.

On the tenth day of the third month of akhet, as the floodwaters of Hap-Ur reached their peak, I prepared to become a wife of Pharaoh, son of Osiris and Ruler of the Two Lands. As a daughter of the Great Royal Wife, it was my duty to marry the king, but still I could not deny the fear that sent tendrils of apprehension through my heart.

On the morning of my wedding day, my father announced that his second-ranking wife, Isnofret, would also be known as the Great Royal Wife. Therefore, he told his courtiers, the day would bring his marriage not only to his daughter Merytamon, but Bint-Anath as well.

I received the news with mixed feelings. Having Bint-Anath present for the ceremony would ease my nervousness, but Pharaoh's recognition of Isnofret as Great Royal Wife seemed disloyal to my mother, who had been the bride of Pharaoh's youth and was still the mother of his first-born son. But she could not function as Royal Wife without her ba, and I did not dare hope it would return in time for the ceremony. I was still child enough to want her near me, to see her smile as I moved through the throne room toward my husband and king.

I trembled as Nema dressed me for the ceremony. Perhaps my mother was not the only incomplete woman in Pharaoh's household. How could a woman who had no womb be a fit wife for a king?

My heart formulated fantastic thoughts as Nema painted my face. Perhaps my mother's ba had gone in search of my womb. Perhaps both had been devoured by a crocodile of Hap-Ur, or a suckling lamb of the Hebrews. Perhaps the child of Pharaoh's dream, the one who would grow to threaten Egypt, had stolen pieces of myself and my mother in revenge for his watery death in Hap-Ur. . . .

"You must hold still, my lady."

Scolded thus by Nema, who seemed unusually fretful, I resolved to rein in my thoughts and emotions. I looked at my dressing stand, which was now heavily laden with gifts presented in honor of my wedding. Along with a silver mirror adorned with golden faces of the goddess Hathor had come a collection of jewelry wrought in gold, electrum, and silver, inlaid with blue and green paste, carnelian, lapis lazuli, turquoise, amethyst, and garnets. The carved jewelry chest at my feet overflowed with bracelets of amethyst, turquoise, lapis, and gold, along with girdles and necklaces featuring the same stones.

Among the gifts from Egyptian nobles were ebony jewel caskets paneled in ivory, gold, and blue faience. Nema had been delighted to discover a bronze rouge dish, a new razor with a golden handle, and an alabaster unguent jar. As my favorite handmaid, she would use these items every day.

The crowning glory of my wedding collection was a personal gift from the king: a broad pectoral bearing his cartouche in the center of the beaded design. Without being told, I knew I should wear it whenever the king sent for me.

Nema tried to behave as if this were an ordinary day, but I knew she sensed my anxiety. "I hear, lady," she murmured, bending forward to apply her weight as she tugged on my heavy wig, "that Pharaoh is planning to leave soon on another military campaign."

I nodded, for I'd heard the same news. If Egypt did not maintain an armed presence in Syria and the other northern tributary states, the Hittites were quick to swoop down and demand that the people in those regions change their allegiance. Pharaoh had been striving against the invasive Hittite Empire for well over a year.

Nema reached out to adjust the golden uraeus upon my wig, the golden cobra that was another gift from the king. "So your father may be gone a long time. And while a king is gone, many things can happen in his house."

I twisted in my seat to look at her. Though she was but twelve years old, Nema was no fool. When not with me, she spent her hours mingling with the other servants of Pharaoh's household, and servants, I had learned, had access to a boundless supply of useful information. She also knew everything about me, including the state of my nonexistent womb.

I placed my hand upon my belly. "Indeed, even an unripe womb may ripen. But what if it does not?"

Nema's dark lips parted in a dazzling display of straight white teeth. "Are you not the firstborn daughter of Nefertari, Rich of Praise and Pharaoh's Lady of Charm? Is the priest Tanut-amon not your friend? Am I not the most devoted handmaid in the Black Land? You are not alone, my lady. Though her ba has flown, your mother has not left you friendless in Pharaoh's house."

Armed with the comforting words of my child-slave, I rode to Pharaoh's throne room in a gold carrying chair engraved with the hieroglyphic images for "Mother of the King of Upper and Lower Egypt, Follower of Horus, Guide of the Ruler, Favorite Lady." Lifted high upon the shoulders of four courtiers and followed by a group of exquisitely dressed handmaids, I arrived at the throne room at the sixth hour, just as the sun reached its zenith. Bint-Anath's retinue followed mine, but I did not glance back to give her comfort. Her mother would be present, mine would not.

Wearing silver anklets, my golden pectoral, and a sheer robe of the finest pleated linen, I stepped into Pharaoh's throne room and faced the Theban nobles who had gathered to witness the event. Behind me, Bint-

Anath tittered nervously as she alighted from her chair, but I did not want to show my trepidation. I was Nefertari's eldest daughter, the opener of her womb, and therefore an important link in my father's claim to the throne of Egypt. I could not fail in what I had been born to do.

High clerestory windows lit the rectangular audience chamber and caught the river breezes. Silence descended upon the crowd as I began to move toward the dais at the far end of the room, and I stepped slowly, with what I hoped was a regal air. Illustrations of the king's exploits in Nubia and Syria lined the walls, depicting him as a victorious warrior. While other pharaohs had been content to show themselves worshiping the gods or relaxing in the company of family members, my father found pride in two things—his wars and his monuments. Even though I could not say I knew the man, like all Thebans, I knew the king.

Placing one foot in front of the other, I strode forward with as much confidence as I could muster. Pharaoh's Medjay warriors—Nubians who served as the king's bodyguards—flanked the sides of the room, standing between me and the onlookers. Wearing loincloths over muscled torsos that gleamed like polished ebony, the guards carried shields and spears even in this protected place.

My eyes focused on the platform at the far end of the room where my father sat on a gilded throne. At his right hand stood his eldest son, my brother Amon-hirwonmef, and at his left lounged a young lion, a souvenir from one of his recent expeditions. My father's principal advisers—the viziers of Upper and Lower Egypt, as well as Rudjek, the chief priest of Amon—were stationed behind the throne, and beyond them a pair of male slaves with feather fans moved the air in perfect synchronization.

Ramesses—father, king, and soon-to-be husband—wore a long white robe with generous pleating. A broad gold pectoral, a larger version of the one over my own breastbone, spread over his chest, while the red-and-white crown symbolizing Upper and Lower Egypt sat upon his head. Attached to the front of his headdress were models of the serpent goddess Wadjet and the vulture goddess Nekhebet, symbolizing the power of the gods against anyone who would dare come against Egypt or her king. In his hands he held the crook and flail, symbols of the king's role as a divine shepherd to his people.

Reaching the dais, I knelt on the marble floor, then prostrated myself, spreading my hands before Pharaoh's throne.

"Rise, Merytamon, the Most Excellent, Most Gracious Royal Daughter, Royal Sister, Divine Consort and Royal Spouse." My father's voice seemed to come from far away, but when I lifted my head to meet his gaze, his dark eyes smiled at me.

"Do you agree to this marriage?"

Who would reply in the negative? "Yes, my lord."

Ptophotep, one of the king's counselors, stepped out from the crowd of officials and offered the traditional words:

"If thou art a man of note, establish for thyself a household and love thy wife at home, as it beseemeth thee. Fill her belly, clothe her back; unguent is the remedy for her limbs. Gladden her heart, so long as she liveth; she is a goodly field for her lord. Hold her back from getting the mastery and the like."

A smattering of giggles rose from some of the women of the court, for no one could imagine a wife trying to master Pharaoh.

In an act heavy with symbolism, Pharaoh rose from his throne and extended his hand, lifting me up from my supplicant's position. As we stood side by side, the high priest of Osiris washed our hands and feet with water freshly drawn from Hap-Ur, to symbolize the purity of our union. Then the king took a corn loaf from the priest and broke off a bit, offering it to my lips. I accepted it, then forced the dry bread down my throat.

During these rituals, the women of the court sang a bridal song that had never seemed more fitting:

> Sweet of love is the daughter of the King!
> Black are her tresses as the blackness of the night,
> Black as the wine-grape are the clusters of her hair.
> The hearts of the women turn toward her with delight,
> Gazing on her beauty with which none can compare.
>
> Sweet of love is the daughter of the King!
> Fair are her arms in the softly swaying dance,

Fairer by far is her bosom's rounded swell!
The hearts of the men are as water at her glance,
Fairer is her beauty than mortal tongue can tell.

Sweet of love is the daughter of the King!
Rosy are her cheeks as the jasper's ruddy hue,
Rosy as the henna that stains her slender hands!
The heart of the King is filled with love anew,
When in all her beauty before his throne she stands.

Despite my apprehensions, my eyes filled with tears at the sound of those sweet voices. I wasn't sure why I wept . . . but I was overcome by a feeling, unanchored but strong, that I had been born for this moment.

There remained but one more act—the crushing of the jar of wedding wine with the sword—and as the pottery cracked with the blow, I pasted a smile upon my face and looked toward the back of the room, where my half sister waited to marry our father and king.

The women sang a different song in her honor, then together we were escorted to the king's banquet hall where we ate from a greater variety of dishes than I had ever been offered. While dancers performed and musicians played, Ramesses, my father, now my husband, sat alone beside a dining tray, his eyes wide and his expression preoccupied. To my right, Bint-Anath ate from several platters, occasionally throwing scraps to the little monkey she kept as a pet. I dined in silence, smiling when my gaze crossed those of my king's advisers, and trying my best to look like a happy and blessed bride.

It was, I am sure, the most sumptuous wedding Thebes had ever seen. And as I peered at my father through lowered lashes, I became convinced the wedding also featured the city's most disinterested bridegroom.

∽✖∽

Hours later, after the feasting and drinking and evening sacrifices, a servant came to my apartment with a message: My husband the king wanted to see me in his chamber.

I looked at the heavy ceremonial wig and flowing gown I had just taken off, then caught Nema's eye. "Would you like me to help you put it all on again?" she asked, a quaver in her voice.

I shook my head. "Something simple, I think. A plain garment, and a short wig."

We took care of my toilette in a few moments, then I twirled for her inspection.

"You look lovely." She clapped her hand to her cheek. "If only your mother were here—"

"Say a prayer to your gods for me." I picked up a mirror to double-check the cosmetics around my eyes. "Pray Pharaoh does not divine that he has married a barren woman."

Pharaoh's royal apartments lay on the far side of the palace complex, near the river where the evening breeze blew strongest. I walked between two guards, my sandals slapping the stone floor in a quick rhythm as we passed through the vestibule, the garden courtyard, the north loggia, and the reception room. From there we traversed the great hall, where a servant led us to the carved door of Pharaoh's bedchamber.

The guards stiffened, making it clear I had to open the door myself. This I did, stepping into a room lit by rush torches high upon the wall. I did not see Pharaoh at first, so I closed the door and moved farther into the room, running my hands over my bare arms as a chill swept over me.

I collapsed in a sudden weakening of knees and arms and elbows when I spied the king reclining on his bed.

"My lord," I whispered, pressing my palms to the tiled floor. "You sent for me."

"Indeed, I did." His voice was heavier than it had been at noon, his words thick and slurry. "Rise, Merytamon, Wife of the King."

I obeyed. And for the first time in my life I beheld Pharaoh without a crown or any of the other fierce symbols of his majesty. The man stretched out before me wore a plain kilt of white linen, a girdle of panther fur, and a simple gold collar. His head was bare, save for a thatch of close-cropped auburn hair, and the eyes focusing upon me were narrowed with something that could have been compassion.

"You are Nefertari's daughter?"

The question was idiotic, but who was I to rebuke him? I bowed my head. "Yes, my lord."

"You can stop bowing in my presence; let us speak as man and woman."

I blinked. He was a god, the king, and my father. How could I ever consider him an ordinary man?

Extending the hand that held a goblet, he gestured to a chair at the side of his bed. After hesitating an instant, I crossed the room and seated myself.

"Tell me, daughter of Nefertari." His eyelids drooped. "Did you know your mother well?"

"Yes, my lord. I am the eldest daughter."

"Do you miss her, now that her ba has flown away?"

Emotion clogged my throat, forcing me to swallow before I could speak. "Very much, my lord."

"Good. A daughter ought to love her mother, even as she loves her father." He squinted at me. "Do you love your father?"

Bewildered, I nodded.

"Also good. So you will obey me?"

"Always, my lord."

"I want you to take Nefertari to Mi-Wer."

I was too surprised to do more than nod again. Mi-Wer was the palace built for the royal harem. With more wives and concubines than he had chambers in which to put them, my father had discovered the wisdom of maintaining a household away from his women. The higher-ranking wives and their children usually resided with him in Thebes, while the king's other women lived at Mi-Wer, awaiting his pleasure.

"Mi-Wer will be good for her." Pharaoh rested his head on his palm. "It is quiet there."

Silently, I agreed. My mother had often taken her children there while Pharaoh journeyed, and I had always enjoyed those visits. Located in the region known as the Faiyum, or Land of the Lakes, I knew Mi-Wer as an area of lush vegetation, a variety of aquatic life, and countless royal females. Given my new marriage and my still-reluctant body, ready access to the counsel of women appealed to me.

Then a new thought struck my heart—was my father trying to be rid of my mother? His next words, however, dispelled that notion.

"I will be departing soon for Syria," he mumbled over his palm as he stared at the floor. "And there will be no company here for Nefertari, Sweet of Love. So you must take her to Mi-Wer, where Mehy will attend to her needs."

I recognized the name—Mehy was the eunuch who ran the harem. A competent man, he obviously had earned Pharaoh's complete trust.

"I will do it." I smiled, grateful that concern, not convenience, had motivated his request. "I will take the most tender care of her, and together we will await your return."

Silently, I blessed the gods for providing this escape. Every day spent away from my husband was another day in which a slumbering womb might awaken.

The king looked directly into my eyes. "You look very much like her," he said, then he rolled onto his back and dropped the empty goblet to the floor. Above the clattering he called, "Did she sing to you?"

"Who, my lord?"

"Your mother—Nefertari. She used to sing to me—songs of Hap-Ur, of the gods. She would put me to sleep with her sweet song."

And in that moment I realized a truth my naïveté had kept from me— my lord the king was drunk. I had little experience with men in general and none with drunken men in particular, but the calm voice of reason instructed my heart from that moment on.

"Yes, she sang to me." With courage I had not known I possessed, I stood and moved to Pharaoh's bedside. Drawing a deep breath, I sang a favorite tune of my mother's: "Come Through the Garden, Love, to Me."

Though his eyes were closed, Pharaoh's powerful hand reached for me. Still singing, I slid my palm into his hand, then allowed him to pull me to his side. Sitting on his bed, I caught my breath when he turned to wrap an arm about my waist and place his head in my lap.

"Sing again," he said, his voice hoarse.

"My love is like each flower that grows," I sang softly, not wanting to agitate him. "Tall and straight as a young palm tree, and in each cheek a sweet blush-rose."

I sang for the better part of an hour, every song I knew, and before the night had swept over Thebes with her dark cloak, Pharaoh, King of Egypt, slept in my arms like a newborn babe.

∾

Ptahmose, the king's ranking servant, found us together the next morning. I slipped out of my still-sleeping husband's bed and hurried away as a parade of attendants—barber, manicurist, chiropodist, and half a dozen priests—entered the king's bedchamber to prepare him for the day.

Not waiting for an official escort, I hurried through the palace passageways, nearly losing myself in the twisting hallways that led to my new chambers.

Nema almost dropped the basin she was carrying when I entered my apartment and stood panting against the closed door.

Her eyes widened. "Well?"

"He slept." I felt a wide and foolish grin o'erspread my face. "Like a pup who has drunk his fill of warm milk, the king slept in my arms. He only asked that I sing to him."

Nema slumped in relief. "You should be pleased."

"I am—but for another reason. The king wants me to take my mother to Mi-Wer, so we will pack at once. Summon Abi, the chamberlain of the Great House, and have him arrange the transportation for our journey."

Nema hurried off to do my bidding. When Abi appeared in my chamber and heard my news, he replied that he would require three days to procure a suitable vessel to transport all of us, so I prepared to patiently wait out the delay. News of my journey rippled through the palace, however, and on the day before my departure, the priest Tanut-amon sought entrance to my chambers.

I was genuinely glad to see him. "Welcome, Tanut-amon," I called, rising to meet him as he entered.

"Greetings to you, daughter of Isis." He bowed before me. "Long life, strength, and health to you!"

I allowed him to genuflect, then bent to catch his gaze. "My old friend— I am glad you have come. I hope all is well with you?"

"I am well, Sweet Royal Wife. But I was saddened to hear of your impending departure."

I made a face. "My problem is still unsolved, so I think it will be good to get away. Pharaoh is allowing me to take Nefertari to Mi-Wer while he marches to Syria, so we may be there many months. I am hoping my womb will awaken while he is away."

Tanut-amon nodded. "The gods may be gracious to you. But if they are not, I have been thinking . . . and I think you should consider your mother's words of wisdom."

My thoughts stuttered to a halt. "About—"

"The Hebrew babies." Tanut-amon lowered his voice as though the walls might be listening. "I have had another thought, Gentle Royal Wife, and I hope you will listen. I believe it is worth considering."

Confused, I nodded, giving him permission to continue.

"You have studied Egyptian history." He crossed his arms. "Doubtless you have heard about the glorious kings of earlier dynasties."

"Of course." I have always liked to read, and as the king's daughter all the houses of the papyri were open to me. Since the time of Narmer, my people had kept careful records of the great kings.

"Nearly every pharaoh," Tanut-amon spoke in a neutral tone, "married his sister or daughter in our tradition, but gradually those families weakened. Yet each time someone outside the royal bloodline was introduced into the divine lineage, Egypt's greatness was restored."

I sank into my chair, momentarily confused. "Egypt has never been anything but great."

His mouth pursed up in a tiny rosette, then unpuckered enough to say: "Pray consider this example—Amenhotep II, a great king, begat Tuthmosis, a great king who died young, who begat Amenhotep III, who begat Akhenaton—"

Reflexively, I made a face. Every Theban knew how Akhenaton had scorned all gods but Aten and moved the royal court to el-Amarna, a city to the south. That king ignored the needs of his own people and did nothing to maintain Egypt's power over the foreign nations. Blindly devoted to one god, he refused to understand that people required many gods to meet their needs. Fortunately, his son, Tutankhamen, had the foresight to move the royal court back to Thebes and restore worship of the old gods, but that king died young and left the nation without a royal heir. His widowed royal consort, Ankhesenamen, begged the king of the Hittites for a royal prince to become her husband and king of Egypt, but a wily old vizier, Aye, married her and stole the throne when mysterious marauders murdered the promised Hittite prince on the journey to Egypt. Yet Aye did not live long, and was succeeded by Horemhab, a military general. Horemhab, a commoner, effectively founded the nineteenth dynasty that had produced my father . . . and me.

"Do you not see?" Tanut-amon spread his hands. "Egypt is mighty for a while, then the royal seed seems to weaken and we suffer kings like Akhenaton who weaken us from within. But Egypt rejoices when fresh seed is spread upon the throne—"

I covered my ears. "Blasphemy! And from you, a priest!"

"'Tis not blasphemy." Tanut-amon leaned closer. "'Tis the truth. And it is the reason you should not fear to take a Hebrew child if your womb does not awaken. They are a strong people, and multiply like rabbits. You would have no trouble finding a child."

Torn by conflicting emotions, I lowered my hands. "Pharaoh fears them because of a dream he had. If I gave him a Hebrew son, he would think of this dream—"

"The prophecy of Pharaoh's dream has been obliterated; he no longer fears the suckling lamb."

"But he would look at the child and know."

"He would not. There is no physical difference between our people and the Hebrews. They are taller, perhaps, but Pharaoh would be pleased to think he sired a strapping son."

"He would know." I spoke more softly this time, and felt a blush burn my cheek. "Pharaoh has not . . . well, when we were together, he fell asleep. So he would know he did not father a son by me."

The priest snorted softly. "Your wedding night? I waited upon Pharaoh before he retired to his chambers. He was drunk. He will not remember that night."

"Are you sure? He was not incapable of thought, for he asked me to take Nefertari to Mi-Wer."

Tanut-amon pressed his fingertips to his lips for a moment, then waggled a finger in my face. "Think, Royal Wife, of the story of Hatshepsut."

I frowned, trying to remember my history lessons. Hatshepsut had been the daughter of Tuthmosis I, and upon his death she married Tuthmosis II as tradition demanded. But when Tuthmosis II died, Hatshepsut declared herself pharaoh.

I lifted my eyes to find the priest watching me. "Hatshepsut was . . . unusual. But what has she to do with me?"

Tanut-amon's smile deepened into laughter. "Do you not see? In order to establish and validate her claim to the throne, Hatshepsut assured her people that the god Amon, her true father, had assumed the form of Tuthmosis in order to conceive a woman who would be king."

I gaped at the paunchy priest pacing before me. "I do not want to be king. And they say Hatshepsut was murdered by her son, so I *definitely* do not want that kind of—"

"I don't want you to be king, my dear. I'm referring to her conception. She claimed that the god fathered her. And after her reign, Tuthmosis III insisted he had been fathered by Amon."

My heart whirled. "So I should say I am—"

"Not you, the *child*. If anyone dares question his parentage, tell them that Amon divinely fathered a son for Pharaoh. No one will dare question you."

I pressed my hand to my heart; I could feel it thumping beneath the fabric of my skin. The idea was unthinkable, yet brilliant in its conception. Pharaoh had to believe in the gods and all their legends, for he claimed to be one of them. Doubting my word would be tantamount to doubting his own history. Furthermore, even if in the basest part of his heart Pharaoh doubted my fidelity, I would have an added proof—I would have been living in a community of women, surrounded night and day by devoted guards, priests, and servants who would die before they would touch a wife of Pharaoh.

I felt a slow smile begin to creep across my face. "Still," I said, thinking through the technicalities, "a few people would know the truth. I would need a wet nurse for the baby, and my maid knows about my condition—"

"Your maid is loyal, and silver can buy silence." The corner of the priest's mouth rose in a satisfied half smile. "It is a good plan, Wise Royal Wife. It requires, however, that I go with you and Nefertari to Mi-Wer."

I laughed. "You want to live at the harem?"

"More than life itself. I will serve you there in whatever office you wish, and I will continue to oversee your mother's care."

I found myself nodding, for Mother would need a physician, and who better to care for her than this priest? Besides, he knew us, and Mother trusted him. I needed no other recommendation.

I stared at him a moment more. "Why would you do this for me?"

He knelt before me, his knees cracking in the silence of my chamber. "Because I loved your mother," he said simply, smiling into my eyes. "With the purest heart and the noblest of intentions, I love her still. Therefore, Merytamon, I find that I must love you, too."

With that, he bowed low, kissed the tiles at my feet, then rose and backed away, keeping his head low as he moved through the doorway. I felt a sweet sorrow at his departure, for true friends are never easy to release, even for a moment. But he had given me a gift. Indeed, for the first time in weeks I felt as though hope—and friendship—might live with me in the house of Pharaoh's wives.

The royal harem, or *per-khenret,* was nearly as ostentatious as Pharaoh's house. The household of lesser wives existed for several reasons, including Pharaoh's convenience, but its primary function was the production and education of the royal sons and daughters. When the ranking wife did not produce a son, a male heir would have to be found among the women of the harem. The king's daughters were valued, too, and often used to sweeten military or trade agreements with foreign lands. Because I was a daughter of the Great Royal Wife, I never feared being sent to Syria, Mittani, or some other foreign land, but my half sisters in the harem lived with the realization that though they had been created from gold, they were still pawns in the king's hands.

Every educated prince and princess also knew of the harem's dangers. On at least two historic occasions, conspiracy to murder the king rose from the harem, and it was generally assumed that the plotters were successful. The first plot rose in the Old Kingdom, when Amtes, a high-ranking wife, killed the king in order to put her son on the throne. The investigation surrounding that treachery was never recorded. And in the twelfth dynasty, King Amenemhet uncovered a harem conspiracy and even fought hand-to-hand with his would-be assassins. He survived the first attempt upon his life, but died while his son and coruler was away from the palace, fueling speculation that the murderers had finally accomplished their goals.

Perhaps it was for these reasons that my father placed Mi-Wer at some distance from his capital. Amenhotep III had located his harem at Malakata, just across the river from his palace, but my father had no patience with plotters.

I had visited Mi-Wer in my childhood, journeying there with my mother when she was heavy with my unborn sister. My brothers and I had been born at the palace in Thebes, but for some reason my mother wished to give birth to her final child among the company of women. And so, only three years ago, she had squatted on the bricks in a room at the per-khenret. I had been allowed to enter and observe—for my education's sake, I suppose. During the course of those few hours I saw many midwives, inhaled much smoke and incense, and heard dozens of incantations for health and fertility. Finally, a royal priest-physician knelt near the mud-brick stool and caught my sister as she slid from my mother's womb. She would survive only a few months, but the memory of her birth would never leave me.

Staring at my bloody sibling, who opened her mouth and promptly began to squall, I felt a child's revulsion toward the unknown . . . and as the royal boat rode the floodwaters and carried us into Lower Egypt, I wondered whether the gods had marked my unwillingness to open my body to the same experience. Did they steal my womb that day? Did Thoth, the god of magic, somehow shut me up?

I dismissed the thought and concentrated on the soft sound of the oars pulling against calm water. With Pharaoh away, I resolved not to fret about my uncooperative womb. I would instead care for my mother, who sat on her chair with an impassive expression, her eyes like empty windows. She ate when we pressed food to her lips, she drank when we offered a cup, she shuffled forward when we led her by the hand. But she did not speak, and her ba did not return.

My eyes drifted to a shallow pool where two boys were fishing. They beat the water at the front of their papyrus skiff with long sticks, then rushed to the back of the boat and dropped a net into the path of the frightened fish. Giggling, the boys hauled up their net, then pulled out several flopping Nile perch and dropped them into the skiff.

I drew a deep breath as we sailed by the boys. My sympathies lay solidly with the fish, who had undoubtedly been lured by the skiff's sheltering shade from the despotic sun . . . just as I had been drawn to my father's embrace in the hope of finding relief from his blinding glory. I could only pray I would not be trapped like those hapless perch.

We traveled for three days, passing Dendera, Amarna, and Herakleopolis, and finally the mud-brick walls of Mi-Wer rose into view. The slaves aboard our ship labored to keep the boat in the channel, for the fields were still covered with the heavy gray floodwaters that would soon turn this land into an emerald paradise. Beyond the walls of Mi-Wer, a few peasants splashed bare-legged through the shallows, restoring the stone boundary markers to their rightful positions.

I turned away from the sight of the poor people. Any man in Egypt could learn to read and write and therefore better his position, so I had little sympathy for those who persisted in working the soil. I knew vendors in Thebes who made a good living selling flour and grain—one woman boasted to me that she and two partners gathered ten and one-half sacks of grain and ground it into seven sacks of flour in a single day. Some women found employment as musicians and dancers; others excelled in weaving or the production of perfumes. The king's house could not function without midwives, serving women, and female musicians. With all Egypt had to offer her daughters, I could see no reason why an intelligent woman would work in the mud—unless, of course, the gods had destined her for no more significant work than farming.

Catching Tanut-amon's eye, I motioned him toward me. Immediately he left his chair and bowed by my side.

"Is it possible," I asked, looking toward the west where the setting sun had tinged the water crimson, "that the gods decide our fates before we are born?"

Tanut-amon tilted his head, rolling his eyes toward the sky. "Surely they know what we will become. But can a man change his fate? I believe he can. Sometimes he does it with one action."

He gestured toward the flooded fields. "Can a slave rise from these fields to become pharaoh? 'Tis not likely. But could he become a scribe, and a trusted member of Pharaoh's house? Yes. Some things are possible, others are not. Our duty is to decide the difference."

"Could a scribe"—I nodded toward the same fields—"commit a murder, and be banished to work in the mud? Yes. Given that, could a royal wife displease her king and be executed for the offense?"

A smile found its way through the mask of uncertainty on the priest's face. "Does that prospect worry you? Banish the thought, Lady of the Two Lands. No one can change who you are—Wife and Beloved Daughter, Most Beloved of Pharaoh."

Messengers had forecast our arrival, so a retinue of servants waited when our felucca docked at the landing. A company of dancers and musicians filled the air with music and movement as I descended, again reminding me of my newly exalted status. I was no longer Merytamon, daughter of the king, but an exalted royal bride of Pharaoh.

"Hail to thee, Most Gracious Royal Wife!" A portly man in a white robe stepped forward, then fell to his knees before me. "Fair of Face, Beautiful in the Palace, the Beloved of the Lord of Two Lands, welcome!"

I had only glimpsed his face, but it would be hard to forget Mehy, the man who had overseen my visits on many other occasions. Yet he had always known me as a king's daughter, and now I was returning with a new title.

Holding Nema's hand, I stepped onto the landing as a dozen other attendants prostrated themselves on the wooden dock. "Thank you, Mehy, for your gracious greeting. Will you welcome my mother as well? And our adviser has come with us from Thebes—Tanut-amon, priest of Amon-Re. He will require suitable quarters."

"Most certainly, Royal Lady." Mehy pushed himself upright, then nodded rapidly, his short wig swinging in the jerky rhythm of his movements. "It is my very great honor to welcome you to the per-khenret."

The eunuch's obsequious bobbing annoyed me, but I returned his smile. "I thank you, Mehy. I appreciate your hospitality and welcome, but my handmaids and I would like to retire to our rooms. We are weary from the journey."

Mehy squinted at me through the bangs of his wig. "I have prepared the finest rooms in the house for you. Pharaoh's vizier also instructed me to set aside a smaller block for the Lady Nefertari and her servants."

An unexpected sob caught in my throat. The finest rooms in this house used to be reserved for my mother . . . but she would no longer need them. Nefertari did nothing these days but stare into empty space.

"Thank you, Mehy." Lifting the hem of my gown, I began to move toward the gleaming entrance to the palace complex. "If I need anything else, I will not hesitate to call for you."

Thus began my life as a wife of Pharaoh. At Mi-Wer, I lived among the multitude of royal women and tried to do all the things expected of a king's wife—I made daily sacrifices to Pharaoh's gods, I established cordial friendships with other women in the harem, and I recited countless prayers to Khonsu, who blessed the earth with fertility; Isis, who instituted marriage in the Beautiful Land; and Bastet, the cat-headed goddess who protected pregnant women. Something in me hoped I might be pregnant already—had I not spent a night in the presence of the divine king, for whom a miracle would not be too great a task? And was not the sign of pregnancy a bloodless womb?

But weeks passed, and my belly remained flat. Each morning I rose and bathed in water suffused with natron, then applied perfumes blended from myrrh, frankincense, broom, and foreign plants. After my bath and anointing, Nema dressed me in finery fit for a queen; then I broke my fast with a meal of dates, figs, bread, and honey. After eating, I attended to the morning sacrifices at a shrine dedicated to Khnum and begged him to fashion a child for me on his potter's wheel. After making my sacrifices and offering my prayers, I retired to my chambers . . . to wait for a miracle.

I had looked forward to the peace of Mi-Wer after the frantic pace of life in Thebes, but I soon discovered that the aloofness of rank kept me from full acceptance by Pharaoh's other women. My mother's vacant condition fright-ened many of them (and resulted in whispers that she had been cursed), and my exalted rank kept others from drawing me into their confidences.

What gossip I heard, however, proved interesting. Though Isnofret currently shared the title of Great Royal Wife, not many in the harem expected her to remain in the king's favor. "She is the royal wife only because you have not yet borne a son," one of the bolder concubines told me. "When you or Bint-Anath presents Pharaoh with an heir, Isnofret will take her place among us old crones."

The woman then cackled a laugh—and I withdrew from her presence, appalled at her frankness and dismayed by her prediction. For if I did not present Pharaoh with a son, what would become of me? Would I be per-manently exiled from my father's presence? I had hoped to know him better now that our situation had changed.

I did not dislike Mi-Wer—the harem palace was lovely, and the sur-rounding settlement a center of agriculture, industry, and knowledge, for Pharaoh's sons and daughters had to be well educated. Scores of slaves and servants tended the palace and workshops, training many of Pharaoh's daughters in the craft of spinning and weaving. The adminis-trator of the growing harem also maintained flocks to supply the house-hold with grain, milk, and meat.

Along with myriad servants to serve the king's women, Mi-Wer offered veteran bureaucrats and retired military officers who made themselves available for the teaching of reading, writing, ethics, etiquette, soldiery, and statecraft. Though any of Pharaoh's women could have learned from these esteemed teachers, most of the students were Ramesses' offspring or children of high-ranking Egyptian officials. The harem school even included foreign princes whose royal parents had sent them to Egypt in order to learn from the most advanced teachers in the civilized world.

My rooms at the harem palace were as elegant as my royal chambers at Pharaoh's house in Thebes. Vibrantly colored tiles and friezes gleamed on the walls, filling my apartments with images of fish, waterfowl, lotus blossoms, and clusters of poppies and grapes. I enjoyed the beauty of the place, but often felt unattached. For friendship I had only Nema, Tanut-amon, and a mother who no longer recognized me.

In order to pass the days, after my prayers and sacrifices, I spent most of my day reading papyri from the *per-ankh,* or House of Life. While lost in the rich rhythms of the poetry of my people, I could momentarily forget my wounded mother, distant father, and unrelenting loneliness. For a while, at least, I could also forget that Khnum had committed an injustice against me and left me a woman only half formed.

But I could never lose myself completely in literature. As Re rode his sun-barque into the west, I would have to set down my papyrus scroll and call for Nema to light the lamp. Then I would have to decide whether to dine alone and in peace, or venture out with the other women.

Each evening, if I wished, I could feast with the king's women in the banquet room, where slaves piled the dinner trays high with pyramids of fruit sprinkled with fragrant flowers. On most nights, however, I dismissed all the servants but Nema and ate with her in my reception room. Together we partook of ibshet-biscuits, tjet-loaves, cakes, dried meat, carob beans, pomegranates, figs, and grapes. Every day we dined on fresh fish or, if the fishermen had not produced a catch that met Mehy's exacting standards, roasted duck and goose flavored with leeks, herbs, and honey.

As one of the most pampered women at the harem, I should have been one of the happiest, but each day found me more miserable and increasingly tense. Shortly after our arrival, Tanut-amon returned to Thebes to settle his affairs there, and I found myself missing his reassuring presence. My mother's ba did not return, and occasionally when I visited her chambers I found that the servants were neglecting her care. Huda remained faithful, of course, but she could not be with my mother day and night. Whenever I found my mother sitting in a soiled garment or with food upon her chin, I personally summoned Mehy and upbraided him for the lack of respect shown to Nefertari, Royal Wife and Consort, Beautiful in the Two Lands. The overseer always apologized with tears and promised to beat the thoughtless servants who had left her in such a state, but his words brought me no satisfaction.

I needed to blame someone for my mother's condition, but who deserved my fury? Tanut-amon had advised the surgery, but he loved my mother and would never purposefully hurt her. Pharaoh had approved of the procedure, but he loved Mother, too . . . and how could I be angry with my husband? Any one of a host of gods might have coveted my mother's ba and stolen it when the priests opened her skull, but which god would be so cruel? Thoth? Seth? I had no way of knowing, but perhaps Tanut-amon could divine the truth for me.

Each afternoon as I left my mother's small apartments and meandered through the halls, the happy chatter of the other women only served to emphasize the distance between us. They all smiled and bowed before me as if I were a woman most blessed; indeed, through Nema I learned that rumor held I was already expecting a child. One of my other maids had made it known that I spent a night with Pharaoh, therefore I was handled with great care and provided with anything I desired, for surely I carried a divine prince within my womb.

Only Nema, Tanut-amon, and I knew the truth. I would not present Pharaoh with a son next year; I might never give him a child. Eventually, my father and husband would realize that honoring me had been a mistake.

In the first month of shemu, the harvest season, and our fifth month at Mi-Wer, Tanut-amon begged permission to see me. When Nema ushered him into my audience chamber, my heart leaped at the sight of the priest's familiar face. Though I had important matters to discuss with him, for the first moments of our reunion I quizzed him on the well-being of my brothers and two younger sisters in Thebes.

"Your little sisters are well," the priest told me, "and your brothers have ridden to Syria with Pharaoh."

"My brothers? Fighting?"

Tanut-amon laughed softly. "You forget, Royal Wife, that Pharaoh rode to Libya with his father when he was only fourteen. Your brothers will need military experience when one of them rises to take your father's place as king."

I lifted a brow at this remark, for to speak of Pharaoh's death was almost blasphemy. But Tanut-amon was nothing if not practical and I appreciated common sense. Though my priest respected the offices of Egypt, he was not afraid to speak plainly . . . and, thankfully, he was not intimidated by a fourteen-year-old royal wife.

"Please." I gestured to a gilded chair next to mine. "Sit, so we can talk."

He accepted the proffered seat, then leaned forward, the folds of his pleated robe flattening at the soft mound of his belly. "And what of you, Merytamon? How are you faring since I have been away?"

'Twas all I could do not to burst into tears. "I am fine." I lowered my gaze as a blush branded my cheek with the lie. "But to speak plainly, Tanut-amon, I am not happy. My mother is no better, and the gods do not answer my prayers. I have been wondering—is it possible that one of the gods stole my mother's ba? Could the source of my unhappiness be divine?"

A melancholy frown flitted across his features. "I suppose it is possible."

"I know Pharaoh is not to blame, and neither are you," I hastened to add. "Neither could my mother's ba remain away by its own choice."

The priest's bottom lip edged forward in thought. "This is true. Your mother would never willingly leave you."

"I have been studying the matter, and I believe Seth may have been jealous of the love between my father and Nefertari. So he who has always been an instigator of confusion kidnapped my mother's ba. But if we make bountiful sacrifices in his temple to assure Seth he is loved and revered, surely we can persuade him to return her."

Tanut-amon said nothing for a moment, but stared at the painted frieze on the wall behind me with deadly concentration. "I think," he finally murmured, "you should look to Nephthys for your answer."

I lifted a brow as I considered his answer. I had assumed the villain to be male, but couldn't a female be just as jealous and adversarial? Nephthys, wife of Seth, was known as "Lady of the Palace" and esteemed for her skill in magic. Furthermore, she had given birth to Anubis, the opener of roads for the dead. That jackal-headed god could well be holding my mother's ba hostage in the Judgment Hall as a favor to the goddess who had borne him.

Leaning forward, I caught Tanut-amon's wrist. "It must be Nephthys! So what shall we do to free my mother's soul?"

The priest looked at me, his dark eyes brimming with tenderness. "Nephthys is very jealous, my dear, and very strong. I do not think she will surrender your mother's ba. And" —he waved his free hand in a gesture of helplessness—"I fear she may have stolen your womb as well. Obviously, she does not want to see you happy. If you are to defeat her malevolent intentions, you must proceed carefully."

Shock caused words to wedge in my throat. I had suspected that the gods had interfered in my life, but to hear the situation described so perfectly by a priest . . .

My heart thrummed with a thousand thoughts. I could not make war with gods . . . no more than I could resist the divine pharaoh. Yet neither could I escape my obligation to bear a son.

"I am defeated," I whispered, my voice breaking. "I thought to escape thoughts of my empty womb by leaving Pharaoh's house, but here I am surrounded by women who talk about nothing but babies and birth. And how can I defeat the gods? If my mother, who is strong, cannot break free—"

"You are not defeated, Sweetest Royal Wife. You are a daughter of Pharaoh, so a spark of divinity animates your own soul." The corners of the old man's eyes crinkled into soft nets as he smiled. "Your mother was strong, and she understood many things. Have you considered the plan she suggested?"

I felt myself flush as memories of my mother's advice came flooding back. "I have not found the courage."

"But you must find it, and soon. For Pharaoh has been away five months, and if you are to provide him with a child, you cannot wait much longer." He extended his spidery hand and rocked it slightly from side to side. "A few weeks will not matter, but the timing must be believable."

Despite the shattering revelation of the last hour, an unexpected bubble of relief rose up within me. I had felt so alone of late, but here was someone who could help me take charge of my life. My mother could not counsel me now, but her favorite priest might yet save my honor.

I took his hand and pressed it against my cheek. "Thank you, wise Tanut-amon." I closed my eyes. "When you are here, I do not feel alone."

"Serving you is my joy." When I released his hand and met his gaze, his dark eyes had narrowed in concentration. "Have you made any arrangements to provide Pharaoh with a son?"

I shook my head. "None."

"Then we will begin immediately. While in Thebes I made several discreet inquiries, and on the journey back to Mi-Wer I devised a plan. We will request a vessel from the administrator—what is his name again?"

"Mehy. He is a kind man, but nervous."

Tanut-amon laughed softly. "I'd be nervous, too, if I were in charge of Pharaoh's women. But to the point—I will tell Mehy that you wish to travel to the city of Pi-Ramesses, your father's ancestral home. Along the way, of course, we will stop to hunt and fish at the river's tributaries. Hebrew settlements are dotted throughout that region, and since they breed like rats upon a grain barge, I do not doubt that we will find a babe within a few days. When we hear squalling, we will fetch the child."

A confusing rush of anticipation and dread whirled inside me. Praying for a child was one thing; acting to obtain one was quite another. Yet Tanut-amon was right, time was fleeting, and I would need a son . . . soon.

I met the priest's gaze. "And when we find a baby?"

Tanut-amon lifted one bony shoulder in a shrug. "If it is a girl child, release it to its mother. If it is a boy and does not please you, 'tis your duty to offer it to Hap-Ur. But if it is a handsome child, claim it as your own."

"And what of the mother?"

"The mother will be grateful her son is not drowning beneath the river waves. You may trust me on this, Royal Wife. I know people . . . and even the Hebrews, dirty as they are, are people."

I brought my fingertips to my lips. "But how will I recognize these Hebrews when I see them? You said they look much like us."

Tanut-amon smiled. "You will recognize them by their dress. The women cover their heads with veils, and the men do not shave their beards. The baby boys are easily identifiable because they are circumcised a few days after birth—a ritual demanded by their ancestral deity. They are generally heavier than our people, though the thickness of their physique depends upon whether they have sufficient food." A frown worked its way into his forehead. "When they do not make bricks fast enough, they are not fed. Many men are so thin you can count their bones."

A faint shudder arose from somewhere within me. "So . . . by taking this child, I will be sparing him a life of hard labor."

His tense expression relaxed into a smile. "You would be like a goddess to him, Gracious Royal Lady."

Again a feeling of gratitude overwhelmed me. Smiling in contentment, I lifted his hand once more, inhaling the faint aroma of frankincense that clung to his skin. "Thank you, Tanut-amon, for being my friend. I know I shall need you in the days ahead."

The twin grooves beside his mouth deepened into a full smile. "Beloved Daughter of Nefertari, my desire is only to serve you."

Within two days, Tanut-amon had made and received an answer to his requests. As ingratiating as ever, Mehy himself came to my chamber, promising me the use of a ship, sailors, servants, guards, and was there anything else the Lady of the Two Lands would need?

I assured him that he had been most gracious, and I trusted Tanut-amon to arrange the details of our trip. But while I was away, I would depend upon Mehy to see to my mother's care, even if he had to check on her comfort every hour by the water clock.

"All twelve hours of the day," he promised, bobbing like a reed in the wind, "I will visit her. She will be tended with the utmost care and concern, as if she were Isis—"

"She is more than Isis," I reminded him. "She is mother of the heir to the throne, and Pharaoh's favorite lady." I smiled. "I thank you, Mehy, for your kind concern."

A week after Tanut-amon's return I found myself riding the waves of the green Nile, the afternoon breeze fanning my face. In shemu, the season of harvest, Hap-Ur shone like the emerald-colored malachite with which Nema adorned my eyes. Green surrounded us—on the river and the riverbanks, where the men who tended the fields labored over outlined plots of wheat, barley, and flax. Men and donkeys tramped along black strips between the emerald rectangles, pouring precious water over the growing crops. The workers often paused to shade their eyes and look up at our ship . . . and I wondered if they had any idea who was passing by.

Gulls dived and shrieked among the ropes as we pulled in the sails and let the felucca ride the current to Memphis, home of past kings and the current vizier of Lower Egypt. From there we traveled to Heliopolis, where many of Pharaoh's sons were educated in the religious arts.

At Heliopolis, Tanut-amon sent the servants into the marketplace to buy food. Later, as we dined on roasted duck, onions, and grapes, he gestured toward the north and told me that just beyond the horizon Hap-Ur would branch into tributaries. "We will ride the easternmost waters." He shifted his hand toward the northeast. "Your father's ancestral home is there, and so are most of the Hebrews. They are building Pi-Ramesses."

I squinted into the distance. "We will be safe on the journey?"

"You, my lady, are safe anywhere in Egypt. Not even the Hebrews would dare harm the wife of a god."

We traveled more slowly as the river narrowed, but a leisurely journey worked to our advantage. Each night we anchored the felucca in a quiet cove, then the servants disembarked to build a fire. While they prepared the evening meal, I sat on the deck and studied the night sky. The stars glistened like precious stones, but were brighter by far than any gem I had ever seen upon Pharaoh's chest. Through some magic of nature, those quiet nights began to restore the peace I had taken for granted when I lived in the shadow of my mother's love. Trusting in Tanut-amon's plan, I set aside my fears about Pharaoh.

When Re-as-Khepri began to cross the sky at dawn each morning, Tanut-amon directed the male servants to tend the boat and bake a fowl while my maids and I went down to the water.

The land of Goshen looked nothing like Thebes—there were fewer fields here, and far fewer irrigation canals. Tanut-amon explained that as Hap-Ur subsided into its bed each year, it left behind large pools that did not dry up until the end of shemu. Water lilies carpeted these marshy places, known as *pehou*, and reeds, papyrus, and bulrushes fringed their boundaries. The tall papyrus reeds often grew in such profusion that the ducks and waterfowl felt secure enough to nest there, so the pools were excellent places to hunt.

My maids and I enjoyed looking for birds in the marshes. With Nema carrying my quiver and arrows, I would take my bow and set out on a short expedition, hoping to bring back a bird or two. We saw all sorts of marvelous things—hens sitting on their nests, screech owls watching us through narrowed eyes as they patiently waited for nightfall, a crocodile hoping for an unwary stork to stride across its snout. Nema delighted in spying batensodas—fish that lazily swam upside down for so long that their backs became pale while their bellies darkened.

We enjoyed ourselves so much in the marshes that I nearly forgot my purpose for journeying into Goshen. My memories, however, came rushing back one morning when we encountered a band of women gathering papyrus.

We came upon them as my maids and I chased a fat duck through the shallows and into the reeds. I was just about to draw my bow when Nema stopped in ankle-deep water and threw out her hand. I halted in midstep, and we remained silent as frantic female voices fell upon our ears. Ahead of us, the rushes were rustling.

Creeping as quietly as cats, we moved forward, forgetting the duck. Severed stalks of papyrus floated on the water near us, along with a papyrus bundle someone had dropped in haste.

Nema parted the reeds. In the distance, just beyond the reedy boundaries of the marsh, a dozen mud-brick huts stood around a common fire pit. Several bundles of papyrus lay on the ground; others had been unbound and spread upon the earth for drying. Thatched roofs covered the primitive structures, and though we saw no sign of the papyrus-gatherers, three young children played in the sand before the entrance to the hovels.

Consumed by curiosity, I moved closer. Unlike Egyptian children, these young ones had thick heads of shaggy hair and wore simple loincloths of dark fabric. They babbled in a tongue I did not recognize, but Tanut-amon was right—if not for their odd hairstyle and coarse clothing, they could have been Egyptian.

At that moment an older girl of eight or nine stepped out of a house with a basket on her hip. Nema and I shrank back into the reeds lest she see us, but she seemed preoccupied with other concerns. "Aharon," she called, glaring at one of the squatting toddlers. The rest of her words were unintelligible, but clearly she wanted him to go inside. When he did not move, she yanked on the small boy's ear, making him wail; then the girl turned him toward the hut and swatted him on the rear.

Nema brought her hand up to cover a smile. "Surely his sister."

I was about to reply, but a new sound stole my breath. Something in the toddler's yelp must have stirred another pair of ears, for a baby's cry cut through the rattle of the insects in the thick morning air. The sound set my blood to rushing through my veins, and for a moment I could not breathe. The child I heard . . . would be mine, if I wanted it. I could step out right now and stride into the house, take the child, and either succor or sacrifice it, whichever I pleased. I was Egypt, and these people were only slaves.

But I could not move. I stood transfixed in the reeds until a woman about my mother's age appeared, but there was nothing vacant about this woman. She searched the reeds and spied me almost instantly, and from the look in her wide eyes I knew she understood that I had heard the baby. A tiny shriek escaped her, then she whirled and rushed back into the house.

"Mistress?" Nema's hand slipped around my wrist. "Should I fetch the guards?"

I shook my head. Too many emotions were surging through my chest; too many thoughts whirled in my heart. I gripped her hand and slipped back through the reeds, retracing our steps.

"Let us return to the ship," I said when I found my voice. "I must speak with Tanut-amon."

MIRYAM

❦

For the first time in my memory, I could not comfort my mother. Despite my attempts to reassure her, she held the infant to her breast and rocked back and forth, weeping because her son was lost, her baby doomed. "She saw me," she cried, tears spilling from her eyes. "And the babe was wailing. She will send soldiers; they will kill him. And my heart will break."

The baby cried with her, so lustily that I feared the other women in the village would soon come to our window to complain. Yet my mother kept lifting her voice in the dreadful ululation of mourning that had become altogether too familiar to the children of Israel.

Secretly, I worried that Mother had lost her senses. Some members of our village whispered that she was crazy for hiding her infant. Since the baby's birth, an event that opened more doors to the world of the women around me, I had learned that some mothers, fearing Pharaoh's edict, quietly smothered their male children as soon as they exited the womb. Others left their babies in the marketplace in hope that some Egyptian woman would rear the child as a slave in her home. But my mother doted on her new son from the moment of his birth, refusing to release him even to the care of the midwives who stood ready to swaddle his limbs.

"He is a handsome boy," my mother had told them. "And I will beg the God of our fathers to protect him."

Shiphrah and Puah, the midwives who had come to assist during my mother's travail, did not argue, though other women in the village did. "You trust in a God whose name you do not know?" some of them shouted the first day my mother returned to work in the fields allotted to our village. "Forget about him! You might as well pray to Nut, the sky goddess, so she will not bake your baby when you are finally forced to leave him in the hot sun! Or perhaps you should pray to Great Hapi, the river god, so he will not drown your son and provide meat for the crocodiles!" Some of the women were so vicious in their attacks I worried they might toss the babe to the river in order to spare us trouble with the Egyptians.

My mother remained resolute beneath their harsh words, but I could not bear to let her hear such criticism. I led her back to our hut, promising to do her share of work in the fields until the babe had been weaned.

That day my gentle mother excused the other women, saying their hard words sprang from shattered hearts. "There is not a woman among them who has not lost a son or a husband to the Egyptians," she told me, her voice heavy as she allowed the baby to suckle at her breast. "They believe the God of our fathers has forgotten us."

Sometimes, when I climbed a tree and looked across the marshes toward Pharaoh's vast city on the horizon, I wondered if the other women were right. My people had lived in Goshen for generations, yet few of them could recall our God's name. The Egyptians had a name for every deity imaginable. They understood the power that resulted from knowing a god's name, for with it you could command the deity's attention and understand his essence.

When I lifted my eyes to the spangled heavens of night, I didn't know how to begin addressing the God of my forefathers. The best I could manage was, "God of Avraham, Yitzhak, Yaakov, and my father Amram, hear my prayer . . ."

Though my mother sympathized with the women in our village, she did not trust Egyptians. In the three months since the baby's birth she had been as nervous as a cat, and today I thought she would jump out of her skin. I had been inside the house, trying to shush the baby and quiet

Aharon, when she ran into the hut and slammed the door, her eyes blazing beneath her veil. "Egyptians!" she hissed, her face going as pale as the sun-bleached palmettos that lined our roof. "Royal Egyptians!"

Before I could stop her, she swept the baby from my arms and sank into the corner, cowering there as if the shadows of the room could hide her from prying eyes.

"Mother, there is no one outside."

"I saw them! An Egyptian and her maids, and they saw me! I'm sure they heard the baby crying!"

I knelt at her side. "Mother, I was outside only a moment before you. And I saw no one, only Aharon and Sari's little girls—"

"She was hiding in the reeds!"

"Who?"

"An Egyptian girl—wearing jewels and a gold collar! She will come for the baby, I know it!"

To shush the crying babe, my mother parted her garment and held the infant to her breast. Leaving her in the corner, I stepped outside and turned slowly toward the reeds.

The slender papyrus reeds bent slightly in the breath of the wind, but there was no girl at the water's edge. No sign of Egypt at all.

MERYTAMON

I was trembling by the time we returned to the felucca. Tanut-amon took one look at me, then had a slave bring me a chair. As I sank into it, one of the servants produced a fan and began to move the air around me.

The priest's dark eyes raked my face as he offered a goblet of cool water. "Gracious Lady, are you ill?"

I shook my head, then lifted the goblet to my lips. Forgetting herself, Nema blurted out the reason for my discomfiture: "She heard a baby crying in the Hebrew village beyond yonder marsh."

Tanut-amon glanced at my maid, then straightened. "Well." A wrinkle appeared in his forehead. "The gods have heard your prayers."

I lowered the goblet as a sudden wave of emotion crested and crashed over me. I wanted a child, I *needed* a child, but could I simply stride up and take one from the woman I'd seen in the village? She was only a slave, true. Probably fashioned from dung—but if so, what would that mean for her child? What if the child was not fit for Pharaoh? After wresting it from her arms, could I fling it into the river as if it were of no more significance than a fish?

Yesterday I might have been able to. Even this morning. But in that

Hebrew woman's eyes I had seen a look I recognized. My mother had worn the same look when I grew ill or when one of the other royal children committed some offense against me.

"That woman," I managed to whisper, "will not release the child easily. She wears the look of a tiger."

"Ah." The muscles worked in Tanut-amon's jaw. "I have seen that look in animals. The drive to protect one's offspring is strong."

I wiped my forehead, for I had begun to perspire beneath my wig. "I don't know if I can do this thing, my friend. Perhaps we should find another way."

"Now you surprise me." Tanut-amon uttered those words in a flat voice, without inflection or affection, and his tone caught me off guard. Not even my younger sisters dared to speak to me in such a voice.

The priest's eyes gleamed like obsidian. "If you are a true daughter of the god Ramesses, if you are the daughter of brave Nefertari, you will draw courage from deep within you and do what must be done. The royal wife who does not produce children is of no value as a consort. So if you do not act now, you will spend your entire life at Mi-Wer, alone and childless. You will spend your days with vapid fools who care for nothing but gowns and food and jewels. When you die, you will be buried in a plain tomb, without the servants and goods you will need to prosper in the afterlife." His lashless lids closed over his eyes. "Consider the eternal consequences, daughter of Pharaoh, before you step away from this opportunity. A wise ruler must always take the long view."

Shame, agony, and indignation whirled in my heart. How dare he speak to me this way! Yet he spoke the truth, and with my mother incapacitated, he was the only one with courage enough to speak bluntly. Perhaps I had been a spoiled and protected child until this moment, but I was a daughter of Pharaoh, a bride of the world's most powerful king. I could sit next to him as the Great Royal Wife and influence the course of Egyptian history.

Was this not what I yearned for as I read ancient stories of other royal women? Had I not longed to do something significant with my life, to accomplish deeds the scribes would record for future generations? And I desperately wanted to please my father, as a daughter, a wife, and a consort.

I drew a deep breath to steady my voice. "Tomorrow, Tanut-amon, you will go with the guards to the Hebrew village beyond. Search every house until you find the baby. Examine him yourself—if he is a goodly child, unblemished and healthy, bring him to me. If he is weak, unattractive, or disfigured, offer him to Hap-Ur according to Pharaoh's edict."

A small, admiring smile crossed the old man's face, then he bowed. "It shall be done as you command."

As he turned to go, I looked at Nema and read the unspoken thought in her eyes.

"I know." I pitched my voice for her ears alone. "He would have preferred that I go to the village myself. As a daughter of Pharaoh, perhaps it is my duty."

I shook my head. Tanut-amon would have to be content with whatever cooperation I could give. Beneath my heavy wig and its circlet of gold, I was still a girl of only fourteen summers.

MIRYAM

◈

Detained again by the overseer, my father did not come home that night. So in the manner of women who must rise up to defend themselves, my mother stopped crying and applied thought to her grief. Working by the dim light of our single oil lamp, she took strips of dried bulrushes from a storage bin outside the house, then began to weave them into a basket. Silently, I watched her, a little terrified by the sad smile dominating her features.

"I may not live to see him under a marriage canopy," Mother murmured, her fingers flying between the long, flat strands, "but I will shelter him under a canopy now."

She might not live? I crouched against the wall, my heart pounding like a drum beneath my breastbone. What was my mother planning?

I shivered as a vision rose before my tired eyes—my mother carrying her baby in this basket, wading into the river until the waters lapped at her knees, her thighs, her waist. Yet she would continue until the river claimed her and the baby. She would give both her soul and the baby's to God before she would let the Egyptians take him.

"Miryam!" Mother's voice, sharp and insistent, woke me from my shallow doze. "Take the jar of pitch outside and heat it in the fire. Do it now."

I stared at her for a moment, not understanding, but there was no dis-obeying the energy in her eyes. Obediently I pulled the jar of pitch from its storage place, then carried it outside to the fire pit. Wood was a luxu-ry slaves could not afford, so we had learned to cook with charcoal and wormwood.

Inside the house, my mother kept weaving, but now she hummed a song she had learned from her mother, a song about God's power and protection. How could she sing that song? We had not known God's pro-tection in years. Our men died at the hand of Pharaoh's taskmasters, our babies drowned in the Nile. Our young men worked until their bones snapped beneath the heavy loads their masters forced upon them.

"Pay attention, Miryam. The pitch will be smoking by now."

So it was. Using a forked branch, I lifted the jar from the coals, then carried it inside to my mother. With a singleness of purpose I rarely saw on her face, she dipped a flat piece of wood into the pitch, then began to slather it on the outside of the woven basket.

Then I understood. She was making—

"A *teba.*" She guessed at my thoughts. "Like that of Noah. As God pre-served Noah and his family in the teba, he will preserve my son."

I sank silently back to the packed earthen floor. I knew my mother loved me, but if I had been born under a decree of death, would she have gone to this extreme for my sake? Now I think so, but as a child of eight I could not understand the depths of a mother's heart.

I pondered these mysteries for the length of the night, watching from the shadows as my mother made an ark for the infant she could no longer hide.

MERYTAMON

T anut-amon and a trio of guards left for the Hebrew settlement shortly after sunrise the next morning. My stomach churned as I watched them go.

"Come, lady," Nema said, reading the troubled state of my heart. "Let us leave the ship and go down to the water. While I wash your hair, the cleansing river will carry your troubles away."

And by the time we returned to the boat, I would have either an answer from Tanut-amon . . . or a child to offer Pharaoh.

Agreeing with Nema's wisdom, I slipped into my cloak, then stepped over the springy gangplank and joined my maids on the shore. Together we walked with bare feet over cool sand not yet warmed by the sun. Tiny turtles in striped gowns of bright green and yellow lifted their heads at our approach, and a school of silvery minnows darted away as our shadows fell upon the shimmering river.

"Mistress, look!" After dropping her gown, one of my maids took a running leap at the water, landing on her belly and sending up a great splash. She meant to lighten my mood, and she did, for soon I was laughing with Nema as she removed my cloak and poured a jar of sweet-scented unguents into my hair. Several of the other girls splashed by us, relaxing in play, and as I waded into the shallows I breathed a prayer of gratitude to Hapi for providing a diversion to occupy my thoughts.

My words died away when my eyes beheld a most unusual sight. A tiny boat floated upon the river a short distance away. The covered vessel had lodged among the reeds and now it bobbed there, each splash of our merrymaking jostling it in its resting place.

I froze as memories flooded over me—stories of Horus, hidden by Isis in the river reeds to protect him from the wrath of his evil uncle Seth. Had someone else hidden a child among the flags at the river's edge?

I lifted a dripping arm from the water and pointed to the object. "Girls! Do you see that? Bring it to me!"

Nema gaped openmouthed as two of the maids sprinted through the shallows. One of them parted the bulrushes while the other bent to pick up the floating basket.

I stepped out of the water, a shiver of apprehension shriveling my skin as the servants approached. Nema hurried after me, holding my cloak. I slid into it as the girls knelt before me. One of them reached out to lift the basket's woven lid.

"Don't." I stepped forward. "I'll do it."

"But mistress, it could contain anything!"

She was right, of course. A Hebrew with malicious intent could have planted a cobra, an asp, or a nest of scorpions in the basket. But my heart knew what the little ark contained.

My fingers trembled as I reached for the lid. A soft mewling sound broke the tense stillness, and as I lifted the covering the creature inside began to wail in earnest.

"Mother Isis, help us!" Nema's hand went to her throat. "Is it Horus?"

"It's a baby . . . of the Hebrews." A perfectly formed, strong and handsome boy, as naked as the day he came from his mother's womb, but undoubtedly a great deal plumper. And already circumcised, which left no doubt as to his origin.

A chorus of delighted exclamations rose from my handmaids.

"He's adorable!"

"How sweet!"

"By the life of Isis, he is precious!"

With a certainty borne of confidence, I lifted the infant and sheltered him in my arms. He nestled there, seeming relieved to find himself in a woman's embrace, but after a moment of sucking his fingers, his red face crinkled in frustration.

Nema arched a dark brow. "He's hungry. And none of us has milk to give him."

I looked around at my maids, most of whom were younger than I. None of us had borne a child, and no one on our small expedition had any way of producing milk for this hungry babe. We didn't even have a goat with us.

From out of the river reeds, a skinny girl-child appeared. "Great Lady," she said, speaking stilted Egyptian. She fell to her knees in the dirt. "Would you like me to find a wet nurse among the Hebrew women for you?"

I smiled in pure relief. Once again, the river god had supplied my answer. "Go." I waved her off, and the skinny girl darted away.

While we waited, my maids and I amused ourselves with the baby. Nema tried to feed him a piece of bread she had chewed to a moist softness, but the infant only spat the pulp out and wailed louder. Finally, with genuine gratitude I looked up and smiled as a Hebrew woman approached. I was not surprised to recognize her.

Our gazes met and held for a long moment, then she fell to her knees as her daughter had. The skinny child, I noticed, had accompanied her mother on this return trip. She hung by the river's edge, as tall and thin as the reeds growing there.

"This child"—I looked at the woman—"needs a wet nurse. Are you able to nurse an infant?"

I knew the answer, and she knew I knew. But for the sake of our charade, she nodded dumbly.

"Your name?"

"Jochebed, of the clan of Levi."

"Jochebed, take my son." Grudgingly, I held the baby out to her; she rose eagerly to accept my gift. "Take the child away and nurse him for me, and I will pay you wages."

She held him tenderly, and if I'd had any doubts that she had borne the child, they vanished when the babe buried his face in the folds of her robe, seeking the life-giving breast.

"When he is weaned, bring him to me." I reluctantly shifted my gaze from the baby to her face. "I will send word so you will know where I am."

"And who," her voice cracked, "shall I inquire for when I bring him?"

"Ask for Pharaoh's daughter," I replied, more out of habit than conscious thought. "Merytamon, who is also Pharaoh's wife."

∾

I knew I would not see my son or the Hebrew woman again for nearly three years, for most children were not weaned until then. Mindful that a pregnancy, even a divine one, would have required a period of confinement, we journeyed upon the river for three months, then I returned to Mi-Wer and went into seclusion. For another three months I kept my distance from the other women of the harem, seeing only my maids, my mother, and Tanut-amon.

A year after my arrival at Mi-Wer, I gradually eased back into the life of the community. I told anyone who asked that I had a son who was with his wet nurse, and I looked forward to the day when I would present him to Pharaoh. I spoke truthfully and with great joy, and no one seemed inclined to doubt me.

While at the harem, I spent hours watching other mothers with their children, observing how they taught, encouraged, and comforted them. Soon I would be doing the same things for my son.

I said my prayers each morning, offering praise to Pharaoh's gods for enabling me to achieve a tentative victory over the machinations of Nephthys, the goddess who had stolen my womb and my mother's ba. My mother's condition did not improve, but I hoped the powerful sight and sound of her first grandchild would summon the missing piece of her soul from the underworld dungeon where Anubis had imprisoned it.

In my morning prayers I also offered supplication, begging the gods to keep my child safe among the Hebrews and my brothers out of harm's way in Syria. Though all the sons of Pharaoh were trained in military skills from a young age, Tanut-amon told me stories of the Hittite warriors that chilled my blood and made me worry for my brothers. The Hittites did not fight in lightweight two-man chariots like those of the Egyptians, Tanut-amon said, but drove heavier conveyances with three-man crews of a shield bearer, a spearman, and a driver. With these strong vehicles they battered their way through an enemy's frontline, then set about slaughtering the foot soldiers.

I soon commanded Tanut-amon not to tell me any more war stories. "I will be raising a son," I reminded him, "and while he must be skilled in the ways of war, I do not think I can bear to think of him suffering on a battlefield."

Wisely, Tanut-amon changed his topics of conversation. As we entered the third year of my sojourn at Mi-Wer, he began to bring news of the building at Pi-Ramesses, which would soon be the most magnificent city in the world. "They have built a bronze-smelting furnace," he boasted, "as long as ten men laid end-to-end. More than three hundred metal-workers there produce tons of bronze each day."

"Are these metalworkers Hebrews?"

If Tanut-amon sensed the concern behind my question, he gave no sign of it. "Not many." He shrugged. "Most of the Hebrews are charged with making bricks. Pharaoh employs skilled artisans to work on the statuary and in the quarries; few of the Hebrews have those skills. Most of them mold bricks. More than anything, the king's city requires bricks."

I brushed Tanut-amon's fascination with brickmaking aside, for what did Pi-Ramesses have to do with me? My thoughts centered on the little boy in a Hebrew village, and the soon-coming day I would take him into my arms and raise him as a son of Pharaoh. When we next saw my father, he would smile with favor upon us. He would invite me to sit at his side and enjoy the radiance of his divine presence.

I filled my days with reading and dreaming of motherhood.

In the third month of *proyet*, the season of the emergence, Tanut-amon arrived at my chambers with auspicious news: "Your son, Merytamon, awaits your pleasure at the harem gate."

"Bring him to me!"

I dashed to my bedchamber to check my appearance in my mirror, then hurried to the central hall in my apartment. As I fretted upon a chair, squeezing Nema's hand, Tanut-amon returned, an odd little family trailing in his wake.

I forgot that they had been traveling for days; I forgot to offer them refreshment and an opportunity to wash the sand from their feet. As they prostrated themselves upon the floor, my eyes fixed on the rounded bundle strapped to the woman's back.

"Stand, please." My voice sounded faint in my own ears.

They rose—a gaunt, bearded man, stooped at the shoulder; the wide-eyed woman I had met at the river's edge; the thin girl, now a young woman of perhaps a dozen years; and a smaller boy, about six. The family features, which I had scarcely noticed in our previous encounter, now loomed apparent. The children of this family shared their father's spareness, their mother's hooked nose, and golden brown eyes that gleamed in the sunlight streaming from the clerestory windows.

I looked at the woman, my eyes pleading with hers. Slowly she untied the knot below her breasts, then unlatched the tiny pair of hands that gripped her shoulders. She bent slightly and turned, allowing a pair of sturdy legs to touch the tiled floor. Soft bare shoulders flexed as the child reached up to her, but she resolutely turned him to face me.

Tears blurred my vision as I beheld my long-awaited son.

How can I express the feeling that welled in my heart at that moment? Few joys can equal the ecstasy of motherhood, and few words can adequately convey the feeling. I felt a warm glow flow through me as I beheld stout arms, a round face, a head full of tousled brown curls. His eyes, when he looked up at me, were soft with sweetness, his lips as pink as acacia petals, his cheeks as full as ripe melons.

Forgetting all protocol, I slipped from my chair and sank to my knees. "Come," I called, extending my arms. The boy looked up at his wet nurse as if asking permission; for a moment I feared the woman would forget our arrangement and beg to keep him. But she nodded solemnly and pressed her hand to his back. The boy stepped forward, his gaze now fixed upon my face.

A thrill shivered through my senses when his chubby fingertips touched mine. Laughing, I drew him into my arms and tipped my face upward, not caring who heard the sound of my joy. I don't know what the Hebrews thought—truth to tell, I little cared. For the past three years, I had instructed Tanut-amon to pay Jochebed a living wage, so the family probably owed the clothing on their backs and the food in their bellies to my largesse. They had given me a precious gift, but I had also provided for them.

I turned to the woman. "What baby name did you give him?"

She glanced at her husband before answering. "I called him Jekuthiel, but his father called him Heber. In our tongue, the name means 'reunited.'"

I gazed at my son in delight. I would give him an Egyptian name, a name fit for a son of Pharaoh. *Mose* was the word used to name a child born on the anniversary of a particular god, but I had no idea when the child had been born. No matter, my son could choose a patron god at his leisure. In time he might call himself Amon-mose, or Thut-mose, but for now, the name was close enough to *mos,* our word for water, to make me smile each time I called him to my side.

"I will call him Moses." I caught Tanut-amon's eye. "Because I drew him out of the water."

Stepping closer, Tanut-amon spoke in a low voice. "Will you not give him a god's name as well? If you call him Seth-mose, you might go far to appease Nephthys—"

"Why should I appease a goddess who has done nothing but hurt me?" I did not look at the priest; the child had captured my eyes as well as my heart. "When he is older, if he wishes a god's name, he may claim one. Until then, he shall simply be Moses."

Scooping the child into my arms, I rose on tiptoe and twirled in the center of the room. Startled, the boy clung to me, then, caught up in the spirit of my impromptu dance, he laughed. Together we raised our happy voices to the gods, then my son and I slipped out a side door, leaving Tanut-amon to say my farewells and give the Hebrew family a bag of silver.

The priest and I had already discussed the terms of our settlement. For Jochebed's silence, Tanut-amon would promise to continue paying wages to the Hebrew woman. Her husband, of course, would still work in the brickyards, but Jochebed's wages would help the family provide for the two remaining children.

I carried the boy to my chambers, delighting in his dusty, earthy scent. No longer would I stare longingly at the other women as they played with their children. Finally, I had a son of my own.

"From today forward you are Moses," I said, watching the boy's eyes grow wide and round. I knew our language sounded strange to him, but surely he could hear the warmth of love in my voice. "Today," I breathed a kiss in the soft folds of his neck, "you have become my son."

∿

I do not think love had ever smitten me before, for a daughter of Pharaoh was not free to dream of other men, but in the weeks that followed love beat me senseless with blows to the heart.

I loved my beautiful son, foolishly and desperately. Having prayed, worried, and waited for him, every day after his arrival revolved around his needs. Within a week he had begun to smile at the sound of my voice; after a month he could babble in the Egyptian language as if he had been born to it. He learned to clap with delight whenever Tanut-amon appeared in our chambers, and the pleased priest usually responded by giving the boy a little cake or other treat.

Hoping for a miracle, one morning I took him to visit my mother. I stood him before the Great Royal Wife, beautiful Nefertari, and prayed that his presence would spark some sign of life in those dark eyes. But my mother and my son beheld each other in silence, and after a few moments I took Moses by the hand and led him away.

Two months passed like two days; then we heard that Pharaoh was returning from his military campaign. Tanut-amon read all the official reports, then helped me discern the truth of the matter. Though Pharaoh was declaring victory, the campaign had been far from decisive. At a battle outside Kadesh, a band of Hittite charioteers had nearly defeated him in a surprise attack, but my father had leaped into his chariot and rallied his personal guards. Stunned that an ambushed king would react with such valor, most of the attacking Hittites retreated across the river in terror.

Impressed by Pharaoh's bravery, the next day the Hittites sent a messenger to sue for peace. Now, under the banner of truce, Ramesses and his army were returning to the Beautiful Land. Along with royal dispatches covering every subject from taxation to his mammoth temple project at Abu Simbel, he had sent a message asking the Royal Wife Merytamon to meet him at Pi-Ramesses.

He wanted me.

I knew, of course, that Isnofret and Bint-Anath had retired to Mi-Wer shortly after Pharaoh's departure for Syria. They had been living at the harem for many months, but I had not even considered the possibility that they might have fallen out of favor. But none of that mattered—my father and king wanted to see me, and his desire would grant me the opportunity to present him with a son.

Tanut-amon and I made immediate plans to leave for Pi-Ramesses. The journey to the Delta would take at least two weeks, and I had to be certain to look my best before Pharaoh. I wanted him to look upon me with approval; then I would present Moses to the king and hope he would recognize the boy as his lawful son. If he did not accept Moses, I would be discarded like an uninteresting concubine. If he suspected me of infidelity, my life would be forfeit.

Two days after receiving the summons from Pharaoh, Tanut-amon, Moses, and I boarded a royal felucca and floated downstream to Pi-Ramesses. At stops along the way, I watched my small son play on the docks. During his first few days in my household he had been quiet, watching much and saying little, but now he delighted in pointing at objects and people and naming them in the Egyptian tongue.

Now he pointed at Tanut-amon. "Bald!"

I laughed softly. "Yes, Moses, Tanut-amon is bald. But he is a priest and worthy of respect, so you should not mock him."

My old friend's lips curved in an expression that hardly deserved to be called a smile. "He has nerve, this boy. He is outspoken."

"He is but a baby, Tanut-amon. Babies do not know what they are doing."

"Even babies should be given boundaries. Pharaoh does not tolerate recklessness, even from children."

I lifted Moses onto my lap, then ran my hands over his sturdy legs. "Pharaoh has not met *this* child. Moses is not like those other whiny little brats."

"That reminds me." The priest was studying my face with considerable absorption. "I know you adore the boy's quirks, but you must make certain this child is virtually invisible at the palace."

I looked up. "Invisible? Why on earth would I do such a thing?"

"The less attention you bring to him, the better off we will be." The priest jerked his chin toward my darling Moses' golden brown curls. "You must cut his hair immediately. He should look like the king's other sons."

I rolled my eyes at this, but I knew he was right. All the young royal princes wore their heads shaved with the exception of one lock over the right ear—the Horus lock, usually braided, signified their royal status. Moses would not look like a king's son without it.

Ruefully, I agreed. "I will ask Nema to shave his head this afternoon. She has already fashioned him a loincloth to wear in the king's audience chamber."

"A loincloth? For one so young?"

"I know it's unusual, but I'd rather not have anyone notice that Moses is circumcised."

Tanut-amon nodded. "You are wise, daughter of Pharaoh. I should have thought of it myself." He hesitated a moment, then finished his thought. "While I know you are proud of the boy's beauty and boldness, you should do as little as possible to draw attention to him. Every eye will be upon you when we meet the king at Pi-Ramesses, but sometimes it is best to remain at a safe distance from the god's attention."

Silence stretched between us as the boat drifted lazily downstream. The waters were low and green, this being the season of drought, and to our right and left harvesters and their donkeys lined the riverbanks. A musician shuffled behind one group, piping a tune on his flute, and the harvesters' sickles flashed in rhythm to his song. They dropped the corn to the ground, where women gathered it up and loaded it into baskets slung across the donkeys' backs. I smiled as I spied a little boy running over a black strip of earth, a sheaf of corn in each hand. He was not much older than Moses.

I leaned back in my chair, feeling the warmth of the sun on my face as I let my thoughts wander. Behind me, the long figure of the pole man who steered the boat fell upon the water, creating shadows where there had been none a moment before. A silver fish swam against the current, hiding in the shade. Did he know that he clung to the shadow of a mere slave? With a word, I could send the man away, and the poor fish would find himself exposed to the harpooners once again.

What would Moses' life be like if I had not rescued him? If any other Egyptian had found him, he might be dead; if by some miracle he had not been discovered, he would be thin and hungry, as frail as the sister with the bony elbows and wide eyes. So taking him had been the right thing to do, and presenting Moses as Pharaoh's son would be right as well. I would not be lying, at least not blatantly, for Moses was my son, legally and emotionally, and therefore Pharaoh's son as well.

I would not be lying . . . would I?

Words from the Book of the Dead echoed in my heart, repeating themselves with increasing intensity. When I stood in the Judgment Hall after death, I would have to place my heart in the scales of justice to be weighed against the feather of ma'at. I would have to say, "There is no sin in me, I have not lied wittingly, nor have I done aught with a false heart. Grant that I may be like unto those favored ones who are around thee . . ."

Could I repeat that prayer with a clear conscience? Or would I be found false on account of the story I planned to tell Pharaoh when I next saw him?

If I told Pharaoh the bald truth—that because I was barren, I plucked a Hebrew child from the river in defiance of the king's own edict—his anger might wax hot enough to result in death for myself and Moses.

If I told him a complete lie—that he had slept with me, that I had conceived his son and borne him from my own womb—the gods would certainly judge me harshly in the afterlife and commit my soul to the Destroyer.

But if I told him a partial truth, perhaps good would prevail. After all, the idea had come from my beloved mother and my trusted priest, and they knew Pharaoh better than I did. And would not even Jochebed prefer that I keep Moses' true identity a secret? She had tacitly played into my hands the day I found Moses at the river. Surely she would not want her son to die now. If the Hebrews worshiped any gods at all, she had probably begged them to preserve her son.

I turned to Tanut-amon, who was watching the horizon with half-closed eyes. "What gods do the Hebrews worship? Is Great Hapi among them?"

The priest pursed his lips into a small circle, then unpursed them enough to answer. "Though some of them have adopted the gods of

Egypt, few of them worship the river. From what I have heard, most of them do not worship any god at all. A few cling to the god of their fathers."

"An older god, then. Like Khnum, the great potter?"

Tanut-amon lifted a bunch of grapes from a golden stand at his side, then plucked one and popped it into his mouth. "From what I understand, yes, they say their god created the world. They believe in the Great Flood, as we do. But they have no images of their god. Most of them do not even know his name."

I digested this news in silence. A god without an image? A spirit, then. We knew the gods were spirits; the statues in our temples represented the attributes of the divinities we served. But we had names for all our gods, some gods even had three or four names, for they were known by different names in different settlements. All cities had at least one patron god, and most people had one or two personal favorites.

Which god, I wondered, watching my son, would Moses choose to make his own? In manhood, would he be known as Khnum-mose, to honor me, or Amon-mose, to honor Tanut-amon? And which god had his mother begged to keep him safe when she lowered him into the water? Whatever god she had petitioned had certainly answered her prayer, for not only had Moses been saved, but he had been restored to her for three years.

"If I knew his name," I whispered, "I would beg him to safeguard us when we kneel before Pharaoh."

Tanut-amon stopped chewing his grapes. "Who?"

I shook my head. "Never mind."

Though I appreciated his willingness to act on Moses' behalf, I would not worry about the nameless Hebrew God. Moses was an Egyptian now. He would learn to serve our gods, and when he became pharaoh, the gods would serve him.

I lifted my gaze to the northern horizon, where the golden walls of Pi-Ramesses had come into view. If Moses were to have a future at all, I knew what I had to do.

⟨⟩

The welcome ceremony began the moment our vessel pulled up to the dock outside Pi-Ramesses. A stele at the quayside proclaimed the wonder of the city to all who approached: "His Majesty has built himself a Residence whose name is 'Great-of-Victories.' It lies between Syria and Egypt, full of food and provisions. The Sun arises and sets within its horizon. Everyone has left his own town and settles in its neighborhood."

Because I had not seen Pi-Ramesses in years, I marveled at the sight. Though the city was still under construction, Pharaoh's workers had surrounded it with tall, gleaming walls that extended as far as I could see in both directions.

A group of courtiers met our traveling party—young men in festival dress, with freshly set wigs and cones of perfumed oil upon their heads. They stood on the dock, their arms laden with greenery and flowers, and bowed as I stepped off the boat.

"Welcome, Royal Lady!" One heavyset man in white came forward and bowed himself to the ground. "Beloved of the King, Most Fair in the Two Lands! Welcome to Pi-Ramesses, which is beauteous of balconies and dazzling with halls of lapis and turquoise. I am Hori, overseer of the Great House at Pi-Ramesses, and devoted to Pharaoh."

I turned for a brief moment to check on Tanut-amon and Nema, who carried Moses, then lifted my chin and followed my escort through the impressive gates.

Hori had not understated the city's beauty. Though the atmosphere was heavy with dust and clamorous with the sound of chisels, considerable progress had been made in a city that had been more functional than lovely before Ramesses' ascent to Egypt's throne. The seaport of Avaris, which had bustled with activity in the day of my father's forefathers, would move from commerce to beauty by the time Pharaoh's plans had been fulfilled.

My garrulous host babbled constantly, taking pains to point out empty spaces from which important buildings would one day rise. "His Majesty plans to build temples for Re, Seth, Amon, and Ptah," he explained, tossing me a quick smile. "All of the important gods will be represented. And all of the high officials will have houses within the city walls—tax collectors, governors, and military captains. But Pharaoh's house will be the most spectacular of all."

At this, he stopped beside a tall wall into which two gilded doors had been set. "This is my humble home, which Pharaoh has desired to use until his palace is complete. Enter it, Beloved Lady, and honor my household with your loveliness."

Thanking him with a smile, I turned to my retinue. "Nema and Tanutamon will walk behind me," I told them. "Everyone else will wait outside."

Escorted by Hori, my people and I moved through the towered gateway and into the courtyard of the overseer's home. From there we passed into the porch, then the vestibule, where we held our hands and feet over the lustration slab as a maid poured water over our exposed flesh. Another servant handed me a towel, and I felt better after swiping Moses' round face with the wet cloth. There could be nothing of the dusty Hebrews about him today.

When servants had finished ministering to us, Hori led us into the north loggia. Plucking a single lotus blossom from a bouquet presented to me by one of Hori's servants, I held the long stem between my hands, then drew a deep breath. The rest of my life would depend upon the next few moments . . . and Pharaoh's attitude when he saw me.

As the doors to the central hall swung open, Hori pointed past the tall red pillars in the center of the chamber. "Pharaoh is holding court in the reception area beyond. Enter at your leisure, Divine Lady."

A knot of people stood just inside—couriers, nobles, tax collectors, priests—but they parted as I moved into the large rectangular chamber. At my right a trumpet blared; then a guard announced my appearance: "O Pharaoh, live forever! The Lady of the Two Lands, Mother of Horus, Beloved of Pharaoh, Merytamon approaches thee!"

My gaze darted over the men who stood at the front of the room. Two empty chairs rested upon a low brick dais. Several men had gathered around a board upon a wooden stand; most wore the loincloths and light armor of warriors. One of the men looked up, and I recognized my father, my husband, the god of my world and all Egypt—Usi-ma-re, "Strong in Right is Re." Ramesses.

My knees turned to water, but I steeled my nerves and kept moving. My lord the king wore the electrum war helmet, not the double crown, and he had chosen a pleated loincloth instead of the more formal kilts he had favored in Thebes. A girdle of leather embraced his waist, and a simple gold collar adorned his neck.

Obviously, thoughts of war still occupied Pharaoh's heart.

I stopped a few feet short of the empty chairs at the front of the room, then sank to my knees. Touching my palms and face to the floor, I called, "My lord the king, life, strength, and health forever! Merytamon, blessed by the king, seeks to bring thee honor!"

"Welcome, God's Wife."

With my face inches from the floor, I smiled in relief. The voice that answered my salutation brimmed with kindness. I lifted my head and beheld Pharaoh advancing toward me. He did not carry the ceremonial crook and flail, but his right hand reached out, helping me from the floor.

I could have melted in relief.

"My lord and king." I smiled at him. "I have offered sacrifices on thy behalf at the temples of Amon-Re and Mut. I have worshiped thee in the temples of Ptah and Bastet, and have made sacrifices to Hapi to ensure that the river would bring thee safely home to the Beautiful Land."

Pharaoh squeezed my hand—the most affection he was likely to demonstrate in such a public place—then gestured toward the empty chairs. "Come, Beloved of Egypt, and smile upon me while I confer with my captains. We are sending fresh forces to the desert garrisons to keep watch on Syria's restless tribes."

He released my hand, then hesitated for a moment as his gaze swept over my attendants. "Is this Tanut-amon, much-esteemed servant of Nefertari, who attends you?"

"Yes, my lord."

Tanut-amon bowed low, touching his palms and wrinkled forehead to the floor.

"You may rise, priest of Amon." As Pharaoh lifted his hand, his small, bright black eyes grew somewhat smaller and brighter, the pupils of them training on the priest with an eager intensity. "And how is Nefertari, Beloved of the Two Lands?"

Tanut-amon dipped his head slightly. "She is . . . the same, my king. Her ba has not returned to us."

Pharaoh blinked slowly as a tremor touched his smooth, marblelike lips, and in that moment I realized how much my father loved my mother. But he would not speak of her. Instead, his gaze slid over my handmaid, lingering on the child riding her hip.

"And who is this?"

I knew he didn't mean Nema; Cushite slaves were practically invisible in the royal court. His eyes were fixed upon Moses, whose shaven head now bore the Horus lock worn by princes of Egypt.

I could not conceal my fear. I trembled with it until I thought my teeth would chatter, but somehow I stepped forward.

"My lord, I have a gift for thee." I don't know how I managed to speak, for my tongue felt thick and heavy in my mouth. "Royal Father! Before thy assembled court I am honored to present thee with a son."

Keenly feeling the pressure of a dozen pairs of eyes, I knelt and stretched out my arms. Moses, confident as always, willingly slid from Nema's grasp and ran to me, then climbed into my lap and wrapped his chubby arms about my neck.

Pharaoh watched with an uplifted brow, and I saw thought working in his outlined eyes. He was thinking, trying to remember if he had slept with me.

"Royal Father." I summoned the words Tanut-amon had given me. "Through the bounty of Great Hapi, god of the river, I have received this boy as a precious gift. As Hapi is the son of Horus, so I present this boy, Moses, as your offspring through the gift of the gods. I have established him as thy son so he might one day be worthy of inheriting thy throne and kingdom. I am praying he will grow in wisdom, skill, and might, as befits a son of Pharaoh."

I looked away, afraid of what I might read in those powerful eyes, but after a long moment my father and husband spoke: "A handsome boy, truly."

"Yes, my lord. He is bright, too."

The king crossed his muscular arms, then lifted one hand to his chin. Still staring at my child, he opened his mouth as if to speak, then smiled. "Will he come to me?"

A ripple of surprise moved through the crowd of onlookers as Pharaoh, the god in flesh, knelt on one knee and held out a hand to my son.

I lowered Moses' bare feet to the stone floor. "Go," I whispered, placing my hand in the small of his back. "Go to thy royal father."

I held my breath—and knew that behind me, Tanut-amon was muttering fervent prayers. Would the Hebrew child advance toward the king who had murdered hundreds of his people?

And then, wonder of wonders, Moses stepped forward, a smile spreading over his round cheeks. He walked straight into Pharaoh's arms, then lifted a hand toward the vulture at the center of the king's glittering electrum crown.

"Halt!" Pharaoh laughed, catching Moses' wayward hand. "You are not king yet, little one!"

As the onlookers behind me twittered, Pharaoh stood and lifted the boy. Moses clapped his hands and smiled at his royal father, but the glittering crown had fascinated him. Again he reached for the vulture, and this time he succeeded in knocking the crown askew before Pharaoh caught his hand.

My smile froze. This meant nothing. Young children reached for things; any mother would have overlooked the act as a simple mistake. But this man was no common father; he was Pharaoh, who never appeared bareheaded in public. And ordinary fathers did not have an attendant corps of dour-faced priests who scanned every action and idle word for signs and portents.

Now one of the priests, a long-faced fellow with a bulbous nose, stepped forward, a frown dominating his features. "Mighty Pharaoh," he said, his voice as dusty as the streets outside, "this is an evil omen. A child so fixated on thy crown might try to assume it against thy will. How can we forget the evil sons of the past who attempted to murder the rightful king?"

I did not move, but from behind me I heard Tanut-amon's quick intake of breath. The priest's unspoken accusation rang in the silent space above our heads—*Here is another woman from the harem, and she may be hatching yet another murder plot!*

My thoughts began to whirl. Pharaoh believed in signs and portents; we all did. And he had other sons, older sons, who stood in line for the throne. I myself had two brothers who were offspring of the Great Royal Wife, and he would undoubtedly want them to rise to greatness before this grasping child. If I could convince him that Moses was not a likely candidate for the throne, that in all my babbling I had only meant that I wanted my son to grow worthy of it—

Fortunately, in that moment Pharaoh was more rational than I. "I do not wish to discount your warning, Rudjek." He lowered Moses to the floor. "But neither do I wish to deny this son his right to greatness. After all, I have lost two sons in recent months. Who can say whether or not this child is destined to rule Egypt when I am united with Osiris?"

I felt my stomach contract. He had lost two sons? He could only mean Amon-hirwonmef and Prehirwonmef, who had gone with him to Syria.

Swallowing hard, I wrapped my arms about myself and tried not to think of my brothers. Later—when I had the time and freedom to mourn— I would weep for them.

The priest narrowed his painted eyes as he stared at Moses; then he looked at me. Behind those eyes I saw naked suspicion. He was probably thinking of how soon Pharaoh had departed after making me his wife, and how long I had been exiled at Mi-Wer. Soon he would be counting the months and judging the age of this child, wondering if Pharaoh could have fathered the boy.

Was this another malevolent trick from Nephthys? Frustrated by my success and happiness, had the goddess conspired against me again?

"Let this child be put to death." Rudjek dismissed me with a glance. "Pharaoh has many wives and many sons. Thy fruitful loins will furnish Egypt with an army of princes, and none of them will be so brash as to seize the crown off thy head."

"O King, live forever!" Stepping to my side, Tanut-amon spoke. "Do not listen, Mighty Pharaoh, to this advice to slay the child. It will be innocent blood thou wilt shed, for this child is still young, and knows not what he is doing."

Pharaoh glanced from Rudjek, his priest, to Tanut-amon, who had served my mother. I lowered my eyes, fearful of the moment's outcome.

"I have an idea." My father spoke slowly. "A test. Let two bowls be brought before me—a bowl of golden rings mixed with sparkling jewels and a bowl of glowing embers. And let us set them before the child to see which attracts his eye."

Rudjek clapped his hands in approval. "A wise test, O King. We shall then determine whether the child is wiser than befits his age. If he stretches out his hand and takes the gold and precious stones, then he is certainly endowed with wisdom and understanding beyond his years—in reaching for thy crown, he must have acted with design and therefore deserves death. But if he grasps the live coals, then his action was the result of a childish fancy and he must be innocent."

I drew a breath, about to protest, but a sharp glance from Tanut-amon stopped my voice. A woman had no right to speak in such matters. Who was I, after all, to protest the decision of a god?

While Moses sat at my feet, happily tracing the lines between the brightly painted floor tiles, servants scurried to bring the items the king had commanded. While we waited, Tanut-amon turned to me. Speaking in a low voice meant for my ears alone, he whispered, "'Tis time to offer prayers, Royal Wife, from your heart. For in his nurse's village this child was undoubtedly taught to avoid the fire, and he will not go near the coals. But, having never seen rings and baubles, he is apt to reach for the king's treasures and seal his doom."

A chill crept over me, freezing my scalp to my wig. I glanced right and left, hoping for some interruption from Hori or one of the other officials, but no one in the room dared move. A moment later two slaves entered, the first carrying a bronze bowl filled with golden rings, necklaces, and gem-studded pectorals. Between two thick cloth mats, the other slave held a brass bowl filled with gleaming coals. A thin stream of smoke rose from the second bowl, and my nostrils filled with the acrid scent.

Reflexively, I bent and lifted my son.

"Set the bowls on the floor," Pharaoh commanded.

The servants obeyed, then the king turned to me. "Set the child on the floor, Merytamon."

No courtly phrases did he use this time, no lofty praise or royal titles. He spoke in an unvarnished tone, and I feared my fate as well as Moses' would be decided in the next few moments. If I, even unwittingly, proved to be an object of threat, I would be forever exiled to Mi-Wer.

Moving woodenly, I stepped forward and lowered Moses to a spot equally distant from the bowl of jewels and the bowl of fire. Tanut-amon's words proved true—Moses did not even look at the fiery bowl, but toddled steadily toward the gleaming baubles.

I closed my eyes and began to pray to a god whose name I did not know. *God of the Hebrews, if you care about your people, if you care about this child, direct his grasp. Save him from this test of fire and gold as you saved him from the water—*

My eyes flew open as a shrill scream echoed through the reception room. Moses sat on the floor before me, his tiny fingers black with soot, his palm already blistering from the heat. Though glowing embers still clung to his moist skin, he was about to thrust his fingers into his mouth—

"No, Moses!" I rushed to his side, brushed the gleaming embers away, then pressed his burning flesh against the coolness of my own cheek. Kneeling by my screaming child, I glared at Rudjek, who wore a look of frank disappointment, then looked at Pharaoh. He was watching me with something like loving pride in his eyes.

"Take your son, Lady of the Two Lands." He raised his hand in a gesture of blessing. "Live with me in peace and keep the son of Pharaoh safe."

Unwilling to bear the tension a moment longer, I lifted my shrieking child and ran from the room.

With tender-loving care and generous applications of aloe, the burns on Moses' hand faded, as did my anxieties. Though we returned to Thebes with Pharaoh, the king rarely saw my son. I did not regret the lack of royal interest—as Tanut-amon had said, sometimes it was best to remain at a safe distance from the god's attention.

Though my father now had scores of women for his pleasure, I truly believe he loved my mother best of all. After our return to Thebes, he ensconced her in the finest apartments in his palace. He visited her often, and I am told he would sit at her knee, one hand reaching up to stroke her placid face as she stared into the distance. Realizing that she needed the healing touch of Amon-Re, he ordered physicians to take her for daily walks in the sunlit gardens.

I continued to visit Nefertari, too, but my living child demanded more time than my vacant mother. After a year of spoiling my child to my heart's content, Tanut-amon declared that Moses should begin his formal education. So at four, my son donned the belt and loincloth of a boy and left babyhood behind. Tanut-amon came to my chamber each morning to instruct Moses in music and writing, and by the time Moses passed his fifth year, the priest declared my son ready for day school.

Each morning my small son accepted from Nema a little basket containing a crust of bread and a jug of beer, then left the palace for the writing school in the temple of Amon-Re. As the sun lowered in the western sky he returned to my chamber, offering me a chance to examine the rough flakes of limestone on which he had traced hieroglyphic signs. As he grew older, the passages he wrote grew longer, until he was learning to write the lengthy Hymn to Hap-Ur by heart.

One day Moses came home bursting with pride. He had memorized a song, he told me, for the priests often taught lessons by encouraging the boys to sing them. As I watched in pleased surprise, Moses sang a little song of this verse: "Always to mother be loving and tender; God will be angry if love you don't render."

Another day Moses' homecoming was not so pleasant. One afternoon he returned to me with a blackened eye. When I demanded to know the cause of such bruising, he reluctantly explained that his schoolfellows had taunted him after the teacher praised his work. "They surrounded me, asking, 'Whose son are you? Haven't you got a father at home?' I did not know how to answer them, so I punched the first boy I could reach. He punched me back."

His quick temper dismayed me, but I understood the frustration that had fueled my son's anger. Sadness pooled in my heart, a heavy and familiar despondency. On many occasions in my own childhood I would have gladly exchanged a father on the throne for a father in the house.

"Oh, Moses." I drew him into an embrace. "You should not strike out against those who are weak and ignorant. You know Pharaoh is your father."

Stubbornly, he pushed away to look into my eyes. "The priest says Pharaoh is father of all Egypt. Who, then, is my father?"

I floundered in an agonizing maelstrom of emotion. Who, indeed? What could I tell him?

I gripped his strong shoulders. "Your father *is* Pharaoh, and you must never doubt it. When you are of age he will call you into his service and you will feel the blessed rays of his favor. None of your little schoolmates will be so honored, Moses. Only you. For you are the son of a god."

In my younger days a niggling worm of guilt might have risen to torment me with those words, but since presenting Moses to Pharaoh I had come to believe that Moses had been unusually blessed by the god whose name I did not know. How else could we have defeated the evil scheming of Nephthys?

At the age of eight, my little godling graduated from schoolboy to student and began to study with the priestly tutors engaged to teach the sons of Pharaoh. He no longer wrote his lessons on limestone slabs, but with carefully prepared red and black inks upon costly papyrus scrolls. To my delight, Moses proved to be an exceptional scribe. His hieroglyphic paintings were not only neat and legible, but beautiful in their artistry. He also learned how to read, write, and speak Akkadian, the international language spoken at court whenever foreigners visited. I once remarked that the written version of this tongue looked like bird footprints to me, but Moses laughed and said he enjoyed learning foreign languages.

As he grew, my athletic son became adept at gymnastics, swimming, and the intricacies of Egyptian religion. Through Tanut-amon's skillful tutelage, he learned how to worship in the temples of the gods, how to offer sacrifices, and how to read the ancient literature with feeling and understanding. Every morning he accompanied me to the temple of Amon-Re, and together we set offerings before the statues of the chief god of Thebes. As we wandered through the forest of columns designed to resemble a papyrus thicket (reminding me of the place where I had found my son), Moses would read the hieroglyphic images high on the walls, beyond the point where my poor eyes could focus.

One morning as we strolled together in the temple of Amon-Re, Moses interrupted his recitation to whisper in my ear. "Royal Mother, you should pray to Hathor for more children. Surely the goddess mother of all kings would give you another son if you asked her."

"I used to sacrifice to Hathor," I replied, taking pains to keep my voice light. "I sacrificed to Thoeris and Min, too, the gods of childbirth and fertility. I also made sacrifices to Shed, the savior and helper of mankind."

Moses cocked a bushy brow at me.

"When the gods sent me you," I said, smiling at my tall and handsome son, "I stopped wishing for other children. You are the son of my heart."

At the age of twelve, when other royal sons underwent circumcision as a rite of adolescence, I told Moses that I had circumcised him as an infant to spare him pain as a youth. He accepted this news gratefully and declared I was the wisest mother in Egypt, for he had heard nothing but moaning from other princes after their encounters with the surgeon's knife.

Now that he stood on the brink of manhood, Moses entered advanced studies with other royal princes. After our evening meal I often paused outside his bedchamber and overheard him muttering his recitations with Nema or Tanut-amon.

"What are the rations for soldiers on campaign?" the prompter would ask, or "How many men are needed to transport an obelisk?" Moses' studies covered everything from history to geography, and demanded that he understand military tactics as well as practical logistics.

But never did he falter. I overheard other women complain about their sons' laziness and obstinacy, but during his youth, Moses rarely brought me anything but pride and pleasure in his accomplishments.

His only noticeable character flaw was a lack of self-control when events pushed him from irritation to anger. His temper did not simmer beneath the surface as some tempers are wont to do, but blazed forth in unthinking actions and harsh words. When his rage had passed, he was always quick to apologize, but the sparks in his dark eyes frightened me when his temper flared into fury. I clung to a sincere hope that his fiery nature would settle as he matured into manhood.

As Moses matured, Pharaoh's interests shifted from war to building. By the winter of my son's fifteenth year, Ramesses and Hattusilis of the Hittites signed a peace treaty. Though Tanut-amon would never speak such things to anyone but me, after he pointed out certain unwritten stip-ulations in the document I realized that Pharaoh had abandoned his claims to Kadesh and Amurru. In return, Hattusilis agreed that Egypt would be assured control over the eastern shores of the Great Sea and granted access to ports as far north as Ugarit, where no Egyptian had set foot for more than one hundred years. According to further terms of the remarkable treaty, the kings of Egypt and the Hittite Empire agreed to come to one another's aid if attacked by a third party.

Much ado was made of the truce. Royal messengers from Hattusilis brought a final copy of the treaty inscribed on a silver tablet. Papyrus copies were stored in the Egyptian state archives of the House of Life, and Pharaoh had the terms of the treaty engraved upon the walls of the temples at Karnak and his mortuary temple at Thebes.

To reciprocate, Pharaoh dispatched official greetings from himself and the Great Royal Wife to the Hittite king's court. My mother, of course, was in no condition to write a message to her counterpart in the Hittite Empire, so I penned a missive for her. As Tanut-amon watched over my shoulder, I dipped my pen in ink and wrote: "With me, your sister, all goes well; with my country all goes well. With you, my sister, may all go well; with your country may all go well. Behold now, I have noted that you, my sister, have written to me, to inquire after my well-being. May the sun god and storm god bring you joy; and may the sun god cause the peace to be good and give good brotherhood to the great king, the king of Egypt, with his brother the great king, the king of Hatti, forever. I am in friendship and sisterly relations with my sister the great queen of Hatti, now and forever."

With the advent of peace, Pi-Ramesses celebrated in festival. Envoys laden with correspondence and gifts of jewels and fine clothing traveled between the royal courts of Egypt and Hatti. Through all the festivities, I felt relief and joy for my father. In battle, he had proved himself a warrior. Now he had proved himself a diplomat, and his people would benefit from peace.

The time had come, my father told his officials, to begin building in earnest. Religion demanded that each king build upon the accomplishments of his predecessors to ensure their immortality as well as his own. At death, each pharaoh was reborn as Osiris, and would be worshiped in Egyptian temples for as long as Egypt remained. Thus it fell to the priests to offer perpetual sacrifices in Pharaoh's name, and thus it fell to the people to remember his name and image. A king's life span lasted as long as his memory, and Ramesses was determined to become immortal.

So not only would he continue to build Pi-Ramesses, but he would complete his father's mortuary temple and build his own in Thebes. The temple at Karnak, in which his father had begun a huge hypostyle hall with more than one hundred thirty ornate columns, needed to be completed. For the outside walls Ramesses commissioned reliefs depicting his military campaigns in Canaan and Syria, as well as a copy of the peace treaty with the Hittites. And in Upper Egypt, at the far southern reaches of the empire, he would carve a temple out of living stone at Abu Simbel. There he would honor the gods and himself.

I cared little for buildings, palaces, or temples. I was content to worship in the palace shrines, content to live my simple life with Nema, Tanut-amon, and Moses. With each passing day I found myself falling a little more in love with my son. I had been married to Pharaoh, and yes, I loved him, but how can you adore a man who is more figurehead than husband? I knew he had other wives, I knew many of them had presented him with royal sons. He was fond of me—I saw affection in his eyes whenever I visited the royal court—and yet fondness is not passion, nor does it engender marital love within a husband's breast.

Though my womb never did ripen, still I had become a woman, with a woman's passions. And as I entered the years of maturity I discovered that I *could* love, I *did* love immensely. I adored the boy I had drawn from Hap-Ur, the child who had twice been saved by the unseen, unnamed god of the Hebrews. I could never admit this to Tanut-amon, but deep within I knew none of my Egyptian gods could have defeated Nephthys and stopped that toddler's grasping hand. Moses should have reached for the jewelry, he *would* have reached for the gold, had not some god misdirected his hand at the last instant. Khnum, the creator and potter, left his creations alone after fashioning them. Amon-Re did little but shine down upon us day after day. But the unseen god to whom I had prayed had power to move his people even after he had formed them.

I yearned to know more about the god of the Hebrews, but was not in a position to learn. I continued to dispatch small bags of silver to the family of Amram and Jochebed, but never did they respond to my letters—

then again, I wasn't sure they could read or write. At the time I thought they might be too proud to contact me, but now I think they were too wounded. What woman who has given up a son wants to be reminded that he is growing to manhood in another woman's care? The wages I continued to send were assurance enough that he was well.

Moses was my life. At fifteen he had grown taller than any of the other sons of Pharaoh, a fact that often elicited comments from members of the king's court, though none of them would dare accuse me of impropriety. Tanut-amon and I kept a careful eye on Rudjek, who had opposed my son in his boyhood, but the crafty priest had little to say about Moses . . . though I often felt him watching us from a distance.

Any honest parent of a teenager will tell you that children are not always a delight. In the summer of his sixteenth year, for reasons that still elude me, Moses withdrew from my embraces and rebelled against my remonstrations. I began to hear reports of daydreaming and distractedness from his tutors. One teacher, a priest called Amenmose, personally visited me to speak of my son's conduct. "He is neglecting his studies and spending all his time dancing, going from tavern to tavern, always reeking of beer."

"Amenmose," I protested, struggling to catch my breath, "surely you have my son confused with someone else!"

"I do not think so." The priest looked down his pointed nose at me. "He is like a shrine without its god, and a house empty of bread. If only he could realize that wine is a thing of the devil and forget his wine jars! But he neglects his own dignity. More than once I have pulled him from establishments of wine and dancing girls, where women of easy virtue entice even the sons of Pharaoh—"

I threw up my hand, cutting him off. "Enough. I will speak to him."

"Forgive me, Gentle Lady, but he needs more than a mother's rebuke. He needs a father's stick, for a young man's ear is on his back; he listens only to the man who beats him. Horses must be trained; monkeys have to be taught to dance before they are of any use—"

"I will speak to him," I repeated wearily. "Do not trouble yourself further."

As Amenmose departed, I lowered my head into my hands and wept.

What could I do? I did not dare trouble Pharaoh with this; he scarcely knew Moses by name and knew his character not at all. Tanut-amon was the closest thing to a father figure in my son's life, but the frail priest now barely came up to Moses' shoulder. A young man flushed with strength would not respect a bald priest who cared more for service than for the pleasures of this world.

I could think of only one answer. In peacetime, most princes of the royal blood entered training for Pharaoh's army in their eighteenth year, but perhaps Moses was ready for military training now. He had completed all the regular courses of study, and undoubtedly his daydreaming stemmed from boredom.

Lifting my head, I wiped the tears from my eyes. When Tanut-amon next visited, I would tell him to contact the captain of Pharaoh's army at Thebes. Moses had too much energy, and though it meant he would be living apart from me, the time had come to bid him a temporary farewell.

In the twenty-fourth year of Ramesses' reign, three years after Moses had begun his military training, my father commanded that my mother and I accompany him to Abu Simbel, to view the shrine he had constructed to honor the gods of Egypt.

With great ceremony, we sailed up Hap-Ur accompanied by Hekanakht, the viceroy of Nubia, and an entourage of courtiers and attendants. Moses, Nema, and Tanut-amon traveled in my boat, while a company of physicians and handmaids accompanied my mother. The journey was long, and we sweltered in the heat despite the breezes that blew our vessels southward. To complicate matters further, Abu Simbel was located at the second cataract, a white-water region filled with boulders and rushing currents. When we reached the first cataract, we had to disembark and ride in carrying chairs while slaves hoisted our boats out of the water and hauled them overland in order to avoid the rocks.

The territory between the first and second cataracts was dotted with trading posts and populated by an assortment of uncivilized people. I found them uninteresting, but nineteen-year-old Moses stood at the railing for hours, drinking in the odd sights and strange languages. "Bring him inside," I complained to Tanut-amon, "or we will lose him to these brutes." But the priest only laughed and told me that young princes would learn about the world one way or another.

"Besides, your son has brought you nothing but honor of late," the priest added. "I hear he is so mighty of arm that none among the soldiers or the captains can bend his bow."

I shrugged away my pride in his accomplishment. "Moses has always been determined. He makes a success of whatever he chooses to do"—a wry smile twisted my lips—"once he chooses to do it."

"I hear he has no rival in the whole of the army—no man can run as swiftly, nor can anyone drive a chariot as well. They say he can mount a horse with a single leap—"

I stiffened on my couch. "And what good will those skills do him in peacetime?" When an expression of hurt filled Tanut-amon's face, I relaxed and sent him a rueful smile. "Peace must prevail in Egypt, my friend. I do not want my son going off to war. Though he is skilled, I can't help worrying about him."

I worried, too, about my mother. The journey was difficult, and her body frail. I feared this trip might harm her, but I could not say such a thing to Pharaoh.

Finally, we reached Abu Simbel. I stood on the deck as the boat moved past the facade of the temple, and what I saw took my breath away.

The temple faced the rising sun, but the structure itself seemed dwarfed by the magnificence of four gigantic enthroned figures of Pharaoh. The rock behind the statues had been carved in the form of a temple pylon, complete with a cornice surmounted with a cresting of dog-headed baboons, who would worship the sun at its rising.

Somehow the temple architect had sculpted the statues of my father in a lighter-colored granite than the background cliffs, so Pharaoh's image stood out against the tapestry of stone behind the colossi. Seated upon his throne, Ramesses wore the double crown of Egypt, complete with uraeus and the false beard that signified his authority as a god. Above the main entrance stood a figure of the falcon-headed Re-Horakhty.

But beyond this huge temple lay another, and on the facade of the second shrine stood another row of colossal statues, four images of Ramesses and two of . . . Nefertari. Suddenly, I understood why my father had want-ed my mother to come. Her eyes would behold this proof of his devotion, and perhaps the sight would compel the gods to awaken her ba and send it back to her body.

Alas, she did not change. We worshiped in the two shrines, Ramesses, Nefertari, and I, yet my mother did little more than follow us as we went through the motions of offering sacrifices. To record the glorious event, the viceroy of Nubia commissioned a stele to be carved into the rock out-side the temple; later, I saw that it depicted Pharaoh and me performing the appropriate rituals for the temple dedications, while Hekanakht made obeisance to a seated Nefertari.

As we returned home, I stood at the railing of my boat and realized that the trip had changed all of us. Pharaoh finally realized that his beloved Nefertari would not awaken from her stupor, I understood the depths of the love my father bore my mother, and Moses caught a glimpse of the world beyond the palace at Thebes.

Whether these insights would work for good or ill . . . I could not say.

Three months later, during the third month of the season of inundation, a weeping Huda brought the news I had been dreading. Grief welled within me, black and cold, as I ran to my mother's apartments. Nefertari had borne Pharaoh six children, four of whom had survived infancy, but I was the opener of her womb and the daughter of her heart. Though in her last years she had been but a shadow of her former self, I mourned for the woman we had lost after the surgery that erased not only her pain, but her essence.

I found her lying in her bedchamber, her flaccid body surrounded by Tanut-amon, two other priests, and two of her maids. The women wept softly as the priests chanted.

I fell to the floor at the side of her bed as grief ripped through my soul. "How long," I cried, "has it been since she crossed to the western bank?"

Tanut-amon dropped his gentle hand upon my head. "Do not despair, daughter of Pharaoh. Her ka still resides in her body, and will remain in her tomb once we place her there. But soon she will be whole again, for her ba will return to dwell with her ka at night. You and your father shall provide all she needs to flourish in the afterworld."

I closed my eyes to the sight of my mother's lifeless body. Tanut-amon spoke the truth, as always. For years my father had employed workmen to construct his tomb, and I knew he had made similar arrangements for my mother. She would be buried in the Valley of the Queens, the necropolis on the western shore of Thebes. My grandfather Seti lay in a magnificent tomb in the Valley of the Kings, and in my younger days, Mother and I had often presented offerings of food and drink at its threshold.

"You should go, daughter of Pharaoh." Tanut-amon's voice was soft with compassion. "Your mother was prepared for death, so you have no worries here. You have always been a loving daughter."

I rose on legs that felt like wooden stumps and left my mother's chambers. The priests would take her body to a house of embalming, and there they would begin the seventy-day process required for a complete mummification. The house of Pharaoh would mourn until the seventy days had been completed; then we would escort Nefertari to a tomb that had been richly provisioned with everything she would need in the afterlife.

I had no doubt that my mother would pass unmolested through the Hall of Judgment. Though she had given me the idea of adopting a Hebrew child, her words had sprung from selfless love. My obedience, on the other hand, had sprung from ambition and self-preservation. I was not as virtuous as she, but, armed with only my wits and the aid of a nameless god, I had dared to battle a goddess . . . and won.

I found Nema waiting when I crossed the threshold of my chamber. I opened my mouth and gestured toward the hallway, but could not speak. Nema seemed to understand, for she drew me into her arms and held me as I wept.

The title *pharaoh* means "great house," and only those who have lived within its sprawling brick walls can truly appreciate its vastness. In all my thirty-four years, I had never visited every room in the king's house at Thebes, nor met everyone who dwelled within it.

But on the morning of my mother's burial, a warm spring day washed with brilliant sunlight, every inhabitant of Pharaoh's houses at Thebes, Mi-Wer, Pi-Ramesses, and Memphis joined an entourage of priests and paraded through the wide streets of Thebes. I found myself one of many among the scribes, advisers, nobles, governors, warriors, guards, wives, concubines, and children who shuffled along the dusty roads.

The city of the living lay upon the east bank of the flooded Nile; the dead occupied the west bank and the towering cliffs. As I walked with Moses and Tanut-amon, I kept my head high. Throngs of Theban citizens lined the streets and peered at us through the doorways of their houses, and I wanted them to see that we were confident of my mother's goodness. We would mourn her no longer; we were freeing her to live in the netherworld.

We crossed the river on flower-festooned barques; we crossed to the western bank and passed irrigation waterways that shone like bright silver veins amid serried folds of black earth. Along the edges of the newly tilled fields, pennants fluttered in the wind, marking the location of small temples dedicated to the gods. Behind them, in the distance, lay the burial chambers of noble Theban dead.

My mother would not rest in one of the small tombs designed for mortals fashioned from mud. She would lie in a chamber fit for a divine wife of Pharaoh.

As we made our way across the coal-black earth, my gaze fell upon servants tilling the fields. Poor men did not even enjoy the provision of a small burial chamber when they died—unprovisioned and unprepared for the afterlife, they were often buried in the desert, where the dry sand desiccated their bodies. If they were virtuous enough to pass Anubis' examination in the Hall of Judgment, they would enter the netherworld, but there they would find themselves as poor and miserable as they had been in this life.

Shuddering, I repressed the thought. I had read of malicious men who stole bodies from grieving families and buried them in the anonymous sand, but I could not imagine what sort of fiend would commit such an act. Such an evil heart could never escape destruction in the Hall of Judgment.

I closed my ears to the mourners' wails and tried to imagine the western bank at nightfall. According to the priests, the dead came from their burial places at sunset and stood on this riverbank, staring over the water toward the living city. Here they could feel the river's wind as I felt it, and breathe in the sweet scent of fertile earth. Perhaps they could even catch the aromas of meat roasting over evening fires, and hear the shrill chatter of children and the lowing of cattle in the fields. Perhaps my mother would search and find me talking to Moses, the love of my life and the fruit of the suggestion she had planted in my heart.

Opening my eyes, I stared at the purple cliffs in the distance. The heat coming off the rocks made the air shimmy as it rose, causing the cliffs to shudder . . . or perhaps the distortion came from my eyes, which had once again filled with tears. Dashing the water from my lower lashes, I lifted my chin and lengthened my stride.

In time, we reached the boundary of the cultivated land, then passed into the foothills of the mountains. The road began to climb beneath our feet, and the journey became more difficult. After more than an hour of travel, we halted before the carved stone portico of my mother's freshly completed tomb. Behind us, the ox-drawn hearse pulled its sorrowful burden to within a few feet of the entrance. For the first time I was close enough to examine Nefertari's funeral sledge.

The sight of it sent a shiver of revulsion through me. My mother's coffin had been concealed beneath a catafalque mounted on a boat and flanked by statues of Isis and Nephthys, troublemaking wife of the god Seth and my personal nemesis. I would not have chosen to honor Nephthys in this way even if she were my mother's favorite goddess, but the decision had been Pharaoh's.

Unable to disclose my reasons for hating that particular goddess, I bit my lip and turned to Tanut-amon, who acknowledged my distasteful expression with a tight smile and barely discernible nod.

Folding my arms, I edged closer to Moses and waited for the drama to unfold. Now the priests were unharnessing the oxen so the catafalque could be dragged toward the tomb. Behind it, other oxen pulled sledges loaded with furniture, clay jars, and other provisions for the afterlife. Two final sledges completed the procession—one bearing the chest containing the four canopic jars, another carrying a multitude of ushabti figures. The canopic jars held my mother's important internal organs; the ushabti were small statues of servants, scribes, handmaids, cooks, and guards. These would go into the tomb with her, and in the afterworld the gods would magically imbue them with life.

A pair of mummers, wearing crowns of reeds, performed a funeral dance for observers while a team of priests removed my mother's coffin from the catafalque. I ignored the mummers, preferring to watch the progress of my mother's gilded casket. Skilled artists had painted the slender box with her image, but the representation did not do her memory justice. There was nothing of the vibrant, loving woman in the picture. The fixed lips upon the coffin were completely unlike my mother's curving smile, and the eyes stared out at the world with an unfeeling expression. The image was the Nefertari of late, not the Nefertari who had blessed us with love.

When the coffin stood upright at the door of the tomb, a masked priest impersonating the dog-headed Anubis came forward to support it. Behind him, the *sem*, or chief mortuary priest, accompanied Pharaoh to perform the opening of the mouth ceremony.

Moses squeezed my elbow. "What are they doing now?"

I closed my eyes, realizing that he had never attended the burial of a close relative. We had gone to other burials over the years, but we had stood at the back of the mourners, content to watch from a distance.

"Her mouth was closed during the mummification." I kept my voice low. "They are restoring her speech so she will be able to speak in the netherworld. She must be able to breathe and say the magical spells from the Book of the Dead in the Hall of Judgment."

Content with my explanation, Moses locked his hands behind his back. My greedy gaze lingered upon him a moment—even in mourning, he was the most handsome of the king's sons—then I remembered to lower my head in respect as the priest's high-pitched, reedy voice reached us: "Thy mouth was closed, but I have set in order for thee thy mouth and thy teeth. I open for thee thy mouth, I open for thee thy two eyes. I have opened thy mouth with the instrument of Anubis, the iron implement with which the mouths of the gods were opened. Horus, open the mouth!"

Dressed in a resplendent leopardskin, the chief priest touched the lips on the coffin with an adz, a ceremonial instrument shaped like an ax with an arched blade. Tipping it toward the painted lips, he uttered the necessary spell: "You are young again, you live again, you are young again, you live again, forever!"

After this final ritual, mourning began in earnest. While Pharaoh, somber and silent, sat in a gilded chair to the right of the coffin, an entire company of female mourners, many of them professionals, moved forward to weep and wail. They tore their garments, threw sand on their heads, and made the very air vibrate with their shrieking.

I could not join them. I had spent all my tears in the previous seventy days. Now I felt as though my own heart had been encased in the painted coffin beyond.

While the women continued their noisy mourning, the pallbearers lifted my mother's coffin and carried it down the carved steps. Pharaoh, Moses, my sisters, and I followed like sleepwalkers. Over the entrance to the burial chamber, Ma'at, goddess of truth and order, spread her brilliant blue-green wings, a gesture of protection for the one Pharaoh had called "the Most Beautiful of Them."

After descending thirteen steps, we passed through a long corridor where artists had painted images of my mother's life on the walls—Nefertari holding a symbol of royal power over a mound of food for the creator god Atum, the Great Royal Wife eating a banquet with the king. Beyond this room lay another room, filled now with furniture and jars of flour, oil, and dried fish.

Without speaking, we moved into the burial chamber, which was dominated by a pink granite sarcophagus, breathtaking in its smooth beauty. At the corners of the rock that would soon become my mother's final bed, two carved and gold-covered hippopotamus heads would keep watch throughout eternity.

Inside the sarcophagus lay three nested boxes. Moses and I stood along the back wall as Pharaoh stepped up to inspect the work. Only after he nodded in approval were the pallbearers allowed to slowly lower my mother's gilded coffin into the smallest of the three containers.

Chanting the necessary prayers for the dead, the priests ceremonially sealed each box with a fitted lid. When a team of servants lifted the pink granite top of the sarcophagus into position, Pharaoh stepped forward with a floral wreath. As he placed the circle of blossoms around the image of my mother's face, a priest recited, "Thy father Atum binds for thee this beautiful wreath of vindication on this thy brow. Live, beloved of the gods, mayest thou live forever."

With that final pronouncement, servants slid the heavy granite lid of the sarcophagus into place. Moses and I followed our father through the hallways and out into the heat of the day. While we stood squinting in the blinding sunlight, a team of servants began carrying provisions into the burial chamber—more furniture, chests of linen, and the canopic jars. Whatever my mother needed must be provided before the tomb was sealed.

As the servants emptied the sledges and the mourners wailed, we of the royal family prepared to eat a ritual last meal in her honor. At the entrance to the tomb, we tied brightly colored pectorals around our necks. Several of my sisters' younger children were naive enough to peacock around the tomb entrance as if the occasion were a festival. I touched the collar of flowers and beads and felt nothing but sadness.

A harpist opened his performance by telling us that because Pharaoh had been generous, the Lady Nefertari was faring well in the afterlife. When he had finished his song of praise to Pharaoh and his Great Royal Wife, another harpist began a more melancholy song.

While we listened in the shadow of my mother's tomb, servants brought us a banquet—lamb, four different kinds of duck, three varieties of geese, fruit, vegetables, and rich wine. We ate without truly tasting, automatically sampling something from each dish. When we had completed the dinner, we handed our dishes to the servants, who smashed them. The broken pieces of pottery, as well as the bones of the sheep and fowl, were placed inside a large storage jar, then carried to a nearby pit.

As workers buried the jars, a priest stood in the center of the gathering and called out a final word: "As long as Re rises each morning and Atum sinks to rest at night, so long will men beget and women conceive. Through their nostrils they will breathe; but one day each one that is born must go to his appointed place. Make a happy day, all ye who hear. Put misfortune out of your heart and think only of pleasure until that day comes when you must travel to the land of Mertseger, the lover of silence. Look on this and drink and take thy pleasure, for when thou art dead, thus wilt thou be."

Nefertari's funeral was finished.

My family and I walked at the head of the mourners who journeyed back to Thebes. All around me, people talked about the funeral and the fine treasures they had glimpsed in my mother's tomb, but I resolved to put thoughts of Nefertari behind me. Her soul had left us years before; we had only buried her body. I had served her as well as I could, but from this day forward I would live to serve my son.

MIRYAM

Despite the ridiculousness of it, Yitzhak's proposal brought a blush to my cheek. The thought that I might once again stand in the center of the village as a bride—but no, my maiden days were long past. I was twenty-seven, a widow, and settled in my solitary ways.

"Thank you for doing me this honor, Yitzhak, but I will not marry you. You should not have spoken to my father before talking to me."

My would-be husband straightened, his cheeks puffing in indignation. "You would refute your father's wishes?"

"My father does not speak for me. I am a woman grown, with property of my own."

"I do not want you for your goats, Miryam."

"I do not want you at all, Yitzhak." The words were far blunter than I'd intended, but Yitzhak was thickheaded. Polite implications did not penetrate.

He spread his hands. "What is wrong with me?"

"Nothing. You are a fine man. But you have six children, and I do not intend to raise them for you. My parents are not strong; I must work in their field. My brother and his wife have four sons, and I help care for them." I folded my arms and gave him a smile. "Thank you, Yitzhak, but you would be happier with a younger woman."

"Bah!" Yitzhak made a face. "What do I need with a young woman? She would only give me more children!"

I waved him away and turned back to the row I had been working. As my hoe cut into the dark earth, I wondered if I had spoken the truth.

I did not want to marry Yitzhak—of that I was certain. I did not want to love the six children of his dead wife, nor did I want to love him. His proposal reeked of desperation, and I did not want to be married under desperate circumstances.

But it would be nice to be loved again . . . to be courted. Nathan had wooed me gently in the summer of my fifteenth year, and it was with great joy that I learned my father would agree to give me to him as wife.

That joy had been short-lived . . . and our baby's life even shorter. I had poured my hopes into that child, and when he died, he took my heart with him.

In that moment, for the first time, I understood what my mother felt when we surrendered Moses to Pharaoh's daughter.

I hacked at the soil, tearing at the weeds' twining roots as if they were the memories that tendriled my heart. My mother was never the same after we lost Moses. The death of my baby had left me a changed woman, too.

MERYTAMON

fter my mother's death, I thought Pharaoh might name another Great Royal Wife; to my surprise, he named three. Isnofret, who had been drifting in and out of Pharaoh's fickle favor, was reassured of the title, yet it was also conferred upon me and my half sister Bint-Anath.

I suppressed a shiver of excitement when I heard the news. Ostensibly, the title meant that we had found favor with our husband; in reality, it meant that our sons had become eligible to succeed Pharaoh. All of us had presented Pharaoh with royal princes, and time alone would tell which of them would ascend to the throne of Egypt.

As Ramesses continued to add wives and concubines to the royal harem, he continued to sire sons and daughters, yet he rarely summoned me to his bedchamber. I worried that I had somehow displeased him until Tanut-amon told me the reason was simple. "Look in your hand mirror the next time Nema dresses you," he remarked, his voice dry. "You are the image of your beautiful mother."

I gave him a sidelong glance of utter disbelief.

"It is true. You are thinner, perhaps, but you have her face and manner."

"If I do, why does Pharaoh detest me? He adored my mother."

"He adores her still, and in that lies the answer to your question. Seeing you reminds him of the treasure he has lost. I am certain he loves you—if he did not, he would have you and Moses sent to Mi-Wer. I am equally certain he suffers pain in his heart every time he sees you smile when his beloved Nefertari lies silent and still in her tomb."

The priest's answer made sense, and accounted for Pharaoh's reluctance to summon me into his presence. I wanted to please him, but since he did not require much of me as a wife, I determined to concentrate on being a good mother. The gods may have thwarted me from giving Pharaoh many sons, but I would do my best to give him an exemplary one.

Unfortunately, far too many of Pharaoh's sons did not outlive him. After my two brothers passed into the netherworld from the Syrian battlefield, two sons of Isnofret died from an illness. A son by Bint-Anath passed over on his fourteenth birthday, then another of her sons was killed in a drinking-house brawl. Three royal princes died in separate hunting accidents, and another prince drowned in a sudden storm that overturned his felucca during the flooding of Hap-Ur.

With each death, Moses moved closer to the throne, and my anxious hope intensified. Pharaoh could have named an heir at any time—at fifty, he was entering the winter of his life. His own father, Seti, had taken the resolute step of naming Ramesses co-regent in order to establish his son's right to rule. But the years passed, and still my father named no heir.

As Moses matured, I began to appreciate what a king he would make. His three-year-stint in Pharaoh's army had done more than settle his wild impulses, it had made him a leader of men . . . and of our household. I began to notice how quickly he interpreted people's personalities, and how easily he could read my mood. He exhibited a strong drive for harmony, and could not bear knowing that one of the servants was upset with Nema, or that Tanut-amon was chafing under some slight in the royal court. Though Moses could be quick with an abrasive comment— he still had a lightning-fast temper—he was also quick to apologize and make amends. I had no way of knowing what Pharaoh was thinking, but he couldn't go amiss if he named Moses his heir.

One afternoon in the summer of my son's twentieth year, I sat on a bal-

cony with Nema. We were playing a quiet game of draughts, and as I
rolled the dice and moved my game pieces across the polished board, I
would occasionally glance down at Moses and the other young men in
Pharaoh's garden. Mentu-amon, one of the king's captains, was training
the royal princes in warfare. The men had spent half the morning
wrestling; now each of them clutched a battle-ax. Under Mentu-amon's
direction, they took turns charging a wooden dummy, delivering what
would certainly be lethal blows upon a human target.

A cat brushed up against my ankles as I turned my attention back to
the game board. "Moses does not seem to handle the ax as well as the
spear," I remarked casually, hoping Nema would not hear the concern
in my voice. Like any mother, I hoped my son would never find it necessary to go to war. The peace treaty with the Hittites had held, and
Ramesses controlled the banks of Hap-Ur as far south as the fourth
cataract. Members of the army were required to serve at the border garrisons where they often engaged in skirmishes with roving bands of
marauders, but few sand-crossers were any match for Pharaoh's trained
warriors.

"Moses is the strongest prince on the field," Nema loyally replied. "See
how Mentu-amon favors him! When the captain wishes to have a tech-
nique demonstrated, he always calls upon Moses."

I squinted at the arrangement of marble game pieces. "I do not know
if that is a good thing. Sometimes I think Moses likes to show off."

"Bah! Moses is stronger than the others, that is all. Look how he stands
a head taller than Kha'emweset!"

I couldn't stop myself from looking down. Though we would never
admit it, a rivalry of sorts existed between the children of Nefertari and
those of Isnofret, and Kha'emweset was one of Isnofret's sons. He was
handsome and only a few months older than Moses, but I did not think
him nearly as accomplished.

I shifted my gaze back to the polished board as a memory closed
around me—my childhood tutors had always claimed that mortals were
like these marble game pieces, moved about by the whims of various
deities. But Tanut-amon and my mother had encouraged me to draw
upon the divine strength within my soul and move against the gods.

Rather than being passive and waiting for Pharaoh to name an heir, perhaps I should do something to further my son's cause.

A slave stepped onto the balcony and bowed before me. "What is it?" I murmured, shifting my attention from the game.

"O lady, live forever! The priest Tanut-amon seeks an audience with you."

"Send him in." I looked at Nema. "I am sorry, but I haven't spoken to Tanut-amon in weeks."

"Of course, mistress." Nema stood and in one smooth motion lifted the marble game board from its carved wooden stand. "Shall I have food and drink prepared?"

"Please do. If he has walked from the temple, Tanut-amon will be thirsty."

Nema had scarcely departed when my old friend joined me on the balcony. He bowed, then looked up when I leaned down and tapped him on the shoulder. "Tanut-amon, it is good to see you."

"Mother of the Two Lands, live forever in beauty. I came as soon as I heard the news."

I cocked a brow. "What news?"

"Pharaoh is planning an expedition into Nubia. And he desires to have Moses and Kha'emweset accompany him."

I sat still as a curious, tingling shock numbed my limbs. Moses and Kha'emweset had been measured against each other for years. What was Ramesses thinking? Would this be some sort of contest to determine which of his two sons was better suited to wear the crown?

"This cannot be good," I whispered, careful to pitch my voice for Tanut-amon's ears alone. "Moses has enemies in the court. I fear many of the royal princes, including Kha'emweset, are consumed with jealousy of him."

Tanut-amon's smile was grim as he moved to the stool Nema had recently vacated. "The journey will certainly be a test of his character, my lady. But is he not ready for this test? He is confident and strong."

I looked down at the garden, where Moses was charging the wooden dummy with a fury that made my stomach clench. "Confidence and strength are good, but Moses is far from being settled in maturity. His temper is still unbridled, his thoughts often confused—"

"As are the thoughts of most young men." Tanut-amon leaned one elbow on the table and traced his nonexistent brow with a fingertip. "I am not worried about him, my lady. I worry more about Kha'emweset. If he picks a fight with Moses, he may find his chest pricked by the sharp end of your son's spear."

"Do you think Moses would actually harm him?" I pressed my hand to my forehead as a fearsome image rose in my heart. From what I'd heard, my half brother was a resentful sort, quick to start a quarrel and slow to mend one.

"Let Moses go, and say nothing to him of your reservations." Tanut-amon leaned forward to whisper in my ear. "Trust the gods, and all will be well."

His comment was so absurd that I actually laughed, though I felt a long way from genuine humor. Trust the gods? How could I, when Nephthys had stolen my mother, my womb, and done everything in her power to destroy my happiness? Some of the gods might be dependable, but I had an archenemy in Nephthys.

"I will pray to my gods." I pulled back to look the priest directly in the eye. "And I will also pray to the unseen god who has preserved Moses in the past. He saved my son twice before; perhaps he will be pleased to save him again."

For the six months of Pharaoh's Nubian campaign, I lived in a state of heightened tension unlike anything I'd ever known. We received few reports from Nubia, but occasionally we did hear that Pharaoh and his party were well. Ramesses had met with the Egyptian governors of Upper and Lower Nubia and offered sacrifices to Dedun, the patron god of Nubia. The area's officials, scribes, bureaucrats, priests, and agents were overjoyed to experience the divine pharaoh's presence, and apparently delighted to meet two of the royal princes.

After completing their diplomatic duties, the messenger told us, Pharaoh was planning to hunt in the savannahs for lion, panther, elephant, and oryx. As I worried about an entirely different threat to my beloved son, a week slipped by, then two. Finally, we heard that Pharaoh and his party had been sighted on the river.

Nema and I flew to the quayside, where the palace overseer situated us according to rank and position. Waiting in the front of the crowd, I found myself weeping with joy as Pharaoh's ornate barque approached. Amid the blaring of trumpets, a contingent of Medjay warriors thundered over the gangplank, then Pharaoh himself, my husband and father, appeared on the platform.

I gave him a smile and bowed, but understood when he did not pause to speak. As dozens of wives and officials cheered his appearance, the king moved quickly past me and through the gates of the palace. I lifted my head, but did not move from my favored spot, for I had not come to see my husband, but my son. Kha'emweset was the next to step off the barque, and my half brother barely glanced in my direction—nor, I noticed, did he deign to bow to his mother. But when Moses alighted, he lifted me from the dock, spinning me in a dizzying circle as he held me against his chest. The arms that held me were thicker now, I noticed, and more defined with muscle.

"Moses!" Laughing, I pulled out of his embrace to better examine my son. "Let me see how you have changed!"

As courtiers, guards, and slaves milled around us, Moses laughed, the sound warming the air where we stood. I looked at him and could not find a single sign of lingering boyishness in him. His skin had grown darker and richer in the hot Nubian sun, while dark stubble grizzled his chin and cheeks.

I drew back in pretend horror. "You have not shaved?"

"I did, this morning." He grinned. "But my beard grows quickly."

Before I could offer another word of critique, my son, the confident warrior, slipped a strong arm about my waist and propelled me toward the city gates. I went with him willingly, realizing that Moses had left Thebes a youth and returned a man.

Perhaps, I mused, this was what Pharaoh had intended.

In the first month of the season of flood, in the thirtieth year of Ramesses' reign, my father observed the *sed* festival, a holy ritual celebrated by few pharaohs in Egypt's history. The festival originated in the ancient custom whereby the king was obliged to prove his physical capabilities every thirty years in a ceremony called *heb sed*, and my father was pleased to rise to the occasion.

I stood with a crowd of royal women to watch him race against his sons, including Moses, outside the temple of Amon-Re. He won, of course, for none of his sons dared defeat him; then Pharaoh entered the temple for the ceremonies of raising the *dd*-pillar, a marble obelisk symbolizing the stability of his reign. While he raised the pillar into an upright position, groups of professional dancers and musicians took part in a sacred performance consisting of mock fighting, the recital of hymns, and the clattering of rhythmic instruments.

After raising the pillar, Pharaoh and Isnofret left the temple accompanied by priests and a host of royal offspring. Considering that he had chosen Isnofret to accompany him, I should have known what Pharaoh would do next, but my adoration for Moses blinded me. As my son and I trailed in his royal wake, the king halted at the top of the temple steps, looked out at his people and his progeny, and announced that he had chosen Kha'emweset as his heir.

I stood rooted to the floor, my arm linked through Moses', as disappointment struck like a blow to my stomach. Moses did not acknowledge the king's remark, but his voice was husky when he asked if I wanted to escape the hot sun.

"By the stinking crust between Seth's toes, yes."

Two months later, as we struggled to accept Kha'emweset as crown prince, Pharaoh announced that the royal household would be moving to Pi-Ramesses, for his palace there had been completed. Though much of the government work would continue from Thebes, the king's announcement set off a frenzy of preparation. All of us in the immediate royal family would have to move, as well as Ramesses' personal priests, his guards, and untold hundreds of scribes, advisers, and military personnel.

Moses and I planned to go, of course, but a sense of uneasiness lay like a mantle upon my shoulders as I directed the slaves in packing our household goods. Thebes lay a considerable distance away from Goshen where I had found Moses, and here his distinct looks and unusual height had been considered a sign of the gods' blessing.

But what would the Egyptians of the Delta think of him? Living so near Goshen, they saw Hebrews nearly every day. One would not have to be an intellectual giant to look at my son and surmise that he had not been born an Egyptian, but a Hebrew.

I wanted to speak of these things to Tanut-amon, but days passed and my old friend did not appear. Finally, however, a message came to my door. I skimmed the papyrus immediately, and learned that the priest lay near death in his quarters at the temple of Amon-Re. If I wished to see him before he crossed over, I would have to hurry.

Wrapping myself in a cloak, I summoned two of my slave girls and slipped away from the palace, trailing the dusty streets in anonymity until I reached the temple. A guard there would have forbidden my entrance, but I parted my cloak and revealed the royal cartouche upon my necklace.

I found my old friend upon a narrow bed in a small, curtained alcove. A platter of meat, cheese, and fruit stood untouched on a tray close by. His eyes were open when I entered, but unblinking.

From some part of my soul that had not been paralyzed by fear, I summoned a trembling voice: "Tanut-amon, live forever."

One eye blinked, but did not swivel toward me. "Merytamon?" The hand across his chest twitched with recognition. "I can't see you, Gracious Royal Wife, but I know your sweet voice. Come closer, please."

His words were slurred, but I knew he had not been drinking. Leaving my slaves in the doorway to guard our privacy, I dropped to my knees by the old man's bedside.

One corner of his mouth rose in a twisted smile. His breathing came quick and heavy, and something in his throat whistled with each inhalation. "Most unlikely to find you here."

"Most unlikely to find you like this." I slipped a smile into my voice, though my heart was weeping. "I did not know you were ill. I would have come sooner—"

He made a soft tsking sound with his tongue. "I was not ill, child. The affliction struck without warning. And because I fear I will die just as suddenly, I sent for you. There are things you must know before I depart for the west."

A lump in my throat crowded out my words, but Tanut-amon did not seem to notice my silence.

"The payments of silver will continue to be made to the family of Amram in Goshen. I have instructed a scribe, Baken-khonsu, to deliver the expenditure each month. It will be paid from my own estate, so there will be no link to you."

I nodded wordlessly, then remembered he could not see me. "Thank you." The words hurt as they slipped over my crowded throat.

"You must beware, child, of certain priests in the king's household—Rudjek has never forgotten the day Moses made him look foolish in Pharaoh's court. He will be no friend to the prince in the days ahead."

I smiled, warmed as much by his calling me a child as by his care for Moses. I was a mature woman, with streaks of gray already in the hair beneath my wig, but to him I would always be Nefertari's beloved daughter.

Sudden tears blinded my eyes. "I will remember, friend."

"Remember this, too—Kha'emweset is not pharaoh yet. Moses may still rise to the throne. He will always be a prince of Egypt, a son of the Great Royal Wife."

The old man's trembling hand lifted and reached toward me. I caught those spidery fingers and wrapped my palms around them, then brought his hand to my wet cheek.

Again, the half smile played at his mouth. His voice softened. "Do not cry, daughter of Pharaoh. The gods have smiled upon thee and thy son. May they shine upon Egypt as well. May Pharaoh seek truth and compassion for as long as he lives. And mayest thou live in the spirit of thy mother, Rich of Praise, Lovely of Face, the Most Beautiful of Them, who was life and goodness and sunlight to me."

The aged priest exhaled a long breath. I waited for him to take another, but his ba departed without even the twitch of a muscle.

"Tanut-amon?" With my free hand I nudged his shoulder, but he did not respond.

My friend and confidant was gone.

I released him, lowered his palm to his sweat-soaked chest, then stood on knees that suddenly felt as insubstantial as air. In a quavering voice, I called to my maids and told them to summon another priest.

Then I stumbled out of the cubicle, pressed my hands to my face, and wept.

❧

Other pharaohs had moved their capital—Akhenaton had moved his household from Thebes to el-Amarna, and the ancient rulers had conducted their affairs from Memphis. But none of those kings had been as wealthy as my father, and none had employed as many people. The quayside at Thebes became a sea of surging chaos as everyone who was anyone of consequence prepared to move their people and possessions to Pi-Ramesses.

Pharaoh's vizier announced that we would devote the entire season of proyet to moving, and the news pleased me well. I wanted to remain in Thebes for Tanut-amon's burial, and the mummification process would require at least seventy days. My son and I might be among the last to journey to Pi-Ramesses, but I did not care.

The news of Tanut-amon's death affected Moses deeply. The priest had been more than a tutor to my son; in many ways, he had been a father. In quiet evenings after dinner, Moses and I sat in my audience chamber and often spoke of the little man who had made such a huge impression on our lives.

"He taught me about women," Moses confided one night. "Did you know that?"

I masked my surprise. "What did Tanut-amon know of women? He never married."

Moses passed his hand over his jaw, and I heard the rasp of stubble. "He knew many things . . . about women, about horses, about life. He told me I should live each day with death in view. That I should pass each day in happiness, for one day I must fare to the land where all men are as one."

"That is true, but I don't think Tanut-amon wanted you to be preoccupied with death." I reached out and gently touched Moses' forearm. "I think he wanted you to know that as long as you live, you should follow your heart's desire. Sprinkle your head with incense, clothe yourself in fine linen, anoint yourself with the rarest of all the perfumes, for you are a prince of Egypt. Follow your heart and seek your happiness as long as you are on earth. Yes, we must all stand before the gods, but your final day is not yet come, Moses."

"How can I follow my heart's desire?" His eyes flew toward me like a pair of blackbirds alarmed out of safe hiding. "What if my heart's desire is something a son of Pharaoh should not want?"

I looked at him, at once puzzled and amused. "And what is it you want? If it is something in Thebes, you have only to ask and one of the servants will fetch it for you."

He looked away as dewy moisture filled his beautiful eyes. "Servants cannot fetch this."

"And what is it?"

He hesitated, then brought a hand to his jaw. "I was thinking it is time I took a wife. There is a servant in the household of Bint-Anath called Makare, and she is most beautiful—"

I cut him off with an uplifted hand. "A prince of Egypt cannot marry a servant. The arrangement is simply not permitted. Pharaoh will want you to marry a titled lady, probably one of the daughters of a Great Royal Wife—"

"But I love her!" He leaned toward me, anguish flashing in his eyes. "Her hair is blacker than the night, her lips redder than ripe dates. My heart swells with words and feelings when I see her—"

"Your heart must remain silent, my son, unless you can persuade Bint-Anath to give you the girl as a concubine. But you can no more marry a servant than you can mix gold and mud to mold a jar." I lifted my hands, struggling to fit motions to my words. "The two are separate, distinct, and they will not cleave together."

He looked at me, his eyes alive with speculation. "Because Khnum made us of gold, and servants of mud?"

"Mortals are created from mud; servants and slaves must be made of dust or something even less valuable. I know it's hard to understand, my son, but servants were put on earth to serve us, not marry us."

"But they must marry someone."

"Let them marry their own kind. Consider how I arranged for Nema to have a child by the Cushite who serves Pharaoh. Her child is now serving at the temple of Amon-Re, and we are all pleased. Yet if you insist upon having this girl, I will speak to Bint-Anath, and we will arrange for you to take her as a concubine—"

"If I want a woman that way, I will find one at the tavern." His lips thinned. "It does not seem right that one so beautiful should be kept from the son of a god."

"Very little in this world seems right from our perspective," I responded coolly, my pulse quickening at the visible sign of his anger. If I was not careful, he would lose his temper, and Moses in a temper was a fearsome sight. His propensity for flaring into sudden rage was his chief flaw, and neither my rebukes nor Tanut-amon's remonstrations had been able to affect it.

I drew a deep breath and gave him a smile, hoping to cool the flame of his indignation. "When you are older, Moses, you will understand. Until your fate is clear, however, you must control your passions. Bend them to your will."

He rose and left me, stalking away in wide, angry strides, and I did not doubt that he would end this night in one of the taverns. He would either drink his frustration into numbness or take it out upon some unfortunate brawler who did not know the strength of his arm.

"Ah, Moses." I closed my eyes as weariness flooded over me. "If only your father would take you under his arm and teach you himself."

After Tanut-amon's burial, Moses and I settled into the glorious city of Pi-Ramesses with little fanfare—on our behalf. As father of the city whose name meant "Domain of Ramesses Great of Victories," Pharaoh received fanfare with his every step, and Moses and I often found ourselves enveloped in his reflected glory. But despite my son's unsteady passions, we found pleasure in furnishing our apartments and exploring the environs of this glorious new city.

Ramesses had established a vast house of papyri at Pi-Ramesses, and the history of our people fascinated both Moses and me. In our pursuit of story, we discovered an unlikely ally in Kha'emweset. Moses' longtime rival on the training field also loved literature, and spent many of his days in the House of Life, recording the proceedings of his father's court with meticulous care. Moses did not care much for life at court, but many nights he remained awake reading long after everyone else had gone to bed.

One night as I lay upon my bed, unable to sleep, I heard soft singing from his bedchamber:

> This army returned in safety,
> It hacked up the land of the sand-dwellers.
> This army returned in safety,
> It destroyed the land of the sand-dwellers.

I smiled, recognizing the chorus from a royal Triumph-Song of the sixth dynasty. My smile faded a few moments later, however, when Moses abruptly switched to a song of a far different nature:

> When in the house I lie all day,
> In pain that will not pass away,
> The neighbors come and go.
> Ah, if my darling to me came,
> The doctors she would put to shame,
> *She* understands my woe.

Sighing deeply, I crossed my hands upon my breast. My son might occasionally suffer from lovesickness, but at least his feelings were easy to discern.

Yet how does a mother pave the road of life for her son? If she forces the gatekeepers to clear the way, her son will resent her intrusion, and the gatekeepers will snicker to think that the mighty son requires his mother's help. If she does nothing, however, she leaves her son open to suffer for his mistakes, misjudgments, and misalliances. Life was a young man's best teacher, true, but no one had prepared me to experience the pain of watching my beloved suffer the consequences of his foolish actions.

Fortunately, however, most of Moses' mistakes were kept from me. He certainly never spoke of them in my presence, and the servants only told me about less serious offenses, such as the occasions he got drunk and emerged the victor in a brawl. When we were together, Moses was the dutiful son, a perfect prince.

When not reading, riding, or training at the military barracks, Moses enjoyed exploring the marshy lands of the Egyptian Delta. At Thebes, a narrow band of fertile land surrounded Hap-Ur; beyond that band lay nothing but empty desert to the east and rugged mountains to the west. But plants bloomed upon the well-watered Delta, and animal life capered about in glorious abandon.

Here, too, were Pharaoh's famous vineyards. Unlike any king before him, Ramesses emphasized viticulture and the wine trade. He appointed gardeners from among his foreign captives to tend his vineyards, and dug pools of water for their irrigation. When Moses expressed an interest in the vineyards, Pharaoh proved his generosity—and his favor—by giving Moses the vineyard of Sebahorkhentipet.

I used to visit him there, for I found winemaking a delightful process. When the fruit ripened, pickers moved among the fragrant vines, carefully plucking the fat black grapes. They lowered the bountiful bunches into baskets, careful to avoid bruising them, then carried the baskets to granite vats that stood as tall as my waist.

Once the vats were full, a barefoot picker would climb up and hold on to horizontal ropes while treading out the grapes. If Moses or I were present, the overseer would invite musicians to honor us with a song during the treading out. The players used *crotals*—small, flat disks that were clicked together—to encourage the workers to tread rhythmically while a singer improvised a tune in Moses' honor: "Come, master, see thy vines which gladden thy heart, while thy vine dressers are busy pressing the grapes. The vines are heavy with fruit and never have they been so full of juice in any year before. The lady of Imit has caused thy vines to grow strong because she wishes thee well. . . ."

After the treaders had flattened the grape skins, slaves shoveled the juicy fruit into a strong sack, which was then wrung out by four men so not a drop of the precious juice would be wasted. The juice was collected in widemouthed containers, then poured into flat-bottomed vessels to ferment. Later, the fermented wine would be poured into long jars designed for transport, then sealed.

As owner, Moses' responsibilities included overseeing the pickers, the irrigators, and the scribe who counted the baskets of grapes and jars of wine, as well as recording the particulars of the yearly harvest. Nor did

Moses neglect his religious duties, for he appointed a slave to make certain fresh offerings appeared daily on the altar to Renoutet, the snake-deity and goddess of the harvest.

In the season of akhet, when the harvest was done and the Nile floods appeared again on our land, Moses would take me out among the marshes on a small papyrus raft. I would sit in the back and applaud his efforts while he speared gray mullet, sheat fish, or the fat Nile perch hiding among the shallows. Often he shot waterfowl with his bow and arrow, reminding me of my own youthful excursions in the marshes.

I tasted such recollections with pleasure, for if I had never ventured into Goshen, I would never have found my son. My former worries about being so close to the territory inhabited by the Hebrews faded away, for in his wig, pleated kilt, golden collar, and kohl-lined eyes, my son had never looked more thoroughly Egyptian.

I was happy to see Moses enjoying his work in the vineyards. A man with busy hands and many servants had no time for moping about love and serving girls. Silently, I blessed whatever benevolent gods had brought us this great favor, and counted the vineyard as further proof that I had soundly defeated Nephthys's evil intentions.

We passed two years and many pleasant hours in Pi-Ramesses. We might have spent the remainder of our lives in such enjoyable pursuits if the malicious goddess had not sent an enemy to intervene.

One afternoon Moses and I returned to our chambers to discover a guest waiting in the vestibule. I caught a glimpse of the visitor through the gauzy curtain that separated the northern loggia from the waiting area, but I did not recognize the man. The stout fellow wore a short wig and the simple tunic of a workman or scribe.

"His name," Nema told me as she took my cloak, "is Baken-khonsu, and he has come from Thebes."

For a moment the name didn't register, then Tanut-amon's parting words came back to me on a tide of memory. Baken-khonsu was an accountant or scribe dealing with the priest's estate.

"I will see him in the garden." I waved Moses away, then moved with a leisurely tread toward the enclosed private space. I could not imagine why this man would come to see me. Tanut-amon had said there was nothing to link me to the monthly payment to the family of Amram, and he would not have lied. Perhaps this was merely a friendly visit, or perhaps the man had a question about Tanut-amon's wishes. As his royal patron, I would naturally be consulted.

I had just seated myself on a bench by the reflecting pool when Nema returned with the stranger. He prostrated himself on the stone path and greeted me with the poetry typical of an anxious mortal: "May the grace of Amon be in thy heart, Royal Lady. May he grant thee a happy old age and let thee pass thy life in joy and attain to honor! May—"

Interrupting, I calmly asked his business.

With a decided effort, the stout man stood. "My business, Great Royal Wife, concerns the affairs of the priest Tanut-amon, who has dwelt in the netherworld for many months."

I lifted my hand, silently urging him to proceed to the point of his business.

He then shot me a sideways look of cunning that I couldn't decipher . . . and didn't like.

"Are you aware, Royal Wife, of a regular stipend of silver paid to a Hebrew family in the region of Goshen? Tanut-amon has been most faithful to make this monthly payment for over twenty years."

I shifted my gaze to the water lilies and blue lotus blossoms at the edge of the pool. "Tanut-amon had dealings with many people. Though we were close, he did not disclose all his business to me."

The heavy man smiled, then squatted in the open space before me. "It seemed logical, Royal Lady, to think you might know of this arrangement. Tanut-amon began making these payments when he served you at Mi-Wer. And after checking his records, I discovered that the arrangements began at the time of your royal son's birth." He squinched his fat face into a questioning expression. "Can you account for the coincidence?"

I met him with a look as impertinent as his manner. "Why, yes, I believe I can. I employed a Hebrew wet nurse after my son was born. It is a common enough practice."

"You were"—the impertinence in his face gave way to a leer—"unable to nurse the child yourself?"

My shock yielded quickly to fury. "You forget yourself, sir!"

"And why," he persisted, rising on one knee and leaning closer, "would you hire a Hebrew wet nurse when you lived among the king's harem? There were probably a dozen Egyptian women capable of nursing this child of yours."

I stood, taking advantage of the momentary difference in our heights to glare down at him. "I will speak to Pharaoh of this! You will pay for this effrontery!"

"I think not." He rose to his feet with a look of cunning in his eye. "You see, Royal Lady, in the last few days I've had a good look at your son. And the more I study him, the more I'm convinced your Moses is no son of Pharaoh at all. He is a Hebrew, probably one you bought from some poor woman."

Astonishment rendered me insensible. I could not speak.

With a wince of false remorse, Baken-khonsu pressed his meaty palm to his chest. "How difficult it must have been for you to hide such a secret! And how hard it would be for Pharaoh to learn that his most excellent son Moses is not a divine prince at all, but the child of wretched slaves!"

I clenched my fist among the folds of my gown. "You lie! And I will tell Pharaoh you lie."

"You will not need to act against me." The scribe calmly folded his hands behind his back. "After all, you are a woman of property and wealth. There is no reason we should not cooperate in this matter."

We stared at each other across a ringing silence, and I knew my next words would establish either his version of the truth or mine. . . . I found myself wishing I had Tanut-amon to settle this matter as he had all my other problems.

I forced my words through clenched teeth. "If Tanut-amon was generous enough to provide for a poor slave family in the Delta, surely it would not be charitable to discontinue such payments now. The soul of Tanut-amon would be grieved."

Baken-khonsu smiled. "Do you not think the spirit of Tanut-amon would be gladdened to know that I was receiving a reward equal to that monthly stipend of silver? After all, I have worked hard to maintain his privacy—and yours. And I have troubled myself to come all this way to see you—two weeks on the river is no easy journey."

I closed my eyes, considering the question. I could easily afford to make regular payments to this scoundrel, but what reason could I give my accountant for sending Baken-khonsu a monthly sum?

The man guessed at my thoughts. "I would be happy to become your scribe," he said, spreading his hands. "I have always wanted to live in a spacious apartment in Pi-Ramesses, the new city of the great king. If I were added to the employees of your household, no one would question the arrangement. And my work for Tanut-amon would not suffer. After all, a dead man does not generate as much paperwork as a living one."

My spirit recoiled from the thought of having this man nearby. "Impossible."

"Then I shall offer my services to the priest Rudjek while I am here." The evil little man showed his yellow teeth in an expression that was more grimace than smile. "I have heard that he has often expressed particular interest in your son. He will be happy to hire me, I am sure. Especially when I tell him all I learned while overseeing Tanut-amon's accounts."

Was there *nothing* this man had not investigated? He had obviously plotted well, scouting out my enemies and rivals as thoroughly as he had searched Tanut-amon's records.

Without answering, I stood and walked the length of the reflecting pool. I needed time to think; and more than that, I needed a friend and adviser. But who did I have, apart from Nema? My mother had been the protector of my youth; Tanut-amon had been my fount of wisdom in adulthood. Now both were gone, and while my name aroused no great passion within Pharaoh's heart, he would crush me like an insect if he learned the full truth.

If only I had approached him with the truth all those years ago. Ramesses had been fonder of me then; if I had spoken prettily or gone to him in private he might have allowed me to rear Moses as a servant in the palace. But no. Lacking faith in his love, I had contrived a fantastic deception, basing it upon the gods my father served.

A shiver spread over me as I remembered the speech I'd memorized and delivered in Pharaoh's audience chamber: *Through the bounty of Great*

Hapi, god of the river, I have received this boy as a precious gift. As Hapi is the son of Horus, so I present this boy, Moses, as your offspring through the gift of the gods.

My father had accepted those words. Whether he believed Moses the son of his loins or the son of his god did not matter; he had acknowledged Moses, and a divine king could not be fooled. If my deception were exposed, if Moses were revealed as the son of Hebrew slaves—

Impossible. The throne of Egypt could not survive such an upheaval. Therefore I and my memory would be erased as completely as the cartouches of the heretic Akhenaton had been chiseled from the statues created in his honor. I would disappear, and so would Moses.

Gathering my slippery courage, I strode back to face Baken-khonsu. "I will not have you come within one hundred paces of myself or my son," I said flatly. "If I see your face again, I will have you killed, do not doubt it."

"Not a wise decision, Great Lady. I could write all I know and leave it for Rudjek to discover."

"And I could write all you have said in this conversation, and 'twould be enough to ensure your death. I could embellish it, say you attempted to molest me—"

"A lie!"

"A lie fit for a traitor!" My strength returned as my heart pumped outrage through my veins. "You would threaten your king and your country in an attempt to enrich yourself. Well, Baken-khonsu, I will arrange to pay you for your services as a scribe, but never a sliver more than you are worth, and never again will I grant you an audience. And if harm comes to my son, Moses, if anyone lifts a hand or a rumor against him, I will send assassins to your house in the dead of night. They will kill you as you sleep and bury your body in the desert sands so no trace of you remains in this life or the next! Do you understand me?"

The offended, indignant expression the man had managed to squeeze into his features soured into an expression of resentment. "Agreed." He sounded as though he were strangling on repressed curses. "But I will live in Pi-Ramesses."

"It is a crowded city," I answered, matching his hostility with my own.

"So take care that our paths do not cross. Send your correspondence regarding my accounts to Hori, overseer of Pharaoh's household, and do not cross my threshold again."

Baken-khonsu nodded, then threw back his shoulders and drew a deep breath. A twisted smile crossed his thick lips. "So be it, Royal Lady. I look forward to serving you."

∿

I immediately instructed Hori, Pharaoh's administrator, to issue Baken-khonsu a regular payment for a personal service he had done me, but for the next few days my bowels tumbled every time I glimpsed a linen-clad scribe in the hallways of Pharaoh's house. Gradually, however, my trepidation faded. Months passed without another word from the scoundrel, and soon it became clear that our arranged truce had satisfied the greedy scribe. In time, I heard that he had expanded his work to include several noble clients: In addition to my estate and Tanut-amon's, the nefarious little toad also supervised the accounts of several high priests, the Lady Isnofret, and Pharaoh's latest Great Royal Wife, Maat-Hor-Neferure.

Was I jealous because another had assumed the title rightly belonging to me alone? Several women of the court hinted that I should feel at least a spark of envy toward the newcomer; in fact, many would have been delighted had I openly snubbed Pharaoh's newest wife. In truth, I felt relieved to know he had become infatuated with another woman. His broken heart was finally mending; the pain of losing Nefertari had eased. The sight of my face would no longer wound him, yet I couldn't help but believe the less Ramesses looked at me and my stunning son, the less risk we ran of offending him.

In order to strengthen the thirteen-year-old peace treaty, Hattusilis, king of the Hittites, had agreed to send his eldest daughter to become my king's newest wife. The betrothal dominated the attention of scribes and ambassadors for more than a year, and with every passing day my father's passion for this unseen bride became more obvious.

Not only did Hattusilis promise his daughter, but with her he agreed to send an extravagant dowry of jewels, rich fabrics, bronze ornaments, precious metals, horses, flocks of sheep, herds of cattle, and a company of skilled slaves. For months Pharaoh waited, but neither the bride nor her treasures materialized on the horizon.

I found myself growing amused by the situation. At fifty-eight, Pharaoh was no longer a young man, but he badgered his courtiers for news of his bride as if he had never known a woman's love.

I was a mature forty-two, and years removed from the young woman who had wept and worried over the prospect of marrying a king. Instead of feeling jealous of the soon-coming bride, I found myself thinking of her with gentle pity.

I also pitied my son. At twenty-eight, Moses was a grown man, yet still a prince-in-waiting. Like the other sons of Pharaoh, he spent a portion of the year serving as a captain of the king's army, and he seemed to enjoy military service without being fulfilled by it. When we were alone together we occasionally spoke of how he might rule if he became king, but neither Kha'emweset nor Ramesses showed any sign of weakening. Some of the priests had begun to whisper that Pharaoh was not only divine, but immortal, and when I considered that few men in Egypt lived past the age of forty or fifty, I thought it might be true.

Undoubtedly, my father also heard the rumors. As if to prove his virility and vigor, he dispatched dozens of impatient letters to his ally Hattusilis, demanding to know when his new bride would arrive. The girl's mother, Lady Puduhepa, chided Pharaoh for his impatience, asking why such a rich king should be so anxious to receive his promised bounty. "My brother possesses nothing?" she once wrote. "That you, my brother, should wish to enrich yourself from me is neither friendly nor honorable!"

But by the season of drought, when my father's ambassadors journeyed to the Hittite Empire to perform the betrothal ceremony, the queen's attitude toward Pharaoh had softened. "When fine oil was poured upon my daughter's head," she wrote our royal court, "the gods of the Netherworld were banished. On that day, the two great countries became one land, and you, the two Great Kings, found real brotherhood."

In the fourth month of the season of flood, in the thirty-third year of my father's reign, a great caravan journeyed from the Hittite Empire to Pi-Ramesses. The foreign bride traveled through treacherous lands in the season of winter, but the weather remained temperate. When news of this miracle reached us, my divine Pharaoh accepted full credit. As the wedding stele would later inform his posterity, Ramesses had made a personal appeal to the gods: "The sky is in your hands, the earth is under your feet, whatever happens is what you command—so may you not send rain, icy blast, or snow, until the marvel you have decreed for me shall reach me!"

When the much longed-for marvel arrived, we of Pharaoh's former favor hid ourselves behind statues and pillars and spied upon the royal assembly. The girl who alighted from a gauzily veiled carrying chair looked a little thick to my eyes, and heavy through the waist. She wore no wig, but her dark hair, wrapped at intervals by gold bands, fell to her hips. Her sheer garment gleamed with color—odd enough, since Egyptian linen did not readily hold dye—and the spun gold at its edges sparkled in the sunlight.

Ramesses was enchanted. Ignoring the officials who had journeyed with the Hittite princess, he escorted his bride into the palace, established her in new apartments, and had his wedding stele engraved upon monuments at Pi-Ramesses, Karnak, and Abu Simbel. According to the words written there, his Hittite bride "was beautiful in the opinion of His Majesty, and he loved her more than anything. She was installed in the Royal Palace, accompanying the Sovereign daily, her name radiant in the land."

So the girl from the Hittite Empire abandoned her old name to receive a new one: Maat-Hor-Neferure, meaning "she who beholds the Royal Falcon that is the visible splendor of Re." With her coming, Moses and I receded further into the shadows of the royal palace—a development that pleased me very well.

The Egyptian word for year, *renpit,* is represented by a hieroglyph depicting a young shoot in bud, and the same sign appears in words like *renpy,* which means "vigorous." As time passed, my father seemed determined to prove himself as vigorous as the years that followed, one after the other, unchanging.

With each passing year Hap-Ur rose and fell, blessing us with fertility

and life-giving harvests from the black earth. At each subsequent sed festival, which Pharaoh now celebrated every three years, the king proved
his virility by taking foreign brides. Once their charms diminished, he
sent them and their offspring to live at Mi-Wer.

The vast number of royal relatives did not bother me. Of his sons, only
a handful had been born of Great Royal Wives, and of that select number,
only I was descended from Nefertari, who had been the Great Royal Wife
when Ramesses ascended to the throne. Therefore, my son, my Moses,
would be the first Pharaoh would consider when he decided to name
another heir . . . because in the forty-fourth year of Ramesses' reign, a furious hippopotamus in the marshes killed patient prince Kha'emweset.

While careful to express my sorrow at the loss of so fine a prince, I was
secretly thrilled with this development. Moses had grown to become a
handsome man, strong, intelligent, and a favorite with the women in the
royal court. He stood a head taller than all his brothers, and his strong
physique made them look like gangly teenagers. Beside Moses,
Kha'emweset had looked like a stump, and Merneptah, a younger son
by Isnofret, seemed a mere boy.

Moses had managed his vineyard so well that Pharaoh had given him
three others, all in the Delta. Each of these was now run by an Egyptian
overseer, for the king had also appointed Moses as a division commander. Pharaoh's army was composed of four divisions of five thousand men,
and a favored son commanded each branch: Merneptah led the troops of
Re, Pekherenptah controlled the division of Sutekh, Amennmesse directed the men of Ptah, and Moses commanded the troops of Amon. In times
of peace the title was primarily honorary, for Pharaoh's sons had other
businesses to run, but duty still required Moses to spend long weeks training his men.

I missed him in the months he spent away from me, though I tried not
to let my sadness show. Occasionally, he and his troops were stationed at
the desert garrisons for months at a time, and though I knew he was doing
what had to be done, still I missed him.

I consoled myself with one sweet realization: As long as Moses was on
patrol, he remained safely away from the king's household and its scores
of fawning women.

At thirty-nine, Moses had not yet taken a wife—but not because he didn't want to marry. He was not inexperienced with women, for I had heard many tales of how Pharaoh's warriors conducted themselves in border towns, nor was he unskilled in the courtly actions and phrases designed to win noblewomen's hearts. On at least four separate occasions he had begged me to ask Pharaoh to sanction his marriage to some girl who caught his eye, but each time I managed to convince him that his future would be better served by waiting.

Why did I insist he wait? Because it is the lioness who must guard and provide for her young. And when the old lion is still preying upon tender fawns, he is not likely to share the feast with a cub.

When Ramesses was still a young prince, his father gave him wives and concubines—indeed, I had been born in that harem. But Ramesses had made no effort to provide women for any of his sons, and if I had encouraged Moses to look for love among noblewomen, I risked him setting his heart upon a lady Ramesses coveted for himself. As long as the old lion remained on the prowl, I advised Moses to wait for marriage.

Reluctantly, Moses accepted my counsel, but something in my heart broke each time I looked at him. A man so strong and handsome deserved a family of his own, but a prince in waiting could do no more than wait.

In one area, however, I urged him to proceed, and Moses stubbornly refused to heed my advice. He had lived far too long without incorporating a god's name into his own, and as a prince of Egypt, the priests were bound to think it odd that he had not done so. In his younger years, I had hinted that he should choose Re to honor his father, but lately I had dropped all pretenses of subtlety and bluntly suggested that he choose any god in the pantheon. "You cannot displease Pharaoh," I pointed out, "if you choose one of the official gods of Thebes. Become Ptah-mose, or Min-mose, or Hap-mose. But do not delay—the priests are waiting to see which you will select as your patron."

Grinning, Moses ignored my nagging. "The priests circle like hungry fish, waiting for offerings to drop in their coffers. But let them wait. What god has helped me thus far?"

I opened my mouth, about to suggest Hapi, who had protected him on the river, then remembered that I could not share that memory.

Moses did not notice my hesitation. "Whichever god delivers my destiny," he finished, tossing his head, "will earn my patronage. Until then, the gods and their priests may wait with me."

I had no idea the gods were about to act. One morning not long after our conversation I was waiting for Moses to visit when Nema burst into my audience chamber. Dropping her market basket on the floor, she bowed, then began babbling about a woman she had encountered outside the city walls.

"She was a Hebrew." Nema squeezed her hands as if she knew the mention of the word would bring me pain. "She called upon your name and begged me to bring you a message. The people of her village have tried to petition Pharaoh, but no one will listen to their complaints—"

"Slow down, Nema." I lowered the papyrus I had been reading and regarded my maid with a level glance. "How did this Hebrew woman know to ask for me?"

Nema rolled her eyes toward the hallway leading to Moses' chambers, and instantly I understood. The woman was one of *them*.

My hand rose to my throat. "The mother?"

"No, my lady. The sister, I believe."

I frowned, absorbing this news, then nodded. "Go on. What is the problem?"

Nema's hand-wringing began again. "Apparently, an overseer has committed an injustice against a Hebrew slave in his service. The Hebrew has a young wife, and the overseer commanded his men to rise before dawn and march to the brickyards outside the city. Once the Hebrew men had left the village, the overseer went into the Hebrew man's house and took advantage of his pretty wife, who went in tears to the woman I met in the marketplace. The Hebrews want vengeance, or at least justice. I tried to tell her you could do nothing, but she insisted I speak to you."

I shook my head. "You were right, I can do nothing."

"Why can't you help, Gentle Mother?"

I flinched as Moses strode into the room, his chest wet with sweat.

"Moses! I didn't hear you come in."

"Excuse my appearance," he said, moving to the bowl and pitcher on a stand in the corner. "I've come from the stables, where we've just received a pair of new stallions from the east." He splashed water into the basin, then wet his hands and looked at me, his eyes narrowing in concentration. "The injustice Nema described is something we should not tolerate, even though the matter concerns slaves. So why do you say you can do nothing?"

"Because—" I floundered, searching for any answer but the truth. "Because I have little influence with Pharaoh," I finished lamely. "What will he care if I present this case to him?"

"Pharaoh does not need to be bothered with this. I can address the matter myself." Moses splashed water on his arms and shoulders, then plucked a square of linen from a golden stand. "Tell me, Nema, where I can find this Hebrew woman. I will investigate and make certain justice is restored."

A thousand protests swirled in my soul—no, he shouldn't seek out this woman, *any* woman of the Hebrews—but my mouth went as dry as the desert and I could only stare at him. Tanut-amon and I had taught Moses to base his life upon justice, order, and peace, the ideals of ma'at, and those ideals could not be cast aside because one situation proved difficult—even risky—for me.

I could not even explain the danger.

Pressing my lips together, I lowered my eyes while Moses accepted my silence as acquiescence. "Nema, will you help me find this Hebrew woman?"

My maid's voice came out in a squeak. "When, my lord?"

"Right away. This kind of evil cannot go unchecked."

Nema looked at me, but I refused to meet her gaze.

"My lady?"

I waved her away. "Do what you must, but do it quickly."

I knew I would not rest until Moses had safely returned.

MIRYAM

~⚬✕⚬~

How did I feel, watching my brother the Egyptian stride toward me? You may think I wanted to weep, rejoice, or fall upon my face and thank the God of heaven that an errant son of Levi had returned to us.

In truth, I wanted to spit.

With the black slave woman trotting by his side, the prince called Moses strutted like a conqueror into our village. Painted, bewigged, and gleaming with gold, he stood in the dusty center of our settlement, thrust his hands on his hips, and called for the woman who had spoken to the Royal Wife's handmaid in the marketplace.

His approach drew my people like rotten meat draws hungry flies. In doorways they clustered, peeping from behind lintels and peering at him over mud-brick windowsills. I joined a knot of women who stood speechless at the fire pit and through lowered lashes observed my brother more closely.

He wore a short wig like those of the Egyptian warriors, and his arms were corded with muscle beneath golden skin—but I knew those arms had never held a plow or pulled the ropes of a weighted sledge. Broad circlets of gold wrapped each wrist; a broad golden collar encircled his neck and covered much of his shoulders. Through his wig ran another circle of gold—and it was this sign of royalty that struck my people speechless. We were accustomed to beholding Egyptian taskmasters in our village, but never in the winding length of a tortured collective memory could we recall a visit from an Egyptian prince.

"Where," he asked, speaking this time in an informal dialect of Akkadian, the language spoken by most slaves brought to the Black Land, "is the woman who spoke to the Royal Wife's handmaid?"

He spoke with hesitation, one eye lowered in a cautious slit, and I suspected that our reticence had caught him off guard. Beside him, the slender Cushite slave trembled as a breeze blew up from the reeds and fluttered the veils at our backs. Then her gaze met mine.

Knowing she would soon identify me, I stepped forward and lifted my eyes to meet the Egyptian's. And then Moses, born of my own mother and father, frowned down at me and demanded my name.

"I am called Miryam." I met his gaze without flinching. "Daughter of Amram and Yokheved, of the clan of Levi. Sister to Aharon, who lives in this village."

"I didn't ask for your pedigree, just your name." The corner of his mouth rose as if he were amused by his own answer, but I saw nothing funny in his retort. Crossing my arms across my thin chest, I glared at the usurper.

He opened his mouth to issue another proclamation, then apparently thought the better of it. Glancing around at the circle of eavesdroppers, he pointed to the river's edge. "May we go there and speak privately?"

Unbidden, tears sprang to my eyes. Why had he pointed to the river? Probably because he did not know which house was mine, or perhaps he did not want to soil his kilt by sitting on the earthen floor in one of our mud hovels. But why the river? Was it possible that something inside his memory recalled the time when I had stood in those same reeds and watched over him?

Moving quickly lest he see my damp eyes, I strode forward, the movement swishing the fabric of the thin tunic that modestly covered my legs. I did not look at him, but by peeking at the shadows on the sand I saw him hesitate a moment, then break into a jog to keep up. With nowhere else to go, the Cushite maid followed at a discreet distance.

I stopped at the river's edge, then whirled to face him, arms crossed and spine stiffened.

"What is your hurry?" he panted, though his long-legged stride had easily caught me.

I returned the frown he had given me. "Why would you bid justice tarry?"

"Well spoken." He spread his feet in a solid stance, then propped his arms upon his hips. "Tell me of the woman who was assaulted by the Egyptian. Give me names, and I will look into the matter."

That's when I spat at his feet. I don't know why I did such a rash thing; perhaps I had been hoping he would offer something more than pompous postures and useless promises. After all, he was one of us. And though at the moment I could not believe, I could still hear my mother fervently assuring me that the God of Avraham, Yitzhak, and Yaakov had miraculously preserved this Moses, her son, for our salvation.

She had died with that assurance on her lips.

But the man standing before me was as Egyptian as the obelisk marking the boundary of our slave village. He was no savior. He carried no sword to avenge us, no shield to defend us. Though he wore a dagger in the girdle at his waist, he had not unsheathed it in our cause. He would be like all the other Egyptians, like the overseers who pretended to bear our petitions to Pharaoh, then promptly forgot that we were people, not animals.

The spittle had no sooner left my lips than his face flushed. I braced myself for the blow that would certainly follow, but he did not lift a hand against me. As I stood there, bracing my will against his, he spoke with a wounded note in his voice: "Why do you hate me?"

I could not believe my ears. Torn between laughter and tears, I brought my hand to my mouth and choked on raw emotion. And while I stood at the river's edge, bent and coughing, the Egyptian prince stepped forward and slapped me between the shoulder blades. I bore one blow only, then spun away. "Don't you touch me!"

He threw up his hands. "You were choking."

"I do not need your help."

"Yet I am here to give it."

This calm response, coupled with his refusal to beat me for my impertinence, cooled my temper. And in that moment, I decided to test his sincerity.

I looked at him, saw his squint tighten as he measured me in an appraising look, then lowered my chin in an abrupt nod. "Come, and I will introduce you to the wronged husband and wife." I spun on the ball of my bare foot and led him back to the village.

The crowd fell silent as we approached, but I did not hesitate. I strode straight to the household that had been violated and threw open the door. Dathan, the husband, came forward at our approach, and his wife, Rivka, stood in a corner by the window, her cheeks visibly flaming even in the shadows.

We waited in silent expectation as Moses extended his hand toward the Cushite handmaid. She took a papyrus scroll from a pouch at her waist, then handed it to him and took a hasty half-step back.

"I know you can't read this," Moses said as he offered the scroll to Dathan, "but tomorrow morning you must give it to the overseer who wronged you and your wife. This order directs him to report to the commander of Pharaoh's Amon company. When he reports, justice will be swiftly served."

Moses might have expected the man to respond with tears of gratitude, but my cousin's reaction was no more civil than mine.

"Bah!" Pushing the papyrus away, Dathan released a torrent of Egyptian words. "What good are you to us, you pretender? Do you not know only a miracle has elevated you from among your Hebrew kinsmen? If there were justice in this world, you would be sweating with us in the mud or dead, broken by the cruel whips of Pharaoh's taskmasters!"

Even I had not felt bold enough to deliver the truth in one brutal rejoinder. Wincing, I peered up at my brother and saw astonishment, anger, and denial flit across his face. For a moment I thought he would strike Dathan for his unmitigated gall . . . then Moses looked away, his eyes filling with a pain so raw something within me shriveled to look upon it. He brought a hand to his brow, looked at me again, then reached out and seized my shoulders in a grip that bruised my flesh. In that instant his eyes widened, as if for the first time he had realized he could have been looking into a mirror.

He cried aloud and released me so suddenly I fell backward, then Moses the Egyptian ran from our village, his feet kicking up clouds of dust with each frantic stride. The Cushite maid hurried after him, feebly calling his name, while I pressed the back of my hand to my forehead and wondered how it would feel to have my world turned upside down in the space of a heartbeat.

I almost pitied him.

MERYTAMON

Without being told, I knew. Nema returned to my chamber without Moses, and one look at her face revealed that the eventuality I had spent forty years dreading had come to pass—Moses had learned the truth about his heritage. Tragically, he had not learned it from me.

Clutching the carved pillars of my bed, I lowered myself to its edge, knowing Moses must surely hate me. He would feel I had deceived him, and hadn't I? I had lied to my son and my husband. I had mocked my father and my only love. My decision to deceive would destroy my child . . . and what remained of my life.

Re had disappeared behind the western mountains by the time Moses returned. I heard the sound of the heavy door at the entrance to our chambers, but he did not come to me. I waited in the oppressive silence, and at length I rose and found him sitting in the audience chamber, his face stark and tense in the flickering light of an oil lamp.

He did not look up, so I slid silently into a chair. Neither of us spoke for a moment woven of eternity.

Though I was fully clothed, I felt naked and exposed . . . and ashamed.

"Would you have ever told me?" Politeness soaked his voice, but I could hear the undertone of anger in it. "Or would you have allowed me to keep believing I am the son of a god, a god myself? I am no golden son of Isis. I am a son of dust!"

Though my heart wept, I could not speak for a moment. I pulled myself off the back of the chair and sat hunched before him, one hand reaching out in mute supplication. "You are not dust, Moses." My words rang with the tinny sound I had heard in the voices of terrified slaves. "You are gold, as golden as Re's first rays. If you are dust, so am I, for you are the son of my heart, as fine a prince as has ever lived and breathed in the Beautiful Land—"

"I am not Pharaoh's son." Moses held up his hands, studying them as if he had never seen those particular palms and fingers before. "I have hunted with him, worshiped with him, ridden in his chariot. We have laughed together, bled together, dined together, and now you tell me he is nothing to me—or rather, I am nothing to him but a slave."

He spoke in an almost casual tone, but the tightening of muscles in his throat betrayed his deep emotion.

"He is your father, Moses." The words tasted like gall, but still I forced them out. "Perhaps not a flesh-and-blood father, but a father nonetheless. He acknowledged you. He cares for you. He stands ready to make you his heir—"

"Only because he believes a lie." He looked at me with a slightly perplexed expression, then found the courage to ask a question: "Why did you do it?"

I lowered my gaze; the quick query needed a thoughtful answer. How could I explain myself after forty years? The fears that had dogged my youth seemed foolish now. My barrenness, my timidity before Pharaoh, my dread of sharing the king's bed in order to give him a son—what did those things matter now that Pharaoh had more than ninety sons, sixty daughters, and two hundred women? And how do you explain maternal love to a man who has never married or loved a child?

My eyes clung to his, desperate to decipher his reactions. "I wanted to share my life. I wanted to share yours. Borne by the love of the woman who gave you birth and the unseen god who protected you in her care, the river guided you into my arms."

With a reasonable attempt at calmness, marred only by the thickness in my voice, I told him of his mother, Jochebed; his father, Amram; and his sister, Miriam, who had watched over him years ago and confronted Nema in the marketplace today. I told him what I knew of his people—that the ancient texts recorded their arrival during a previous dynasty, and that one of them had served as vizier to one of the mightiest pharaohs of Egypt. But in time, as they grew populous, the kings of Egypt feared they would unite with Egypt's enemies and drive native Egyptians from the fertile land. And there was the matter of Ramesses' dream . . .

"So my father sought to break the spirit of your people through hard labor. When that failed, he tried to kill baby boys upon their birth. When that failed, he tried to make sure all the male infants of the Hebrews were thrown to Hap-Ur—"

"Which is why you never told Pharaoh the truth." Moses' eyes gleamed with calculation as he looked at me in the flickering lamplight. "For he would not have accepted the son of a Hebrew."

"I don't know what Pharaoh would have done had I told him the entire story," I answered honestly. "Who can divine the heart of the king? But I knew I couldn't risk it, even as you cannot risk the truth now. Whatever you do, do not tell Pharaoh what you have learned today. The Hebrews will keep quiet; they have remained silent for years. Stay away from them and forget the troubles of those people. You are a prince, Moses; you are a commander of Pharaoh's army. You are loved, you are held in high esteem, and Pharaoh himself considers you his most favored son."

"But I am not *divine*." He pronounced the word as if it had sprung from a foreign language with unfamiliar sounds.

I forced a laugh. "Of course you are. All of Pharaoh's children are divine. We are all golden creations of Khnum the potter, put on earth to fulfill his purposes, to uphold the principles of ma'at."

He was not looking at me. In desperation I reached out and caught his hand, then held it tenderly between both of my own. "Forgive me, Moses, for not telling you the truth sooner. I lied to Pharaoh, but I did it to preserve your life and defeat the evil goddess who has persecuted me for years. Nephthys was jealous, you see, of the great love between my mother and father, so she stole my womb, she stole my mother, and she would have stolen you had I not defeated her with a few well-chosen words. And though you may not understand, I know I did right, for when Nephthys tried to attack us again, I prayed to the unseen god of the Hebrews who had sheltered you in the river. And you were saved."

Moses' eyes, usually so brilliant and alive, flicked toward me, then settled on the floor. "Is it right to do wrong . . . to do right?"

I faltered in the silence, then the power of speech escaped me as he resolutely pulled his hand from mine, then stood and left the room.

I had no answers and no more excuses. Years ago I had made a decision to deceive and tonight I had begun to pay the price for my wrongdoing.

Nephthys had awakened from her lethargy and struck where I was most vulnerable. But this time I had no priest to aid me, no mother to guide me. And it had been so many years since I had even thought about the nameless Hebrew god that he probably wouldn't recognize my feeble voice.

I might pay for my rebellion against the gods with the love of my son . . . but I would have to pray my folly would not cost both our lives.

MIRYAM

ᘰᕽᘱ

Moses kept coming.

The first time he reappeared at the outskirts of our village, surprise stole my breath. I had convinced myself that the haughty Egyptian prince would decide his encounter with us was a mistake, an inauspicious omen, and therefore he would never seek the circle of our village again. He did not speak on his second visit, but hovered at the outskirts like a shy youth afraid to speak to a pretty girl, then retreated into the marshes.

Yet the next day he came again. This time he stalked boldly into the center of our settlement and stood on the stone rim of the fire pit, scattering the women who usually congregated there. He came at noon, when the men were out working, and after a few moments of awkward silence the bright prince realized he had deigned to call on us at the wrong hour. Modest women did not speak to strange men when their husbands and brothers were not in attendance.

Yet I do not always behave like a modest woman.

He turned, probably about to leave, and I approached with a water jar on my shoulder. I lowered it at his feet, then boldly met his gaze and spoke in Akkadian: "Would you like a drink of water, Moses the Egyptian?"

He looked at me, his eyes hungrily absorbing the details of my face. "You are Miryam."

"True."

"You are my sister."

"That is debatable."

I tipped my water jar to fill the smaller containers we kept by the fire. To my surprise, Moses grasped the bottom of the heavy jug and lifted it, considerably speeding my task.

"Your parents are living?"

"Both dead. But I have a brother, Aharon."

His brows shot up to the fringe of his wig. "I have a living brother?"

"My brother is part of the crew working on the south side of the city. Each day he must make two thousand bricks or he will be made to suffer."

I feared Moses would drop the jar, but after a moment of hesitation he lowered it to the ground.

"Can you take me to the work site? I'd like to meet our brother . . . but I'm not sure he will speak to me if I go alone."

I hoisted the empty jar to my hip and studied Moses through narrowed eyes. This sun-baked man of forty years was no youth, but a certain boyish enthusiasm snapped in his eyes. I saw no trace of treachery there, only a certain desperate eagerness.

"Why do you want to do this? You are a prince of Egypt; you should stay in your palace."

Clamping his jaw tight, Moses stared at the horizon for a long moment, then spoke. "Perhaps I have lived in the palace too long. Have you never questioned why the gods gave you life? For years I have wondered why I am here. And now I would know whether or not I am to help . . . you people."

"We *people*," I retorted in cold sarcasm, "do not need you. We do not need Egypt, we do not need princes, we do not need Pharaoh or his gods . . ."

My words trailed away as my irritation abated. In truth, we did need a deliverer, and who was I to say whether this Moses would deliver us? He had wealth and position, influence with the king, and I myself had been witness to the way he had been miraculously preserved as an infant.

Our God, my father used to say, works in mystifying ways.

"Come." I jerked my chin toward the worn path that led toward Pi-Ramesses. "I make no promises as to whether Aharon will speak to you, but I'll take you to the work site."

We set out together, walking side by side in a silence broken only by the soft slapping of his sandals. He looked up and out as we traveled, and I suspected that the mighty prince had never traversed the rough foot-paths that led to the royal city. These were the back ways that led through marshy pastureland and stagnant pools that remained even in the stifling heat of this season of drought.

The sight of one of my kinswomen caught my attention. She was struggling to slip a heavy yoke over an ox's head, and the stubborn animal stiffened his neck and held his head upright, frustrating her efforts.

Moses jerked his hand toward the village. "Will none of the men come to help her?"

I caught my veil, which the hot wind was threatening to rip from my head. "Our men work for Pharaoh. Our women work wherever we can. Pharaoh gives our men a small portion of rice in return for their labor; anything else our women must provide."

I had assumed Moses understood the organization of Pharaoh's slave corps, but apparently he did not. "Our men do not work for wages, but for their lives. If they do not produce their daily quota of bricks, they are beaten." My heart suddenly squeezed so tight I could scarcely draw breath to speak, but I forced the words out. "Many of our men have died from their blows."

Including my husband . . . but Moses did not need to know of my pain.

"Surely you are mistaken." He glanced my way as if searching for signs of exaggeration on my face. "The servants of Pharaoh are always well treated. Our overseers make certain the principles of justice and goodness are perpetuated throughout the land—"

I released a bitter laugh. "Those principles are watered down by the time they reach the level of slaves. You would have to live in our territory before you would understand."

"I know the king. He is good; his laws are just."

"Pharaoh is evil; his laws are corrupt."

Abruptly halting, Moses turned and met my accusing eyes without flinching. "Pharaoh's very name means 'Strong in Right is Re.' How can a man be false to his own name?"

"Do you speak Hebrew? No, of course you do not, for what man would trouble to learn the language of a conquered people?"

The wind gusted, blowing sand into my eyes and hair. "In our tongue," I continued, struggling to keep the bile from my voice, "*Ra'a* means 'evil,' and *mses* sounds like the word meaning 'to bring forth.' So to our ears, the king is 'he who brings forth evil.'"

A tiny flicker of shock widened his eyes, so I pressed on, not wanting to lose the advantage. "Do you know anything about the children of Israel? Do you know how we work, or how we are organized?"

His mouth spread into a thin-lipped smile. "I'm sorry you find me so deficient."

"Then learn, so you will no longer be ignorant. You should know there are ten slaves to each Israelite overseer, and ten Israelite overseers to each Egyptian captain. Dathan, the man whose wife was assaulted, is an overseer, and a man of integrity."

Moses nodded, absorbing my words, and as we began to walk I tried to explain the organization of our villages and clans. Later, when we moved past a crew of workers at a brickyard, he studied them as if he had never seen bricks being molded. As an Israelite in Egypt, I had seen little else.

I pointed to a muddy crew dressed in leather loincloths. "Mud is mixed with chopped barley straw until it forms a thick paste, then the mix is poured into the molds you see there. The molds are turned upside down and removed, then the bricks are left to dry in the sun."

Moses shook his head, proving my suspicions. "I have never been around brickmakers. The king is much more interested in his quarries. Only cut stone is used in the monuments and temples."

"Brick is used for everything else, Prince of Egypt." I spoke in a wry voice, and again I felt a wave of pity for the man.

"I know what bricks are used for. I'm not stupid." He shot me a glance of exasperation, and I felt a lopsided grin cross my face. So . . . the mighty prince of Mizraim had a human side.

We passed that work crew, then entered a stretch of wind-combed sand. Lowering our heads into the current of air, we pressed on. The river gleamed at our left, thickly bordered by reeds, and at a natural clearing Moses gestured toward the water. "Are you thirsty?"

I shook my head.

"I am."

As I halted, he strode to the river and knelt, scooping water in his cupped palm. After drinking, he pulled off his wig, then splashed his face and neck. I looked away, suddenly embarrassed by these intimate moments of ablution. The man who knelt before me was my brother—if God had willed otherwise, I should have seen him wash this way a hundred times. Odder still was the realization that with Moses' close-cropped head bent just so and his arm outstretched, he reminded me of Aharon, who often bent in the same sort of posture.

The sound of singing snapped me out of my thoughts. "Someone's coming!"

Moses looked at me, water dripping from the end of his nose. "What?"

I did not wait to explain, but darted into the tall reeds beyond the clearing. Hiding was a reflexive action, for no Israelite woman felt safe on the road, and I did not trust Moses to defend either my life or my honor.

I stepped into the cool water, retreating farther into the reeds as a chariot spun over the smooth sand. The trotting horse slowed to a walk, and at the clearing the Egyptian driver stopped singing and pulled the animal to a halt. After dismounting, he yanked on a length of leather tied to a ring at the back of his conveyance.

Peering through the rushes, I saw that the driver was not leading another horse, but an Israelite slave, whose long hair obscured his face. The Egyptian untied the leather straps, then dragged the stumbling slave toward the water. When he spied Moses, he wrapped one hand in the man's dark hair and forced the slave to his knees.

"Hail, Prince of Egypt," he called, but before Moses could stand, the man pulled a smooth stick from his girdle and proceeded to beat the Israelite with a fury that made me cringe. I covered my ears as the air filled with the sounds and smells of male sweat and fury.

Perhaps he thought to impress Moses. I am sure he had no idea which of Ramesses' many sons he had stumbled upon, but from my vantage point it was clear he meant to inflict as many blows as possible before the prince asked to share the pleasure.

Moses surprised both the Egyptian and me. The reeds blocked my view of my brother's initial reaction, but his subsequent roar lifted the hair on my forearms. I leaned forward, momentarily forgetting my own safety, and beheld a series of images that will be forever engraved in my memory—Moses rising up to strike the Egyptian with the grace of a springing cat, his dagger flashing in the blinding sun, blood splattering across the smooth skin of my brother's chest, then dripping from the golden collar at his neck.

The Egyptian hit the ground with a thud that reverberated even in my hiding place. Gasping, I staggered back into the reeds, suddenly afraid for my life, my clan, and my people. What sort of murderer had we produced? We were farmers and shepherds, not bloodthirsty warriors. And yet in this man, this Moses, violence and murder flowed close to the surface, just beneath that smooth skin of which the Egyptians were so proud.

I pressed my hand over my mouth and felt tears sting my eyes. Water had crept up the length of my tunic; now the thin garment clung like a leech to my chilly legs, but I did not dare call out or make a splash. My heart seemed to have stopped beating in the instant Moses struck; now it pounded harder than usual, to make up for the missing beats.

And my brother? I heard him say something, and a moment later, I saw the dazed slave staggering on the path, his hands untied and his back a patchwork of bloody bruises. His face twisted with each painful step, but I did not think he would die.

The Egyptian, however . . .

Silence, thick as wool, wrapped around me. Then I saw Moses on the path, searching, I was certain, for me.

Like a child, I pressed my hands over my eyes and ducked deeper in the reeds, grateful that my brown veil and tunic would blend into the bulrushes.

Insects whirred from the tall grasses as Moses walked to the horse, briefly stroked the animal's jaw, then stepped back to give the beast a solid swat on the rump. The animal lurched forward, then settled into a steady trot, following the path.

After another cautious look around, Moses knelt in the soft sand beside the reeds and began to dig.

The skin at my ankles and calves had begun to pucker by the time he finished burying the Egyptian. Moses returned to the water, washed the blood and sand and sweat from his hands and chest, then pulled his wig back into place, smoothed his wet kilt, and lifted his chin. The sun had begun to lower in the west, and against this blaze of burning light the silhouettes of distant palm trees stood black against the bloody sky. Moses stared at the crimson horizon for a long moment, then began to walk—not toward our village, but toward Pi-Ramesses.

When I was certain he had gone, I crept out of my hiding place and hurried home.

MERYTAMON

As a dry eastern wind swept over the city, I wrapped a thin shawl around my shoulders and set off on foot in search of my son. Moses had not joined us at the midday meal, nor had he come to my apartment for dinner. I did not see him every day, but today my soul yearned to touch his, to know the extent of the wounds I had inflicted so many years ago.

The city shadows had pooled and thickened around the columns of the garrison by the time I approached the gate. The guard cast a lazy eye over my form and figure, then stiffened in apprehension when he caught sight of the royal pectoral at my neck.

"Hail to thee, Royal Lady!"

"Greetings." I peered past him for a glimpse of the one I sought. "Captain, I wonder if you have seen our most favored Moses?"

If possible, the man went even stiffer as color flooded his face. "Moses?"

"That is the name." I regarded him with a level gaze. "You need not fear me, friend. I am his mother, and I wish him no harm."

His shoulders relaxed as he exhaled. "I saw Moses a short while ago, in the temple of Amon-Re."

Of course. Tanut-amon, priest of Amon-Re, had been more of a father than any man my son had ever known.

"Thank you, Captain." I turned and left him, then wended my way through the streets until I reached the chiseled marble steps of the temple. Silently I climbed the stairs and walked through the spacious festival court surrounded by carved pillars and open to the sparkling stars. Overhead, the moon hid her face in a thin swipe of cloud, like a nosy servant spying through a sheer curtain.

I startled a pair of priests bearing fruit at the entrance to the colonnade, but after one glance at my royal attire, they slunk away like scolded dogs. Steadily I progressed into the heart of the temple, the strong scent of incense filling my head as I peered around the silent statues of Ramesses.

Finally I moved into the innermost court, and there I saw my son. He was not kneeling before the idol, but off to the side, before an empty altar the priests would soon fill with food for the god's evening meal. The priests in the outer court must be growing anxious, I realized, given the late hour, but they would not interrupt Pharaoh's son in his prayers.

I stepped forward, about to summon Moses, but stopped short when I heard him speak.

"You are powerless, Amon-Re." His voice was soft, almost taunting. "I have been taught to revere you, to consider you the father of life, yet my strength, vile though it may be, is greater than yours."

I froze in midstep, terror lifting the hair at the back of my neck. What had Moses done?

He bent forward like a broken man, his hands clinging to the edge of the empty altar. "Am I the son of gods, Amon-Re? Or am I the son of mud, related only to the sand in the Delta beyond? Am I to rule the greatest kingdom on earth or serve it as the meanest of slaves?"

I brought my fingers to my lips as emotions clogged my throat.

"If there is any justice in earth"—Moses turned his face toward the motionless statue that stared out in apathy—"I would be struck dead on this spot! If you had power, you would take my life! For I am not worthy to live or to be called a son of Egypt!"

I could remain silent no longer. "Moses!" I hurried forward, knelt before him like a supplicant, and placed my trembling hands upon his shoulders. "Son, you should not say these things. Come home. Let me get you a good dinner, and let us talk of the future. The past is done; you need not dwell in it. Forget the things that lie behind you, and look to tomorrow."

His eyes, when they met mine, were filled with undecipherable emotions. "Tanut-amon once told me to live each day with death in mind."

I brought my hand to his cheek. "Yes, my love, but he did not mean it literally. Come home, Moses. Your place is in the palace—"

"Not anymore." As he pulled free of my grasp and stood, I could see vestiges of weariness and pain upon his face. In the torchlight he looked every day of his forty years. In that moment, for the first time, I felt old.

Without another word he turned and walked away, leaving me upon my knees before the altar. "Moses!" I cried, not caring what the priests thought of my wailing.

There was no answer, only the ghostly echo of my voice amid the statuary.

MIRYAM

I did not sleep that night, and was still feeling sandy-eyed and irritable at the fire pit the next morning when one of the children tugged on my tunic and pointed toward the path from the river. "He's back!"

I looked up and saw Moses again, as bold as ever. This time he had come early, before the men left for the brickyards. Few of my kinsmen offered a greeting as they passed; most studied him with outward suspicion.

Dathan and Elezar, however, had not yet noticed the Egyptian prince. They stood outside Dathan's house, where Rivka had tried to give her husband a crust of bread to eat on the long walk to the brickyard. Dathan had refused his wife's offering, and Elezar was scolding the husband for his hard-heartedness. He had just landed an ineffectual and pointless punch on Dathan's arm when Moses sauntered into the midst of the domestic argument as if he had every right to adjudicate the matter.

"What are you doing, hitting your neighbor like that?" Moses said to Elezar. "Come now, you are brothers. Why would you want to hurt one another?"

Caught by surprise, Elezar gaped at Moses, but Dathan turned on my princely brother in a flash of defensive fury. "Who do you think you are? Who appointed you to be our prince and judge? Do you plan to kill me as you killed the Egyptian yesterday?"

Surprise siphoned the blood from Moses' face. He turned slowly, his eyes searching the curious crowd, and stopped when he met my gaze.

I pressed my hand to my chest. *No,* I wanted to tell him, *I didn't say anything,* but before I could find the words Moses whirled and departed as suddenly as he had come.

The women at the fire began buzzing like a swarm of bees. The story, of course, had come from Zuriel, the slave Moses saved from the hot-headed overseer. He had seen my brother's murderous act, and while he felt grateful for being rescued, he knew the supervisors at the brickyard would report him as the last person to have seen the Egyptian captain alive.

"He stands a better chance of surviving Pharaoh's wrath than I," Zuriel repeated, nodding in a frightened, jerky motion to a circle of cousins. "Better him to face the king than a poor slave."

"He brought it on himself." A sly smile flashed in the thicket of Dathan's beard. "And he's the murderer, no doubt. Rest easy, Zuriel, no one blames you . . . and no one trusts him."

No one in my village seemed inclined to trust the man who looked like a Hebrew but dressed, talked, and murdered like an Egyptian.

I did not add to the conversation but carried my thoughts to the quiet house I had once shared with my parents. For the first time in months, I was glad they no longer dwelled in the land of the living.

MERYTAMON

Two weeks passed with no word of Moses. The morning after my meeting with him in the temple I sent my servants out to look for him, and though they searched his vineyards and every garrison, stable, and watering hole where a soldier might stop for food and drink, they found no trace of my son. I even sent Nema back to the Hebrew village, but the women threw stones and drove her away.

We Egyptians were not welcome in the Hebrew world. Hebrews were not accepted in Pharaoh's palace. What, then, must my son be feeling?

I could not eat. Nema tried to awaken my appetite with my favorite dishes and sweet fruits, but I could no longer take pleasure in food. She then tried to tempt me with jewels and a painted tunic of bright colors, but I could not wear a festival dress in such a dark mood.

Moses, the light of my life, had learned of my treachery. I had wounded the person I loved most in the world, and I did not know if I would ever be able to restore our relationship.

I was lying on my bed in the quiet stillness of morning when Nema came in and touched my shoulder. "My lady," she whispered, a tremor in her voice.

Instantly, I tensed. "Is there news of Moses?"

"No, Gentle Lady. But a courier is here to escort you to Pharaoh's audience chamber."

I felt my breath being suddenly whipped away. Pharaoh had not summoned me in years. Sometimes I wondered if he knew I still lived.

So why had he sent for me? Had he heard about Moses' disappearance? Or was he planning to finally announce Moses as his heir?

I rose from my bed and walked out to the antechamber, where a royal guard and courtier stood waiting. After accepting their obeisance, I clasped my hands and pasted on a smile. "Did my lord the king make mention of his royal son Moses? Is he to accompany me?"

The courtier lifted his head. "Indeed, my lady, the king does wish to see your son. But we were under the impression he is not here."

"You are correct; he is not." I forced a smile, then gestured to a gilded bench against the wall. "Please, sit, while I prepare myself. I will be quick."

Nema was waiting in my dressing room. I sat at my stool before the tray of cosmetics, then lowered my lids as she deftly painted my eyes in broad black strokes, the better to camouflage the wrinkles of fifty-four years. I opened my eyes in time to see the trembling of her hand. "Find me something to wear." I took the alabaster rod from her fingers. "I'll finish my face."

I spread the malachite over my eyelids while she rummaged through my cedar chest; finally she produced the painted linen gown I had spurned earlier in the week. "This one?"

I glanced at it. The painted designs rendered the sheer fabric opaque, which was good. A woman my age had no business wearing a transparent gown in the presence of a king.

"That will do." I turned to the cabinet where six of my wigs stood on stands, then pointed to the one with human hair braided around a royal diadem. "And that wig. Whatever matter lies on Pharaoh's heart, I must look every inch a queen."

The day would probably bring good news, I assured myself. After all, the revelation that had been sprung upon Moses was personal, and not a story he was likely to repeat. Neither would the Hebrews betray my secret, for Miriam's entire village probably benefited from my monthly payments to Moses' birth family.

Why was I dreading this encounter? The day would likely bring good news. After all, Moses had distinguished himself in Pharaoh's service. He was forty years old and more than ready for the responsibility of leading the kingdom.

Nema must have followed my thoughts. "Pharaoh cannot have heard of Moses' encounter with the Hebrews." She pulled the gown over my head. "The king does not concern himself with such low matters."

"No, he does not."

"And the Hebrews—who listens to them? Even if the woman Miriam and her brother shout the story from the cliffs, no one would listen. The rantings of the Hebrews are as nonsensical as their prayers to a god they cannot call by name."

"You're right, of course. Pharaoh surely means to honor Moses. I only hope the king's men find him soon."

Nema dressed me with as much haste as she dared, then I stood and paused in the doorway to take a deep breath. My eyes fell upon the shrine in the corner of my dressing room, where chains of fragrant flowers wreathed statues of Amon and Khnum.

My sacrifices to them had been in vain, for Moses had not yet returned. Nephthys had moved against me, but I would resist with all my might and defeat her again. I was the golden daughter of the divine Pharaoh, and I had powers, too.

My thoughts drifted to the nameless god I had not begged for news of Moses. I had never brought him an offering, never chanted a single song in his praise. Perhaps it would be wise to murmur a prayer, just in case—

I shook off the thought. I wouldn't need him, for this day would bring good news, not bad. Moses would soon recover from his unpleasant shock and fulfill his destiny as a leader of a mighty kingdom. The gods had intended him for greatness; he could not settle for anything less.

Girding my courage about me, I went out to meet the men who would escort me to Pharaoh, my husband, father, and king.

My heart was pounding like the relentless beat of barrel drums when I entered the king's audience chamber at Pi-Ramesses. Though I had not entered this room in ages, it had little changed. The customary crowd of sycophants still crowded the doorway; the usual Nubian guards, somber and vigilant, lined the pathway to the king, punctuating the prevalent colors of white and gold with their ebony bodies and dark spears. A bewildering array of scents assaulted my nostrils—the reek of perfume borne in melting cones of fat atop the women's wigs, sweet incense burning in the four corners of the room, and the spicy fragrance of lotus-blossom wreaths adorning the nobles who awaited the king's pleasure.

Apparently I was expected, for the crowd at the doorway parted to let me pass. Though I tried not to look at the faces turning my way like flowers seeking the sun, I couldn't help but notice several openly curious expressions.

My confidence shriveled the moment I looked up at Pharaoh and recognized his companions. The priest Rudjek occupied the space at Pharaoh's right hand, and beside the priest stood the accountant, Baken-khonsu.

This was no welcoming committee. It was an ambush.

"Mighty Pharaoh." I knelt on the floor. "Life, strength, and health to you!"

Pharaoh, who usually greeted visitors with a practiced nonchalance, rose halfway out of his chair and disregarded the traditional phrases of greeting. "Merytamon, did you know your son has murdered a captain of the Egyptian workers?"

My heart went blank with shock even as my thoughts came rushing together. Moses in the temple—he had been there to confess a crime, and I had been too blind to understand.

My right arm began to tremble—instinctively seeking support, I suppose, but neither Nema nor Moses stood by my side. I knelt there, a quivering composite of wig, flesh, and linen, and stared at the man who had always been the center of my universe.

"Surely the king has been misinformed," I whispered when I had caught my breath. "Moses is no killer."

Ramesses, upon whose face I could now see full evidence of the passing of seventy years, gestured toward the vile little accountant. "This scribe, Baken-khonsu, employs a spy in a certain Hebrew village. This morning he has learned what the Hebrews have known for days—your son, Moses, killed a captain in the king's workforce and buried the man's body in the sand. He has committed a double crime, murdering a man in this life and the next, but he cannot hide his transgression! He will most surely die for this."

Strength fled my body; only the quick reflexes of a Nubian guard prevented me from collapsing like a creature without bones. The evil I had expected had been supplanted by something far worse.

The world went fuzzy as I leaned on the guard, then my eyes filled with Baken-khonsu's surly face. I breathed deep and felt a stab of memory, a sharp shard from an afternoon when I threatened that wily little eel: *I will send assassins to your house in the dead of night. They will kill you as you sleep and bury your body in the desert sands so no trace of you remains in this life or the next!"*

Nephthys must be gloating. Not only had she struck the love of my life, but she had destroyed him with my own words.

"I have also learned," the king continued, his face a mask of rage, "that you, a daughter of Pharaoh, lied about the child's birth! You claimed he was the son of a god, but he is nothing but a slave! You have brought a viper into the Great House; you have allowed a murderer to dwell among the god's royal children, to train alongside them with the lethal weapons of sword, mace, and spear—"

"As Pharaoh lives," I cried, choosing the most serious vow an Egyptian could utter, "I meant no harm!"

My words fell like stones into water, vanishing with no more than a ripple. Pharaoh's mouth did not soften; his eyes did not glimmer with affection or memory. Instead, his hand curled around the crook and flail, the symbols of his authority; then he extended his right arm toward me.

"You, Merytamon, are hereby exiled to the women's palace at Mi-Wer, to live out your days apart from the great god of Egypt. And when this usurper, this false prince, is apprehended, he shall be executed without recourse. I, Ramesses, decree it, and as long as I live this edict shall stand!"

Rudjek signaled the trumpeters, who released a metallic blast that shattered the stillness of the throne room and sent a frisson of terror through my bones.

"Let it be known," Pharaoh called, his stentorian voice resonating throughout the chamber, "that Moses, once known as a prince of Egypt, is banished from our sight, our house, and our kingdom! Death to him if he crosses our threshold! Let what belonged to him be given to another, and let his name be struck from the walls of our temples, our palaces, and our stele here and throughout the land!"

As the trumpets blasted again, the scribes picked up their brushes to record the proclamation. At a signal from the smirking Rudjek, two of the Nubian guards moved to stand beside me.

I did not need to be told what to do. I rose upon shaky legs and retreated from the presence of the divine king.

I knew it was the last time I would ever look upon Ramesses' living face.

Though to my knowledge no one had ever hired professional mourners to wail over a banishment, that night my servants wept with professional fervor as we contemplated our exile to Mi-Wer. I did not know how long we would be allowed to prepare for the journey, and, truth to tell, I didn't care. Without Moses my life would be as empty at Mi-Wer as it would be at Pi-Ramesses.

I cared only about saving Moses. I wanted him to be safe, yet I feared he had already fled into the desert. Selfishly, I wanted him to remain in Egypt long enough for me to kiss his face and tell him good-bye.

After directing the other servants to begin packing our household goods, Nema found me sitting in my bedchamber, my hands empty, my heart occupied with thoughts of my son.

Sinking to the rush-covered floor, she folded her hands in her lap. "There are guards at the doors to your apartment, Gentle Lady. But there is a servants' passage that leads to the main hall, and a window on the west wall. If you are willing, we could slip away tonight. In darkness, we could find our way to the Hebrew village and see if they have news of Moses."

I stared at her in total incredulity. "How are we to get there? We cannot take a chariot—"

"We'll take a horse." Her dark brow arched. "Unless you've forgotten how to ride."

I managed a choking laugh. I hadn't ridden astride a horse since my youth, and most of Pharaoh's animals were trained to pull chariots, not carry riders.

"You can do it, Sweet Lady. And I fear it is the only way."

Amazed by her thoughtful and generous concern, I clasped her hand. "I would not ask you to accompany me. In darkness, a guard might attack anything that moves, and I cannot ask you to risk your life."

"My life, Gentle Lady, has always been yours."

We waited until the twelfth hour when Re disappeared behind the western hills; then Nema helped me don a simple wig and a plain gown. Together we slipped out of my chambers through the servants' entrance; then Nema led me to a staircase. We climbed, and found ourselves on a balcony that circled the interior of the palace walls. We followed the wall in darkness, then came to a lookout window.

In daylight, the window's height might have frightened me, but the dim light from a sliver of moon revealed nothing of the ground below. From the basket she'd been carrying Nema produced a length of rope, then bent to tie it around a support in the balcony railing. "This will hold us both, I think."

Knowing every moment counted, I waited until she completed the knot, then I gripped the rope and gave it a tug. Propelled by sheer determination, I climbed onto the wide windowsill, then pulled my knees close to my chest and turned to face the night. Nema threw the remaining length of rope out the window; I watched it disappear into darkness.

Slipping the rope between my legs, I closed my eyes and concentrated on the rough fibers itching my damp palms. "I'll meet you at the bottom," I whispered, then leaned out into blackness. My arms had long since lost the strength of youth, so I slid painfully down, the rope burning my hands and the inside of my thighs. My legs gave way when I hit the sand, and momentum slammed me to the ground. For a long moment I could not catch my breath, then I rolled over and pushed myself out of Nema's way. Within a few moments she huddled beside me, trembling with exertion.

Despite her fears, she took my hand. "This way." Like fleeting shadows we ran toward the royal stables, then Nema positioned me against a dark wall. "Wait here."

As brash and confident as Moses, she slipped through the fence, then crept into a stall. From my hiding place I heard the creak of leather and a metallic clanking; then Nema emerged leading a horse. Unfortunately, she could not exit the courtyard without leading the animal past three guards who were playing a game beneath a burning torch.

One of the guards looked up as she entered the circle of firelight. "Hold there," he called, rattling a pair of dice, "what do you think you're doing?"

Nema tossed her head. "My lady wishes to see her new chariot horse."

Another of the guards stood, his hand at his dagger. "And which lady is yours, slave?"

Nema flashed a smile, dazzling in the darkness. "The Royal Lady Isnofret," she called, moving steadily toward me. "Mother of Merneptah."

I winced at her lie, but the bemused guards seemed to accept it. The tallest of them, however, stood motionless, his eyes upon Nema. "I've never known any royal wife to ask for such a thing at night. And why would she send her handmaid to the stable?"

Nema grinned and tossed her head as if she would answer, but one look at her trembling arm told me she had run out of answers. I ran toward the gate, reaching it just as the tall man had begun to move toward Nema.

She looked at me and held out the leather reins. "Go," she cried, turning the animal toward me.

I caught the reins. As Nema sauntered bravely toward the threatening guard, I stepped onto a mounting block, then leaped onto the back of the startled animal. The chariot horse shied beneath my unfamiliar weight, but I wrapped my hand in its mane and pummeled its ribs with my heels.

I heard a slap, then a woman's cry, but to turn back would be to void everything Nema had risked for this hour. As the other guards shouted, I urged the skittish beast through the courtyard, then cantered past a pair of heavy-eyed guards who had not expected a solitary rider to come out of the palace gates after dark.

Before they could respond, I kicked the horse into a gallop. By the light of a crescent moon, I rode toward the Hebrew settlements on the Delta and prayed that the unnamed god of the Hebrews would lead me to the right place.

∿

The moon had faded into a brightening sky by the time I found the Levite village. I had ridden through the marshes all night, often backtracking when I realized the moon had changed position and I had lost my way. I remembered that Miriam's village lay south of Pi-Ramesses and by a tributary of Hap-Ur. I passed by three other settlements, but did not recognize the arrangement of the huts. Finally, by some miracle, I thought I might have found it.

Stopping well outside the circle of mud-brick structures, I led the mare to the river, then slipped off her broad back. As the horse drank, I stood barefoot in the shallows and braced myself against her sturdy flank. What would I say to my son if I found him here? Would he still be angry with me? Would he care that Pharaoh had banished us?

Most important, would his temper lead him to defy the king's edict, or would he have sense enough to flee?

I held no great hope for his life in either case. If Moses tried to enter Pi-Ramesses or even Thebes, Pharaoh's warriors would carry out the king's order whether they found Moses at the garrison, the gates, or the entrance to the palace. Whoever killed my son would drop Moses' head and severed hands at the king's feet as proof of obedience and loyalty.

But death also crouched at Egypt's borders. With harsh desert to the west and wilderness to the east, Moses would struggle to survive. Foreign kings had been known to lose entire armies in desert sandstorms.

I looked to the east, where the barque of Re had already begun to streak the pinking sky. Leaving the horse to browse the river grasses, I moved to a clearing and sank to the ground. Shivering with chill and fatigue, I pulled the wig from my head, then raked my fingers through the short gray hair at my scalp.

I had come to the end of my dreams. In the beginning I had wanted to provide Pharaoh with a son. Later I had wanted that son to rule Egypt. Now I would be content to know my son would live.

But what god could answer that prayer? Khnum, Amon, and Hapi had failed me. My own divinity had proved powerless when matched against Pharaoh's. For years I had trusted my gods and my own semidivine nature to protect my little family, but in the long hours of the past night I realized that bad decisions and blind self-reliance had corrupted my soul. I had lied to my son, the court, and Pharaoh, and then compounded the lie by lying to myself.

I had no power. I was no god. I had no allies, save a brave Cushite slave . . . and a nameless foreign deity who was probably furious with me for ignoring his role in Moses' life.

I hugged my knees, then lowered my head onto my arms. I had no idea how to approach a Hebrew god, nor did I have sacrifices to bring him pleasure. All I had to offer was a wounded heart and a sincere confession.

"To thee, unseen god of the Hebrews, I lift this prayer. Forgive my inattention, and hear this request from thy broken and contrite servant."

I paused, listening for some sign, but heard nothing but the far-off cry of a waking heron and the flutter of a duck settling upon the water.

"Be with my son, Moses," I whispered. "Keep him safe, I pray thee, and guard his life. Because I know you have preserved him for greater things than exile."

I felt my stomach drop when I heard an answering sound—not the rumbling voice of a god, but the soft murmur of melodic humming. I lifted my head in time to see a veiled Hebrew woman approaching the river, a basket upon her hip. I crouched lower, trying to make myself disappear into the weeds along the bank, then caught my breath when the woman seemed to disappear into the cattails. Rising as soundlessly as I could, I crept toward the sound of voices, then parted the reeds and beheld the woman . . . with Moses.

I thought I might burst from the sudden swell of happiness rising in my chest.

My son's mouth went slack. "Mother?"

Suddenly limp with weariness, I sank to the damp ground and whispered the words uppermost in my heart: "My son! You must not stay here!"

Coming forward, Moses caught my shoulders and lifted me, his dark eyes searching my face. "You're here alone?"

I nodded. "I rode all night to find this place. Pharaoh is sending me to Mi-Wer."

"Why? What happened?"

I lifted my hand to touch his stubbled chin. "Did you kill a man?"

Moses looked at the woman, and in that moment I recognized her. She was no longer a skinny child, but the bright eyes and bold manner remained. The sister who had concealed Moses in the bulrushes had hidden him yet again.

A swift shadow of anger swept across my son's face. "I was defending another man, for injustice should not exist in Egypt. Did not the ancient Ptahhetep write, 'Thou shalt make neither man nor woman to be afraid, for God is opposed thereto'?"

I pressed a hand to my brow. "Why didn't you take this matter to the king? He knows only that you killed a man and buried the body."

Miriam pulled a loaf of bread from her basket, handed it to Moses, then looked at me. "There is no justice in Egypt. Your son killed an evil man and an evil man seeks his life. So Moses must flee."

"But where can he go?"

"I will go to the wilderness." Wrapping the bread in his cloak, Moses jerked his chin toward the eastern horizon. "I know the area; we traversed it often when I served at the border garrisons."

"But you dare not encounter any of the king's men! They will kill you!"

Something like a smile flitted across my son's face. "Pharaoh does not rule the entire world, Mother. I will go where people do not bow to Ramesses."

He turned to his sister and gave her a tentative smile. "Thank you for your kindness, Miriam."

"I will remember you in my prayers." A thread of tenderness lined her husky voice. "May God go with you, Moshe."

His mouth quirked in a half smile. "You are giving me a new name?"

His sister's face lit with a quiet glow. "It's Hebrew. It's like your Egyptian name, but different. To us it means—"

"'To bring forth,'" Moses finished her thought. "It's the same sound you used to explain Ramesses' name."

She looked away for an instant, then smiled. "Well, Moshe, may God bring you forth out of all your troubles." The warmth of her smile echoed in her voice. "I had begun to hope you would be our deliverer."

"He can't deliver anyone, he has to flee." Spurred by fear that grew more intense as Re climbed the morning sky, I reached for his hand. "Take my horse, Moses. Outrun the king's edict by moving south, then flee across the borders. But you must hurry!"

Drawing me into his arms, he pressed his cheek to mine. "Does this," I asked, clinging to him, "mean you have forgiven me?"

"You did me no wrong, Royal Lady." Something caught in his throat, and I squeezed him once before letting go. Stepping back, I tried to smile at him, but the corners of my mouth wobbled with the effort.

He did not embrace Miriam—her reserved manner kept both of us at arm's length—but nodded soberly and looked directly into her eyes. "I will not forget you, sister."

Beneath the impassive surface of her face there was a suggestion of movement, as though a hidden spring were trying to break through. Finally, she reached out and touched his sleeve. "May the God of our fathers watch between us while we are apart."

Moses snorted softly as he moved toward the horse. "I have no more use for gods—I was one, remember?"

He caught the reins, mounted the mare, and gave us one final wave before turning the horse toward the south.

As he rode away, I stood absolutely still and heard my heart break.

MIRYAM

◄─×─►

A s Moshe moved away, the Egyptian woman and I watched
without speaking. We stood there, two adversaries bound by
a single man, until the tiny speck of his figure disappeared on
the horizon. Then I took a step back and looked at Pharaoh's daughter.
In my stilted Egyptian I asked, "What would you have me do for you,
lady?"

She met my inquiring look with a chilly stare. "You owe me nothing.
Yet I owe you . . . a debt of gratitude."

Her answer left me momentarily speechless, for I had been expecting
her to demand a carrying chair, a meal, and clean clothes. I would not
have been surprised if she had demanded that I return the silver she had
sent our family over the years.

But with more dignity than I would have exhibited in the same situation, she picked up her wig, lifted the hem of her garment, and began to
make her way over the sun-baked path that led to Pi-Ramesses.

I couldn't contain a soft laugh. The high-and-mighty queen of Egypt,
daughter of the greatest king on earth, looked like one of us—mud-
streaked, dirty, and thoroughly defeated. She had gambled her hopes and
dreams on Moshe, and she had lost.

But hadn't I done the same thing? I had helped my mother keep Moshe alive because we believed he was special. And though I hated him for embracing the people who had stolen him from us, in the last few days I had begun to hope he might yet be the key to our deliverance. His temper needed bridling, his knowledge needed expanding, but in killing the Egyptian he had at least demonstrated a sense of loyalty.

I had also pinned my hopes on Moshe. And I, too, had lost.

Watching Merytamon walk away, I recalled the last time we met. She had been a young woman of seventeen; I had been a mere girl of eleven. Now we were both mature women. Though we lived at opposite ends of Egyptian society . . . perhaps the gulf between us was not as wide as it seemed.

BOOK TWO

MIDIAN

Now the priest of Midyan had seven daughters; they came, they drew (water) and they filled the troughs, to give-drink to their father's sheep.

Shepherds came and drove them away.

But Moshe rose up, he delivered them and gave-drink to their sheep.

When they came (home) to Re'uel their father, he said: Why have you come (home) so quickly today?

They said: An Egyptian man rescued us from the hand of the shepherds, and moreover he drew, yes, drew for us and watered the sheep.

He said to his daughters: So-where-is-he? For-what-reason then have you left the man behind? Call him, so that he may eat bread (with us)!

EXODUS 2:16-20

ZIPPORAH

Life changed forever the day my mother went into labor with her ninth child. When the infant would not come, my brother rode for the midwife while my father offered sacrifices. We girls set images of the gods of childbirth around my mother as she crouched on the bricks; we burned incense and parroted every chant the midwife uttered, but to no avail.

After two days of suffering, my mother lay down and reached out for me. I took her hand, but while I watched, the flickering spark of life slipped out of her eyes. The midwife hastily cut her belly in an effort to see if the child still lived, but the little girl was the white-blue color of the desert sky at midday. My father failed, the midwife failed, my sisters and I failed.

I also think the gods failed. And I, who had believed in them as steadfastly as I believed in my mother's love, began to wonder if they had any power at all.

She who had been as warm as a breeze off the red rocks of the Sinai left a husband, Reuel; a son, Hobab; and seven daughters, of whom I was the sixth to enter the world. My mother had been a lovely woman, and my father wept many tears at her death. He buried her in the foothills of the

Sinai and sacrificed a dozen goats, one to each of his principal gods, in order to ensure her safe passage to the next world.

My father was a priest in the land of Midian, and therefore a man of some importance. Because he knew how to implore the gods of Canaan, Egypt, and Edom, desert-dwellers came from all directions to seek his counsel and give him offerings with which he made sacrifices on their behalf. Because of my father's position, and because hospitality to strangers was a necessary part of life in the inhospitable wilderness, life in our compound was much like life in a small city. I've never lived in a city, much less a kingdom, but merchants who traveled to us from the Black Land assured me that my father was no less gracious a host than any noble in Egypt.

Before my mother died, my sisters and I had been charged with the duties of tending to the flocks. But everything changed when my mother left us. Suddenly, the duties of the household fell to my oldest sister, Noura, who had to oversee not only my sisters and the flocks, but the servants as well.

I daresay she managed as well as any sixteen-year-old girl might.

Within a few days, Noura had convinced my brother, Hobab, that one of his responsibilities would be to remain near the compound in order to greet visitors who came to petition my father. This appealed to Hobab, who could almost taste the respect that would one day be his if he assumed my father's priestly calling. At eighteen, Hobab considered himself ready to marry and establish a family of his own, but I knew he would not leave our father. If he had been a second son, he would have departed, but as the eldest child and only son among so many girls, he remained in our camp, eager to do what he could to keep our father happy. So each morning, after setting our two slaves to grinding the grain, Noura would wake Hobab, remind him of any important guests sleeping within our compound, then join us girls as we set out with the flocks.

Though Noura, Talibah, and Rima were of marriageable age, I think our father intended to keep them at home as long as possible. With many animals and two slaves, he had no great need of dowries, and no desire to enrich himself. According to my father, riches lay not in gold or goats, but in reputation. He gloried in the people who came to seek his advice;

he reveled in revealing the ways of gods to men. Though he would never admit it, I believe he saw his beautiful daughters as proof of his expertise (if that sounds prideful, forgive me, but it is true). As long as we lived in his camp, we were evidence that Reu-el, the "friend of gods," knew how to invoke the deities' blessing.

My father, I also think, genuinely delighted in us. In a time when so many men ate, drank, and slept apart from their women, my father enjoyed calling for us at the end of the day. While he and Hobab sat on carpets inside my father's goatskin tent, we girls would dance to music provided by the blind harpist he had bought from an Egyptian trader. Raja and I would join the twins, Halah and Almira, and swirl the dust as we twirled and clapped, laughing all the while. Talibah, Rima, and Noura would often dance with us, but since the brunt of the work had fallen upon their shoulders, they usually allowed us younger ones to steal our father's favor.

Raja, whose name means "hope," was the youngest. At six, she knew how to bend our father's will to suit her every whim, and usually did.

At nine, I was probably the boldest of the lot. My name means "little bird," but Talibah used to say I was more like a little vulture, always circling and prying. Noura often scolded me for being too brash and outspoken, especially with men. But I didn't care. Father never scolded me; in fact, he often laughed at my tart tongue.

Almira and Halah, our twins, were so inseparable I sincerely hoped my father would marry them to the same man. Almira, our princess, had inherited my mother's graceful beauty, while Halah lived up to her name, which meant "nimble." She was by far the best dancer in our family, and the fastest runner. I have seen her overtake a galloping goat, not an easy feat, especially when one is swathed in a long tunic and veil.

At thirteen, Rima was a pale girl with odd eyes—more gold than brown. Fifteen-year-old Talibah wanted to read more than anything, but lacked a tutor.

My brother was a man—separate, different, and a mystery to me. I do not think our mother's death affected Hobab as deeply as it did us girls, but he had not brushed her hair, listened to her songs, or helped her sew our tunics. We had been bound by womanhood, and no man can understand the sorts of things shared in the women's tent.

Now I am my mother's shadow. I walk where she walked, I wear her veil to breathe in her scent, I serve the evening meal to my father and brother, then join my sisters in our tent.

My father smiles at me and says he is pleased by my hard work, but I also think he is sad. And I fear nothing for us will ever be the same.

I cannot tell you the exact month my life turned in another direction, but I remember the morning well. After waking Hobab as a favor for Noura, I returned to the women's tent to tie back my hair, then draped a light woolen veil over my head. The wind had not begun to blow, yet one never knew when a sudden sandstorm might threaten to scour the skin from our faces.

By the time I joined my sisters, Talibah and Rima had already driven the goats out of their pen. Halah, Almira, and Noura were trying to rouse the sheep, but the smelly animals were resisting the prod of their sharpened goads.

I pulled my staff from the sand by the fire and jabbed a stubborn old ewe in her hindquarters. The animal bleated in protest, then leaped forward, kicking up dust with each mincing step. Her lamb followed, and soon the herd was moving toward the west, where scrubby grass still grew in abundance. We would remain at this spot until the grass disappeared; then my father would move us to another location.

We lived in a changing land of broad plains, narrow valleys, dry riverbeds, and rocks—lots of rocks, particularly around the mountains. The limestone and granite boulders were as varied as my sisters' faces, composed of gorgeous colors and fashioned in unpredictable shapes. My father said the wind and water carved the stones, but I liked to imagine that one of the gods reached down and squeezed them between his fingers, molding them when the land was young and pliable.

Father said the Egyptians called our land *Mafkat*, or "land of copper," but "land of sand" would be a more appropriate name. We had more sand than anything; it permeated every aspect of our clothing and bodies. I couldn't sneeze or cough without expelling sand with my breath, and as a child I believed sand coated the inside as well as the outside of my body.

The land of sand might have been a dustbowl if not for the dew. Rainfall was rare, yet we did get occasional flooding thunderstorms in the winter. Father assured me that floods were the gods' way of keeping our land in balance. The floodwaters fed the fragrant herbs and grasses upon which our flocks fed, and rains replenished the oases where we camped.

Skipping in my shadow, Raja sang as we drove the flocks down a dry wadi, her little voice scattering the birds that had roosted overnight in a twisted acacia tree. Like the rest of us, a leather scrip containing her mid-day meal hung at her waist, suspended from a strap that crossed her chest and shoulder. Unlike the rest of us, Raja carried neither a sling nor a staff. Because she was too young to wield much authority with the animals, to her fell the tasks of scouting for honey and streams of water.

None of us carried extra water that morning, for we planned to graze the flocks within walking distance of the well near our compound. Water was a luxury in the desert no matter what its source, but this well had certain disadvantages, the chief being the youthful sons of an Edomite tribe who had established a camp not far away. Two weeks ago we had tried to water the flocks at day's end, but a band of unruly boys had come out of the desert to mock us, one going so far as to pin Talibah against a stone. Before he could damage her honor, I bounced a good-sized rock off his turban, surprising him long enough for Talibah to slip under his arms and escape. Since that day, however, we had played a waiting game with our flocks, not daring to approach the well if we saw any strangers in the area.

The gods smiled on us that morning. Not only did we graze the flocks in peace, but Raja found a honeycomb in the stump of a broken tree. While Halah made a fire and smoked the bees into a stupor, Rima scooped out the comb and dropped it into a leather pouch.

We ate bread and cheese in the shadow of a stone outcropping, then drained our goatskin water bags. Raja worked on a new song about bees buzzing in a tree, while Almira practiced making faces in a bronze mirror she'd tucked into her scrip.

I lay in a bit of shade on the rocks and looked up at the sky. The sun gleamed white and hot over our heads, heating the rocks around us and the air that sucked moisture from my body like a leech. If I lay here too long, the sun would crack my skin and split my lips, just as it inflated the bodies of sheep that died in the wilds.

"Noura," Rima whined, holding her goatskin upside down to emphasize its emptiness. "I'm thirsty. Isn't it time to go to the well?"

I glanced at my older sister, who had shaded her eyes to check the angle
of the sun. As a rule, no one moved in the hottest part of the day, so this
might be a good time to visit the well. Still, if we moved in the heat, we'd
be bone tired and drenched with sweat by the time we arrived, and we
would still have to fill the troughs for the animals.

The prospect of encountering the Edomite boys, however, was less
appealing. Noura leaned on her staff as she rose. "We can go to the well
and have a look around. Talibah and Rima, bring the flocks, but remain two
hundred paces behind me. If the well is deserted, I'll whistle for you. If
there are people about, we'll have to wait beyond the rocks."

Unable to imagine lagging behind, I stood and danced into my older
sister's line of vision. "Can't I come with you, Noura? I'm thirsty, too."

Sighing, Noura looked down at me. At nine, I was no baby, but sometimes it proved advantageous to behave like one. I also think Noura did
not have the energy to argue.

"You can come, Zipporah, but do not make a sound, particularly if
there are people about."

Obediently, I fell into step beside her as she set out. Noura walked with
a quick step, eager to finish our task and retreat before the local bullies
came out of hiding.

The sun attacked us as soon as we left the shadows. I squinted against
its blinding brightness, then took several steps with my eyes closed, following the sounds of Noura's sandals. A thin ribbon of sweat wandered
down my back as my feet crunched the pebbly scree underfoot.

At last we came to the trail that led to the well. Turning to my sisters,
Noura motioned for Talibah to halt; then she crept forward, with me following in her shadow. We peered around a rock at the rim of the canyon,
and my heart sank when I saw that the well was not deserted.

A solitary man sat upon the short brick wall, one leg swinging in a
mindless rhythm while he drank from a curved bowl someone had left
upon the sand. He had watered his beast as well, for a large black horse
drank from one of the troughs.

The horse held my attention. This was no scrawny desert pony, but a regal beast with an arched neck, braided mane, and long tail. The mare's chest was broad, a sure sign that she'd been bred to pull chariots, and her hooves gleamed with wax, an affectation more common among wealthy Egyptians than desert-dwellers. Hobab had taught me to admire proper horseflesh, and some of the neighboring nomadic tribes produced fine animals. But this was a stunning chariot horse, and since desert-dwellers rarely rode in chariots, the horse had to have come from the Black Land.

I let out a low, admiring whistle.

Startled, Noura darted back into the shadows of the stones, but I remained in place and shifted my gaze to the stranger. He wore a short tunic, a garment indicating an Egyptian influence, and traces of kohl lined his eyes. But he wore no wig. His graying hair had been cut close to the scalp, and a short beard covered his cheeks and chin. If this man was Egyptian, he hadn't held a razor in weeks.

Noura tugged on the hem of my tunic. "Zipporah, get back here! He'll see you."

I waved her off. "What will he care about a little girl?"

Noura's hiss intensified. "Come away! Now!"

"I don't think he'll hurt us. He's alone . . . and I see no weapons."

Convinced either by my observation or by her increasing thirst, Noura stepped forward and peered again at the man. If wagering were a proper activity for girls, I'd have bet my only gold ring that the stranger had come from the Black Land, but I had never seen an Egyptian traveling alone. Merchants from that kingdom always moved in large caravans, their goods carried on donkeys or camels and guarded by chariots and archers. If this man was Egyptian, he was either lost or a renegade.

I pulled back as a thrill shot through me. What if the man were dangerous? Where was Hobab when we needed him? For that matter, where was our father?

I jumped when a masculine voice broke into my thoughts. "Do not be afraid, child." The stranger's voice bounced from the rocks sheltering the well, creating a ghostly echo. "I will not harm you."

I swallowed hard as a tide of gooseflesh rippled up my arms. He had seen us, so to hide now would only demonstrate cowardice. I glanced at Noura. Her eyes were round with anxiety, but the restless flocks behind her were stirring up dust. We couldn't hold them much longer. We would either have to retreat or go forward, but if we retreated we'd have to return later.

Ignoring my paralyzed older sister, I decided it would be better to face the calm, mysterious stranger than the riotous youths from the desert. The man had spoken Akkadian with an Egyptian accent, and Egyptian traders were usually respectful. Those with many goods to sell were always friendly, for no one wanted to barter with an enemy.

I peered out at the man again. His horse carried only two small bags, so he didn't have many goods to trade, if any, but perhaps his servants and pack animals would follow later.

"I'm going down."

"You are not!"

"Watch me." Leaving Noura sputtering on the rocks, I edged out from our hiding place and strode toward the well, stopping when I stood within ten paces of the stranger. He was taller than I had first supposed, and his arms gleamed like oily bronze. His face featured a prominent nose, high cheekbones, and dark eyes that looked up and out but did not seem inclined to let anyone look in.

From my girlish perspective he looked tough, sinewy, and unmistakably foreign.

As I approached, he stood and bowed with a gallantry rare in the wilderness. "Greetings, young lady."

I broke every rule of decorum and gaped, for never had any man bowed to me. I clapped my hand over my mouth, suppressing a giggle, then remembered that I should respond.

Making an attempt to achieve dignity, I lowered my hand. "Greetings, traveler." Pretending nonchalance, I moved past him and descended the steps leading to the well, then picked up a pitcher.

My heart thumped against my rib cage when I heard the stranger's tread on the stairs. Startled, I whirled to face him, but he only gestured to the jar in my hands. "May I draw water for you?"

His lips curved in a polite smile that did not reach his eyes. Too surprised to reply, I stared in silence while he took the pitcher, knelt to dip it into the water, then carried it up the stairs.

Delighted with this unexpected turn of events, I ran after him, then slipped my fingers into my mouth and whistled. I heard him chuckle softly, but as my sisters and their flocks came into view, his smile turned into a look of bemusement.

Trouble, however, followed on my sisters' heels. As Halah and Talibah drove in the last of the bleating sheep, four of the troublesome Edomite youths thundered in on their ponies. One of them struck Talibah on the rear as he rode past, and the obscenity he called after her brought a flush to the stranger's face.

Oblivious to the Egyptian, the boys rode their mounts through the midst of our herds, stirring up dust even as they stirred my fury. I might have been satisfied with shaking my fist at them, but one of the boys scooped up little Raja and held her by one bent arm as he pressed his grimy lips against her cheek. The sight of my little sister's helplessness drove me into a frenzy. Lifting the hem of my tunic, I ran into the swirling melee.

The Egyptian was quicker. With a speed that surprised me, he charged into the churning animals and sprinted toward the oldest of the youths. He caught the young man by the hair, then dragged him off his pony and knocked him on the temple. When the youth went limp, the Egyptian dropped him in the dust and swiveled toward the boy holding Raja. Bending, he picked up a stone and sent it flying. The rock caught my sister's assailant between the shoulder blades, a solid blow that left the target gasping for breath. As Raja wriggled from his grasp and dropped to the ground, the third youth caught sight of our defender. With his undulating battle cry echoing among the rocks, he kicked his pony, but the Egyptian grasped the reins as the confused animal trotted past. Pony, man, and youth disappeared in a cloud of dust; then the Egyptian reappeared, dragging the boy by the neck of his garment. When the squirming youth yelled out an insult, the Egyptian reached back and thunked his opponent squarely in the jaw, then dropped him on the sand. The fourth Edomite youth, finding himself alone, turned his mount and raced for the horizon.

I stopped in the center of the swirling mayhem to count heads. All my sisters were present and unharmed, as were all the animals.

By the time I finished counting, the Egyptian had returned to the well. As he poured water over his head and arms, Raja stood at his knee, her face tilted toward him and a look of adoration in her eyes.

I hurried down the steps to claim my sister. "Thank you." I placed my hands on Raja's shoulders. "We appreciate your kindness and your help with those troublemakers. But you need not have bothered. We are used to those terrible boys—"

"Indeed." He smiled, and I was struck by the beautiful condition of his teeth—few men of my acquaintance had so many. "I noticed how brave you were, little one. I'm not sure I could have charged into the fray had you not inspired me."

I'm sure he intended the words as a compliment, but even at that tender age I could recognize condescension in a man's voice. I narrowed my gaze. "I am not so little, sir. I don't know where you've journeyed from, but we grow up quickly in this land. I know its dangers full well."

"I do not doubt you, young lady." Again a smile gleamed through his dark beard. "And pray forgive me; I did not mean to offend."

Not knowing what else to say, I dismissed myself with an abrupt nod and set about the task of watering our animals. The Egyptian, however, helped us, and each time he came up the steps he cast wary looks toward the three Edomites who still lay stunned among our herds. He nodded with satisfaction, however, when finally they stood, gathered their ponies, and rode away.

Moving with more speed than usual, I helped my sisters drive the livestock toward the troughs. When the animals had drunk, we refilled our water bags, then, still conscious of the Egyptian's dark eyes upon us, I fell into step behind Noura as she herded Reuel's daughters and flocks toward home.

Raja ran ahead as we neared our camp, announcing our arrival with squeals of excitement. Father met Noura at the door of his tent, an expression of concern upon his face. "How did you get the flocks watered so quickly today?"

"An Egyptian rescued us from the other shepherds," Talibah answered, driving the she-goats into the milking pen.

"A handsome Egyptian," Rima chimed in.

Raja tugged on our father's sleeve, the gap between her teeth showing as she smiled. "Then he drew water for us and watered our flocks."

Father's gaze met Noura's. "Well." He spoke in a low tone of rebuke. "Where is he? Did you just leave him at the well? Go and invite him for a meal!"

Noura lifted her hands in weary exasperation. "I can't go back out there, Father. I have to see to the dinner."

Halah grinned at me. "Zipporah will go. She is his special friend."

Father turned, his brows lifting. "A special friend, little bird?"

"She spoke to him first," Almira answered, brushing sand from her toes. "She should go out to find him."

Father's eyes twinkled at me. "My brave Zipporah. All right then, take the donkey and find this man. He will be hungry."

I made a face and pretended to resent my father's command, but something in my heart leaped at the chance to see the Egyptian again.

My father used to say there is no such thing as luck, for the gods rule every aspect of our lives. While I was not as devoted to the gods as he was (I often thought he played the role of priest with more flair than necessary), neither luck nor the gods were with me when I returned to the well. The troublemaking Edomites had vanished, but so had the Egyptian. Furthermore, my donkey knew dinnertime was approaching and he wanted his oats.

Holding my stubborn beast by his halter, I hesitated at the well, torn between returning home empty-handed and making an extra effort to please my father. The shadows under the overhanging rocks were already cold and blue, the western sky blazing with shades of copper and amethyst.

Sighing, I looked at the ground. The Egyptian's trail was clear enough—I'd have to be as giddy as Almira to miss the massive hoofprints in the sand. I decided to follow the trail until the sun dipped halfway behind the hills on the horizon. Then, for safety's sake, I'd turn and truthfully tell my father that the Egyptian had departed on a horse much swifter than my humble donkey.

I hopped upon my donkey's sweaty back and urged him forward, rhythmically kicking his ribs in time to the song I hummed beneath my breath. I hoped Noura was preparing a generous dinner. Our Libyan slave, Rakia, was a good cook, but required a watchful eye to make sure she did not fall asleep by the fire and scorch the food. But if we were lucky, there would be bread, leben cheese, and perhaps a nice lamb stew.

I smiled at the thought, and suddenly realized that being outside under the cooling sky was far more pleasant than sweating over the fire with Rakia and my sisters. A few stars had already risen to spangle the eastern sky, and as I followed the Egyptian's trail I wondered why he had come our way. Why would an Egyptian travel alone through the lands of Midian? I had thought him a merchant who rode ahead of his servants and pack animals, but none had appeared. He did not look diseased, so he was no outcast. He was no thief, or he'd have helped himself to our animals. Furthermore, he seemed to respect women—a quality rarely found among desert-dwellers. The females of my world quietly accepted the authority of men as easily as they accepted the separation between the sexes. I obeyed my father without question, and expected to marry a man who would command me in exactly the same way.

But this man had not commanded, he had *served* me. Protected me. As well as my sisters, of course, but he had spoken to me first.

When my donkey's hooves struck hard rock, I pulled on the lead and brought him to a stop. The Egyptian's tracks had led to a rocky slab, but here they vanished. From this point he could have gone into the silken dunes of the northern desert or the sandy hills and beige canyons of the east. He might have even gone south toward the mountains, but with night falling, he'd soon want to stop and build a fire.

Somehow I knew he wouldn't go toward Egypt.

I sat straighter, scanning the horizon for a curl of smoke or rising dust, but saw nothing. And I could no longer follow a trail I could not see.

As I turned the donkey, I was surprised to feel a sharp stab of disappointment. "Silly," I rebuked myself, "why should you care if an Egyptian sleeps in our camp tonight? Your father attracts strangers like raw meat draws jackals, so why would you want another mouth to feed?"

Feeling the cool approach of evening, I hunched deeper into my tunic, then stopped breathing when an elongated shadow fell across my path.

"Are you lost, young friend?"

My panic melted into irritation when I recognized the cultured, clipped tones of the Egyptian. A boulder at my right had concealed the man and his horse. Now man and beast moved into my line of sight, and as the man looked down, his curved brow indicated humorous surprise.

"I'm not lost. My father wishes to invite you to dinner. Reuel the priest of Midian wants to extend his gratitude."

The Egyptian did not answer, but looked toward the western horizon. I followed his gaze, then turned back to him. "So? Will you come?"

"You tracked me?" He smiled. "You are good."

"Anyone could track a horse as big as yours." I waited another moment, then shrugged and kicked my lowly donkey. "Come or not, it's your decision. I will tell Father I invited you."

"I will come. To refuse would be unforgivably rude." He made a clicking sound with his tongue, then turned his mount. "Lead on, little lady, and I will follow."

I think he agreed to come with me because he was hungry. I also think he was lonely, for a man who will stop to talk to a mere girl is desperate for companionship.

My father greeted the stranger with an embrace, a kiss on both cheeks, and the traditional tribal greeting: "Had I known you would honor me by coming this way, I would have strewn the path between your house and mine with mint and rose petals!"

The Egyptian returned the embrace and bore the greeting with grace. "You are too kind, Reuel. Indeed, I am honored by your hospitality."

A glow rose in my father's face, as if he contained a lamp that had just been lit. "May I know the name of the kind man who rescued my daughters?"

The stranger smiled. "I am called Moses."

"Son of water?" My father cocked a brow. "Forgive me if I misinterpret your name. Most Egyptians of high estate—and you are obviously of high estate, my friend—have a god's name attached."

"I am not attached to any god. I have no use for them."

I nearly dropped the jar of wine I carried. What sort of man did not claim allegiance to any deity? Everyone I knew called upon the gods to aid them with everything from rising out of bed to choosing a spouse. My father had made the gods his livelihood, and even the most villainous people we met in the wilds worshiped some force of nature and called it god.

I halted in midstep, staring at the Egyptian as a rush of admiration poured through my veins.

"No use for the gods?" My father spoke in an incredulous whisper, then lifted his hands and inclined his head in a deep bow. "You are a seeker, then. Perhaps I can help you find a god to suit your needs."

"I appreciate your kind intentions, Reuel, but I really prefer to speak of other things."

My father lifted both brows at this, then cast about for another topic of conversation. With a relieved smile, his gaze settled on Hobab and he introduced my brother. Hobab welcomed the Egyptian with an embrace, too; then the three men went into my father's tent for dinner.

Noura and Talibah served the meal, while Rima, Halah, Almira, Raja, and I crouched on the other side of the goatskin wall and strained to hear the conversation. With his love for people, my father had a gift for extracting their secrets, so we were sure we'd learn all about our mysterious rescuer if we sat quietly.

As the men talked and ate, Noura and Talibah trotted past us, their arms laden with carved bowls containing savory meat, boiled onions, and bread. My sisters said little, but once I thought I saw a blush upon Noura's cheek.

The flush was significant, and turned my thoughts in a new direction—though the man inside Father's tent was probably more than twice Noura's age, she was certainly old enough to be married. One did not have to be a soothsayer to know my father had begun to think about finding her a suitable husband. By the end of tonight's dinner, we might discover if Moses the Egyptian had become a worthy contender.

Raja had begun to sing her bee song again, so I pressed my finger to her lips and bent lower to listen.

"Where are you going?" My father's voice carried over the clink of brass utensils. "We do not encounter many Egyptians traveling alone in this area."

"I'm just . . . going." The answer was purposefully evasive, but I could hear no trace of annoyance in the stranger's voice.

"The man who has no use for the gods is wandering through the desert for no reason." My father laughed softly. "You had better be careful, then. The wilds of Sinai are dangerous even for men who pay homage to all the gods."

"I'm no stranger to the wilderness." Again, his answer tantalized without giving information, but his voice remained smooth and polite.

"Really? Then perhaps you would be content to reside a while with us. We can always use an experienced man in the compound. My son would enjoy your company, and my daughters owe you a great debt."

Almira giggled, forcing Halah to slap her hand over her twin's mouth. We all knew what Father had in mind—a cultured, intelligent Egyptian was about to find himself being measured for a bride.

Noura trudged past us again, a pitcher of wine on her hip. My eyes followed her, wondering how she would enjoy being married to the Egyptian. This Moses seemed kind, but who knew what secrets lurked in the heart of a stranger? He was obviously hiding his past, but at least he was being honest. He could have spun us any story he liked and we would not have known the difference between truth and deception.

My father apparently placed great confidence in his ability to bring speech from a rock, for he continued to question our patient guest. "They say the great temples of Amon-Re in Memphis are spectacular."

"They are."

"And I hear the mortuary temple of Ramesses in Thebes is a wonder to behold."

"It is."

"And yet . . . the beauty of these temples does not elicit worship from your soul?"

Silence swelled for a moment, then Moses spoke in a tone of infinite tolerance. "The buildings you mention are outstanding works of men, and in my youth I regularly worshiped in them. But I am no longer a youth; time and experience have opened my eyes. I have come to see—to *know*—

that temples are works of men, and men are not gods. If they are, then the gods are not all-powerful. They are certainly not good or just."

My eyes widened at this deluge of words, then I cringed in anticipation of my father's rebuke of Moses' blasphemy. But my father remained silent, as did Hobab, who seemed to have been struck dumb by the entire conversation.

Finally, in a voice heavy with resignation, Father said, "Stay with us a while, Moses of Egypt, and I will ask the gods of heaven and earth to reveal themselves to you. In this vast emptiness beneath the vault of heaven one cannot help but think of eternity and mortality. One cannot escape the realization that man is not god, therefore someone else must be."

"Thank you," Moses answered, his tone purposefully polite. "Perhaps time will prove you right."

According to nomadic hospitality, visitors stayed for at least three days. The first day was dedicated to *salaam*, or greeting; the second to *ta'aam*, eating; and the third to *kelaam*, speaking. By twisting my father's arm, on Moses' second day in camp I was excused from the herding in order to help Noura prepare a feast.

As the sun rose over the edge of the golden hills around us, Noura assigned me to make loaves of bread, a task even Harkhuf, our blind harpist, could have accomplished with ease. After mixing the dough with leavening and shaping it into fist-sized balls, I dug small pits in the sand beneath Noura's fire pit. After dropping the balls of dough into the pits, I covered them with sand and stepped away.

The baking would occur when Noura roasted a lamb, which left me with more than enough time to investigate our guest. Moses had not yet come out of his tent, so I crept toward the pen where his mare had been hobbled with our donkeys.

The animal stamped the earth as I approached, churning the dust with her tail. "Sorry, girl," I whispered, running my hand over the velvet flesh at her jaw. "I don't have any oats now. But maybe later."

Running my hand along her silky nose, I saw that Moses had ridden with no saddle of any kind. Two bags hung on either side of the horse's neck, though—rough linen sacks that probably contained every possession he had brought from the Black Land. My hand fell upon the first bag, which felt soft. Glancing toward the place where he slept, I saw that the tent flap remained lowered. Emboldened by my luck, I wrapped my hand in the horse's mane, turned her until she stood between me and Moses' tent, then rose on tiptoe to undo the drawstring bag.

Inside I felt fabric—the medium weight of a woven shawl of no particular richness—then my fingers encountered the cool touch of metal. I pulled out two earrings of solid silver, then thrust my hand in again. This time I withdrew a wide collar and bracelets of hammered gold.

Ripples of shock spread from a point in my stomach, making the crown of my head tingle and my toes go numb. I held the collar, its golden fastening chains spilling over my fingertips, and realized the gold in this adornment alone would probably purchase every animal in our herd five times over.

A cold quiver ascended to the back of my neck. Who was this man? A murderer? A thief? This Moses could have happened upon a caravan, where he killed someone for these jewels and this horse. He must have murdered someone important, for only high officials wore bracelets like these, and I had only seen collars like this in painted pictures of Egyptian royalty.

My heart congealed into a small lump of terror. Had Moses murdered a prince of Egypt? Such a crime might explain his presence here, his evasiveness, and his reluctance to call upon the gods who would surely want to strike him down for his crime—

"Are all little girls as inquisitive as you, Zipporah?"

Flinching, I looked up and saw Moses standing on the other side of the horse. His gaze took in my gold-strewn hands and my horrified expression, but he only lifted his arms to stroke the mare.

"I'm—I'm sorry." As heat suffused my neck and cheeks I stuffed the jewelry back into the bag. "I was looking for something—"

"Don't lie, little one. Lying is one of the worst things a woman can do."

I stepped back as warning spasms of alarm erupted within me. I wanted to scream, to run for my father, but what could I say? Having jewelry was not a crime, even though it was not the sort of jewelry that should ever have appeared in a Midianite camp.

I stood there, frozen in shame; then Noura's shrill cry echoed across the compound. "Zipporah! Where are you, lazy girl?"

I lifted my eyes to meet the Egyptian's. "I have to go."

Moses' eyes remained gentle and unthreatening. "Go, then."

I sprinted away as fast as my feet would carry me, and could not find the courage to look back.

I carried my doubts and questions throughout the day, holding numerous silent conversations with myself. If Moses were a murderer, I supposed he would kill me, for I had discovered his secret. But he had not moved to harm me in the moment he discovered my prying eyes, and he could have done so. I had seen him expertly strike the Edomite youths, and I did not doubt that those strong hands knew how to kill with one blow. He could have clouted me behind the horse and carried my lifeless body to my father, explaining that I had spooked his mare and suffered a kick.

On the other hand, perhaps he thought a little girl posed no threat. But surely he knew I could speak to my father, and he'd had enough experience with my outspoken parent to know Reuel would not hesitate to discuss the matter. My father's tongue respected few boundaries, and he would wheedle Moses until we had an answer for the golden bracelets and the unusual collar.

Yet he had warned me not to lie . . . and lies were the language of thieves and murderers.

Still musing, I went back to the fire pit, lifted the roasting lamb with one stick and poked at my buried bread with another. Not satisfied with the springy consistency of the dough beneath the sand, I dropped the lamb and settled back to wait.

Why not wait on Moses? As long as he did not threaten us, why not wait to see when and how he would reveal his past? I could not forget his bravery or his kindness, and it seemed uncharitable to betray his privacy when I had been the one guilty of snooping.

A few moments later I pulled the baked bread from the sand, then took a smaller stick and beat each loaf like a dusty carpet. Sand flew with each blow, but soon I had chipped all the brown crust away. I thrust my fingers into the center of one loaf, pulled out a hunk of soft, steaming bread, and popped it into my mouth.

Delicious.

Squatting in the sand, I decided to watch and wait before saying anything to our father about Moses.

We girls had just begun to serve the men's evening meal when a crazed bull wandered out of the desert and entered our compound. With the bread bowl on my hip, I scurried toward the fire pit. The huge beast circled slowly, surveying our tents as if he couldn't decide which one best suited his fury, then charged the largest dwelling. He did little damage, for my father, Hobab, and Moses sat deep inside, beyond the entrance, but after collapsing the front wall, the bull shook his horns free of the ropes and goatskins and glared around for another target.

Raja had joined me behind the fire pit, and perhaps the scent of roasting lamb drew the bull's attention. The animal shook his head, then snorted heavily, blowing clouds of dust with each exhalation. The unexpected sight had rooted me to the ground, but Raja's frightened whine spurred me to action. Moving slowly, I stepped behind her and placed my hands on her shoulders, never taking my eyes from the bull.

"Careful now," I whispered. "When I give the word, run like the wind to the animal pen. Stay in front of me, and don't look back, whatever you do."

Too frightened for words, Raja nodded, the back of her head rubbing against my belly.

The bull blinked. For a moment dark little eyes seemed to roll up inside its skull, then it shook its mighty head and charged.

"Run, Raja!"

She took off and I followed, but I kept my eyes on the bull. The beast had not advanced six steps before a flying spear struck its neck. The animal tripped over the dangling handle and fell, then quivered in the heat, bellowing in muted fury. Great gouts of blood spurted from the wound, and after a few moments the animal's movements stilled.

My father and Hobab peered out from behind the rumpled goatskins of the tent. Rakia, our cook, stood shrieking, her tunic smeared with greasy drippings from the dish she'd been carrying. But like an avenging warrior-god, Moses stood alone in the clearing, his spear arm still flexed, his eyes narrowed in concentration.

Pulling himself free of the tent coverings, my father stared at the huge beast with undisguised wonder in his eyes. "Praise to the gods! They have sent us a feast!"

"Not today." Moses pressed his hands to his face, drew a deep breath, then lowered his arms and strode toward the still-quivering animal. "This beast is diseased. The carcass must be burned and the meat discarded. Do not even give it to the dogs."

Hobab's face fell, but my father was not about to let a gift from the gods go to waste. "So be it. We'll burn the creature, but as an offering. Tonight the gods shall smell the sweet and generous gift we lay before them, and tomorrow they may reward us yet again!"

My father clapped his hand upon Moses' back. "Come, friend. We will eat under the shade of yonder terebinth tree while Hobab restores our tent."

My sisters buzzed about the event as they gathered their bowls and dishes. Talibah proclaimed Moses the most intelligent man in the world for knowing exactly where to strike the bull while Halah proclaimed him the strongest for being able to throw Hobab's spear with enough force to bring the animal down. Noura said nothing, but blushed with each mention of his name. Almira smoothed her hair, then picked up a bowl of dried dates and said, "I think he's a very pretty man. Don't you, Zipporah?"

I did not care if he was pretty. I was still wondering if the powerful arm that had slain the bull might turn on one of us.

No gift from the gods appeared the following day, but Hobab did encounter a bit of mischief. After taking a short trip to meet with a spice trader, he returned with the news that a band of Edomites had stolen a sheep from one of our kinsmen. My sisters and I were about to take the flocks out to graze, but we stopped in the center of the compound, staves in hand, to watch the drama unfold.

My father received Hobab's news in silence, as did Moses, who had girded on his sandals. After spending three days in our camp, he was preparing to leave.

"Come, Moses," Hobab called, strapping on his sword. "We shall find them and slit their throats where they stand! There were only three of them, so you and I can overpower them with ease. All you have to do is let your spear fly, and that blow will even the odds."

I think we were all a bit surprised when Moses shook his head. "You would fare better if you calmed your anger." He stroked the silky flank of his horse. "Your kinsman is not hurt, and he has lost nothing more than a sheep. Is one sheep worth a war between tribes? Forget this trespass, and save your anger for something more important."

Hobab gaped at Moses like a man faced with an indecipherable papyrus. "Forget it? They have injured the honor of our clan; they have stolen what is rightfully ours! We are within our rights to wreak vengeance upon them!"

"All they have injured is your pride." Moses had lowered his voice, but I could still hear the censure in his tone. "And do you think you are the only one who must bear injustice? The world is full of unfairness, and scores of others have suffered far worse than you. So yes, my friend, forget this incident and counsel your kinsman to keep a closer watch on his flocks."

Hobab's face crumpled with frustration. "I can't believe you're saying this! You, a warrior! You attacked the Edomites who were harassing my sisters—"

"I didn't intend to kill those boys." Moses glanced up and caught my eye, then shifted his gaze to Hobab. "There was a time when my temper was hotter and harder to restrain, but it has cooled with time. There is a time for killing, but men should never lift their weapons without first weighing all the consequences."

I looked at Noura, who blushed again, then I glanced at Talibah. Her eyes had gone wide with alarm at Hobab's first words, but now her mouth settled into a thin line. Apparently, she was eager for Moses to spill blood for the sake of our clan.

I turned to my father, expecting to see Talibah's expression mirrored on his face, but a small smile twitched at the corners of his mouth.

"Moses." He gripped the Egyptian's shoulder. "Do not depart from us today. Come inside my tent and hear the proposal I will make in your honor."

Behind me, Talibah and Rima twittered in anticipation while Noura stalked away, her head lowered and her face obscured by her veil. If Father meant to propose a marriage joining Noura and Moses . . . should I tell him what I had found in Moses' bags? Should I cast doubt on a man who had behaved so honorably in our camp?

Halah elbowed me as she moved past. "Come, Zipporah, don't dream the day away."

Urged out of my quandary by my sister's sharp elbow, I decided to leave the matter in my father's hands. Pulling my staff from the sand, I hurried to join my sisters.

I never learned whether my father mentioned marriage that morning; I only know Moses did not leave. Persuaded by Reuel's glib tongue and our obvious need for another man to help protect our camp, the mysterious Egyptian became part of a Midianite priest's household.

His decision to stay brought me great hope. For several weeks I had been wondering whether a girl who wanted nothing to do with the gods should remain in a priest's household. I had begun to entertain the idea of slipping away with a traveling caravan or running off to live with a less religious kinsman, but if a skeptical Egyptian could live with Reuel, why not a skeptical daughter? After all, Moses worshiped no gods, but he tolerated my father's religious rituals with equanimity. Surely I could do the same.

Soon we discovered that Moses possessed an outstanding skill that boosted my father's prominence to the heavens—the Egyptian could read and write hieroglyphics, hieratic script, and Akkadian, the language of the desert tribes. When word of Reuel's scribe began to filter into the wilds, men from even distant territories sought our camp to have contracts validated, documents read, and covenants recorded. Relationships with the gods were always contractual, and the local sand-crossers delighted to know they could now be written down. Many times I came in from keeping the flocks to find Moses recording a covenant as my father dictated for a guest: "I, Tewfik, promise to worship El, father of the gods, if he will bless me abundantly with life, health, strength, wives, and children as numerous as the sand of the desert. . . ."

My father was delighted to discover Moses' ability for another, more personal reason. Within his heart he carried stories of the Creation, the Deluge, the Tower of Babel, and Abraham, the ancestor who had left Ur and established many nations. By rights, Hobab should have become the inheritor of those stories, but my brother had little patience for sitting still and no aptitude for storytelling.

So every night after dinner, while the wind blew sand against the tent and almost tricked us into believing the sky had brought forth rain, we girls huddled in the shadows of my father's dwelling and listened as he spun the stories of El-ohim, the plural God who had created the earth and sent the worldwide flood. El Shaddai, God of the Mountains, had called Abraham from Ur. The priest Melchizedek had blessed Abraham in the name of El-Elyon, the Exalted One. Hagar had called upon El Roi, the God Who Sees, and later Abraham had planted a tamarisk tree in Beersheba and called upon El Olam, or God the Everlasting One.

Moses rarely commented as my father spun his stories, but sat cross-legged upon a carpet, dipping a reed pen into wet mixtures of red and black, then painting symbols upon rolls of cured leather.

At first I didn't understand what Moses scribbled upon his scrolls, but when I expressed an interest, he asked Father for permission to teach me. Talibah, who had longed to read and write in her younger years, complained that I was shirking my duties, but Father told her to leave me alone. He would have been happier, I think, if Hobab had become Moses' student, but my brother was too busy scouring the wilds for adventure to apply himself to brush and ink.

Every morning after breaking our fast, I would sit across from Moses and learn how to make images on rocks or whatever resources were available. When Moses was busy helping my father entertain his guests, I would set about the work of providing materials for our writing practice—grinding raw pigments into paste and mixing the paste with water until it made a suitable ink. Because papyrus was expensive when purchased from trade caravans, I gathered reeds at oases and chewed the ends to separate the stiff plant fibers. After I had loosened the fibers, I flattened the strips of pith and arranged them in two layers, one perpendicular to the other, upon a flat stone. I then moistened the woven sheet, pounded it with a rock, and allowed it to dry in the sun.

Because we had no wooden stands, Moses taught me to sit like the scribes in Egypt—with folded legs so the taut fabric of my tunic served as a foundation for writing. The stiff surface of the papyrus was more than sturdy enough to withstand the pressure of my reed pen.

Moses taught me many things, including how to carve a wooden palette to hold small cakes of ink and a dozen reed brushes. With his help, I created my own writing kit, complete with a dozen brushes, three colors of ink, and a stone to hold the papyrus flat while I wrote.

Ordinarily, Moses told me, a scribe would recite prayers before starting his work, but he maintained that my father routinely said enough prayers for both of us. Quietly delighted to discover a soul as dubious as my own, at Moses' side I learned how to convert our language into symbols and draw more than seven hundred hieroglyphic signs.

Moses used to laugh when I crouched low over my papyrus, my tongue protruding between my teeth as I concentrated, but he always stopped laughing when I showed him my work. I was, he assured me, as fine a scribe as any youth in Egypt.

I think he was trying to be kind . . . but I also think he spoke the truth. As the years passed, my pen grew quicker, my strokes more fluid and graceful, until my father could not tell the difference between my writing and Moses'.

If that sounds prideful, I am sorry.

By the time Moses had spent a year with us, my father had given Noura to a cousin from a nearby clan. I think my father was more than a little disappointed that Moses never asked to marry her. Father would have offered his eldest daughter in a moment, but a veil of silence surrounded Moses in those days, a veil my less brash sisters were afraid to approach.

Talibah married the next year, with Rima following soon after. As Moses entered his fourth year with us, he danced at the wedding of Halah and Almira, both of whom were married to a wealthy warrior of the Kenite tribe.

For a while only Raja and I remained at home, but the gods took my younger sister before a husband could. One night as she brought the flocks home, a leopard sprang at her from the rocks, killing her and scattering the sheep.

We mourned for Raja, our hope. My sisters and their husbands moved their tents near ours, and for thirty days we camped in sorrowful silence. Then my sisters embraced me, told me to be careful, and took their leave of us.

Noura held me close before leaving. "You are all Father has left," she whispered in my ear. "Do not be quick to leave him, Zipporah. He needs a woman in his camp, for how can he survive alone?"

I did not want to leave my father's household, for my fourteen-year-old heart had settled upon Moses. He had become so many things to me—protector, teacher, and guide—and I could not imagine marrying anyone else. As long as he remained content to live with Reuel's people, so would I.

One night not long after Raja's death, I was helping Rakia serve dinner in my father's tent. From the corner, Harkhuf strummed his harp while Rakia bent to lower a bowl of lamb stew. I stood behind her, a pitcher of wine in my hands.

"Now that Raja has departed," Moses spoke slowly, as if he were carefully choosing his words, "do not send Zipporah out with the flocks. There are other leopards in the desert, along with panthers and wolves. She is an excellent scribe, so let her serve you in the camp."

Spreading his hands, my father gave Moses a look of sheer astonishment. "Who, then, am I to send with the flocks? I have only Zipporah and Hobab, and Hobab must remain in the camp. As my son, it is his place."

"Send me."

My father laughed. "You? You are a learned man, and a more skilled warrior than Hobab. I need you here."

I stiffened, chagrined that a conversation so openly about me had not been addressed to me. But in mixed company women did not speak unless spoken to, and neither Moses nor my father had even looked my way.

Moses smoothed the beard at his chin. "You do not need me here.

Zipporah can handle any requests for covenants or papyri, as well oversee the household duties. You are a wealthy man; you could easily buy another slave to help Rakia with the cooking. And I will tend your flocks."

A faint line appeared between my father's graying brows, and I knew he was pondering the motivation behind Moses' request. Was the man thinking of leaving us?

Father reached for his cup. "Your suggestion has merit, Moses, but—if you'll excuse the question—do you know anything about shepherding?"

Moses actually laughed as his gaze caught mine. "Zipporah can teach me. She owes me a few lessons."

I turned to Father, who looked up as if he'd never seen me before. "Zipporah will teach," he muttered, "and *Moses* will tend the sheep?"

Lowering my eyes, I shifted the heavy pitcher from one hand to the other. The notion was unconventional, and my father would surely think the wilds a great waste of the Egyptian's talents.

Yet I had to admire Moses' cunning. He had been gracious, serving my father to the best of his ability, but on many occasions I had glimpsed a look of defiance in his eyes as he stood beside my father's guests at the stone altars. Of all the men who entered the circle of stones to worship, only Moses did not chant, make sacrifices, or bow before the shrines. Father usually excused Moses' apparent irreverence by saying he worshiped in solitude, but if Moses took himself to the wilderness in daylight hours, those who sought my father's religious guidance would no longer have to wonder about the unbeliever in their midst.

Unable to speak directly to my father, I turned toward Rakia and poured the wine. "Moses' plan makes sense," I said, little caring that the old woman could barely hear even when I yelled in her ear. "I would be happy to record covenants for those who visit us."

Oblivious to my comments, Rakia continued to spoon lamb stew into Moses' bowl.

"A woman? Writing in plain view?" My father's forehead creased in concern. "It's . . . unthinkable."

"It's completely practical." Pulling off a chunk of bread, Moses winked at me. "Zipporah is a woman now. Let her assume a woman's duties."

My father sent him a sharp look, though I doubt Moses saw it. He kept smiling at me, and from the corner of my eye I could see my father watching him, an appraising expression on his face.

I turned and left my father's tent, knowing full well what thoughts filled his heart. For the first time in five years with us, Moses had uttered a personal compliment about a daughter of Reuel . . . a comment that would not be taken lightly.

Nor did I want it to be. Though I had been in awe of his manhood since the day of our first meeting, Moses had finally noticed that I had become a woman.

~⚬~

By the time the kiss of sunrise summoned a rosy flush to the southern mountains, the matter had been settled. Moses would join me with the flocks for a few weeks; then he would assume their care so I could remain in the camp. And since I would be helping my father with his guests, from the next traveling caravan he would buy another slave to help Rakia with the cooking.

Moses wore a pleased expression when he joined me at the animal pen. I noted it, but said nothing as we pulled back the branches that served as a gate. Moses stood there, a branch in his hand, but the animals did not move.

"They won't come by themselves." Suppressing a giggle, I pulled my staff from the sand. "You have to goad them. They huddle together for warmth at night. They'd stay together all day long if we didn't break them apart."

Moses laughed. "I'm afraid you're going to have to think of me as a novice shepherd." He pulled another staff—Raja's—from the sand, then poked a sleepy ewe in the hindquarters. "I've never had to work flocks before."

"I'm not surprised."

As the sheep stumbled forward, I equipped Moses with a sling (which I knew he could use with skill), a short rod to tuck into his girdle, a scrip, and a goatskin water bag. Similarly burdened, I set out, leading the mingled flock of sheep and goats toward a pass in the mountains, beyond which lay a stand of scrub brush and wild grasses. The sun had been up only an hour, but already my skin was soaked beneath my woolen tunic. I found myself thinking of the linen garment Moses had worn when we first met him—how cool it had seemed, and how light! But we had no linen here, and no use for such a fragile material.

We walked through sunlight and shadows thrown by the rocks, moving the animals through a dry riverbed toward the life-giving grass. Once we had settled the flock, Moses and I moved to a shady spot beneath a twisted terebinth tree and sat on the sand. Feeling awkward in the silence, I pulled a reed pipe from my scrip and began to blow a simple tune.

Moses leaned forward, a look of surprise upon his face. "You make music, Zipporah?"

I pulled the pipe from my lips. "When there's nothing else to do. Raja and I used to play together."

Sadness for my departed sister welled in my chest. I put the pipe away.

Moses deftly changed the subject. "Tell me about the animals. What should a shepherd do?"

Clearing my throat, I gestured toward the high rocks. "You watch for dangers. Though there are no more lions in these wilds, occasionally we see wolves. Once Noura and I caught a huge hyena trying to bring down a lamb."

"And how do you stop a hyena without a bow and arrows?"

I shrugged. "Noura screamed, but I strode toward it, my left arm stretched forth to hold its attention. I held my staff like a spear and stared the creature in the eye, never wavering until it turned and ran."

Moses tipped back his head and laughed. The sudden sound startled a couple of the goats, who bleated and trotted a few steps before settling down to graze.

"You must also look for sand snakes." I felt a little foolish teaching a man nearly my father's age, but he *had* asked. "In unfamiliar areas, you must prod the sand with your staff to be sure of your footing. All sorts of strange creatures inhabit the wilds—others have told me of griffins with human heads, winged panthers, and cheetahs with necks longer than a giraffe's. Some say there are dogs in the wilds with square ears and tails as stiff as arrows."

A thoughtful smile bowed my companion's mouth. "Surely you don't believe those stories."

I shrugged again. "Who am I to say whether or not they are true? I have not seen every animal in the world, so how do I know these creatures don't exist? Unless a woman knows *everything*, how can she know *anything* is a lie?"

Moses stared at me a moment, his eyes soft with thought; then he smiled. "Zipporah, you are a wonder. I like the way you think."

If he had said this in the camp, I would have made no reply. But we were alone, surrounded by the painted vastness of the wilderness and canopied by a great bowl of sky. In such a setting, imposed reticence falls away.

"You agree?" I turned to look him full in the face. "Then how can you worship no gods at all? You say you know they are not real, yet you do not know everything. A man cannot say he knows all gods are false unless he has tried *every* god and found all of them unworthy of his devotion. And there are so many gods, I cannot believe you have tried them all."

"I have tried more than you could know." His eyes left mine and shifted to the landscape. "I have worshiped at more shrines than you could count."

"But you worshiped only the gods of the Egyptians. There are other gods, you know. My father's tribe worships Baal-peor—"

"Another name for the sun god. The Egyptians knew him well. Besides"—a smile lifted his lined cheeks—"I haven't seen *you* worshiping at your father's altars."

Emboldened by his honesty, I waved away his words. "I haven't yet found a god worth worshiping. We invoked all of them when my mother was ill, but none of them had power to save her."

"Ah." Moses transferred his gaze to the flock. "So you are waiting for some god to prove himself to you?"

"I don't know. Perhaps. But I do know I'm not bold enough to say there are no gods at all, for perhaps there is a truly powerful god above the others. Consider Abraham of Ur—he worshiped El Shaddai, God of the Mountains, and El-Elyon, the Most High God—"

"*Who* did he worship?"

I blinked, wondering if Moses had suddenly gone deaf. "I *told* you. El Shaddai, El-Elyon—"

Ever the teacher, he waggled a finger at me. "Those are only descriptive terms, Zipporah—attributes combined with *el*. I could call you Bright Scribe, Pretty Girl, Daughter of Reuel, and Brave Shepherdess—those words describe you, but they do not tell me your name."

For a moment the pit of my stomach tingled and I could not speak. I wondered if he would look at me to gauge the effect of his words, but he kept face turned toward the flocks.

I drew a deep breath and struggled to keep my voice steady as I studied the flocks, too. "Those names are attributes, yes, but I think Abraham's God had a personal name. I don't know it. I don't even know if my father knows it—"

Moses' hand wrapped around my wrist. "What was the name of this Abraham's tribe?"

I stared at him, surprised by the sudden snapping in his eyes. "I don't know, but my father does. Surely you've heard him speak of Abraham— Midian, the father of our tribe, was Abraham's son by his wife Keturah."

"Abraham." Moses thoughtfully whispered the name. "Was he also called Israel?"

"No. Abraham begat Isaac, who begat Jacob, who was later called Isra-el, 'one who is ruled by God.' The sand-crossers say the children of Isra-el are in Egypt under hard bondage, for they forgot the God of their fathers—"

"Not all of them." The hand around my wrist tightened as Moses stared past the horizon. "Some of them remembered. And some of them prayed for a deliverer."

Something in his countenance troubled me. In that moment we were no longer teacher and student, but strangers. "What do you know of the children of Isra-el?"

For a long moment he did not answer; then his eyes narrowed at the corners. "I am one of them."

My face must have gone idiotic with surprise. I lowered my gaze, astounded to silence by Moses' confession. If he spoke the truth . . . why, the stranger who had dwelt among us for five years was no stranger at all, but a kinsman.

Moses, a descendant of Abraham? Impossible to believe, for he was as Egyptian as a hieroglyph. Though I had never mentioned the golden jewelry in his possession to anyone, I had long ago convinced myself that he was an Egyptian noble on the run, an important official who had been unfairly set up to take the blame for a crime he did not commit.

Moses, a cousin? My heart could not accept the notion.

Finally, I found my voice. "Why did you not tell us?"

"I did not think it important. After all, the Hebrews are a defeated people."

"The children of Isra-el?"

"The Egyptians call them Hebrews. They call them mud people. They kill the Hebrew children and force the men to make bricks for Pharaoh, a task for the lowest and dullest of slaves. Their women are bent with hard labor, their men scrawny and ill-used. They are a wretched lot."

He looked at me, and in his eyes I saw the glow of a long-buried fire. I wanted to shrink from the sight, yet it fascinated me.

"If they are wretched, you cannot be one of them. You are far from—"

"I was raised as an Egyptian. Pharaoh's daughter wanted a son, and she found me on the banks of the river. I did not know the truth about my birth until . . . well, shortly before I met you."

Perhaps it was the word *you,* or the sudden softness in his voice, but in that moment I felt closer to Moses than to any being alive. His fingers still clasped my wrist, so I dropped my trembling hand over his with all the tenderness I could summon.

"Your story explains a mystery," I said, wondering if he would be willing to tell my father the same tale. "Including the jewelry I found on your horse so long ago."

He exhaled softly. "You kept that secret. Not many women hold their tongues so well."

I lifted one shoulder in a shrug. "You never gave me any cause to doubt you. I always wondered how you came to be with us. I imagined you a thief, then a murderer, then a runaway slave. Now I think I understand. You discovered you were a Hebrew, so you left Egypt to make your own way in the world?"

A muscle worked at his jaw; abruptly, he pulled his hand out of my grip. "Your imaginings weren't far off the mark, little bird. I left Egypt because I killed a man. Pharaoh decreed that I should pay for the crime with my life, so I outran his edict and found my way here."

My breath caught in my lungs. This man, a murderer? The thought was inconceivable, but with one look at his face I knew he was not lying. And I had seen his skill with weapons, the power in his hands.

Oblivious to my pained silence, Moses kept talking. The act of confession must have loosed something in him, for words began to flow from him with an ease I had never witnessed. "I said good-bye to everything I loved—my home, my mother, my position in the house of Pharaoh. I had been taught to think of myself as a god—indeed, I believed it, for whatever I touched was blessed with favor and fortune. I served as a captain in Pharaoh's army; I commanded twenty thousand men. I wore gold and fine linen, I had royal apartments in a half-dozen palaces. Everything in Egypt could have been mine, including Pharaoh's throne, but then I learned that my mother had lied about who I was. I was not the son of a god; I wasn't even the son of Ramesses. I was the son of Hebrew slaves, a baby discovered in the mud of the Nile. All my royal brothers, all the warriors I had bested in contests, had supposed me their superior, but I knew they would soon learn the truth. I was nothing, a man of mud."

As a thunderous scowl darkened his brow, I cringed, feeling suddenly weak and vulnerable in the face of his anger. I had hoped to know Moses better, but perhaps some secrets should remain buried.

"Then I began to reconsider," he said, barely bridled anger in his voice. "What did my origin matter? What if the gods had placed me in Pharaoh's palace for a purpose? What if I were to use my power and position to help the Hebrews rise out of slavery and restore ma'at in their poor lives? I was a perfect combination of Hebrew blood and Egyptian learning. I walked about in a Hebrew body, tall and wiry, but I had an Egyptian soul. I had been educated in mathematics and writing and literature. I could name the stars and interpret dreams. I was acquainted with geometry and art, chemistry and metallurgy. I had been trained in music, song, and dance.

"I resolved to help the Hebrews, to show them I was not the enemy. So I went out to Goshen, determined to know them."

As Moses held up his hands and stared at the smooth palms, I took advantage of the lull. "Surely they welcomed you. They must have been astounded to learn that one of their kinsmen had been living in Pharaoh's palace—"

"They hated me." His nostrils flared. "My own sister spat upon me. And when I tried to save one of them from a severe beating, anger overtook me, rage mixed with a sense of prideful justice. I defended the man, yes, but I killed an Egyptian captain in the process. Shaken, the next day I went to the village where I had been born, hoping they'd realize that I had set my heart to defend them, but they turned on me in fury."

His eyes filled with infinite distress. "How do you help people who will not be helped?" He gestured to the fields, where our flocks grazed on the scrubby grass. "They are like the sheep in the fold this morning—they will not move unless you goad them with a sharp stick, but I had no stick—at least, none they would respect."

He reached for his staff, then jabbed the sharpened point into the sand. "Sheep respond to pain, but the Hebrews have grown accustomed to suffering. Goats respond to sound, but the children of Israel have plugged their ears. I tried to help them, and for my effort I was banished from my home and my people. Worst of all, I discovered that the family I had loved—my mother and yes, even Pharaoh—was no family at all, only a facade."

He fell silent, and we sat without speaking for a long while. Moses would not meet my gaze, so I stared at the jagged horizon, trying to imagine scenes from the life he had described. I could easily picture him as a king's son—the sandy winds of the desert could never strip away the princely mien that permeated the very fiber of his being. I found it more difficult to envision him as a slave or a murderer, though the anger I'd just witnessed gnawed at my confidence in him.

I think Moses was desperately seeking a place to belong. And though he now wore the long robe and full beard of a desert-dweller, I also think he had not found his place among us. He had lived in our household for five years, accepting our customs, language, and clothing, but he had not truly accepted us. A man who trusts his companions does not need to hold secrets, yet Moses still possessed many.

In many ways, he was as much an outsider as he had been the day we met him at the well. But not to me. He had lifted the veil and allowed me to see his true face, and in that hour I knew I would one day become his wife.

ᖇᘛ

Three years passed. Breaking every tradition of our people, Moses kept our flocks, and under his administration our livestock multiplied at an unprecedented rate. My father blessed the gods for this happy situation, and told one and all that tradition should never stand in the way of common sense.

I managed my father's household and acted as a scribe whenever the need for one arose. Hobab negotiated with traveling merchants, sending our leather goods, terebinth-resin, and cheeses abroad while helping me purchase the fruits, vegetables, and spices we needed. The slaves cooperated with one another, my sisters visited occasionally with their children, and one day slid seamlessly into the next as we passed through a prolonged season of calm and prosperity.

I wandered through those years in happy frustration. As I matured, my feelings of infatuation for Moses grew into love, and though he continued to treat me as a special confidante, never did his eyes burn with the particular ardor I had seen in the eyes of men who came to seek my sisters. Moses was fond of me, he appreciated my keeping of his secrets, but the gap in our ages stood like a wall between us. I feared in his eyes I would always be the little girl at the well.

My father, apparently, was growing as frustrated as I. One summer morning Father called me into his tent and looked me directly in the eye. "You, Zipporah, are well past the age of maturity. Would it please you to marry Moses the Egyptian?"

Would it please me? My first reaction was not apprehension for myself, but for Moses. He seemed out of sorts here, welcomed but not belonging, so could he be happy bound to a Midianite wife?

My father did not waste time on such worries. After receiving an assurance that I would have no objection to the marriage (his asking my opinion was a rare honor, to be sure, for most fathers little cared what their daughters thought), at dinner he summoned Moses and mentioned that he had a favor to ask and a favor to grant.

Hiding behind the goatskin wall, I silently shooed the servants away.

"The favor I must ask," my father continued, "concerns my daughter Zipporah, with whom you are well acquainted."

Moses did not speak, though I am sure he nodded.

"She is seventeen and I must soon find her a husband. If you would not mind sharing your opinion, what do you think of Gal the Edomite, who often visits with his father. Is he not well suited for Zipporah?"

"Gal?" Derision rang in Moses' voice. "Gal is far too bossy for Zipporah; she would fight with him every day. I respect your wishes, Reuel, but I do not think Gal would be a good husband for our little bird."

"Hmmm."

I pressed a hand over my mouth to subdue my smile. Though I could not see inside the tent, in my heart's eye I could see my father with his hand pressed to his beard, one gray brow uplifted as he dangled the bait before his intended prey.

"Perhaps Elan, then. He is a fine lad, and intelligent. He has a gentle nature, too—"

"Elan, begging your pardon, would break like a reed beneath Zipporah's force of will. She is not a hot-tempered girl, but she definitely knows her own heart, while Elan is like a feather in the wind. No, Reuel—since you asked my opinion, I'd hate to think of Zipporah married to Elan."

"Aksel, then. Only last week he was mentioning Zipporah's beauty, comparing her to a delicate lotus blossom on the river Nile—"

"Aksel is older than you! I'm sorry, Reuel, but surely you don't mean to marry Zipporah to a man old enough to be her father?"

"I might." Father's voice went oddly gentle. "What I want most, Moses, is to marry her to a man who will love her. I care nothing about his age as long as he is strong enough to love her and soft enough to support her odd little ways."

I closed my eyes in frustration, for I could not imagine the look on Moses' face.

Father kept speaking. "I would not like to send my Zipporah away.

She is a delight to me, and an important part of my household. Therefore, I should prefer it if the gods would allow her to remain nearby with her husband."

When Moses answered, a trace of laughter lined his voice. "You asked my opinion as a favor; I gave it. So what is the favor you'd like to grant?"

"I'd like to grant you the honor of marriage to my daughter. You are a worthy man. I would be honored to call you my son."

"First, Reuel, there is something about me you must know."

I listened as Moses told the story of his life in Egypt, concluding with the reason he left. He spoke calmly, without any trace of the anger he'd exhibited when he shared the story with me. With each word my heart knocked harder in anticipation.

When he had finished, I held my breath and listened vainly for sounds of my father's reaction. I heard nothing, *nothing;* then my father's voice lifted. "Zipporah! Come, and bring wine!"

My heart overflowing, I snatched up the wine jar, then entered the tent and encountered my father's broad smile. "Congratulations, daughter." He lifted his cup. "This Moses, a kinsman, will marry you at the full moon. Prepare yourself for a fine husband!"

Feeling awkward and embarrassed, I met Moses' gaze, and in his eyes I saw something that looked like nervousness. For all his experience, age, and skill, could he be as insecure in matters of marriage as I?

I gave him a fleeting smile, then ducked my head and slipped out of the tent, leaving the wine with the men. At forty-eight, Moses would be an older husband, but he was the only man I had ever wanted.

That night, as I lay in the women's tent shivering beneath a wool blanket, I almost found myself wishing that I shared my father's devotion to the gods. But deities, if they existed at all, surely drifted on a lofty plane above our mortal existence. The gods who had not saved my mother could not have decreed my happiness . . . but it would have been nice to have someone to thank for the blessing of knowing and loving a man like Moses.

∽

Due to my father's insistence that all things be accomplished in accordance with myriad religious rituals, Moses and I were married at the full moon, when the gods had the most power to combat evil spirits. With my brother, several kinsmen, and our slaves in attendance, I dressed in my finest tunic and veil, then stepped out to meet my husband. Father placed a bound lamb upon the stone altar, slit the animal's throat, and drained the blood into a brass goblet. This he lifted in symbolic offering to us in celebration of our marriage, then poured the libation over the stones.

Privately, I was relieved that this would be the only bloodletting at our wedding. Among many of the desert tribes, including ours, it was customary for the priest to circumcise the bridegroom in a ritual known as *hattan*. I had cringed as all five of my sister's husbands underwent the rite beneath a full moon, and I was not eagerly anticipating that moment in my own wedding. My father had been perfectly willing to perform the ritual, but Moses assured him it would not be necessary.

"The Egyptians circumcise males when a boy attains manhood, but Moses said he was circumcised as an infant," my father had confided before the ceremony. "So someone must have performed the rite when he lived among the children of Isra-el."

I made a face. "They cut *babies?*"

"Yes, on the eighth day after birth. So El Shaddai commanded Abraham, and so the men of Isra-el bear the mark of their God's covenant on their bodies."

When I stood before Moses and slipped my hand into his, however, my thoughts had nothing to do with blood or babies. I smiled up into the eyes of a man I had come to love, admire, and respect. Though I suspected he still held mysteries, I was willing to wait until he revealed them all.

As my father and his friends feasted, Moses and I retreated to our bridal tent. A small oil lamp burned on an overturned pot near the door, providing the only light. Steeped in shadows, Moses came to me, then slowly pulled the opaque veil from my head.

I felt a trembling rise from my chest and belly, but was determined not to let him see my anxiety. "Zipporah," he said simply, his eyes caressing my face. His hand rose to my cheek, stroking it for a moment; then he reached back to undo the leather ties that bound my hair.

Breathing slowly, with both hands he fanned out the long tendrils with his fingertips, then stepped back and beheld me. "Come." Taking my hands, he led me to the mountain of furs and skins that made our bridal bed, then pulled me down to his side.

We kissed nose to nose in the manner of the Egyptians while music and the sound of voices drifted in from outside. "I hope," he spoke in a hushed voice, "that you will never be disappointed in me."

"Disappointed?" Forgetting my nervousness, I propped my head on my hand, studying his face. "How could I be disappointed in you? You are a prince."

"I am nothing. A man without a country."

"You are everything. And you shall make your home with me, with the tribe of Midian, and you will never have to feel lost again."

My heart lurched within me as he brought his palm to my cheek, then Moses swept his hand to my waist and drew me to him.

I trembled, completely in awe of the magnificent man in my arms.

MERYTAMON

Because I was born on the auspicious fourth day of the first month of proyet, the priests told my mother I was destined to outlive the rest of my family. As I entered my sixty-first year, however, I knew the priests had lied.

Something within me had weakened, and the priests had no remedy for it. I could barely walk the length of my bedchamber without losing my breath, and sitting upright became a struggle.

As I entered the fourth year of my exile at Mi-Wer, I knew the time had come to tell Moses good-bye.

I would not see him, of course. Four years were not enough to cool Ramesses' wrath. So I sent my handmaid for a stylus and papyrus, then gathered my strength to pen the words on my heart.

For a long time I sat and stared at the crinkled parchment, running my trembling fingers over its uneven surface. We had been connected through letters once, my son and I. We had loved to read together, to share stories and poetry and prayers. Moses had been as educated and literary as any prince of Egypt in history.

Was he using any part of that knowledge now? Or had he put his former life behind him?

Did he think of me fondly . . . or with bitterness?

I swiped a tear from my cheek. I could not know these things now, but I had every confidence I would know them in the otherworld. One day, Moses and I would be reunited.

With an effort, I drew a deep breath and began to write.

ZIPPORAH

The years fell away like petals from a desert rose, one after the other, indistinguishable. I lived as daughter, wife, and scribe. Yet the one title I most yearned for eluded me. In desperation I sought my father's priestly advice, and finally, after an endless succession of offerings to Baal and Isis, I told my husband I had succeeded in becoming a mother.

Our son was born on a cool winter night in my twenty-seventh year. When the midwife delivered our firstborn into Moses' waiting hands, he took the child outside and lifted it toward the rising moon. Watching from the open tent, I observed the gesture and wondered if it sprang from tradition, hope, or pure instinct.

When Moses brought the baby back inside, he gently lowered the child into my arms. "We will call him Gershom," he said, his voice heavy, "for I have been a stranger in a foreign land."

The comment struck like an arrow through my heart, but I lowered my gaze lest Moses see the hurt in my eyes. After so long with us, how could he still feel isolated? My family and I had welcomed him in every way we knew, yet still he kept himself aloof.

I pressed a kiss to my beautiful baby's forehead and kept silent. At least

I had given Moses a son. Our world might be dry and barren compared to the verdant paradise of Egypt, but it possessed a breathless barren beauty of its own. Our people did not boast of gold, rich varieties of food, or temples and marble houses, but we possessed courage, loyalty, and love in abundance.

But Moses would have to learn to appreciate those things himself.

Eight days after Gershom's birth, Moses came into my tent. He took a moment to admire the healthy baby suckling at my breast; then he squatted and touched my knee. "It is time for Gershom to be circumcised."

I don't know how to describe the feeling that rose up within me. People often speak of the fury of a lioness guarding her cub, but my feeling involved far more than defensiveness. I thought of my husband, who had abandoned the traditions of the Hebrews even more completely than he had abandoned those of the Egyptians. I recalled the pain in Moses' eyes when he told me about how the children of Isra-el had scorned him and betrayed him to Ramesses. I considered how we had accepted, welcomed, and loved him, and yet he still kept himself at arm's length, unveiling his heart and innermost thoughts only when he felt inclined to do so—and he had not opened his heart to me in a long, long time.

Something in me snapped. With more rage than I knew I possessed, I clutched the baby to my breast and looked at my husband with a narrowed eye. "If you come near this child with a knife," I said, my voice as steely and cold as any blade he might find, "I will strike you with it."

A tide of resentment washed through his eyes, and I was sure he saw the same dark currents in mine. "I will not," I added, "have my son marked with the covenant of a god you cannot even call by name."

Unable to answer my objection, Moses rose and left the tent. He did not mention the subject again.

Out of anger, indifference, or spite, Moses stopped seeking my bed after Gershom's birth. He often led the flocks on long journeys and dozed under the stars. When he was in camp, he slept in the corner of my tent or by the dim light of the fire pit. Though he remained polite in my company, he treated me with the same detachment he displayed toward the serving women. My father noticed the change, for I often caught him watching me with a speculative light in his eye.

One day my father tugged on my sleeve as I passed. "You must talk to him." His eyes widened with concern. "Every day it will become harder until you do."

"Moses and I are no longer young." I shifted the baby on my hip and gave my father a smile. "Neither of us expects to be coddled. If he has something to say, he will say it."

"Only if he thinks you are listening."

I lowered my head and walked on, shaking my head. My father had been alone for too long; he had forgotten that married love, like the wilderness, had seasons. Moses and I had passed through a difficult spring when babies did not come, but we had successfully eased into summer. We did not need constant reassurance, touching, or rapturous words of affection. We were a mature married couple, well-accustomed to each other, and my husband was more than sixty years old.

Yet I could not deny that I missed hearing the heavy buzz of his snoring, the scent of male sweat in the furs on my bed, the sight of his strong form shadowed upon the tent wall. As a young bride, I had hoped my husband and I would be close, but since Gershom's birth the shell around Moses' heart seemed to thicken a little each day.

The solitary life of a shepherd affects people in one of two ways—either they grow more desirous of fellowship with other people or they grow more silent. Shepherding seemed to close Moses' mouth, but until the baby came I had been able to help Moses relax when he returned to camp. Now that he so often stayed away, I feared the solitude of the wilderness would close his heart as well.

My husband was not the only person affected by Gershom's birth—his arrival triggered something within my own heart, and for the first time in years I yielded to my father's urgings to pay more attention to the gods. Conscious that I now bore responsibility for a life other than my own, inside my tent I established a small shrine to the goddess Athirat. I still held a deep skepticism about the gods, but one could not hold a living, breathing child and not know there were forces stronger than things we mortals can see and feel. So I chose Athirat as my personal deity, for she was the loving consort of El, father of the gods, and a protective mother to her seventy children. Benign as a breeze, she was neither a destroyer nor a usurper.

Moses did not mention my tiny shrine. He made a strangled sound deep in his throat the first time he saw it, then quietly turned to his corner, wrapped himself in a fur, and lay down to sleep.

I said nothing, but patted my dozing son's back.

Gershom had just entered his third year when we learned that Ramesses of Egypt had died. The trade caravans from Egypt were full of the news, for few kings could match Ramesses' reign of sixty-seven years. In his lifetime the great king had fathered ninety-six sons and sixty daughters, outliving twelve princes. His thirteenth son, Merneptah, had inherited Egypt's throne.

"Merneptah brags about his conquest of every race of peoples," a miner from the Black Land told us. "In his funerary temple at Thebes he erected a stele that reads:

> The princes are prostrate, saying "Peace!"
> Not one is raising his head among the Nine Bows.
> Now that Libya has come to ruin,
> Hatti is pacified.
> The Canaan has been plundered into every sort of woe;
> Ashkelon has been overcome;
> Gezer has been captured;
> Yanoam is made nonexistent;
> Israel is laid waste and his seed is not;
> Hurru is become a widow because of Egypt.

Moses listened to this news with a granite face, but I sensed that deep emotions rioted within him. Ramesses had been his father, in affection if not in fact, and my husband had been reared as Merneptah's brother. I worried lest the news kindle within him a desire to return to Egypt in order to claim the rights and responsibilities from which he had been exiled.

Yet he said nothing about a journey. Tamping whatever emotions this news might have awakened, he rose the next morning and took the flocks out, then returned at sunset. Weather-beaten and as brown as umber, he ate silently while my garrulous father rattled on about visiting chieftains, their petitions to the gods, and the scarcity of decent cattle for sacrifices.

That night Moses sought my bed. He did not speak as he pulled me into his arms, but I placed my hands against his chest, holding him at a distance so I could look into his eyes.

"Do you love me, Moses?"

He lifted his hand to touch my hair, and creases angled at the corners of his eyes as he smiled. "Should I have stopped?"

"You've been so quiet . . . removed. I was beginning to think you wished yourself back in Egypt."

"Zipporah." He caught my hand and brought it to his lips, sending heat through every nerve in my body. "My life is here, with you."

"Then why have you withdrawn from us? You have been like a stranger to me and Gershom."

He cringed slightly as I pronounced our son's name, and in the wavering light of the lamp I saw a glazed look of despair spread over his face. "Forgive me, Zipporah."

"For what, Moses? I have to know what you're thinking."

Closing his eyes, he pressed his hands to my head. For a moment I feared he would crush it like a melon; then the pressure eased.

"I don't know how to explain, but you deserve an answer. In the beginning, I was angry because you would not let me circumcise our son."

I pressed my lips together and nodded; that much had been obvious . . . and undoubtedly my fault.

"Then . . . I began to wonder what sort of a father I could be. The only father I ever knew was Ramesses, who was not a father at all, but a god. I knew I could never be a god to Gershom."

I grimaced in good humor. "We have enough gods around this camp. We do not need another."

"No." His mouth quirked. "But I did not know any other way to be, and I could not forget Ramesses. Did you know some of the priests claimed he was immortal? I did not think it could be true, but he remained strong and he kept living. . . ."

I felt the truth all at once, like a tingle in the pit of my stomach. Moses had left Egypt years ago, but Egypt—and Ramesses—had never left him. The boy who had grown up to revere a divine father had never been able to break free of that reverence . . . until now.

I caught my breath as a series of revelations opened in my heart. Despite his oft-repeated pronouncements of disbelief, in the deepest part of Moses' soul he must have wondered if he had been forever cursed by a god.

"You didn't believe you deserved happiness." I whispered the admission, dredged from a place beyond logic and reason.

He did not speak, but closed his eyes. In a wave of tenderness, I pulled his head to my shoulder and stroked his hair, comforting the boy who still struggled with losing the only father he had ever known.

Almost a year later, in the season of winter, a rush of wet heat swamped over us in the middle of a quiet afternoon. Abruptly the wind rose, skirling across the sand. My father lifted his lined face to the bruised and swollen sky, then raised his hand. "Zipporah, Hobab!" he called above the bawling wind. "Take everything you can carry and run for the mountains!"

Something in his tone quickened my blood. Though heavily pregnant, I scooped Gershom up with one arm, settled him upon my hip, and tried to snatch a jar of flour with the other. Hobab sprinted toward the pen where our horses and donkeys waited, then threw open the gate. Sand blew across our compound, moving snakelike in long, thin lines, piling up at the edges of our tents.

Father hurried to help Rakia, who was so stooped she could barely walk, while our third slave, Efra, led blind Harkhuf out of the tent where he'd been grinding corn.

I had heard about flash floods, but never had I lived through one. While Gershom wept in my arms, a slash of lightning stabbed at the roiling clouds. Suddenly, without warning, the skies opened. A few warning drops fell like stones on the sand at my feet; then the rain increased to a great roaring current, a torrent so heavy we had to hold our heads down in order to breathe. Gershom's cry rose to a frenzied wail, but I barely heard him, so heavy was the sound of rain in my ears.

Struggling to walk, I moved toward the rocks I used to climb as easily as a goat; then I felt a strong arm around my waist and Moses appeared at my side. He took Gershom with one arm and with the other supported me until we had climbed to a sheltering spot in the mountains above my father's compound.

Soaked to the skin, we sat in silence, listening to the storm as the raging waters took our tents, the trees, and our flocks. We knew many of the pasturelands would be bare when the storm had passed, for such floods carried even the soil away.

"The gods are often cruel," my father said, his black-and-white beard shimmering in the ethereal greenish light of the storm. "But in the spring, new life will burst forth. The desert will bloom as never before."

After a day and a night of rain, the storm passed. The next morning we stepped out of the grotto into a world washed clean. Below us, on the plain where we had camped, the sand lay like a smooth blanket, with nary a ripple to mar its surface. Not a tent remained, not a goat, not a clay pot.

"May the gods be praised." My father lifted his hands. "We have lost everything, but we are safe."

The sun rose as bright as before; the sky extended in all directions, an unending canopy of blue. Rakia, Efra, and I remained in the sheltering fissure, which would serve as home until the men had rounded up as many of our belongings as could be salvaged.

I gave birth to my second son in the tiny cave. Efra delivered him, and as she placed the child in Moses' hands, again he took the child outside and lifted him toward the heavens. I watched, knowing that any man who would do such a thing had to believe in a god. Somewhere in the recesses of his soul, Moses believed . . . but he couldn't seem to pin a name on the deity he sought.

I almost pitied him. When he returned to me with the baby, he announced that the child's name would be Eliezer.

I stared up at Moses in wonder. The name was simple enough to decipher, for *el* meant "god," and *ezer* had to do with "help," but I wanted to hear the explanation from my husband's lips.

"Why, Moses?"

He looked down, his lashes hiding his eyes, and hesitated for a moment. "Because the god of my fathers was my helper; he delivered me from Pharaoh."

Not all that long ago.

Awareness stretched between us. Bending forward, I pressed a kiss to the face of my newborn son, then reached up and took my husband's hand. "Have you learned his name, this god of your fathers'?"

An unutterably lonely expression filled his eyes as he looked through me. "I don't know. But only he could have saved me, and now I know he exists."

The men of our household found several animals alive, mostly goats who had managed to scamper up onto the rocks. But they also discovered many dead sheep and horses, including those of other tribes. The waters had carried carcasses for miles before depositing them along the rocky ridges.

That night, as the baby slept in my arms, Moses lay beside me and told me all he'd been thinking as he searched for our missing livestock.

"I kept remembering the man I murdered." His voice, echoing in the rocks of the cave, seemed to come from far away. "The Egyptians believe that existence ends if the body is not mummified and prepared for the afterlife, so I not only cut off the man's mortal being, but his immortal being as well. Then I found myself thinking that perhaps the priests of Egypt were right—as a man born a slave, perhaps I was as unfeeling and unthinking as an animal. Yet I was not unfeeling! The priests would say I had feelings only because I had been trained like one of the monkeys in Pharaoh's court—was I really of no more value than a beast?"

As he fell silent, I shifted the babe and settled him between us. Moses lay flat on his back, one arm bent under his head as he contemplated the rose-colored rocks of our shelter. Hobab and my father snored loudly at the mouth of the cavern, while Gershom slept near them with the servants.

"Suddenly, I understood the reasons I have never wanted to join Hobab or your clansmen when they ride off to defend the grazing grounds. I told myself it was because I did not feel involved in the matter, but that's not really the truth. I think I also felt . . . somehow unworthy. If I was not a prince, I was not a man. I was more akin to an animal."

I brought my free hand to his chest. "You are a man, Moses."

He shook his head. "Sometimes I find that hard to believe. A man would not fall prey to an unthinking impulse and commit murder. Yet I know I must be a man, created for higher things, but why? And what god would create me in order to lead me down this insane path? The gods of Egypt would not, for they found their purpose and pinnacle in Pharaoh, and he wanted me dead. If he was god, if I was his son, he should have been able to take my life; I should have surrendered it gladly. But I could not, nor did he have the power to kill me. I slipped past his guards easily and escaped his reach in the desert. So Pharaoh is not god, nor are his gods true.

"Then I came to your father's camp and saw his panoply of deities. Many of them are similar to the gods of Egypt, always crying for blood and sacrifice and food and pleasure, but what god needs those things from us? If a god is higher than human beings, why does he care for us at all? Why is he concerned with us, and why would he desire our worship?"

I did not speak, but let the silence stretch. These weighty thoughts had been troubling my husband for years, and I knew a few compassionate wifely words could not dissipate them.

"Is there a god who despises the way Pharaoh imprisons people and blinds them to compassion? If so, what is his name, and how do I invoke his presence? The Hebrews worship an unseen god, but so did Akhenaton, the pharaoh all Egyptians now curse. The Egyptians spend their entire lives preparing for death, so perhaps the true God concerns himself with *life*, with the birth of children and the well-being of his people. And if this God honors life, then I committed a grave sin against him when I slew the Egyptian; therefore I cannot seek him until I win atonement by making a sacrifice. But how can I sacrifice to this God if I do not know what he desires? How can I get his attention if I do not know his name?"

Reminded of something I had read shortly before the storm, I patted my husband's chest. "Moses, not long ago I read a papyrus from an Egyptian trader. Some of Abraham's children settled in Edom, you know, and the papyrus referred to Edom as a land of the Bedouin of . . . well, I don't know how to pronounce the word. But it looked like the symbols for this."

By the dim light of the moon, I saw Moses lift his head to study the symbols I traced in the sand.

"How did the trader pronounce the name?"

"He didn't. He simply said they were the Bedouin of the Lord."

After descending from the mountains, we gathered what belongings we could find and went in search of grasslands for our remaining flocks. We camped near an oasis at the base of the mountain called Sinai, and in the spring, as Father had predicted, the wilderness bloomed with life. Tamarisk trees that had washed up on sand-covered rocks put out new roots and feathered out with fresh leaves. Plants that had settled in the low places continued to grow there, while clusters of palms, eucalyptus, and terebinth trees huddled around the life-giving spring near our compound. After the flood, the landscape seemed even more random than before, with trees and shrubs protruding from the rocks at odd angles. Those that were strong enough to send forth roots flourished; those that had landed in an awkward position withered in the heat.

I feared that my husband had not yet managed to put down roots in our homeland. Though his attitude had relaxed considerably since we learned of Ramesses' death, he had received a deep heart-wound in Egypt—from his mother and his people as well as his king—and though I had watched him try to ignore the pain, he could not escape it. His wound kept bleeding, haunting his sleep and hounding him throughout his days. I initially thought he had volunteered to keep the flocks in order to escape his private agony—in time, I came to believe he went to the wilderness in order to try to conquer that dull ache.

But some wounds cannot be healed even by time.

I lived with Moses' uncertainties for seventeen years. His questions evolved over the passage of seasons, and often he put them to chieftains and traders who came seeking my father's counsel. From other tribesmen descended from Abraham's Keturah, we learned that the unseen God of Abraham had been called *adonai,* meaning "Lord." Another sand-crosser told us that Abraham had called his God *El Shaddai* in view of his covenant to make Jacob's descendants a mighty nation. But those, Moses insisted, were titles, not a personal name, and since one summoned a god by using his name, how were his followers to invoke his power?

The Egyptian papyrus I had read held the only clue to the actual name of Abraham's God. We were tantalized by the possibility that the reference might pertain to the God of the Hebrews, but none of the tribes we met knew how to pronounce the name YHWH, much less explain its significance. "I'm sure someone knew this name long ago," my father assured Moses. "But his people have been lost. And why do we need this YHWH? There are so many gods today; a man can pick and choose from them as he pleases."

"Man is utterly foolish," Moses muttered. "He can't make a worm, but he makes gods by the dozens."

Silently, I agreed, but Father could not let an opportunity for worship pass by. Inside the circle of stones in the center of our camp he built a special altar to YHWH, though he had no clear idea what to do with it. Every day when he offered the morning sacrifices, he split a goat into a dozen pieces, dripped blood upon the altars, then dropped pieces of meat before the stone idols. YHWH had no idol, only the altar, but at least Reuel had done what he could to honor the God of Moses' forefathers.

As Moses guarded our livestock in the wilderness, I concentrated on the care of our sons. Once the boys were old enough to hold a staff, however, they joined their father in the wilds.

I listened in silent pride as my boys came running back into camp to repeat lessons I'd once taught Moses. "Did you know, Mama," Gershom would babble, "that hares and foxes lead you to water, while jackals and hyena always lead you to higher ground?"

"Really?" I feigned surprise. "What a smart boy you are becoming!"

I watched my sweet babies evolve into men of the desert—tanned, veiled, and wary. With their father they braved sandstorms, thirst, blistering heat, and all the hazards associated with the care of livestock. Like Moses, they grew strong and narrow-eyed, their ears tuned to hear unnatural sounds, their eyes quick to notice anything out of the ordinary.

By the time our sons reached maturity, however, they preferred roaming with their adventurous uncle Hobab over the dull work of keeping sheep. Once again Moses found himself alone in the wilderness of Midian.

As I entered my fiftieth summer, I looked forward to growing old with my family about me. My father, robust and strong at ninety-one, continued to serve every god under the sun and stars. Gershom had grown into a mature man of twenty-one. Attracted by a pretty girl who lived with a nearby tribe, he inquired about marriage, but Moses asked him to wait. Eliezer, at seventeen, had not yet expressed an interest in marriage, and for that I was grateful. I must admit, I had grown accustomed to being the only woman in our camp. Though I knew I would one day surrender my place to my sons' wives, I was in no hurry to sit on the sidelines and watch life unfold around me. For too long I had been my father's scribe, my husband's confidante, and my sons' support.

Though he spent every day beneath a desert sun that could melt weaker men, at eighty Moses was as strong as he'd been when I met him. He could still spot a hare at one hundred paces and bring down a vulture with a pebble from his sling. His body was straight and lean, his hearing keen to the nuances of the desert winds. Upon hearing tales of Ramesses' longevity, I was almost tempted to believe Moses *was* the son of Pharaoh, for it seemed likely he had inherited his father's predisposition toward long life.

But what good would long life do him, I wondered, if he did not live in happiness?

MIRYAM

In the time of half-light just before sunrise, Aharon woke me with a terrific banging. I rose, my bones grumbling as sharply as my tongue, and limped to the door, then scowled at my younger brother with all the annoyance I could muster.

"I've had a dream." The words came from his lips in a ragged whisper, and traces of fear and wonder glimmered in his wide eyes. "The God of our fathers spoke to me."

Reaching across the threshold, Aharon grabbed my arms, the force of his grip bringing fresh pain to my weary bones. "Did you hear me, Miryam? After so much silence for so many years, God spoke to me!"

With an effort, I pried Aharon's hands from my arms. "If the God of our fathers truly spoke to you, the fact that he spoke is not as important as what he said. What did you dream?"

Aharon brought his finger to his lips. "Inside. I will tell you inside."

Mindful that our tiny village had few secrets, I stepped aside to allow Aharon to enter my small house. The mud-brick building had stood empty after our father died during the last inundation, so I took it, shoving aside memories of my mother at the window as ruthlessly as I swept rat droppings from the packed floor. After losing a husband and baby in

217

my own home, I didn't mind moving into a house with fewer unhappy memories. My father, Amram, had passed a relatively peaceful life here, living one hundred thirty-seven years before lying down to die.

Aharon closed the door while I lit the lamp. When I turned, my brother was sitting on a low three-legged stool by the window, his eyes shining with a secret he had not yet shared.

I sank to my straw-stuffed mattress. "What did God say in this dream?"

I asked the question he expected, though I was fully prepared to dismiss whatever Aharon told me. If God had said, "Endure to the end," or "A better day is coming," I would have told my brother to comfort himself with those words and go about his business. Though many of the twelve tribes had forgotten the God of Avraham, Yitzhak, and Yaakov, we Levites continued to remember him. We circumcised our babies; most of us prayed. But for as long as I could remember, no one had spoken God's name, and he had spoken to no one.

Men occasionally claimed that God had promised to send us a deliverer, but those declarations were usually followed by requests for weapons, allegiance, or supplies. Once, shortly after Moshe had gone to live in Pharaoh's palace, a man of Judah called Beniel had claimed to hear God speak in the night. The Almighty, the fellow insisted, declared he would deliver the children of Israel if a certain young woman would promise to visit Beniel in the night. Desperate for hope, the young woman had complied, the terms of the dream had been fulfilled, and the foolish Beniel had attacked his Egyptian overseer the next day. After murdering the Egyptian, the brazen fool ran for the river, but a sentry's arrow struck him between the shoulder blades.

Shivering, I drew my shawl more closely about my shoulders, dreading my brother's news. At eighty-three, Aharon was not likely to say the God of Avraham had commanded him to bed a virgin or murder an Egyptian, but one never knew what a dream could bring forth.

I sighed. "And God said?"

Light from the lamp glimmered over my younger brother's strong face. "Go meet Moshe in the wilderness."

I stared at him, momentarily tongue-tied.

"That's what he told me—I am to meet Moshe in the wilderness!"

Looking away, I struggled to curb my amazement. This dream could have stemmed from anything—indigestion, fear, even nostalgia for the brother we had lost.

When I was certain I could look at Aharon without laughing or screeching, I lifted my head. "How are you supposed to go meet Moshe?"

It was a reasonable question, but Aharon stiffened as though I had stabbed him with it. I persevered. "How are you supposed to leave Goshen and find Moshe? You don't even know where he is. You don't know if he's still alive! You are a slave, Aharon. Don't be a fool as well."

Concern and confusion flitted in his eyes; then he pressed his lips into a thin line. "I know Moshe is alive because God would not command me to meet a dead man. Moshe is to be our deliverer, Miryam. So I will trust God to guide my steps. I must only start walking."

I ran my hand through my unbound hair, wondering how I could prevent another tragedy. Aharon was still strong, but he was an old man. Perhaps his thoughts had begun to wander and I should summon a physician. The Egyptians did not enjoy coming to the village to treat old people, but I couldn't be faulted for neglecting to explain that the ailing brickmaker was also aged.

"I am old," Aharon said, startling me with his intuition, "and my quota at the brickyard is lighter than most. I do not think the overseers will notice if one day I do not report for work. They will most likely think that I have died and not trouble themselves further."

"But the journey, Aharon! How are you to manage it?"

"I'll take a donkey from the village pen. When I explain my need to the others, they will understand."

"You'll tell the others?" My heart began to race—if news of Aharon's journey became common knowledge, someone would slip the story to the Egyptians. They'd publicly beat Aharon for even *thinking* of escape, lest others nurture the same idea.

"You can't tell the others."

"But I must!" His dark eyes glittered with determination. "I want them to pray that God will guide my footsteps, that he will bring Moshe back to us and deliver our people from this bondage—"

"Hush, Aharon, let me think!"

I pressed my hands to my ears in an effort to block his urgent insistence. He *would* do this. Aharon didn't often voice strong opinions, but once he fixed his heart on an idea, he persevered until the thing was done. But telling the others would be like releasing an asp in a cluster of horses; soon they'd be skittish with anxiety and whirling in anticipation. Aharon couldn't tell the entire village, nor could he take many men with him. The overseers would notice if more than a few able-bodied workers disappeared from the brickyards, and a large traveling party would attract attention from thieves.

Propping my chin in my hand, I studied my younger brother, who lowered his gaze beneath the intensity of my stare. Several men could not leave, but an old couple might be able to slip by the border garrisons without notice. We could tell a few people of our intention—Aharon's wife and sons, of course, and perhaps two of the village elders—so if we did not return at least we would be remembered as Israelites who believed in God enough to journey into the desert in search of him.

"This is what you will do." I lowered my hand. "You will speak of this to no one, do you hear, except your wife, your sons, and two village elders. Charge them with saying nothing until after we are safely away. We will take two donkeys—"

Aharon gazed at me, his jaw slack. "We?"

"No one will care if an old man and woman decide to journey into the desert. And so we will go, you and I, to meet Moshe. If God has truly spoken, we will find him and rejoice. If the dream was an invention of your own heart, we will doubtless die together in the wilderness."

Aharon smiled, a glint of wonder in his eyes. "It is a good plan, Miryam."

"It is a foolish plan, but I would rather die of starvation and thirst than at the hands of the Egyptians. Now"—I cocked a brow—"when do we go?"

"Today." Aharon rose. "There is no time to lose."

I would have launched into another discourse on why we could not leave immediately, but Aharon did not linger to hear my reasons. I heard the door close, then sat in silence as the rising sun sent the first streamers of morning into my small house.

Immediately, then. Like an obstinate donkey, Aharon could be led, but he could not be forced.

I bent to blow out the lamp, then unfolded my shawl and began to gather my meager possessions.

ZIPPORAH

The morning had dawned sullen and gray, and the rising sun struggled to penetrate a mass of dark, boiling clouds that came up from the western horizon. Fearing a sudden sandstorm, I kept one eye on the horizon as I worked.

The other women were restless, and sweat beaded Efra's forehead as we ground grain in the supply tent. The air was heavy with foreboding, and the troubling aspect of the sky sent nervous flutterings through my chest. I had not seen anything like it since the flash flood that swept our tents away years before.

I took a quick headcount of my loved ones. All three slaves were present, as was my father. The rising wind had blown Hobab, Gershom, and Eliezer safely home, and they were now sharing a loaf of bread and jug of wine in my father's tent. Moses alone remained outside the camp, but he had braved many sandstorms.

I had nearly convinced myself that my fears were groundless when Moses staggered into camp barefoot, disheveled, and without the animals. When Eliezer asked what had happened, Moses gestured toward the wilderness and gasped, "Bring in the flock."

"Were you attacked?"

Moses shook his head slowly, like an ox stunned by the slaughterer's blow. His long gray hair had come loose from its lacing, and stray wisps flickered past his face.

Despite Moses' assertion that there had been no attack, Hobab and our sons gathered their weapons and took off on horseback, leaving Moses at the entrance to our tent. Alarmed by his pale face and trembling limbs, my feeling of uneasiness turned into a deeper and more immediate fear.

Was this sunstroke? I didn't see how it could be on such a cloudy day, but many a man had misjudged the despotic sun.

I led my husband into the shade and relative coolness of our tent, then checked his skin—victims of sun sickness did not sweat, but Moses' tunic was drenched with perspiration.

"Can you speak?" I knelt to look into his eyes. "Tell me what happened."

I was completely unprepared for his next words.

"I met YHWH."

He pronounced the name with certainty. I sank onto a mound of animal skins, too astounded to reply.

Moses lifted his hand, stared at the trembling fingers as if he'd never seen them before, then closed his eyes. "I was tending the flock near the mountain at Sinai, trying to keep an eye on the clouds in the west." His voice, like his nerves, was ragged. "I had just sat down to drink when out of the midst of a thorny shrub upon the rocks, I saw a flame of fire. 'How can this be?' I wondered. 'How can the bush burn, yet not be consumed?'"

I nodded silently, urging him to continue. I knew the blood-colored place our people called the Mountain of God. Sinai was not one peak, but many, and its red rocks contained a series of protected caverns, hidden caves, and isolated nooks. If the storm clouds had discharged a bolt of lightning into the mountain, Moses might have seen a flaming bush.

He tugged on his beard. "I said to myself, 'Now let me turn aside so I may see why the bush does not burn up!' And when YHWH saw that I had turned aside, he called to me out of the midst of the bush. He said, 'Moses! Moses!'"

I stiffened at something I heard in my husband's voice—sharp conviction, pointed and relentless. I had believed his story until that moment, for a bush hidden high on the rocks might well appear to burn without burning up, but it had to be a trick of the mountain, a matter of perspective. The gods did *not* dwell in burning bushes, nor did they speak from them.

Oblivious to my skepticism, Moses continued. "'Here I am,' I answered. Then YHWH said, 'Do not come near; put off your sandal from your foot, for the place on which you stand is holy ground!' As I slipped out of my sandals, YHWH said, 'I am the God of your fathers, the God of Abraham, the God of Isaac, and the God of Jacob.' Then I concealed my face, for I was afraid to gaze upon God in the bush."

I lifted my hand, about to check Moses' forehead for signs of fever, then pulled it back to my chest. Fire glowed deep in his eyes, but I was inclined to believe it a portent of illness rather than a lingering afterimage of what he had seen in the wilderness.

"Then YHWH said, 'I have seen, yes, seen the affliction of my people in Egypt, their cry have I heard in the face of their slave-drivers; indeed, I have known their sufferings! So I have come down to rescue them from the hand of Egypt, to bring them up from that land to a land goodly and spacious, a land flowing with milk and honey, to the place of the Canaanites and the Hittites, of the Amorites and the Perizzites, of the Hivites and the Jebusites. So now the cry of the children of Israel has come to me, and I have seen the oppression with which the Egyptians oppress them. So now, go, for I sent you to Pharaoh—bring my people, the children of Israel, out of Egypt!'"

Moses looked at me, his face rippling with an anguish that mirrored my own. What had happened to my husband in the wilds? His tormented heart, troubled for years by memories of Egypt, had undoubtedly played tricks upon his eyes and ears. For how could he, the misbegotten Egyptian prince, return to the people who had scorned and cast him out? Both races had rejected him, and he had been exiled under a death sentence!

When he spoke again, his voice was whispery soft and tinged with terror. "I stared at YHWH's messenger, a man-creature lit with flame, and wondered if I had lost my senses. I said to him, 'Who am I, that I should go to Pharaoh, that I should bring the children of Israel out of Egypt?' He said, 'Indeed, I will be there with you, and this is the sign that I myself have sent you: When you have brought the people out of Egypt, you will all serve God by this mountain.'"

Moses raked his hand through his disheveled hair. "I looked around at the cliffs, the red rocks, the endless sand. I could not imagine any landscape farther removed from the green marshlands of Goshen, nor could I imagine any people less at home in the wilds of Sinai than the children of Israel. Turning back to the messenger, I said, 'Suppose I go to the children of Israel and say, "The God of your fathers has sent me to you." They will say to me, "What is his name?" And how shall I reply?'"

I felt an icy finger touch the base of my spine. We had searched so long for this name. . . . Was it possible the unseen God heard our questions?

Moses looked directly into my eyes. "Then God said to me: 'EHYEH ASHER EHYEH, which is *I will be there howsoever I will be there*. Thus shall you say to the children of Israel: EHYEH/I WILL BE THERE sends me to you.'"

I stared at my husband, whose inward gaze had drifted to some apparition I could not begin to imagine.

"'I will be there?'"

Moses shuddered slightly. "I cannot describe what I heard. The name resonated in many tongues, probably every tongue spoken by men. I heard it in Egyptian, Canaanite, Akkadian, and other languages I do not understand. I heard it as I AM WHO I AM, and I AM HE WHO CAUSES THINGS TO BE, and I WILL BE THERE WITH YOU. In the rush of the wind and the rumble of the mountain I heard all these things, and I knew I had found the God for whom we have been searching."

Moses' eyes met mine, and beneath his tanned skin a flush bloomed on his cheekbones. "In that moment I knew he is not a god who must be summoned by the recitation of his name. He is everywhere, he is all that exists, he is all that will ever be. And he has been waiting."

"Why?" The question slipped involuntarily from my lips. "Why would he come to you today and not before?"

Moses' mouth spread into a faint smile. "Who am I to ask? I only know that today I was ready to hear, he was ready to speak, and perhaps the children of Israel are finally ready to leave the slavery they have endured for so long. God told me, 'Thus shall you say to the children of Israel: YHWH, the God of your fathers, the God of Abraham, the God of Isaac, and the God of Jacob, sends me to you. YHWH is my name for the ages; that is my title from generation to generation.'"

I absorbed this information without comment. This was not news—it was merely a confirmation of what we had suspected for years. In a sun-induced stupor, Moses could have merged my father's stories with what we had read and gleaned from the Bedouin. The wavering heat of the wilds often provoked mirages, and the desert echoed with unexplained sounds. The winds screamed through the rocks, while sand sprinkled against stones like rain. With vultures playing tag overhead, insects droning beneath the sand, and stones tumbling down hills in the breath of the wind, the desert was never silent.

Moses looked up, his eyes still brimming with wonder. "Then he said to me, 'Go, gather the elders of Israel, and say to them, "YHWH, the God of Abraham, of Isaac, and of Jacob, has been seen by me, saying, 'I have taken account, yes, account of you and of what is being done to you in Egypt, and I have declared that I will bring you up from the affliction of Egypt to a land flowing with milk and honey.'" They will hearken to your voice, and you will go, you and the elders of Israel, to the king of Egypt and say to him, "YHWH, the God of the Hebrews, has met with us, so pray let us go a three days' journey into the wilderness and let us slaughter offerings to YHWH our God!" But I know the king of Egypt will not give you leave to go. So I will send forth my hand and I will strike Egypt with all my wonders—after that he will send you free! And I will give this people favor in the eyes of Egypt; and it will be that when you go, you shall not go out empty-handed. Each woman shall ask her neighbor for objects of silver, objects of gold, and clothing. You shall put them on your sons and on your daughters—so shall you strip Egypt!'"

Unable to believe my ears, I stared at him in a paralysis of astonishment. Finding YHWH in the wilds was one thing, returning to plunder Egypt was quite another matter.

Moses gave me a quick, gleaming look before dropping his gaze. "I looked at the messenger and said, 'They will not trust me, nor will they listen. Indeed, they will say, "YHWH has not been seen by you!"'"

Prickles of cold dread crawled along my spine as Moses' voice began to tremble. "Then YHWH said to me, 'What is that in your hand?'

"'A staff,' I said.

"'Throw it to the ground.'

"I did. I threw it to the ground, and it became a snake, and I fled from its bite. Then YHWH called to me, 'Stretch forth your hand and seize it by its tail!'

"I did. I stretched forth my trembling hand, took hold of its tail, and it became a staff in my fist. Then God said, 'So they may trust that YHWH, the God of their fathers, has been seen by you, pray put your hand in your bosom!'"

"I put my hand into my tunic, against the skin of my chest, and when I withdrew it, it was white with *tzaraat,* like snow!"

Despite my intention to listen calmly, I gasped. *Tzaraat* was a skin disease, usually viewed by the priests as a divine sign of wrongdoing on the part of the victim. People were cured of tzaraat only after many sacrifices and prayers.

I reached for Moses' hand. The skin appeared blessedly normal, tanned and whole.

Caught up in his story, Moses scarcely seemed to notice my skeptical investigation. "God said to me, 'Return your hand to your bosom!' So I did, and when I took it out again, it had returned to wellness. Then God said, 'So it shall be, if they do not trust you, and do not hearken to the voice of the former sign, they will put their trust in the voice of the latter sign. And it shall be, if they do not put their trust in even these two signs, and do not hearken to your voice, then take some of the water of the Nile and pour it on the dry land. The water you take from the Nile will become blood on the land.'"

Gently lowering his hand, I drew a deep breath to still my storming heart. My father, a holy man of considerable reputation, had never been able to work wonders like these. And yet—I peered at Moses from beneath the edge of my veil. I had no proof my husband could perform these wonders, either.

"I know what you're thinking." The corner of Moses' mouth twisted as he met my eyes. "I know the story is hard to believe. I didn't want to believe it myself, and I did not want to obey. I said to YHWH, 'Please, my Lord, no man of words am I, not from yesterday, not from the day before, not even since you have spoken to your servant, for I am clumsy with words!'"

Moses rubbed a hand over his face. "I do not speak Hebrew, so how am I to convince those people that God sent me to deliver them? How am I supposed to stand before their elders and win their hearts when I cannot speak their language?"

I bit my lip, unable to reply, but Moses didn't need an answer from me.

"As I stood there, fumbling for excuses, YHWH said, 'Who placed a mouth in human beings, and who makes one mute or deaf or open-eyed or blind? Is it not I, YHWH? So now, go! I myself will be with your mouth and will instruct you as to what you are to speak.'"

He gave me a brief, distracted glance, and attempted to smile. "I tried, Zipporah, to persuade him otherwise. I was too old, too slow, and surely an all-powerful God would understand my weaknesses. I said, 'Please, my Lord, send whomever you want to send, but find someone else!'

"In that moment, I knew I had angered YHWH. But he did not thunder or strike me with flame. He said, 'Is there not Aharon your brother, the Levite? I know he can speak, yes, speak well, and even now he is coming out to meet you. When he sees you, he will rejoice in his heart. You shall speak to him, you shall put the words in his mouth! I myself will be with your mouth and his mouth, and will instruct you as to what you shall do. He shall speak for you to the people, he shall be for you a mouth, and you shall be for him a spokesman for God. And take this staff in your hand with you, for with it you shall do the signs.'"

I shifted my gaze to Moses' staff, the worn pole he had carried for years. Over time, the sharp edges of stones had nicked its surface while the oils from Moses' hands had darkened its color. I could not imagine Moses leaving our camp without it, but I had never imagined it as a tool for God.

His hoarse whisper broke the silence. "Then YHWH said to me, 'When you return to Egypt, you are to perform before Pharaoh all the portents I have put in your hand. But I will make his heart strong-willed, so he will not send the people free. Then you are to say to Pharaoh, "Thus says YHWH, 'My son, my firstborn, is Israel! I said to you, "Send free my son that he may serve me, but you have refused to send him free, so here, I will kill your son, your firstborn!"'"'"

The talk of killing sent a shiver down my spine and desperation forced words from my heart. "Moses, how can you return to Egypt? Pharaoh decreed that you must die! To stand before his son would mean certain death for you! So you must forget what you thought you heard today. Tomorrow you will feel better, and all these things will fade away—"

"No." He looked at me in patient compassion, as if I were the one suffering the effects of a delusion. "Yнwн said all the men who sought my life have died. Ramesses and Merneptah are gone."

I blinked at this, for though we had heard of Ramesses' death, we had not yet heard that a new king occupied Egypt's throne.

We sat in silence for a long moment, the only sounds coming from beyond the tent. Outside, Efra scolded Harkhuf for kicking sand in the flour while Gershom and Eliezer brought in the flocks, the sound of their laughter trailing into our tent on a soft tide of animal bleating.

But not even the voices of our sons could wrest my husband from dreams of death and freedom.

Desperate for some touchstone that would anchor my husband to reality, I closed my eyes and struggled to recall his stories of Egypt.

"Your Hebrew brother." I opened my eyes. "I never knew his name."

"I never knew him, not really." Moses' mouth went soft as a trace of unguarded hope filled his face. "But Yнwн said he is on his way to meet me."

"Surely he is an old man now. And a slave. So how is he to journey into the wilds to meet you?"

Moses frowned, weighing the question, then his face cleared. "I don't know how he will come. But I know he will."

"You really believe that?"

"That is why we must hurry. We will leave at sunup tomorrow."

My shock gave way to indignation. "Tomorrow? Moses, we can't just pick up and leave. There are the flocks to consider, and our livestock will have to be culled from my father's. If you insist upon going, I suppose we could go in a month or so. . . ." *Perhaps by then you will have forgotten about Pharaoh, your brother, and serpents at the base of Sinai.*

"Leave the animals, we will depart at sunup."

My husband's face filled with resolute calmness, and I knew there would be no more debate. Moses did not often force his opinions upon me, but in this he would not waver. The man who had sought God for forty years had found him . . . or thought he had.

Frustrated beyond words, I pushed myself up and hurried toward my father's tent. Reuel, friend of all the gods, would know if Moses suffered from the delusions of sunstroke. The heat had surely addled my husband's good sense; the monotony of shepherding had inflated his heart with dreams of grandeur. I might not be able to change Moses' intention, but surely my father could.

※

I was in the midst of relaying Moses' story to my father when my husband stepped into the tent. Though his presence unnerved me, forcing me to omit certain questions I had about the believability of Moses' tale, he did not interrupt.

I finished the recitation with a single comment: "And now, Father, Moses wants us to leave at sunup. But I don't see how it's possible, for our goods as well as our hearts are thoroughly intermingled with yours."

My father did not seem surprised by this turn of events. When I had finished, he looked at Moses. "You are determined to make this journey?"

"By my life, I am." Moses bowed respectfully. "Pray let me go and return to my brothers that are in Egypt, so I may see whether they are still alive. I will not take anything more than provisions for the journey. YHWH has promised that I will return to you, I and all my people. We will worship the Lord here at the Mountain of God."

My father stroked his beard. "You will take Zipporah and your sons?"

"Of course. I want them to see the hand of YHWH as he reaches out to save his people."

"And smite the Egyptians." Reuel lifted a brow. "Are you certain, Moses, that it was not the voice of pride speaking to you in the desert heat? The sun can play tricks upon an old man's eyes—this is no shame, it has happened to me on many occasions. And I know you bear the house of Pharaoh no love for having cast you out—"

"'Twas not the voice of pride I heard." Moses' words came out hoarse, as if forced through a tight throat. "I have little pride left, Reuel. To the desert, the sun, and finally the God of the mountain I have confessed that in imagining myself a mighty deliverer I smote an Egyptian, killing him as thoughtlessly as the Egyptians killed the children of Israel. It has taken me years to understand the truth. In Egypt, I thought myself a god; when I fled I cast all gods aside. But the same pride that led me to murder also led me to consider myself a stranger in the bosom of a family who sheltered and protected me, giving me everything I needed to find wholeness again."

In the shadows of my father's tent, my husband hung his head. "I do not deserve to be called your son, Reuel, nor Zipporah's husband. Those fine boys outside have lived with a false father. But in the last few months I have come to see myself as *the* God sees me: a prideful, arrogant man who could not be a vessel for deliverance until he emptied himself. When I became empty, YHWH filled me."

Still stroking his beard, my father nodded slowly. "I will have the servants pack donkeys with food enough for the journey. Take gifts for your family, if any remain in the Black Land, and go with my blessing, Moses. I ask only one thing of you."

He looked at me and his resolute eyes softened. "If my children face danger, send them back to me. I do not know whether this YHWH is mighty enough to protect them from the gods of Egypt, and I would keep them safe."

Moses inclined his head. "I will, Reuel. I owe you too much to disregard your wishes."

"Go in peace, Moses. We will wait for your return."

～⌖～

Being a man—and by that I mean that he did what was expected and nothing more—after his conversation with Reuel, Moses went into our tent and promptly fell into a deep sleep. The setting sun, however, found me wandering through our compound, preparing for the journey. I had to choose the sturdiest donkeys, check the goatskins for leaks, make a mental list of provisions. We would take several goats to slaughter on the journey, several bushels of ground grain, and two vessels of oil. In an effort to travel quickly and inconspicuously, we would take skins, rope, and poles to erect only one tent. The donkeys would carry the load while Moses, Gershom, Eliezer, and I rode on horseback.

Still marveling over the lunacy of my husband's plan, I shook my head as I ran my hand down one donkey's foreleg and checked the tender underside of his hoof. Gershom and Eliezer had responded to the news with unrestrained glee; to them, Egypt was a paradise to be explored, the trip an adventure. Besides, hadn't Moses promised we would return?

"Zipporah?"

Waddling under the weight of a clay jar, Efra approached. I lifted the pottery lid, inspected the contents by the fading light of the sun, then nodded. "It's good flour. Set it with the other things, will you?"

I counted off supplies on my fingertips as she shuffled away. We would proceed on a direct course to the Black Land, but who could say if we would find a trader on the way? We'd be fortunate if we did not encounter a band of brigands who'd slit our throats and steal the animals.

The sun had slipped below the horizon before I left the livestock pen. I sighed as I checked the final donkey, then paused by the gate to fill my senses with the only home I'd ever known. I breathed in the scents of animals, manure, and arid air. The night overhead was deep black, the great stars little more than distant points and the small ones lost in an inky sky. The animals bleated out a soft melody while the wind rattled the palms at the oasis.

Was I being cowardly? Surely not, for I trusted Moses to care for us. Even at eighty, his skill as a warrior had not diminished. If this "divine calling" had resulted from sunstroke, we would be in no danger on the journey, not even in Egypt, for Midianite traders often traveled there.

I trusted my husband implicitly . . . yet I did not trust this vision.

"Why not?" I asked the air. Did my distrust of Moses' divine revelation spring from a hidden reluctance to part from my father . . . or was it Moses' God I resisted?

My thoughts drifted back to the time of Gershom's birth. Moses had wanted to circumcise our son as he had been circumcised, but what sort of god demanded the blood of innocents? Baal did, but neither my father nor I had ever offered an infant's blood on his altars. And I could not shed my son's blood to placate Moses' ancestral god.

Apparently, my stern refusal to allow Gershom's circumcision had made an impression upon my husband, for though he had lifted our second child to the God of his fathers, he hadn't mentioned the bloody ritual at Eliezer's birth. Yet this afternoon he had told me that Israel was YHWH's firstborn . . . and since there were no papyri to record the agreement, the proof of that covenant was marked in flesh.

At least it was marked in Moses'. But not in the flesh of his sons.

Weary with thoughts of blood and gods, I crept into our tent, then stretched out on the lambskin that served as my bed. Shivering with unease, I reached for my woolen blanket, but Moses' hand crossed the empty space between us and caught my wrist.

"Will you come, Zipporah," he asked in a broken whisper, "with an open heart?"

I was glad he couldn't see my face in the darkness, for I knew a trace of defiant resistance still shone in my eyes.

"I am your wife, Moses." I caught his hand and threaded my fingers through his. "I will go with you. But I do not understand this God of yours, and I may not be open to everything you suggest we do for him. I want our sons to remain safe."

Moses relaxed his grip, and when he spoke again, his voice had gone soft with awe. "YHWH is powerful, he is the Almighty, and I believe he is good. But he is not safe, and he is not one with whom you can be half-hearted." His voice faltered when he added, "I only hope he will find me worthy."

We lay there, linked by the flesh of fingertips and palms, as a new realization began to shadow my heart. Moses' unwillingness to worship my father's gods had kept him at a polite distance from the people of Midian. Now, after a single debatable encounter with a burning bush, Moses' willingness to embrace the fiery YHWH might make that distance permanent.

I certainly did not want to worship a burning God who worked signs with blood and snakes and disease. I preferred my gentle goddess, who sat quietly in her corner and listened to my prayers without demanding anything from me.

A few moments later, Moses' breathing had drifted into the regular rhythm of sleep. I followed him into the shadowy chambers where dreams dwell, but his warning flowed on the currents and echoed in my ears.

∽

Hobab must have ridden out just after Moses shared the news with my father, for by the time I had supervised the loading of the pack animals, my sisters and their families had come from their compounds to bid us farewell. Noura hugged me and draped my neck with flowers, Talibah gave me a jar of perfumed unguent, and in my honor Rima offered sacrifices of food and incense upon the altar dedicated to Athirat. Halah and Almira had their children sing a special song for my pleasure, and before they had finished, tears were flowing down my cheeks.

Then my father called Moses, Gershom, Eliezer, and me into the circle of stones surrounding his altars. In a thick voice that betrayed his emotion, he blessed us in the names of all the gods he represented, ending with "and in the name of YHWH, whom you serve, may you return to us safely and in good health."

The sun had climbed to the center of the sky before we mounted our animals and turned them toward the west. My sisters lifted their voices in keening wails as we rode away, and my heart fluttered with every ululation.

My brother and my brothers-in-law rode with us for the better part of an hour, then Hobab embraced Moses, wished him a safe journey, and turned for home. The riders from my sisters' tribes turned and thundered away as well, their horses raising clouds of dust over the silent sands.

In the center of a vast wilderness stretching toward a bloodred horizon, we were alone.

We rode until nightfall, then found a small tree-fringed spring behind a rocky ridge. Judging from the charred remains of a fire pit, the sheltered spot was popular with travelers.

As I slid off my horse, bone sore and weary, Gershom led the goats to water. Eliezer set about hobbling the horses, while Moses began to pull the loads from our donkeys.

I made flat barley cakes from the flour and oil, then looked at our tent with undisguised relief. Soon enough, I would lie down and the day would end. While our sons jabbered about the things they hoped to see in Egypt, Moses and I kept silent throughout the simple meal.

I looked at my husband, who kept glancing toward the horizon as if he expected to see someone approaching. *Are you looking for Aaron?* I wanted to ask. *If he can come this far to meet you, why can't* he *lead your people out of the Black Land?*

A white moon, round and full, had replaced the sun by the time we settled the animals for the night. I went into the tent and loosened my girdle, then stretched out upon the sheepskin nearest the wall. Moses followed, leaving the boys to douse the fire. As young people will, they stayed awake for some time, their masculine voices lulling me into a deep and dreamless sleep.

At some point in that eternal night, I woke. I'm not sure what roused me, but as I sat up the skin on my arms began to tingle. I have been awakened by winds, sandstorms, and animals, but never before had I felt the empty air around me vibrate, the silence fill with dread.

Outside the tent, I heard the plaintive bleating of the goats, followed by the horses' whinnies and whickers. So . . . something was afoot. Drawing my woolen blanket around my shoulders, I stood and pulled back the tent flap.

All seemed calm in our camp—at least I could see nothing amiss. The hobbled animals whickered nervously, but nothing moved on the vast desert plain, well lit by the round moon. I lifted my eyes to the heavens, then felt my heart stutter as a dazzling star raced across the ebony sky, then swooped toward me as if heaven and earth lay only a hand's breadth apart.

My lips parted in a silent gasp, then curved in a smile. I had to be dreaming. But as I studied the glittering object, I saw that it was no star at all, but a ball of light so bright I had to squint in order to look upon it. It hung in the motionless air above my head, turning and sparkling like the reflection of sun on water; then it moved lightly past me and entered our dwelling.

Scared speechless, I turned. The sparkling orb hung in the center of our tent, above my sleeping men. It whirled brighter and faster than before; then shapes began to emerge from the round mass. I saw a hand, as fluid as water, then an arm, glowing and bright, followed by legs. The odd sight made my skin crawl, but my heart nearly stopped beating when the whirling light expanded into a radiant figure unlike any man I had ever seen. Before my transfixed eyes this sparkling being crept toward

Moses, extending a shimmering hand toward my husband . . . and suddenly I was overcome by the dreadful certainty that we were in mortal danger. Moses did not wake until this midnight foe touched his neck; then he began to thrash and struggle for breath. I scrambled for a weapon, seeking my sons' daggers, but the only serviceable item within reach was the flint I had used to strike the fire.

The sound of gasping now filled the tent, and I knew Moses would die if I did not do something. But how could I prevail against a heavenly being? Frustrated with my helplessness, I struck the sharpened flint on the pottery oil lamp, but the resulting spark did not catch the wick.

I shoved the lamp away. What was I doing? In the ethereal light emanating from the visitor I could see my sleeping sons, my struggling husband, the yawning space where I had been sleeping. What I could not see was a reason for this horrific attack.

With one hand our foe held Moses' neck, choking off his breath; with the other he reached toward heaven as if waiting for some sign, some permission to be granted. I felt a scream rise in my throat and choked it off, for screaming would not help. Nor could I fight this attacker with physical strength, for this being had come from a god I did not know or understand. . . .

In that instant, comprehension flooded my dim heart. Moses' words came back to me in a surge of memory—

I only hope I will be found worthy

— mingled with the words of Yhwh—

My son, my firstborn, is Israel!

—and my own words, offered so carelessly and so long ago—

I will not have my son marked with the covenant of a god you cannot even call by name.

A rock of truth had to exist in the midst of this confusion, and I strove to grasp it. My thoughts ran backward, clicking off the things I knew:

Moses' God required sons to be circumcised.

Moses had wanted to circumcise Gershom, but I had not allowed it.

Now Moses was on his way to redeem the children of Israel, the Lord's firstborn, but he had not obeyed the covenant command God had given his people long ago.

I had prevented him. But I could still correct my mistake.

Without thinking further, I grasped the flint between my thumb and forefinger, stepped over Eliezer, and lifted Gershom's tunic. In one swift movement I circumcised my firstborn son, then, as Gershom howled, lifted the bit of bloody flesh between my fingers.

"Look!" Stumbling toward my husband's assailant, I touched the severed flesh to the intruder's translucent thighs. Not knowing the proper ritual for a Hebrew circumcision, I recited the phrase I had heard over and over at my sisters' weddings: "Surely a bridegroom of blood you are to me!"

Immediately, the stranger released Moses and stepped back. I stared into his bland, nearly transparent face, and thought I saw the start of a smile, but I had no time to ponder the matter. While Moses grasped his throat and struggled to sit up, the night visitor retreated into his sparkling sphere and departed as suddenly as he had come.

"A bridegroom of blood," I whispered, my voice breaking as I sank to the tent floor in darkness. Every ounce of strength poured from my bones, leaving me as soft and malleable as wax. On the other side of the tent, Gershom's cry had awakened Eliezer, and both of them were fumbling for their weapons, assuming we were under attack.

But Moses, when he came to himself, understood. After lighting the lamp and checking on Gershom, he caught Eliezer's eye. "Tomorrow, son," he rasped, his voice threadbare from the struggle, "you will also wear the covenant of YHWH in your flesh."

Eliezer nodded solemnly; then Moses turned to me. "Blessings upon you, Zipporah."

If the eyes of our sons had not been fixed upon us, I think he might have pulled me into a grateful embrace.

The next morning, after breaking our fast, Moses summoned Gershom and Eliezer to an altar of stones before the Mountain of God we called Sinai.

"In the land of Goshen, on the eighth day of my birth," he said, speaking with a certainty I rarely heard in his voice, "my father followed the command of YHWH, who declared that among all the nations, Israel was his firstborn. And so, in obedience to his command, I circumcise you, my son Eliezer, as heir to the covenant God promised the children of Israel."

I cringed as the blade did its work, then embraced my sons and began the walk back to our camp to prepare dinner.

We stayed at the oasis for three days, giving our sons time to heal from the circumcision. Those days were unusual periods of relative inactivity, yet I learned something during our brief sojourn there: the God of Israel was an aggressive deity more concerned with his people's obedience than any divinity in my father's pantheon. As Moses had warned me, YHWH was definitely not safe.

I was not yet ready to pronounce him *good*.

On the fourth day, as we were preparing to pack up the donkeys and resume travel toward the Black Land, I squinted at a pair of travelers on the horizon. They were not Egyptians, for no self-respecting Egyptian would ever ride astride a lowly donkey. They could have been desert-dwellers, for the man wore a long beard and the woman covered her head with a dark veil.

Gershom paused by my side and pointed to the pair. "Are they dangerous, do you think?"

"Not likely," I answered, setting my jar of flour into a bag hanging over the donkey's back. "Perhaps they are Edomites."

As they drew within hailing distance, I saw the woman staring at us, her lined face searching ours with the intensity of the noon sun. The man, tall and aged, slid off his beast and began shuffling toward Moses with an outstretched hand. My husband tightened his grip on his staff. Despite the old man's harmless appearance, I knew my sons were reaching for their swords and spears, for one never knew what to expect in the rocky wilds.

I watched in quiet wonder as my husband walked toward the man, then bowed as a sign of respect.

"Do not bow to me." The aged stranger spoke in a tremulous voice. "I am looking for the mountain the desert-crossers call Sinai."

Moses turned and gestured to the mountain behind us. "That is Sinai, the Mountain of God."

"Good." The man clasped his hands together, then sighed in satisfaction. "I have come a long way."

Moses laughed. "To see a mountain?"

"To see a man. YHWH sent me here to meet a man called Moshe. Like me, he is a child of Israel."

A tremor passed over my husband's face and a sudden spasm knit his brows. "I am Moses."

The stranger cried out with a loud voice, then fell upon my husband's neck with cries and weeping. I looked at my sons, who watched the reunion with undisguised bewilderment, and through the tumult I recognized a name I had not heard until recently.

As he promised, YHWH had sent Aaron to meet us.

MIRYAM

❧

U ntil the moment I beheld my brother again, I was not truly convinced the Lord had heard our cries for deliverance. My decision to accompany Aharon was based more on loving tolerance
for a brother's stubborn whims than any real conviction that the God Who
Sees had noticed our misery.

Then Moshe appeared before us, sober and alive, looking every inch a
prince of Israel, not Egypt. He traveled on fine horses with a woman, two
young men, and a small train of donkeys, but for the first few moments
I had eyes only for my brother.

The baby I had guarded in the bulrushes had thrived . . . and, according to Aharon's word from Yhwh, that baby would be our deliverer.

While the men embraced, I slid off my donkey, then lifted my hands
and began a slow and steady dance of rejoicing, not at all caring what the
sand-crossers thought.

ZIPPORAH

After the greetings and introductions, through which I walked like a dreaming sleepwalker, I found myself compressed into an ever-shrinking space between the weight of my husband's revelation and my own driving doubts.

Aaron had come to Sinai. Somehow the old man had escaped Egypt and found his way to the Mountain of God and our small camp.

So . . . Moses *had* encountered Yhwh on the mountain. My husband had heard the voice of a god, and that god obviously possessed a gift of prophecy. But my father often prophesied in the name of the gods, and sometimes his predictions also came to pass.

The night visitor had possessed unearthly power, but that incident still filled me with confusion. If not for the shriveled bit of skin in our tent and my son's moaning the next morning, I might have been able to convince myself that the entire night had been an awful dream.

Moses had no doubts. He had expected Aaron to appear, and now walked with an arm about his brother's shoulder, leading him into the shade of the tent. He struggled with understanding the tongue of the Hebrews when Aaron and Miriam spoke together, but each of them spoke a simple form of Akkadian, so they were managing to communicate.

We broke bread together in the shade of our tent. I had thought that Miriam would join me in serving the meal, but she sat in the shade by Aaron's side, as bold as any man. I lifted a brow at this, but since there were no other women to share my amazement, no one noted my disapproval.

So I made bread and baked it beneath the sand and slaughtered a goat and roasted the meat and unearthed the bread and beat it clean. And as I served the meal I felt the silent pressure of Miriam's censorious eyes upon me.

Why should the old woman dislike me? I had borne Moses two fine sons, and I was no ignorant girl. I was a mature woman, though judging by her looks Miriam had been living nearly four decades longer than I had. Red spiderwebs of tiny broken veins netted her jaws, and her mouth was a dry, lipless line, like a cut in dead flesh. Her narrow breasts hung as low as the girdle around her waist, and the hands that lifted her cup were spotted with age and rough with hard use. I knew without looking that the hair beneath her veil was as coarse and as colorless as the blowing sand.

As they ate, Moses asked of the world he had known. "Where is Pharaoh living? Thebes?"

His brother, whose bearded face was as raw-edged as the stony landscape, smiled a grim smile—Moses' smile. "The king has been at Pi-Ramesses for several months, and intends to stay there. Seti is not the warrior his father was."

Moses' brow furrowed. "Seti? The second king of that name?"

"Yes, he is the son of Merneptah and Isetnofret. This is the fifth year of his reign."

Moses gave me a look heavy with meaning. YHWH had spoken truly, for Moses did not know the new king. Most important, the new king did not know Moses.

Nodding, I silently acknowledged another victory for YHWH.

My husband lifted his hand when he and Aaron had eaten their fill, and I obeyed the silent signal to leave the men alone. Miriam, however, lingered in their company, and indignation stiffened my spine as I put away my jars and cups. What sort of stiff-necked woman was Moses' sister? Only the saving grace of second thought kept me from hating her on the spot. Perhaps, I told myself, if Hobab and I had been separated for a lifetime, I would be reluctant to leave his side.

I finished my work, then sat outside the tent and let my thoughts dissipate in a mist of fatigue. I was beginning to feel drowsy when I heard Moses calling. Spurred by a desire to prove he had married an obedient and loyal wife, I hurried to answer, then found him in the tent with Aaron and Miriam.

I stared at Miriam, who sat on a folded sheepskin and refused to meet my eyes.

"Zipporah." Moses gentled his voice. "Aaron and I have been talking about the struggle that lies ahead. We do not know how long YHWH will require to free the children of Israel, nor do we know what Pharaoh might do in retaliation for the strength God will demonstrate on our behalf." His eyes flickered toward his sister. "So I have decided to honor my promise to your father and send you back to Reuel's tents—you and our sons. You will be safe there, and you will be more comfortable."

My senses reeled at this announcement. "You are sending us away?"

"It will only be for a short while, YHWH willing. When we leave the Black Land, I will send for you. Then you will go with me into the land God has promised our people."

Seething with frustration and humiliation, I clenched my fists. I wanted to lash out and pound Moses' chest, but I could do nothing with his brother and sister sitting in our tent. Though I could not prove it, I felt certain Miriam had something to do with this dismissal. I had grown up in a family of women, and I recognized her narrow-eyed, hunted look.

"Why did you not think of this sooner?" I struggled to keep my voice low. "You could have spared us the hardship of the journey. You could have spared us that awful encounter in the night—no, perhaps you couldn't. For if I had not been with you, Moses, you would be dead. If I had not saved your life the other night—"

"If God had wanted me dead," Moses answered, a warning look flitting over his face, "he would have struck me swiftly. No, Zipporah, the other night he wanted to show *you* his power. Now he wants to show all Egypt. YHWH will demonstrate his authority over creation, over all other gods, and over life itself."

"If YHWH is so powerful," I pressed on, finding courage in my anger, "why can't you trust him to protect your family? If he will protect Israel, won't he protect your wife and sons? If you have faith, Moses, why can't you trust him for our safety?"

I intended the words to sting, but Moses did not flinch. Without looking to either his sister or brother, he folded his hands in his lap. "Tell Eliezer and Gershom to pull out a single pack animal for me. Tomorrow morning they will escort you back to your father's encampment."

A Midianite woman typically bid her husband a respectful farewell by bowing her way out of his presence, but my fury would not allow such genuflection. I spun on the ball of my foot and swept out of the tent, leaving my husband with his brother and narrow-hearted sister.

We took our leave of Moses the next morning. Not knowing when they would see him again, Gershom and Eliezer embraced their father and bravely bid him farewell. I sat on my horse and kept my eyes fixed on the eastern horizon. A public display of affection would be out of character for us, and Moses had not approached me in the night. He and Aaron had stayed up late talking around the fire, and I suspected they slept under the stars. In my usual spot, deep within the shadows on the far side of the tent, Miriam slept soundlessly, if she slept at all. I lay next to my sons, but a few times I woke with the feeling, unfounded but strong, that Miriam watched me through the dark with jealous, accusing eyes.

Finally, I heard the soft sound of sandals upon the sand. Moses stood beside my horse, one hand gripping his staff, the other tugging at his beard. "It is nothing you have done." He lowered his voice. "But your leaving is for the best. I will be able to apply myself more fully to my task if I do not have to be concerned for my family."

Silently, I considered this remark. Yesterday he had spoken of protecting us; today he spoke of protecting himself. Today's statement may not have been completely truthful, but it sounded far more honest.

"Farewell, husband." I gathered the leather reins. "I hope your god protects you as ferociously as he corrects you."

I was about to kick the horse, but stopped when I felt a gentle pressure upon my foot. Moses' hand had wrapped around my ankle, the most public and spontaneous display of affection he had ever dared. For a moment I was too startled to react; then my throat clogged with emotions I could not verbalize.

I gave him a fleeting smile when he looked up, then slapped the reins and urged the horse away. As I cantered toward my father's camp, leaving the boys to bring the donkeys, one thought struck me—Moses had come out of Egypt with a wounded heart because the people he loved sent him away. Could he not see that he was doing the same thing to us?

BOOK THREE

WILDERNESS

It was, many years later, the king of Egypt died. The Children of Israel groaned from the servitude, and they cried out; and their plea for help went up to God, from the servitude.

God hearkened to their moaning, God called to mind his covenant with Avraham, with Yitzhak, and with Yaakov.

God saw the Children of Israel.

God knew.

*Moshe and Aharon went, they gathered all the elders of the Children of Israel, and Aharon spoke all the words which Y*HWH *had spoken to Moshe, he did the signs before the people's eyes.*

*The people trusted, they hearkened that Y*HWH *had taken account of the Children of Israel, that he had seen their affliction.*

And they bowed low and did homage.

*—*EXODUS *2:23-25; 4:29-31*

MIRYAM

◆

S carcely feeling the sweaty donkey beneath me, I floated on a cloud of confidence as we crossed into Mizraim. Aharon had not been dreaming when he heard the voice of God and, miracle of miracles, the guards at the border garrisons had paid scant attention to two aged foreigners on donkeys. Though I suspected Moshe's fine horse might attract a bit of notice upon our return, I felt as certain as a pharaoh.

I had lived in Goshen all my life, but I was unprepared for the sight that greeted me when we crested a hill on the eastern banks of the Nile. We had left Egypt in a hurry, with nary a backward glance, so I had never glimpsed the Black Land from this perspective. After traveling through an arid, desiccated territory in which beige and blush seemed the only colors, Egypt bloomed before us like a vision of Eden. The river had begun to cover the earth while we were away (the Egyptians would say Isis had watered the kingdom with her tears), and the floodwaters lay upon the valley like a spill of liquid silver. Tall palm trees, vibrant with life and color, shivered in the prevailing winds while the sun that had baked us all afternoon stood poised above the valley, its rays shimmering upon the river in coppery brilliance.

Looking down, I understood why they called Mizraim "the Beautiful Land." Beyond the fields lay Pharaoh's cities, with tall brick walls, gleaming granite statues, and colorful pennants that fluttered from the towers.

I wasn't the only one who'd been captured by the sight. I glanced at Moshe and saw that his face had gone soft with some emotion—nostalgia? Affection?

"Has it changed?" I asked.

For a moment he did not answer; then he nodded. "It has changed somewhat. But it is still beautiful."

Aharon, however, felt no such tenderness for Pharaoh's city. "It *is* beautiful." He kicked his donkey's ribs. "But it is the land of slavery, and was never meant to be our home."

I glared at him—did he think he needed to remind me of our people's plight?—then swallowed my irritation and urged my donkey forward. After sitting astride the beast for several days, I could understand why the Egyptians never rode them. The recalcitrant animals were neither swift nor agile, and their bony backs offered no comfort for my aging frame.

Moshe led the way to yet another garrison where an Egyptian officer in a braided wig and a pleated linen kilt stepped out to inspect our small traveling party.

"Where are you from?" he asked in formal Akkadian.

Aharon and I bowed our heads and kept silent, but Moshe did not hesitate. "I am from Midian," he answered in the same tongue. "We are traveling to the land of Goshen."

The guard laughed. "Why would you want to visit the land of slaves? There are no markets there, no temples—" He paused, looked at Aharon and me upon our lowly donkeys, then smiled broadly. "Ah, now I see. You want to buy slaves to replace these worn-out servants. Very well, then, I wish you well."

"Thank you. So if there is nothing else—"

"Nothing."

As I battled resentment that Moshe not only looked younger but more prosperous than his siblings, the guard stepped back and waved us forward. We rode over a soft road of muddy black earth, then approached a ferry that waited for travelers. Moshe leaned forward upon his horse, crossing his arms as he scanned the vessels upon the river.

"I had nearly forgotten," he said, his voice husky, "how busy the river is."

After the solitude of the wilderness I could understand why the bustling Nile impressed him, yet I had the feeling Moshe's words conveyed only a fragment of his emotions. His eyes followed the crowds at the riverbank, but they also lifted to take in the blazing river, the expansive fields, and Ramesses' magnificent city.

How would I feel returning to the greatest kingdom in the world as a disinherited son?

I kept silent, appraising my brother as he studied our surroundings. Moshe said nothing else, but wore a look that told me his heart was working hard at a new and unexpected set of problems.

God had called him, and Aharon had confirmed the call. But Moshe had not expected to be swamped with nostalgia when he beheld Mizraim again.

Would he be able to perform the task to which God had summoned him? Moshe did know the Egyptians—at least he had known the Egyptians of forty years ago. But were we wise to trust someone who had actually *loved* Ramesses? Did the people of Mizraim still hold a claim on his heart?

"Look at that." Moshe pointed to a *shaduf* on the other bank. The base of the device was submerged, but in a few months it would be situated on the riverbank and used to haul water from the river to the irrigation ditches. "There were not as many shadufs on the river when I left. I saw them only in cities."

"There are none in our villages," I answered, my voice dry. "We still carry water as we always have, on a pole across our shoulders."

His mouth twitched with amusement. "At least you *have* water. The Midianites often travel miles in search of it."

He may not have intended that remark to sting, but it did. I shifted uncomfortably on the saddle and looked away, lest my irritation boil over into some cutting comment I'd later regret.

Why had God not called Aharon to deliver the children of Israel . . . or even me? Were we not children of Levi as well? Aharon was older than Moshe, and eloquent in our tongue, but I knew more about our people than Aharon could ever hope to know. Aharon had spent his life sweating over mud molds in the brickyards while I had stood by the village fire pit and absorbed the thoughts, dreams, and despairs of our clan.

Perhaps this forthcoming deliverance would require all of us working together. Moshe could not handle the upcoming task alone, so God had sent Aharon and me to aid him. I smiled as an indefinable feeling of *rightness* rose within my breast.

Finally noticing us, the Egyptian on the ferry nodded, then gestured to a dock a short distance away.

Moshe turned. "We'll have to go to the dock, then dismount and lead the animals aboard the ferry." He lifted a brow and gave me a small smile. "I assume the river was not in flood when you left?"

"No," Aharon answered for me. "The river here was only a few feet wide. We rode across on our animals."

"I'm not about to ride across now." I kicked at my donkey's ribs, driving him toward the quayside. A few moments later Moshe rode up beside me, grinning.

"For a woman, you have a tart tongue, Miriam."

"Miryam," I corrected. "If you are going to speak for the children of Israel, Moshe, you should learn to pronounce our names properly."

Still grinning, he inclined his head in silent acknowledgment of my advice, then pointed to Aharon, who rode behind us. "I have never spoken Hebrew and it has been years since I conversed in Egyptian." He paused, then added, "I told YHWH I would have trouble with the language."

I rolled my eyes at his last remark, for how could one speak with God as casually as one spoke to a neighbor? After all, YHWH had spoken to Aharon in a dream. He spoke to Avraham and Yaakov in dreams and visions. The great Yosef interpreted dreams sent from the Almighty, but even he never had a conversation with God.

I decided to let Moshe's misguided remarks pass. "Egyptian is not so difficult a language," I said. "I have visited the marketplace outside Pi-Ramesses often enough to pick up an elementary understanding of the tongue. Most of our men speak some Egyptian; some of them manage it quite well." I cast him a sharp glance. "Did Egyptian traders not visit your camp?"

He shrugged. "Many traders came through our camp, but I did not often speak with my father-in-law's guests. I preferred the silence of the wilderness to the chanting of worshipers around Reuel's altars."

I kept my eyes on the watery horizon ahead as we reached the quayside and dismounted. With every word Moshe spoke, I became more and more afraid that God—I was still a little shy about using his name—had sent the wrong man. How could a desert hermit respond to the needs of a multitude? How could a man with the bad judgment to marry a pagan priest's daughter lead the covenant people?

Burdened with questions, I said little else as I pulled the reins over my donkey's head, then followed Moshe onto the barge that would take us back to Goshen and a certain village of Levi.

The village erupted in celebration when we returned. The small circle of relatives who had bid us farewell in the certainty they would never see us again heralded our return with shouts and embraces. The news of our mission had spread during our absence, so our return validated Aharon's dream, YHWH's promise, and Moshe's role as our deliverer.

While Moshe settled into my small house, Aharon sent his four sons to all the other villages, summoning the elders of each clan. As the setting sun stretched glowing fingers across the sky, representatives from each of the twelve tribes came from all over Goshen on foot, on donkeys, and one old man even came on a stretcher. Our people were ready to hear the details of their deliverance.

When a goodly crowd had assembled, Moshe and Aharon stepped out to address them. I stood with the women, eager to judge Moshe's ability to relate to the people he had scarcely known and barely understood. At least now he looked every inch an Israelite. He wore a long tunic, not a short kilt, and a full beard outlined his jaw. His hair was long and tied back, as was Aharon's, and anyone with eyes could see the family resemblance between the two men.

Still, I worried. My youngest brother had spent the last forty years living with a pagan priest who probably worshiped as many gods as the Egyptians. Would Moshe lead us to engage in pagan practices? Would he introduce us to gods other than YHWH?

My fears abated when my brothers began to speak. Because Moshe did not speak our language, he whispered Akkadian to Aharon, who translated all the words YHWH had spoken to Moshe. Then, to my utter amazement, Moshe worked wonders before our eyes. The staff he carried became a snake when he threw it to the ground, but it reverted back to its original state when he bent to pick it up. He held up his tanned arm, bared it to the elbow, then thrust it inside the slit at the neck of his tunic. When he withdrew it, we gasped, for it was white with tzaraat, but when he placed it next to his flesh again, the arm was restored to full health.

When one of the elders protested that Moshe was working tricks undoubtedly learned from a Midianite magician-priest, Aharon handed the man a pitcher and told him to fill it with water from the flooded marshes nearby. While the man went to fulfill this errand, I tried to gauge Moshe's reaction to this skepticism, but he seemed neither intimidated nor concerned by the man's questions. Finally, the elder returned, the front of his tunic dark where the water had sloshed upon him.

After handing the pitcher to Aharon, not Moshe, the elder placed his hands on his hips and gave Moshe a hard look. "You could have hidden a snake in the sleeve of your robe. You could have painted your arm with powder hidden inside your tunic. But this is water from the Nile, and you have not touched it."

Aharon handed the pitcher to Moshe. Without gestures of any kind, Moshe tilted it so the liquid splashed upon the black earth at our feet—only the liquid was not water, but bright, heavy blood!

The women shrieked in delighted horror; the men recoiled in alarmed awe. And then, one by one, the elders fell to their knees and bowed before my brothers.

"Go tomorrow." The doubter lifted both hands in supplication. "Go to Pharaoh and work these signs before him. Surely he will free us when he sees what wonders YHWH has empowered you to perform."

"We will go," Aharon answered, "but not tomorrow. We will spend tomorrow in prayer, and you must purify yourselves. Go back to your villages and tell your people that YHWH, the God of your fathers, has been seen by Moshe. The God of Avraham, Yitzhak, and Yaakov has taken account of what is being done to you in Mizraim. And he declares that he will bring you up from the affliction of Mizraim, to the land of the Canaanites and of the Hittites, of the Amorites and of the Perizzites, of the Hivites and of the Jebusites, to a land flowing with milk and honey. And he will give you favor in the eyes of Mizraim, so when you go, you shall not go empty-handed. Each woman shall ask her neighbor for objects of silver, gold, and clothing, and so shall you strip Mizraim!"

Some of the women around me murmured in confusion, so I stepped forward to clarify my brother's words. "So shall we be paid for our years of labor!" I called, lifting my hand to the sky. "So shall we be recompensed for the food we have not eaten, the clothing we have not worn, and the husbands and children we have lost!"

Shouts of joy mingled with wails of mourning at my words, for every man and woman among us had lost a husband, a brother, or a child to Pharaoh's cruelties. But joy prevailed, and soon drums and tambourines began to beat in a stately rhythm. We divided into two circles, the men dancing to celebrate their freedom from cruel taskmasters; the women dancing to rejoice in freedom from murder, grief, and mourning.

We clapped and danced through the star-spangled night. By the time I fell onto my straw pallet to sleep, I had become convinced that Moshe would be our deliverer, and YHWH our God.

I slept until streamers of sunlight jabbed at my eyelids, then pushed myself up and stared. Across the room, Moshe slept on a thick lambskin he'd brought from Midyan. Aharon had apparently retreated to his own home.

Rising to my knees, I peered over the dusty ledge of my windowsill. Only a scrawny dog moved in the village courtyard; for once, the fire pit stood cold and abandoned. A few women might still be sleeping, or perhaps they had stayed inside to obey Moshe's admonition to pray. I should have felt comforted, but the eerie stillness set an eel of fear to wriggling in my bowels. For the first time I could remember, there were no little girls squatting in the dirt, no women exchanging gossip on their way to wash clothes at the river.

Standing, I smoothed my hair, then draped my veil over my head. After picking up my water jars, I set them into the two rope nooses that hung from my yoke, then held it up and stepped beneath it, settling the load upon my shoulders. I walked as quickly as I could to the water's edge—not a great distance, in the season of flood—then carried my load back to the house.

As the door rasped against the threshold, Moshe pushed himself upright and gazed at me through bleary, bloodshot eyes.

"Good morning, brother." I sloshed water into a wooden cup. "Did you sleep well?"

"I slept well, but not long." He ran a hand over his grizzled face, then stood. "Is there—"

Wordlessly, I pointed toward the door. "Outside, and to your left. You'll see the privy on the path."

While he was gone, I pulled a loaf of hard bread from a basket, carved off a bit of mold, and tossed the refuse out the window. I cut slices of goat's-milk cheese, then pulled a stalk of grapes from the bunch my neighbor had given me last night. I spread the fruit, cheese, and bread on a square of wool, then set it on the floor between Moshe's lambskin and my straw pallet. Stepping back, I admired the artful arrangement. Moshe would certainly realize that I had prepared him a meal fit for a prince.

When he returned, he sank onto his lambskin without comment, pulling the cloth toward him. I sat on my pallet, watching in undisguised disbelief as he set about eating my portion *and* his, but he never seemed to notice my reaction. Instead, he leaned back and reclined on one elbow, then tossed a grape into his mouth.

"Miryam." He pronounced it correctly this time. "I am sorry we do not know each other better."

Still amazed that he had not noticed my lack of food, I stared at him. "We know each other well enough. I have known you since the day you were born, and Yhwh has seen to bring us back together under one roof. How many siblings can say that?"

I leaned forward, pointedly lifting portions of bread and cheese from the cloth, then settled back upon my pallet with the food in my hand.

An expression of confusion crossed his face; then he grinned. "I am sorry. In Midyan, women serve the men first and eat later."

"That is the usual practice here, as well," I admitted, "but we are not husband and wife. We are brother and sister, and I am older than you by eight years. It is hard for me to think of you as a master."

Moshe smiled, then broke off a piece of the goat cheese. His expression grew more serious. "Have you no husband?"

"I had one." I kept my voice light, skirting around an old but still-painful topic. "I married at fifteen, and had a baby the following year. But the child was stillborn, and my husband died soon after."

Moshe's bushy brows slanted the unspoken question.

"He was killed by an Egyptian overseer for failing to fulfill his quota of two thousand bricks a day. After the baby's death, he worried about me, and one afternoon he slipped away early from the brickyard. The next day his overseer beat him until he died." I released a choked laugh. "You know the Egyptians and their sticks. They do not hesitate to use them."

Something like outrage flared in Moshe's eyes, but it was secondhand emotion, and nothing like the agonizing fire that had seared my soul. I lowered my gaze, not certain I wanted to share an old agony with the brother who had been but a shadow in those years.

Moshe suddenly straightened. "Wait—I would have been living in Pharaoh's house at the time. You should have gone to my mother; you should have reported the crime. My mother had a soft heart; she treated her servants and slaves with great gentleness and the justice of ma'at—"

I shook my head. "You were but a boy, and Merytamon was living at the harem in those days. We would not have been allowed to approach her if we had wanted to."

A frown settled upon Moshe's features, and I wondered how much of his childhood he remembered. Few of us can recall many events of our early years, and I doubted he had any recollections of me or our parents. Now he was preparing to demand justice for us, but he had passed his formative years in a completely different world.

"You left us," I said simply. "First you went to Pharaoh's house. When you returned as a mature man we held great hopes for you, but when you slew the Egyptian—"

"I ruined everything." He grimaced, the veins at the sides of his neck standing out like ropes. "I lost my temper and with it, my best chance to help these people."

I noticed he could not yet say *our* people.

I chewed a bit of bread, then shrugged. "Who knows what would have happened had you stayed? But when you left the second time, I was certain we'd seen the last of you. I thought you were dead, but had I known you were living among the pagan Midianites, I would have counted you just as lost—"

He arched one eyebrow, employing the same nonverbal rebuke Aharon favored. "God does not confine himself to the marshes of Goshen. His Spirit moves even among the Midianites."

"Who am I to say where God is? I have seen little of him these past years."

He wagged his finger at me. "The Midianites are also children of Avraham. As I fled from Mizraim, I was often welcomed into their tents and offered food and shelter. I would not have survived the wilderness if not for their hospitality."

I dropped the bread in my hand and stared at him. "Gratitude, you owe them. Appreciation, certainly. But did you have to marry one of their women?"

A change came over Moshe's features, a sudden shock of realization. "You disapprove of Zipporah? Why?"

"She is a pagan."

"She is a fine woman. She is a hard worker, intelligent, and she has borne me two sons."

"But does she believe in YHWH as we do? Will she obey him?"

Moshe's chin jutted forward. "She obeys me. That is enough."

"Is it?" The sharp question slipped from my lips before I could stop it, and in my brother's eyes I read the answer—Moshe wasn't certain of his wife at all. Perhaps that is why he had not resisted when I suggested she would be better off in Midyan than in Mizraim.

Leaving the question suspended in midair, I snatched another bit of cheese from Moshe's meal, then stood and left him alone with his thoughts.

᷍

At the end of the day, as our workers began to trudge home from the brick-yards, I went in search of Aharon and found him greeting his four sons at the boundary marker outside our village. He had not gone to work with the others, for he wore a clean tunic instead of a muddy leather loincloth. But he could not break old habits, so here he was, trying to connect with the slaves who trudged home after a hot day of working in the thick heat.

I inclined my head toward several of the men from our village, whose answering nods now seemed weighted with a new measure of deference, then pulled Aharon aside so we could talk privately.

"What is it, Miryam? Has something happened to Moshe?"

"Nothing is wrong." I swayed slightly, feeling a little dizzy from a lack of sleep. "But I'm concerned about him. We are going to send him before Pharaoh tomorrow, but do we really know what he's thinking? After all, he married a Midianite, and you have seen what pagans they are."

Aharon did not dispute me, for in the market all of us had observed the pagan rituals of the Midianites. The children of Israel were not the only slaves in Mizraim; Pharaoh's warriors routinely conscripted men from wandering tribes or defeated kingdoms and forced them to slave in the Egyptian navy, the king's mines in the Sinai, or the brickyards of Goshen. We had heard stories of the king's men taking captives from the lands of Midyan, Edom, Nubia, Libya, Canaan, and Syria. When Pharaoh finished with them, they were either sold in the slave markets or sent to work in the quarries.

So we were acquainted with many pagan tribes . . . and we had seen demonstrations of their worship. Some of them spilled the virgin blood of their daughters into the earth during fertility rituals; others sacrificed their firstborn children to gods who neither heard nor saved them. In the end, they died believing that the souls of the blessed ate with Baal-Hadad in the underworld, while the souls of the not-blessed went to Mot's city, a filth-filled pit.

I shuddered at the thought of becoming entwined, however remotely, with pagans, but Aharon did not seem concerned. "You were confident of Moshe last night."

"Last night I did not hear him defend his wife. This morning, I did."

Aharon rubbed the back of his neck. "YHWH reunited us with Moshe. We trusted God to give us power to work signs for the people, and he did not fail us. Why should he fail us on the morrow? The matter of Moshe's wife is a small thing."

"For want of a brick the wall fell," I hissed. "Small things become large things in time. Moreover, a man will never consider his wife a small thing. Moshe intends to bring his wife and her children to dwell with us, and what will we do then? She will bring the pagan ways of her people to ours, and her sons will teach their heathen rituals and fertility rites to our sons and grandsons—"

"You worry too much, Miryam." Aharon crossed his arms as the beginnings of a smile tipped the corners of his mouth. "YHWH is working among us, and Moshe is his messenger. Do not borrow trouble, for it is certain we shall have plenty of it before we leave this place."

"You mean *Pharaoh* will have trouble. Surely God would not trouble us, not after all we have endured."

Aharon took my elbow as we entered the village, then squinted toward the setting sun. "YHWH told Moshe that he will have to work many wonders and signs to convince Pharaoh that he is Almighty and should be obeyed. I fear he will have to convince our people, too. In any case, the days ahead will not be easy . . . beginning with tomorrow."

I clasped my hand over his in an attempt to comfort my brother, but his words only intensified the storm of unrest in my soul.

The first pale hint of sunrise had lit the eastern sky by the time I woke the next morning. Moshe did not break his fast, but rose, dressed in a clean tunic Aharon had provided, then asked me to leave him alone so he could seek YHWH.

I stepped outside and found that I was not the only villager restless with anticipation. Several other people lingered in the courtyard, their eyes wide with expectancy and lit with hope. They were watching my house, waiting for Moshe.

I spotted Aharon and his wife, Elisheba, by the fire pit and went to join them. Aharon had combed his beard and dressed in his finest tunic; there was little of the slave about him now, save for the gauntness of his tanned face. I nodded to Elisheba, and together we waited for Moshe to appear.

The tangerine tints of the rising sun were warming our rooftops when Moshe stepped out of my house. He looked around, motioned to Aharon, then pulled his shepherd's staff from the sand where he had thrust it the night before. Taking it firmly in hand, he looked around at the assembled group. "Thank you all for praying." His words were simple, his expression serene. "Today we will relay YHWH's words to Pharaoh."

Carrying nothing but his staff, he and Aharon began moving toward Pi-Ramesses with bold, broad strides. Small children dogged their footsteps, laughing with delight, while their parents followed at a respectful distance.

Drawn by curiosity and the undeniable conviction that YHWH had assigned me a role in the coming drama, I followed, too. Had I not been the one to guard Moshe in the bulrushes? Had I not bravely spoken to Pharaoh's daughter and volunteered my mother as a wet nurse? I had not been afraid to speak that day, and, if the occasion demanded it, I would not be afraid to speak up again.

A light, celebratory air animated our group as we marched past luxurious sprouts of marsh grass and swaying cattails. Men spoke of what they would do with freedom; women murmured, "Remember this day," as they held their children's damp hands. Our noisy approach startled the waterfowl, launching disgruntled loons, herons, and storks into the cloudless sky. One young Egyptian couple, hunting in a light papyrus skiff, watched in openmouthed curiosity as we trekked past.

But Pi-Ramesses lay a good two hours northeast of our village, and people fell away at various stages of the journey. The young men left us first, knowing they risked a beating if they did not meet their quota of bricks for the day, and the mothers with small ones fell behind soon after. Some of the elders weakened halfway to Pi-Ramesses, and others abandoned us to escort the elders back to our village.

But a stalwart handful remained as we approached the pair of gray granite statues of Ramesses at the gates of the city. I must admit that the sight of those giant statues, intended to intimidate, strummed a shiver from me. But we passed through the gates, then followed narrow streets that led to temples and homes grander than anything of my imagining. Flowers bloomed in profusion, covering walkways and dripping from baskets, and every man and woman on the street wore spotless white linen and gold jewelry. The tinkling sounds of harp and the soft thump of drums rolled over the walls surrounding private homes while the sweet scents of incense wafted from temples like the perfume of paradise.

Saturated with unfamiliar sights, sounds, and scents, my head was reeling by the time we reached a yellow wall edged with bold red stripes. A corps of warriors armed with swords, spears, and shields stood guard outside the gate.

"The palace," Moshe said simply.

Aharon and I stood in abashed silence as our younger brother strode up to the captain of the guards and asked, in perfect Egyptian, for an audience with Pharaoh.

The captain looked at us, then turned to his companion. "Have they no quotas in the brickyards today?" he asked, his voice high and reedy. "Has the king declared a holiday and neglected to inform us?"

"By the life of Pharaoh," Moshe retorted, speaking with a confident assurance Ramesses himself might have envied, "I command you to make way so I may address the king. I bring news from a God mightier than Amon-Re, Thoth, Ptah, or Isis, so you must make way for me and these who have come with me."

I pressed my lips together as the guards looked at one another. They had undoubtedly been approached by common citizens before, brave fools who wished to complain about one thing or another, but few would have had the audacity—and the ability—to recite the king's most-favored gods in one breath.

The captain widened his stance and met Moshe's gaze head-on. "You will not enter."

"I must."

An aged priest stepped forward to settle the stalemate. An odd, bald man dressed from neck to ankle in white linen, he looked out at us with a bemused expression on his lined face.

"One who can recite the names of Egypt's gods so easily must have

spent some time in her temples," he said, squinting at Moshe with interest. "Yet you wear the headdress of a desert-dweller. If you would care
to introduce yourself and state your reason for seeking the divine Horus,
I will represent you in the king's audience chamber."

Moshe thumped the end of his staff upon the baked earth. "In the name
of Merytamon, my mother, I seek an audience with Seti, son of Merneptah
. . . who was my brother."

Like a cat scenting the breeze, the priest lifted his head and narrowed
his eyes. "Merneptah had many brothers, for Ramesses had many sons.
Which are you?"

"I am called Moses."

A strange, livid hue overspread the priest's face, and that flush told
me he remembered my brother's name. But he shook his head slightly
and gestured to a courtyard beyond the guards at the gate. "Wait in there,
Moses, you and your traveling party. I will send servants to bring you
water while I approach Pharaoh with your request."

I waited until the bald priest walked away, then tugged upon Moshe's
sleeve. "Why did you give him your name? Have you forgotten that your
life is forfeit in Egypt?"

"Should I hide who I am?" Amusement flickered in the eyes that met
mine. "Do not worry, Miryam. No harm will come to me here."

I released his sleeve and attempted to smile, but beneath the pleasant
expression my emotions were spinning like a piece of flotsam caught up
in the river's flood. Moshe might be acting upon orders from YHWH, but
he was proceeding in an unaccountably brash manner. He no longer wore
the garb of an Egyptian prince, and when one wore rough wool, one had
to bow a little lower and speak a little softer to survive.

Under the watchful eye of the guards, we shuffled forward—Moshe,
Aharon, and a half-dozen others, of whom I was the only woman. We
stood in a vestibule, upon a tiled floor painted with delicate scenes of
water and papyrus, and I felt my heart knocking as for the second time
in my life I entered a royal palace. The first time I had gone with my parents to deliver Moshe to the king's daughter; now I came to deliver that
same child to Pharaoh.

The harem palace at Mi-Wer had impressed me as a place of glory and vast spaces; the palace at Pi-Ramesses impressed me as a city of art and power. Paintings on the sandstone walls depicted lotus blossoms and river marshes, images of Pharaoh and his consort hunting birds among the reeds. Carved columns towered like trees before me, while a vaulted ceiling soared overhead.

Moshe had left all this—for the wilderness? As I lowered my gaze, an inner voice reminded me that he had left the palace for us even before he committed the act that resulted in his exile.

My reverie vanished as a pair of tall bronze doors swung open. A team of guards dressed in stiffly pleated linen kilts and striped headdresses snapped to attention, their arms crossing their chests as their fists thumped the flesh above their hearts. The old priest appeared behind them and nodded slightly to Moshe. "You and your company may enter."

Moshe turned to look at me. I think he may have been about to suggest that I remain in the anteroom, but Aharon, my champion, lifted his hand. "Let her witness. Let her be your voice to the women, so they will understand."

Moshe tilted his head, then nodded. And so I fell into step behind my brothers while the other men from our village trailed behind me. We entered the doubled-columned hall and walked over a floor tiled with a gold-veined marble that gleamed in the light from the high windows along the tall walls. The elaborate paintings on the walls bedazzled my eyes. The art in this chamber showed Pharaoh worshiping the god Amon-Re, conquering his enemies, and celebrating a sacrifice with his wife and firstborn son, Seti-Merneptah. If the room's designers meant to intimidate those who entered, they had admirably succeeded.

Then my eyes fell upon Pharaoh. The second king known as Seti occupied an almost dainty gold-covered chair on a stone dais. The king wore a white kilt more heavily pleated than those of his guards, and a girdle of leopard skin. A gem-studded pectoral hung over his bare chest, while a golden collar gleamed against his bronzed skin. Upon his head he wore a pleated cloth headdress much like his guards', but above his brow I could see the golden heads of a cobra and vulture, symbols of Upper and Lower Egypt, the two lands.

His eyes, gleaming green and heavily edged in kohl, stared out at us with deadly concentration. Though it had not occurred to me in the vestibule, immediately I understood why Pharaoh had agreed to see us so quickly—Moshe had claimed to be Merneptah's brother, therefore Seti feared a royal rival.

He called out a challenge before we were near enough to bow. "Who are you?" As his nasal voice echoed through the chamber, assorted priests, guards, wives, and courtiers fell silent. Feeling dingy and dusty among so many spotlessly clad women, I lifted my chin in defiance.

My attitude did not go unnoticed. Pharaoh frowned when his gaze crossed mine; then he turned his irritation on Moshe.

Moshe stepped forward and inclined his head. "I am called Moses."

"My father, the Divine Merneptah, never spoke of any *Moses.*" The king's mouth curled as if he wanted to spit. "What sort of a half-name is that? There are no records of that name in our temples, no cartouches bearing witness to Moses' presence in our great house."

Something like a smile flitted across Moshe's face. "You Egyptians are fond of scratching through inscriptions that bear record of anyone who displeased the king." He spoke flawless Egyptian in a low rumble that was at once authoritative and gentle. "But I have not come to advance my own petition. I have come to speak for the children of Israel, and to bring you a message from their God."

Laugh lines radiated from the corners of Pharaoh's eyes like cracks. "Does Egypt not have enough gods to suit the dusty ones? Must they now invent their own?"

Moshe struck the tiled floor with the bottom of his staff, sending a sharp crack through the echoing vastness of the throne room. Even I flinched at the sound.

"Thus says Yʜᴡʜ, the God of Israel." Moshe's voice boomed throughout the chamber. "'Send free my people, that they may hold a festival to me in the wilderness!'"

The king blinked, stared at Moshe for a long moment, then tipped back his head and hooted. The sound of laughter rolled into the room, spreading among his courtiers and women until the sounds of mirth surrounded us like a rising tide.

"Who is Yʜᴡʜ," Pharaoh said when he finally caught his breath, "that

I should hearken to his voice to send Israel free? I do not know YHWH, moreover, I will not send the mud people free!"

"The God of the Hebrews has met with us," Moshe answered, "so pray let us go a three days' journey into the wilderness, and let us slaughter offerings to YHWH our God lest he confront us with the pestilence or the sword!"

Pharaoh lifted a brow in amused contempt. "If you are confronted with a sword, it will be mine. But tell me—for what reason would you release the people from their tasks? Go, all of you, back to your work!"

The villagers behind me stirred at this, but Moshe and Aharon did not move. As solid as the granite statues outside the city walls, with perfect confidence they waited for Pharaoh to capitulate.

The king stood, anger blossoming in his thin face. "Who do you think you are, distracting these people from their tasks? Flee from my presence, and do not return!"

For a long moment Moshe and Aharon stood motionless; then Moshe slowly and deliberately turned his back on the king. The rest of us did so as well, then began to move with quick strides toward the bronze doors. But we did not walk so quickly that we failed to hear the king's parting words: "Tell the officers and brickyard overseers that they are no longer to give straw to the people to make the bricks as they did yesterday and the day before. Let the mud people go and gather straw for themselves! But you are to impose the same quota on them, you are not to subtract from it! For they are lax, they are lazy, therefore they beg to slaughter offerings to their god! So let the servitude weigh heavily on the men. They shall work harder so they will pay no more regard to false words!"

I knew Pharaoh was only a man . . . and in that moment I believed YHWH was eager to help us. But as the king's voice resonated throughout the hall designed to honor his glory, my courage shrank within me. I hurried my aging bones toward the door lest I drown in Pharaoh's power and be swept out on a tide of discouragement.

I had spent my entire life in a land where Pharaoh was god and his word law. Even in the presence of Moshe and Aharon, I could not deny that I feared the king . . . and the consequences of our rash actions.

∾

Nine days passed; then the elders who had danced in our village visited us again. This time, however, their thoughts were far from dancing. They complained to Aharon and the other elders, they criticized my youngest brother to anyone who would listen, and I heard many of them say that Moshe should return to the wilderness from which he had come, for his arrival had brought us nothing but grief.

Pharaoh's order had gone out the day we visited Pi-Ramesses, and the next day the overseers forced our men not only to make two thousand bricks each, but also to glean the flooded fields for enough straw to act as a binding agent with the heavy mud. The overseers pressed the children of Israel, chiding the brickmakers to work faster and harder, and most of our men had to rise before sunup to journey inland to find dry fields beyond the inundation's reach. A man could make bricks without straw, I learned, but the dense mud took longer to dry in the sun, and therefore the laborer would not produce his quota of finished bricks by sundown. Pure mud bricks were also more apt to crumble, and the overseers were quick to subtract broken bricks from a man's total. If a man came up short at day's end, the overseers and their sticks waited.

Not only were the individual laborers beaten, but the Israelite captains of work crews were thrashed when their teams fell short of the required number of bricks. After only a few days, a group of Israelite overseers traveled to Pi-Ramesses to complain to Pharaoh. Being warned of this visit, Moshe and Aharon journeyed to the king's city and waited outside the walls until their kinsmen appeared.

I did not go on that trip, but Moshe later told me what had happened. The leader of the Israelite captains had spat at his feet, then said, "May this YHWH see you and judge you harshly, for having made us reek in the nostrils of Pharaoh and his servants. You have put a sword into his hand, to kill us!"

Downcast and dispirited, that night Moshe sat at dinner in my humble house and idly ran his fingers over the vegetables I had prepared. He did not speak nor did he eat, but after dinner he went outside and trudged through the marshes behind the village. I crept after him, drawn as much by concern as by curiosity, and hid in a stand of reeds where I could hear his frantic pleas to the God I could not see.

"My Lord"—his voice brimmed with tears—"for what reason have you dealt so brutally with this people? For what reason have you sent me? Since I went to Pharaoh to speak in your name, he has dealt only ill with this people, and you have not even begun to rescue them!"

The wind blew past me with gentle moans, and I heard nothing . . . but from watching Moshe's face, I knew *he* heard something. As he squinted into the wind, lines appeared upon his forehead and at the corners of his eyes. "But, Lord! My own people won't listen to me, so how can I expect Pharaoh to hearken to my words? I am no orator!"

I heard nothing but the wind and the furious cricking of insects in the river grasses, but at length Moshe came back into the house. By the dim light of my only lamp, he told me what we would do. We would continue to visit Pharaoh, whenever and however YHWH commanded, until he decided to let our people go. First we would ask to be allowed to sacrifice—

"Why, Moshe," I interrupted, "are you asking for less than what God has promised? Did he not tell you we would be led to freedom in our own land? At first I thought you were trying to trick Pharaoh, but now you say God is telling you to ask only for a three-day journey."

Moshe cocked his head and squinted slightly as he considered my question. "I am asking what YHWH commands me to ask. I think God may be grading our requests in order to prepare Pharaoh's heart. YHWH knows how Pharaoh will respond, and he knows we will soon be free. But he also wants to prepare Pharaoh for what he will finally do. If the king were to grant our request for the three-day journey, we would be bound to honor the three-day limit; but by his refusal he is setting the stage for YHWH to do a mightier work."

I wasn't certain I understood, but there were many things about Moshe and his relationship to the Almighty that I did not comprehend. So I blew out the lamp and settled down to sleep, eager to see what God would do next.

✧

On the eleventh day, one full Egyptian week since our first visit to Pi-Ramesses, we returned to Pharaoh's palace and waited a full two hours before the king admitted our tired traveling party. Standing in the same spot he had occupied a week before, Moshe repeated his request from YHWH.

Pharaoh replied with a great deal more irritation than before. "Show me." His upper lip curled in derision. "Show me a sign to prove your god has power!"

Moshe pointed to the staff in Aharon's hand. "So you may know that YHWH has power," he said, his voice matching Pharaoh's in intensity, "behold!"

Aharon threw the staff on the floor, where it clattered and bounced, then . . . writhed. Twosre, the king's Great Royal Wife, shrieked as the thick staff became an equally thick cobra, which reared back its head and hissed pointedly at Pharaoh.

For the first time, respect gleamed in the king's eyes. Ignoring his screeching wife, he stiffened in his chair, never taking his eyes off the snake until Aharon calmly reached down and gripped the creature's tail. Instantly, the cobra stiffened and returned to the wood from which it had appeared.

Pharaoh tilted his head thoughtfully, then waggled a finger at his bevy of priests. "Priests of Wadjet, the serpent goddess!" He lifted his eyes to meet Moshe's. "Show these Hebrews that the gods of Egypt have equal power."

A trio of priests consulted a moment, then approached with the polished ebony walking sticks of wealthy men. With muttered incantations and great ceremony, they tossed their sticks on the floor and all three became black serpents. As the snakes slithered over the tiles, the king's courtiers squealed in feigned terror and scrambled toward the walls.

Smiling, Pharaoh lifted his gaze to us. "The world is full of gods." The corner of his mouth drooped. "Go away."

Without a word, Aharon dropped Moshe's staff; the worn branch again became a cobra. As the priests' snakes swam harmlessly over the slick tiles, the cobra attacked, swallowing the smaller serpents in quick, jerky gulps. The wide-eyed priests turned to Pharaoh in confusion, their faces flushing in shame.

Pharaoh did not look at them. "Go," he repeated, his voice constricted with anger. "Do not let me see you Hebrews in this room again."

Moshe and Aharon turned and led us away, but before we departed I noticed a Cushite woman peering at us from the fringe of the crowd in the king's audience chamber. She wore the simple garment of a slave, but her eyes were fixed upon Moshe, and on her face I saw wonder mingled with admiration.

Our visit had ended in defeat, but I found some consolation in the woman's expression. Moshe and Aharon might not have swayed Pharaoh with their signs and wonders, but they had managed to impress at least one of his palace slaves.

∽×∽

I slept like a dead woman that evening, but Moshe passed the night in prayer. When I fell asleep, he was sitting on his lambskin, his hands upon his crossed knees, his eyes closed. He said not a word, but his concentrated expression assured me he was not sleeping. He was communing with YHWH, and though I lay upon my straw pallet and strained my ears, I heard not a word.

He was still sitting in that position when I stirred in the gloom of dawn, but by the time the first rays of sunlight streamed through my open window, Moshe was ready to act. Swimming to full wakefulness when I heard sounds of movement, I sat up in time to see Moshe slipping his cloak over his tunic.

"YHWH has commanded me to go to Pharaoh this morning." He glanced toward me. "I am to meet him at the Nile with my staff. Aharon is to come, too."

I rose and reached for my veil. "I'll fetch him at once."

"Good." Moshe folded his hands and stared out at the eastern horizon, which was just beginning to brighten behind the thatched roofs of our homes. "We must leave soon."

Aharon was already awake when I reached his house, and Elisheba bid him farewell with a silent nod. As was my custom, I walked behind my brothers, not speaking as we strode swiftly toward the branch of the river that would take us to the gates of Pi-Ramesses.

I do not know how Moshe knew the king would go down to the river that morning, but we had been waiting on the riverbank only a short while when we heard the sound of trumpets. Feathery plumes moved behind a procession of soldiers; then Pharaoh and his guards appeared, surrounded by fan-bearing slaves.

Upon seeing us, Pharaoh halted, annoyance and irritation flooding his face. "I thought I told you I did not want to see you again." He glanced toward his guards. For an instant I feared he would have the warriors strike my brothers or take them prisoner, but Moshe stepped forward and took control of the situation.

"YHWH, the God of the children of Israel, has sent me to give you this message: 'Send free my people, that they may serve me in the wilderness!'" His voice rose on the wind like the mournful call of a wandering spirit. "But you have not hearkened to my voice. Thus says YHWH: 'By this shall you know that I am God: Here, with the staff that is in my hand, I will strike upon the water of the Nile, and it will change into blood. The fish that are in the water will die, the river will reek, and your people will be unable to drink water from the Nile.'"

Pharaoh stared, one corner of his mouth rising in a smirk. "You would command the great Hap-Ur, the river that makes Egypt fertile? You and your god do not have enough power, Moses of the Hebrews."

Moshe did not answer his challenge, but nodded to Aharon, who took Moshe's staff and stretched it out over the waters at their feet. He struck the waters of the Nile, and before the eyes of Pharaoh and all who watched, the water rippled, then blossomed with the horrid brightness of blood. Within the space of three breaths I saw fish bob to the surface, limp and unseeing upon a crimson carpet.

Understand this: I have seen the gray Egyptian floodwaters brighten to green as they recede and fill with plants from faraway places. I have seen the waters become orange as they flushed with soil from lands beyond Goshen. The Nile is a changeable river. But I had never seen it turn this bloody color, or felt the stench of it rise off the water in waves.

I brought my hand to my nostrils, for the water reeked with the metallic tang of spilled blood. Still, Pharaoh did not seem impressed. He tipped his head back, then uncrossed his arms long enough to summon one of his attendant priests. "Have you a pitcher of holy water with you?"

"Yes, my lord."

"Then show this Moses that you have power to equal his."

The priest—later I learned his name was Jannes—motioned to a slave who stood behind him with an alabaster pitcher. The priest dipped his hand into the water, held it up to display that his fingers came out wet, but clean, then murmured an incantation over the pitcher. Calling upon Great Hapi, god of the river, he clapped his hands over the pitcher, then poured its bloody contents across his startled slave's outstretched hand.

As he glared at Moshe and Aharon, Pharaoh's mouth tightened enough to wiggle the false beard upon his chin. "Be gone from me, and know this—I will never send your people free."

The waters of the Nile turned to blood at the worst possible time in the Egyptian calendar. We had returned to Egypt at the beginning of the inundation; when Yhwh struck the Nile, the floodwaters had not yet reached their crest. As the days passed, the entire valley between the deserts became a lake in which cities were islands, towns were islets, and dikes formed the roads. The terrified people of Mizraim, for whom the floodwaters had always meant life and fertility, found themselves surrounded by a sea of blood.

For a full week, the Egyptians sought locations where they could dig new wells, but most of the land lay under floodwaters. During this time, our men did not report to the brickyards—no one, not even the cruel overseers, wanted to face Pharaoh's builders with a load of bloody bricks.

So Moshe, Aharon, and the rest of the children of Israel waited in Goshen, where the water of the marshes sparkled as clear as before. Though our villages lay within walking distance from Pi-Ramesses, none of the Egyptians came near to drink. At dinner one night I remarked that they must be avoiding our villages out of pride, but Moshe gently reminded me that the average Egyptian scarcely knew of our existence.

"Pi-Ramesses is another world, and Thebes far beyond our realm." A look of nostalgia settled upon his face. "When I lived in Pharaoh's house,

I never took time to even consider the slaves who lived elsewhere." His brow furrowed as he looked at me. "It may sound heartless, Miryam, but you should know the truth. I did not scorn or dislike the children of Israel; I honestly never thought about them. Even so, the average Egyptian thinks only of his home and his family."

"Ignorance does not excuse their evil."

"No, it does not. But sometimes people have to be made aware that they are part of a system based upon injustice. The people who live in Memphis and Thebes have no idea what Pharaoh has done to the children of Israel in Goshen . . . but they will learn."

After the week had passed, Moshe again woke me at daybreak. Moving toward the window with a resolute look on his face, he nodded toward Aharon's house. "Today we go again to see Pharaoh."

I drew on my veil and ran to wake Elisheba. When she had roused Aharon, I strapped on my sandals and followed my brothers to Pi-Ramesses.

We again found Pharaoh at the river's edge, where the bloody waters had finally cleared. His arrogant smile faded when Moshe leaned on his staff and began to speak: "Thus says YHWH: 'Send free my people, that they may serve me! If you refuse to send them free, I will smite your entire territory with frogs. The Nile will swarm with them; they will ascend, they will come into your house, into your bedroom, upon your couch, into your servants' houses, in among your people, into your ovens and into your dough-pans, onto you, onto your people, onto all your servants will the frogs ascend!'"

Pharaoh regarded my brothers with a look of loathing, then crossed his arms and silently stared at the sparkling waters of the river.

Aharon stretched out his hand over the river of Egypt and a frog-horde ascended to cover the land. Not a few frogs, not a frog here and a frog there, but a wave of croaking creatures rose up out of the waters as if they had been waiting for my brother's signal.

Even Pharaoh could not disguise the disbelief in his eyes. The frogs were not alike—some were green and smooth, others black and bumpy. Some were mottled with yellow, like sunlight falling through a tree canopy; others looked out at us with red, bulging eyes. In the torrent of creatures I saw burrowing frogs, striped frogs, golden frogs, flat-headed flogs, tiny tree frogs, and big-bellied frogs the size of a man's outstretched palm.

They streamed forward, hopping and climbing over the bodies of decaying fish along the riverbank. How had they survived in the bloody waters that poisoned the fish?

Pharaoh gestured to another of his priests. "Jambres—show this Moses that our gods can perform the same miracle. Call upon Heket, goddess of regeneration and fertility."

Instantly obedient, the priest stepped forward. Muttering an incantation, he placed a small statue of the frog goddess into a standing puddle near Pharaoh's feet, then waved his hand over the idol. A moment later, frogs streamed from that puddle, too, though they were smaller than the frogs from the Nile.

Pharaoh nodded at his priest. "Very well. Now make them go away." But no matter how hard Jambres and the other priests chanted and clapped and waved their arms, frogs continued to pour from the puddle, the flooded river, the canals, the tributaries, and every source of water within sight. I looked at one of Pharaoh's servants who carried a goatskin water bag—a frog was climbing out of the ruched mouth of the carrier, his black eyes bulging above slippery limbs.

"Call upon Heket!" Pharaoh roared, lifting his feet in an agitated rhythm as the animals surged over his sandals. I glanced down. The stream of frogs had avoided Moshe, Aharon, and me—as if YHWH had erected an invisible shield around our bodies. But the animals were covering the Egyptians, climbing the warriors' shields, leaping on the guards' bare legs, crunching underfoot as Pharaoh's retinue tried, unsuccessfully, to shake the persistent creatures from their feet.

The priests called upon Heket, but their cries could not stem the endless tide of croakers. "I suppose," Moshe called, catching Pharaoh's eye, "that Heket is sleeping."

Without another word, he turned and led Aharon and me away. The frogs on the path fled from our approach as if we walked on feet of flame, while behind us Pharaoh's men cried out in fright and frustration as they slipped and fell into the living tide of frogs.

If the situation had not been so serious, I might have laughed. The Egyptians expected frogs during the inundation, and usually welcomed them, for frogs were a natural product of the sustaining floodwaters and therefore a harbinger of good harvests. But YHWH had turned Heket's power against the Egyptians, and I suspected they would not soon forget this lesson.

✑

Three days after the advance of the frog-horde, Elisheba came to my house and leaned into the window. "We have a visitor." A slight frown marred her gentle face. "She asks for the woman who walks with Moses."

The use of Moshe's Egyptian name should have been a clue, but still I was surprised when I stepped outside and saw a bewigged black woman wearing sheer white linen. She stood alone beneath a tamarisk tree, her arms crossed tightly over her chest, a simple leather bag hanging from her shoulder. Green shone from her painted eyelids, and a golden girdle at her waist emphasized its small size. Her face was round, but unlined, so I judged her to have lived about thirty years, and when she turned to greet me I noticed something familiar in her expression. It was not until she began to speak that I remembered who she was.

"I saw you," she spoke in courtly Egyptian, "when you came into Pharaoh's throne room. And now I have come because I have something for the man called Moses, something I must place in his hand alone."

I couldn't imagine what the woman meant, and all sorts of suspicions tightened my nerves. Furthermore, my Egyptian was not good.

"I am Miryam, Moshe's—Moses'—sister." I gave our visitor a tense smile. "Whatever you have for my brother, I will gladly give it to him."

"No." The woman took a step back, and her hands went reflexively to the leather pouch at her side. "I will give this only to Moses."

I looked at Elisheba. Switching to the language of our people, I asked, "Are there any men about?"

My sister-in-law's brow creased with worry. "There might be a few. None of them went to the brickyards on account of the frogs, but most are hunting in the marshes."

"Have you checked the path? Are there any signs of soldiers about?"

"No, none." Her voice drifted into a hushed whisper. "Do you fear a trap?"

"I'm not sure." Looking up, I gave the Cushite woman a stiff smile, then turned back to Elisheba. "Run and see if you can find one of our men. Tell him to find the others . . . and tell them to arm themselves."

Elisheba nodded rapidly, then held on to her veil with one hand as she darted behind the circle of houses. I turned to the visitor, then gestured toward my home. "Come," I said, speaking in my halting Egyptian. "I will get you some water. I am familiar with the long journey from Pi-Ramesses."

The woman gave me a grateful smile, but said nothing else as she followed me into the house. I pointed to the small three-legged stool, my only piece of real furniture. She sat on it while I drew water, then handed it to her in a stone cup.

She sipped from the cup, then held it on her palm. "I must admit," she said, lowering her gaze, "I had another reason for coming here. I have come not only to give something to Moses, but also to beg you for shelter. I do not wish to suffer the judgment of your god. I believe he is mightier than the gods of Egypt, and I believe he will overpower Pharaoh."

Folding my hands, I sat on my straw pallet and gave the woman a patient smile. "Who are you?"

The woman bowed her head. "I am called Femi. I am a handmaid to Twosre, the Great Royal Wife."

Instinctively, I threw up my hands. "A slave of the king's wife? You cannot stay here. Your mistress will send warriors to look for you. When they find you they will beat all of us for your foolishness."

Clasping her hands, the woman slipped from the stool to her knees. "Please, lady! I cannot stay in the palace! Pharaoh's house is overflowing with frogs! You cannot take a step without squashing one of them, and flattened frogs litter the floor tiles. Yesterday my mistress slipped and fell in the goo, then lay on her bed and wept for hours. Last night she demanded that we construct for her a linen tent so the frogs could not touch her!"

"I am sorry." I injected a note of firmness into my voice. "But you cannot stay here. If you want to run away, I suggest you go south, toward the land where your people come from."

Fresh misery darkened her face. "My people, lady, have been slaves for generations. My mother was a slave in Pharaoh's house, and my grandmother served in his temple, while my grandmother's mother served—"

"What, daughter, was your mother's name?"

The voice coming through the window was Moshe's, and the Egyptian language flowed from his tongue as if he had never left the Black Land.

The young woman turned at the sound of his voice, then lifted her arms and clutched at the dusty windowsill.

"Please, my lord Moses, don't send me away! I must escape Pharaoh's house. By my mother, Mandisa, my grandmother Intisar, and my grandmother's mother, Nema, I beg you to give me sanctuary!"

Moshe brought his hand to his lips, then stroked his beard. His long face and bright eyes, which could intimidate most men even from a good distance, filled with a beaten sadness. When he spoke again, his voice was rough. "Your grandmother's mother was called Nema?"

"Yes, my lord. She served Merytamon."

"She served my mother."

The woman looked up in wonder as tears streamed down her dark cheeks. "She did. And before Nema died, she gave something to Intisar, who gave it to Mandisa, who gave it to me."

Not wanting my brother to fall into a trap, I stood. "She says she has something for you, Moshe, but you should be careful—"

"Then I will come inside." Leaving the window, Moshe came through the door and caught the woman's hands before she could prostrate herself. "Femi." He lifted her to her feet. "What an honor to meet you. Nema was very special to me."

The woman's chin wobbled. "Thank you, my lord."

Moshe smiled. "I'm not your master, nor will I be. But you are welcome here."

"I have something for you."

I lifted my hand, about to protest, but Moshe silenced me with a swift glance.

Twisting her torso, Femi pulled the pouch to her stomach, then loosened the drawstrings and withdrew a sealed papyrus scroll. This she handed to Moshe, who stared at it in bewilderment.

"Nema wrote this?"

"Nema could not write, nor can I. This comes from the hand of Merytamon, who now lies in her tomb."

I stared at the woman, beginning to wonder just what she wanted of us. At first I'd thought she must be carrying an adder in that leather bag, but those fears fled the moment she began to loosen the drawstring. A scroll seemed harmless enough . . . unless it was a curse from one of Pharaoh's priests. But even if it was, I was certain Moshe and YHWH could defeat it.

Moshe took the scroll, weighed it in his palm, then looked at me.

"She will stay in our house," he said, apparently harboring no fears at all. "And when YHWH leads us out, she shall go with us, she and anyone else who wishes to serve our God. For he has sent me to liberate anyone who chooses him."

I opened my mouth, about to remind Moshe that he was a guest in *my* house, but at that moment Femi crumpled forward in an excess of gratitude. Rather than have her cling to Moshe, I stepped forward and caught her. I didn't know what to do next, but at that moment Elisheba came in, gathered the weeping woman into her arms, and led her outside. I watched them go—Elisheba murmuring soothing Hebrew words and Femi choking on her gratefulness in Egyptian—and wondered what they would ever find to talk about.

"Moshe." I turned to my brother. "Are you sure this is wise? If word of this woman gets out, every slave in Pharaoh's house will come running to Goshen. And she is not of our tribe, nor of our people. YHWH's covenant was with the children of Israel, not the tribes of Cush, yet you have welcomed her to join us as if—"

"Is YHWH not the creator of the entire world, and all that dwell within it?"

The question caught me off guard. I considered it a moment, then nodded. "Of course he is."

"Then he is God of Cush, too. And Nubia, and Midyan, and all the kingdoms around us. And he will prove himself loyal to all who worship and obey him."

I lifted a brow, about to ask how Moshe had gleaned this nugget of knowledge, but he cut me off with an uplifted hand. "See to her, please."

He pointed toward the girl. "Nema performed many kindnesses for me in my youth, and I will not allow this one to suffer."

He sat down, the papyrus scroll in his hand, and his unspoken message was clear—he wanted privacy in which to read.

Taking the hint, I stepped out of the house. As I moved toward Elisheba's hut, I found myself thinking that though my husband and father were long gone, still I found myself bending in obedience to a man. But such was the fate of women, even in the slave huts of Mizraim.

But Moshe wasn't just any man—I had seen the hand of God working in his life. Furthermore, cooperation flowed in both directions. Moshe would take me out of Mizraim, but I would help him in return. I had already fed him, clothed him, and provided my home as his shelter. Moshe had Aharon to be his interpreter, but he needed me as well, for I represented him to the women of Israel.

If Aharon would be Moshe's right hand, I would be his left. And together, the children of Amram and Yokheved would lead the children of Israel to freedom.

I did not see Moshe again until dinner. He and Aharon joined the men in a circle while we women tore apart the goat we had roasted in the firepit. Elisheba kept Femi by her side, and from the woman's awkwardness with the roasted carcass, I could tell she had certainly never served as her mistress's cook.

I took my turn at the stone oven, where the wind-tattered fire fitfully danced in the gathering darkness. We were fortunate with this meal—though none of Egypt's wonderful fruits were in season during the inundation, we had dried radishes, onions, and garlic to season the food. One of the women had produced a store of dried peas and beans, while several men brought fish they had caught while hunting in the marshes.

A light, jovial mood prevailed at dinner. One of the men joked that we were fortunate not to be eating frog, for the Egyptians had known little else for the last several days. Femi looked startled when we all laughed, and Elisheba made us all giggle anew when she tried to translate the joke with exaggerated pantomime.

Everyone seemed content, but Moshe seemed absolutely radiant. I found myself watching him, wondering at the cause of his joy, but could think of no news that would have changed his mood since leaving him that afternoon. He had been pleased to see Femi and happy to offer her shelter, but something had changed him since that hour.

One of the women threw a handful of dried rushes onto the fire, setting a stream of sparks free to race hot and red among the stars. I leaned toward Elisheba. "Did anyone else come to the village this afternoon? A runner from Pharaoh, perhaps?"

She threw me a startled glance. "I didn't see anyone. Why? Is there trouble?"

"No, no trouble." I waved the matter away, then sat down with the women to eat my portion. As I chewed on a piece of dark goat meat, careful to avoid the loose teeth in the right side of my jaw, comprehension seeped into my puzzlement. Of course! Moshe had received no other visitors, but Femi had given him a papyrus. I had convinced myself that it contained dreary, insignificant news, but apparently it had brightened his spirits.

I ate quickly, did my part to clean up the evening meal, then visited Rivka, who had promised to lend me a straw pallet she no longer used. I brought it back to my house and tossed it on the floor, and when Elisheba brought Femi to me, I explained that the pallet would serve as her bed. She nodded, obviously grateful for anything, then lay down. A few moments later, she slept.

I lay down, too, but did not rest. Darkness filled the house and pressed against my open eyes, but I would not sleep until I had talked to Moshe.

Finally, I heard him speaking to Aharon outside my window. They parted, and as Moshe opened the door, I leaned over to light the lamp.

The light wavered over his features. "You're awake, Miryam?"

"Shh." I pointed to the sleeping woman he had invited into our home. He lowered his voice. "Is something wrong?"

"You tell me." I sat up and leaned against the wall. "You seemed *different* at dinner, but you did not explain your smile." I tilted my head. "Did your mood have anything to do with the papyrus you received today?"

"Ah, sister, I'm glad you asked." Sinking to his lambskin, Moshe pulled the papyrus from a space between the thick wool and the wall. "This is a letter from Merytamon."

I chuckled. "Who was she writing?"

"Me."

Abruptly, I stopped laughing. "You? But she had to believe you were dead."

He smiled, and it was clear he hadn't noticed the subtle shift in my attitude. "She knew I would come back. She writes—wait, I'll read it to you."

Crossing his legs, Moshe scooted closer and hunched over the lamp, stretching the papyrus between his hands. "'Greetings, Most Favored Son and Honored Moses! I, Merytamon, write this with my own hand, in the confident hope that you will receive it when the God of the Hebrews brings you back to the Beautiful Land. For you will come back, Moses, I know it as surely as I know this God lives.

"'I should have realized the truth earlier. When you were but a small child, I took you before Pharaoh, where the priests forced you to undergo a test. By all the laws of the gods and nature, you should have failed, but in my moment of desperation I prayed to the God who had protected you in the river, the same God your Hebrew mother and father worshiped. And he kept you safe! That is why I know that you are still alive and you will return to Egypt where your destiny lies.

"'Many years have passed since we parted, dear son, and I have spent many hours thinking of you. I do not regret taking you into my heart and loving you, for now I understand that my act was the plan of your God. But I should never have lied to you or Pharaoh. I lied rather than trust the God who had kept you safe, and by lying I created a falsehood that wounded you in manhood. I pray you will forgive me. I pray that the Hebrew God will pardon me for my lack of trust.'"

Moshe paused as his voice broke, then drew a deep breath and continued reading more slowly, his finger moving lightly over the hieroglyphics. "'I loved you, Moses, as ever a mother can love a son, and I have not ceased to pray for you since you left. Pharaoh, unfortunately, is not inclined to forgiveness, so he has not called me back into his presence in all these many years. But I am not unhappy. I shall spend my remaining days in full confidence that your God will bring you back, and you will receive this letter.

"'Until then, know that I love you with everything in my heart. I shall always be your loving mother, Merytamon.'"

Strong words rose to my lips, words to question the right of an Egyptian to honor our God, but my objections fell away when I saw my brother's face. Moshe did not look up as he rolled the papyrus, but something had transformed his countenance, peeled back the strong veneer to reveal the vulnerability beneath it.

"She believed." He whispered the words like a prayer.

I lay down upon my pallet, propping my head on one bent arm as Moshe tucked the papyrus back into its hiding place.

Despite her youth, beauty, and generosity, I had never liked Merytamon. She had stolen my brother while her people murdered my loved ones . . . but she was dead in her tomb, and no longer a threat. I could remind Moshe of how her people had beaten, starved, and murdered us, but how could I deny him this small joy? He was my brother, and he needed me to lighten his load.

Like my mother and the other women of our clan, I would silently bear my burden. Like Sarah, Rachel, and Leah, I would remain in the shadows while our men stepped out to wrestle with God.

Such was the lot of women.

"Thank you, Moshe," I finally said, blowing out the lamp. "Sleep well."

When I look back, I recall the rest of the season of inundation as a test of wills. Frogs still swarmed over the Egyptian areas of the Black Land, but Pharaoh refused to call for Moshe, and Moshe refused to visit Pharaoh without an invitation. Pharaoh doubtless assumed that the frogs would retreat as the waters did, but as the waters began to retreat in the third month of akhet, the frogs remained.

By the arrival of proyet, the four-month season of seedtime and planting, the frogs were as numerous as ever. Women who journeyed to the marketplace outside Pi-Ramesses told me that the fertile fields stood empty, for the frogs lay so thickly upon the ground that the Egyptians could not plant.

Three days into the new month, Moshe received a summons from

Pharaoh. We went again to the king, and this time an official immediately escorted our traveling party into the chamber where Pharaoh sat upon his throne, his head bent in abject misery. Frogs, dead and alive, oozing and whole, covered the floor, and the sound of their ratcheting chorus rose to the barrel-vaulted ceiling and echoed throughout the vast chamber.

Only a handful of priests and guards stood beside Pharaoh this time. The courtiers, women, and slave girls had all vanished—to their rooms, I supposed, or behind linen tents such as Femi had described.

Pharaoh looked at Moshe. The thin line of his mouth clamped tight for a moment, and his gold-encircled throat bobbed once as he swallowed. "Plead with YHWH that he may remove the frogs from me and from my people. And I will send the people free, that they may slaughter offerings to their god."

A slow, almost teasing smile blossomed from out of Moshe's beard. "You set the time. When shall I plead for you, your servants, and your people, to cut off the frogs from you and your houses?"

Pharaoh narrowed his dark-rimmed eyes, understanding the unspoken implication. Anyone could say, "Frogs be gone," and eventually they would disappear. But never had they appeared in this number and with such suddenness, and never had they vanished at a man's word.

The king pressed his hands together. "On the morrow, let them be gone."

Moshe inclined his head. "Be it according to your word, then. In order that you may know there is no god like YHWH, the frogs shall remove from you, from your houses, from your servants, and from your people on the morrow. Only in the Nile shall they remain."

We left Pharaoh, and on the way back to our village Moshe stopped by the river's edge. Lifting his hands to the heavens, he cried out to YHWH, asking that the frogs be removed the next day.

The next morning, I drew on my veil and went to fetch my sister-in-law; then Elisheba and I walked to the river's edge. From the gates of the market to the vessels on the river, the Egyptians were busy cleaning up. Masters and slaves alike were wielding rakes, shovels, and hoes, piling up heaps upon heaps of dead frogs. The creatures had not disappeared, but died.

I had thought the dead fish stank, but the smell of dead and bloating frogs was far worse. Elisheba held her nose as she tugged on my arm. "Come, I've seen enough."

She did not have to beg me. We rejoiced on the journey home, for Pharaoh had agreed to Moshe's request, and YHWH's powerful hand had humbled once-mighty Mizraim.

Our lightheartedness did not last. The people of our clan had no sooner begun to pack our donkeys for the trip into the wilderness than a contingent of Egyptian overseers arrived with news that any man not reporting to the brickyards the next day would be beaten.

"Why?" Aharon stepped forward. "We are going to sacrifice to YHWH in the wilderness."

An armed captain answered Aharon's protest. "No, you're not. Pharaoh has given new orders. You Hebrews are not going anywhere."

The negotiation began again. Moshe journeyed to Pi-Ramesses, Pharaoh dared the Almighty to prove himself, and YHWH sent terrible pestilences to afflict the land once called "beautiful."

What can I say of the other plagues? Each was unendurable; each an offense to a particular Egyptian god. Gnats followed the frogs, a storm of small biting bugs that filled the air like grit swirling in a sandstorm. The priests of Geb, the earth god, could not replicate or control this pestilence, and they did not hesitate to tell Pharaoh that the gnats were "the finger of a god!"

But Pharaoh's heart remained strong-willed, and he did not relent.

When every man and beast in Mizraim wore red welts from gnat stings and every woman and child had choked on the buzzing creatures, Moshe and Aharon again met Pharaoh at the edge of the Nile. Moshe threatened Pharaoh and his people with flies; Pharaoh did not relent.

This time Moshe added, "In order that you may know that YHWH is God even in the heart of your land, there will be no insects in Goshen. God will make a clear distinction between your people and his people. On the morrow will this sign occur."

And it was so. Heavy swarms of stinging flies filled Pharaoh's house and all the houses of Mizraim, but not a single fly buzzed in the homes of the Israelites. Our houses, however, filled with a different sort of vermin—runaway slaves. Though only Femi shared my home, I heard stories of dozens of runaways who had fled to Goshen to escape the wrath of YHWH. They lived in our huts; they camped by our fire pits and the Nile's tributaries. Though most of our people welcomed them with hospitality, I considered them mere opportunists. If by some miracle Pharaoh's magicians managed to overcome YHWH, I was certain the slaves would return to Pharaoh's house. He was the god they knew, while YHWH was still an unknown entity.

After several days of flies, Pharaoh sent his guards to summon Aharon and Moshe. We went to the palace and again received Pharaoh's promise that our people would be allowed to go and slaughter offerings to our God . . . as long as we remained within Egypt's borders.

Moshe shook his head. "It would not be wise to do as you suggest, for your people would detest the offerings we sacrifice to our God. If we were to slaughter cattle before their eyes, would your people not stone us?"

Pharaoh pursed his lips, and I knew he had grasped Moshe's point. Though I did not understand everything in the Egyptians' confused theology, from my encounters with merchants in the marketplace, I knew they thought of certain bulls as gods incarnate. The sacred animals were used as oracles on festival days, with worshipers' questions answered by whether the bull ran to a "yes" or "no" passageway. The sacred Apis bull, one with a white crescent on its side or a white triangle on its forehead, was believed to have been born from a virgin cow impregnated by Ptah and conceived for a life of service in the temple. These animals were worshiped for a period of twenty-five years, then drowned, embalmed, and placed in a necropolis.

Moshe thumped the floor with his shepherd's staff. "Let us go a three days' journey into the wilderness. There we shall slaughter offerings to YHWH our God as he has commanded us."

I thought I saw a flicker of desperation in the king's eyes as he swatted a fly buzzing at his ear. "I will send you free and you may slaughter offerings to your god in the wilderness, only you are not to go far. Now hurry, and plead for me with your god!"

Moshe smiled. "When I go out from you I will plead with God. The insects will remove from Pharaoh, from his servants, and from his people on the morrow. But do not continue to trifle with us by not sending our people free to slaughter offerings to YHWH!"

We left the audience chamber, and Moshe pleaded with God. The flies had vanished by the next day, but with them went Pharaoh's willingness to release our people.

The confrontation continued. YHWH commanded Moshe to warn Pharaoh of the next plague, which would strike the livestock: horses, donkeys, camels, oxen, and sheep. The plague would not touch the flocks of Israel, but the animals of Egypt would suffer an exceedingly heavy pestilence.

The event came to pass just as YHWH had said. Among the Egyptians there was not a healthy animal to be found. The marketplaces emptied. The oxen used to haul marble slabs died; the milk-giving cattle died, and, most significantly, the Apis bulls died. I later learned that their caretakers, the priests of Ptah in Memphis, entered the animals' gilded stalls at sunrise to dress them in golden robes, but found every bull dead on the floor.

Pharaoh sent runners to inquire if our livestock had suffered the same fate, but even when he heard that the Hebrew animals survived, he refused to let our people go.

Then Moshe took a fistful of soot from a furnace and tossed it heavenward before Pharaoh's eyes. It blew in the wind, becoming a fine dust that covered all the land of Egypt, and every man, woman, and remaining beast developed boils. I saw dogs and cats slinking through the bulrushes, driven by the pain of their blisters and blains to seek solace in the Nile's cooling waters.

When Pharaoh next summoned us to his palace, he sat—uncomfortably, judging from his pained expression—upon a pillow of silk, but his priests could not stand beside him for the pain of the boils upon their feet. Yet even the sight of oozing sores on the faces of his favorite wife and son could not crack the hardness of Pharaoh's heart.

Then YHWH gave Moshe a new message for Pharaoh. As Egyptian and Israelite alike shivered in dread of what YHWH would do next, Moshe delivered the words of God: "Send free my people that they may serve me!

Indeed, this time I will send my blows upon your heart, and against your servants, and against your people, so you may know there is none like me throughout all the land. Indeed, by now I could have sent out my hand and struck you and your people with the pestilence, and you would have vanished from the earth; however, I have allowed you to withstand so you may see my power, and in order that your people might recount my name throughout all the land. But still you set yourself up over my people by not sending them free. So around this time tomorrow I will cause to rain down an exceedingly heavy hail, the like of which has never been in Egypt from the days of its founding until now! So now, send word! Give refuge to your livestock and to all that is yours in the field; all men and beasts who have not been gathered into the house, the hail will come down upon them, and they will die!"

As we returned to our village, the men of our clan told us that Moshe's warning had spread throughout Pi-Ramesses. The overseers had dismissed them early, without even counting the bricks, so each captain could hurry home to protect his remaining livestock—mostly goats, pigs, and nursing young that had been spared from the former plague. Not every Egyptian heeded Moshe's words, and not all had time to hear it.

At sunset that evening, Moshe strode to the bank of the Nile and lifted his staff toward the heavens. In response, YHWH rumbled the clouds, and fire flashed upon the earth. Hail stormed down upon Mizraim, a land that rarely saw rain and had never seen anything like this.

Drawn by the terrible sight, we climbed to a knoll on the path to Pi-Ramesses and looked toward the cultivated fields that lined the riverbank south of us. Hail poured from the sky, flattening the greening flax, pounding the young barley, and ripping through the tender green herbs as if YHWH had taken a great garden scythe to the fields. Tender young animals, left to fend for themselves in the hayfields, bleated under the blows of hail or were scorched by fire as it blazed intermittently from the heavens. Solid terebinth trees, some of which had stood from my childhood, split in the flash of lightning and flattened under the steady pounding of the hail.

The priests of Shu, god of the air, stood helpless in their temples as the heavens spewed fire and ice.

But in the land of Goshen, where we watched in quiet awe, neither hail, nor rain, nor fire fell.

Pharaoh did not wait for daylight to summon Moshe. After four hours of firestorm and hail, he sent a company of guards in chariots to fetch us. By the light of a burning sky we rode over earth pockmarked by the force of hail and scorched by fire. Even the walls of his palace had been scarred, but we moved untouched through the land of Mizraim and the city of Pi-Ramesses.

Once again we stood before Pharaoh in the audience chamber, lit now by a row of glowing rush torches. The king's face was lined with fatigue; and I could tell he had passed a sleepless night. Only two priests stood with him; their faces looked even more woebegone than his.

The king's voice was heavy in the nearly deserted room. "I have sinned. YHWH is the one in the right; my people and I are the ones in the wrong. Plead with YHWH! For enough is the god-thunder and this hail! Let me send you free—do not continue staying here!"

Moshe nodded soberly. "As soon as I have gone out of the city, I will spread out my hands to YHWH, who will stop the thunder and the hail. He does this in order that you may know the land, even Egypt, belongs to him." His eyes narrowed as he studied the weary king. "But as for you and your servants, I know well that you do not yet stand in fear before the face of YHWH."

I had hoped that the ensuing nocturnal silence would break Pharaoh's stony heart, but the next morning, when the balmy breath of dawn swept over us, Moshe told me that Pharaoh had again hardened his heart. When I asked him why God would allow the plagues to continue, his answer sent a tremor of mingled fear and anticipation through me.

"YHWH told me," he said as he sank to the floor to eat the meager meal I had spread before him, "that he has made Pharaoh's heart heavy with stubbornness in order that he may put signs among the children of Israel, in order that we may tell our children and our children's children how God dealt with Mizraim . . . so we may know without doubt that he is YHWH."

I could not believe that anyone living in Goshen could fail to realize YHWH's power, but few people had journeyed into the Egyptian areas to witness the devastation.

Moshe ate his bread and cheese, then together we went to Aharon's house. The three of us journeyed silently to Pi-Ramesses, a trail I had taken so frequently I could have followed it in the dark.

We found Pharaoh inside his audience chamber, collecting reports from officials on the extent of damage from the hailstorm. Without hesitation, Moshe launched into the message YHWH had told him to convey: "Thus says YHWH, God of the Hebrews: 'How long will you refuse to humble yourself before me? Send free my people, so they may serve me! But if you refuse to send my people free, on the morrow I will bring the locust-horde into your territory! They will cover the earth, so a man will not be able to see the ground. They will consume what is left of your crops, they will devour all the trees in the field, they will fill your houses, the houses of all your servants, and the houses of all Egypt, as neither your father nor your father's fathers have seen from the day of their occupying the soil until now.'"

When Pharaoh did not reply or even acknowledge Moshe's words, we turned and began to leave. Yet a commotion at the door halted our progress.

To my great surprise, the vizier of Lower Egypt, a tall, dour-faced man wearing a white robe trimmed in leopard fur, limped toward Pharaoh on feet that must have still borne the evidence of boils. In a clearly audible voice, he called, "How long shall these people be a snare to us? Send the men free so they may serve their god! Do you not yet realize that Egypt is lost?"

Something in his words must have stirred the king. "Stop the Hebrews!" Pharaoh called, extending his ceremonial flail. "Return them to me!"

A moment later Moshe, Aharon, and I again stood before the king. I slipped my hands into the sleeves of my robe, scarcely daring to hope the king would change his heart.

Pharaoh looked steadfastly at Moshe. "Go, serve YHWH your god. But first tell me—who, exactly, will go?"

Moshe dipped his head in a gesture of gratitude. "With our young ones and our elders we will go, with our sons and daughters. With our sheep and oxen we will go into the wilderness, for it is YHWH's pilgrimage festival for us."

Seti's face darkened with rage. "May YHWH be with you if you try to take your little ones along! I can see that your faces are set toward mischief! Never! Only the males may go and serve YHWH, for that is what you originally requested. Now leave me!"

With those words we were driven out of Pharaoh's presence. As we stepped outside the city walls, Moshe stretched out his staff over the land of Mizraim. YHWH sent an east wind against the land all that day and all night, and when the next morning dawned, the east wind had brought in the locust-horde.

Like a winged army, the locusts covered every measure of ground and consumed all the plants and all the fruit of trees remaining after the hail. The hailstorm had spared the unripened wheat and spelt, for their buds had not yet ripened, but now the locusts devoured the tender plants so not a single sliver of green remained in the black fields. As the locusts devoured the crops Mizraim needed to feed her people through the coming year, Pharaoh called for us.

Exuding weariness like a miasma, he rose from his throne, stepped from the dais, and met us on the tiled floor. He spoke in an apologetic tone. "I have sinned against YHWH your god, and against you. So now, tolerate my sin one more time and plead with YHWH so he may only remove this death from me!"

Moshe led us out of Pharaoh's presence and went outside to plead with God. The eastern wind reversed, carrying the locusts away.

When not one locust remained throughout all the territory of Mizraim, Moshe sent a message to Pharaoh: We were ready and trusted that we would be able to depart in peace. But YHWH again made Pharaoh's heart strong-willed, and he refused to set the children of Israel free.

Then Moshe stretched out his hand toward the kingdom of Amon-Re, god of the sun, and thick night moved over the land, an oily darkness that made breathing difficult and set the Egyptians' hearts to pounding. Lamplight could not penetrate the gloom, nor could torches. Even Pharaoh's astrologers, who testified of occasional brief periods of untimely darkness, could not explain why Amon-Re had been confined so long to his chambers in the underworld.

The unwavering night affected more than the living inhabitants of

Egypt. According to their religious beliefs, the souls of the dead came from their tombs at night and sought rest only when Re appeared as Khepri at dawn. Since Re had somehow been prevented from charting his usual course across the sky, the priests proclaimed that the souls of the dead could not seek their tombs. Trapped in darkness, they had to be wandering the western bank of the Nile, restless and irritated.

In the sunless cities of mortals, husbands could not see the wives who sat by their sides, and women were afraid to rise from their places lest they trip over their babies in the unyielding murk.

Yet in Goshen the sun continued to shine. We went about our business, grinding grain, tending our livestock, and hearing secondhand reports of the Egyptians' terror.

After three days, an abject Pharaoh sent for us. Before leaving our village, Moshe asked God to remove the darkness. We rode to Pi-Ramesses with chariot drivers who had crept toward us in dense darkness, though morning had streaked the sky of Goshen.

When we reached Pharaoh's house, the sun had just begun to creep over the rooftops of his royal city.

The king slouched before us, bleary-eyed and weary. "Go, serve YHWH. Even your little ones may go with you. But your sheep and your oxen shall remain here."

Moshe would not agree. "We must take our animals for slaughter-offerings to YHWH our God. Even our livestock must go with us, not a hoof may remain behind. We must use some of them to serve YHWH our God, and we will not know how we are to serve him until we arrive there."

Pharaoh, who had probably been planning to resupply his impoverished people with our herds, abruptly turned on Moshe in a rage that felt like a hot wind on the back of my neck. "Go from me, this instant! And be on your guard—you are not to see my face again, for on the day you do, you shall surely die!"

Moshe flushed to the roots of his hair. "You have spoken well. Indeed, I will not see your face again, not like this."

Moshe turned to go, but I remained in place, confused and annoyed by his sudden surrender. Was my brother giving up? Were we finished with the struggle? We had come so close; surely we could offer some compromise the king would accept. Perhaps we could leave half our herds, or only the firstborn of the flocks. . . .

I smiled when Moshe whirled to face the king again. He had not finished.

"Yнwн will cause . . . one more blow . . . to come upon Pharaoh and Egypt." He spoke in clipped, abrupt phrases, as if delivering a longer stream of words would dilute his concentration. "Afterward, he will send us free from this place. When he sends us free . . . it is finished. He will drive us, yes, drive us out of here, and we will go quickly."

Moshe's voice fell to an intense whisper, and strength flowed from a power born of conviction. "Thus says Yнwн: 'In the middle of the night I will go forth throughout the midst of Egypt, and every firstborn shall die throughout the land, from the firstborn of Pharaoh who sits on his throne to the firstborn of the maid who is behind the grindstone, and the firstborn of every beast. Then shall there be a cry throughout all the land, the like of which has never been heard, the like of which will never be heard again. But among all the children of Israel, it will be so peaceful not even a dog will bark.' Then you will know, yes, you will know that Yнwн makes a distinction between Egypt and Israel."

Pharaoh's eyes flashed. "Go!"

"I am going." A thin chill hung on the edge of my brother's last words. "But you should know that soon all the officials of Egypt will come running to *me*, they shall bow to *me*, saying 'Go out, you and all the people who follow in your footsteps!' Then I will go out, and you will not be able to stop me."

He delivered these final words in a hoarse whisper, as if they were too momentous to utter in a normal voice. His forecast of merciless death and destruction had frightened me, but I would soon discover I had nothing to fear. Pharaoh—he of the Great House, many wives, and many children—had far more to lose than I.

Moshe seemed preoccupied on the journey home, so neither Aharon nor I spoke. Aharon and I had lived in houses a stone's throw apart our entire lives; we usually knew what the other was thinking. Moshe was the enigma, confusing me at every turn.

Just before we reached the village, he extended his hand and stopped us on the path. "I must explain to you what YHWH will do next." He looked first at Aharon, then at me. "The elders of every clan must come to our village at once."

Aharon and I nodded in unison. Whatever YHWH had planned, we were ready.

"Many foreigners will join us tonight." Moshe placed a hand on Aharon's shoulder. "The words I spoke to Pharaoh will spread like locusts, and those who fear our God will come to us for safety. We must shelter them, and we must make ready for YHWH to visit the land of Egypt."

Aharon lifted his hand. "I will send runners. My sons will go at once."

"Send them. We must give the word of YHWH to our own people. So hurry, summon the elders, while I seek the Lord."

∾

With Moshe by his side, Aharon stood on an overturned clay pot, a large vessel that boosted him high above the anxious elders. While Moshe gave him the words of God, Aharon repeated them to the people: "Pick out, take for yourselves a lamb for your clans, and slay the animal. Then take a branch of hyssop, dip it into the blood which you shall catch in a basin, and touch the lintel and the two posts of your house with some of the blood. Now you are not to go out, any man from the entrance to his house, until daybreak on the morrow, for YHWH will deal blows to all Egypt. But when he sees the blood on the lintel and on the two posts of your doors, YHWH will pass over the entrance, and will not give the bringer-of-ruin permission to come into your houses to deal the death blow."

A flutter of alarm ran through the assembled group, but Aharon pressed on. "We are to keep this word as a law for ourselves and for our children, into the ages. Put on your traveling clothes before you eat." He touched the cloak that covered his tunic. "Check the straps on your sandals and be sure to put your clothing in something easy to carry.

"From now on, this month will be the first month of the year for our people. On the tenth day of this month, each family will choose a lamb, one lamb per household. The animal must be a one-year-old male, and wholly sound, without blemish. You shall keep the lamb safe until the evening of the fourteenth day of this first month. Then each family in the community will slaughter its lamb. You are to take some of the lamb's blood and smear it on the top and sides of the doorframe of the house where the lamb will be eaten. That evening you are to eat the flesh, roasted in fire; with matzo and bitter herbs you are to eat it. Do not eat any of it raw or boiled in water, but rather roasted in fire. And you are not to leave any of it until morning."

We stood in a quiet so deep the only sound was the gentle whisper of the wind stirring the ashes of our fire pit.

"Tonight and in years to come you are to eat the meal with your hips girded and your clothing ready, as though prepared for a long journey. You will wear your sandals, and carry your walking sticks in your hands. You will eat the food quickly, for this is the Lord's Passover. For on this night, YHWH will pass through the land of Mizraim and kill all the firstborn sons and firstborn male animals. He will execute judgment against all the gods of Egypt, for he is the Lord! The blood we have smeared on our doorposts will serve as a sign, and when he sees the blood, he will pass over us. This plague of death will not touch us when YHWH strikes the land of Egypt."

Femi did not speak our tongue, but she obviously understood Moshe's Akkadian, for she began to whimper. I sent her a sharp look of rebuke, then crossed my arms and ignored her distress. Why was she afraid? Moshe had promised to shelter her.

"When you come to the land which YHWH will give you," Aharon went on, translating Moshe's words, "you are to keep this service. When your children say to you, 'What does all this mean?' we will reply, 'It is the celebration of the Passover to YHWH, who passed over the houses of the children of Israel when he dealt the death-blow to Egypt, but our houses he rescued.'"

Aharon smiled as he looked around. "Remember this night, my brothers. On this fourteenth day of the month, God will deliver us from bondage."

Awed by this pronouncement, the elders bowed and did homage to YHWH, then rose and hurried back to their own villages.

With Moshe's warning ringing in our ears, I began to prepare the evening meal. I selected a young male lamb from the village herd; then, while Femi squeamishly held it, I cut the animal's throat above an earthenware basin.

Acting according to instructions Moshe had given us, I dressed the lamb quickly, then wrapped it in leaves and set it in the glowing coals of the fire pit. We had more mouths to feed than usual, for not only had Femi joined us, but two others as well. As I feared, runaway slaves had inundated our village, and so the elders had apportioned them out to each household. These foreign slaves did not understand all that had happened, but the signs and wonders had convinced them that YHWH was greater than the gods of Mizraim.

Our guests, a Nubian woman and her child, sat next to Femi. The child, a toddling girl, kept her wide eyes upon me as I chopped the herbs.

As the sun lowered in the west, I turned toward the door in time to see Moshe dip a branch into the basin of blood. First he stroked the lintel, then he moved the stick from side to side, splashing blood upon the doorposts. The Nubian woman cried out as blood began to drip down the doorframe, then muttered some sort of incantation in a foreign tongue. Reassuring her with a small smile, Moshe came inside and sat down for the meal.

When the lamb had finished roasting, we ate it off the bone, dipping pieces of the meat in bowls of bitter herbs. We ate bread from Elisheba's basket, for I had made no bread that day.

Moshe smiled at me. "On the morrow women will bind their kneading-troughs in their clothing and carry them upon their shoulders." He dipped a bit of lamb into a bowl of greens from my garden plot. "There will be no time for their bread to rise."

We listened, our ears straining for unusual noises in the night, but like blood out of a wound, silence welled from our homes into the courtyard. On any other night we would have heard the sounds of women opening their doors to splash dirty water onto the ground, the wheedling voices of tired children, and the baritone rumbles of men who gathered at the livestock pen. Yet on that night we remained inside, speaking in hushed voices, our hearts in our throats as our eyes gravitated to the crimson splashes of blood on the lintel and doorposts.

After eating, as our guests stretched out to sleep on the floor, Moshe sat against the wall, his eyes closed, his forearms resting casually on his crossed legs. I could neither sit nor sleep, for my spirit roiled within me. I knew Yʜwʜ could do miracles—had I not seen them with my own eyes? But could he truly deliver us in one night?

Creeping to the window, I peered out into the moonlit courtyard, afraid to lean forward lest the wandering spirit of destruction lop off my head. I could see nothing in the darkness beyond—no stars, no moon, no movement. Nothing but dense black and the heavy sound of silence.

Sighing, I lay upon my pallet and stared into the dark. The Nubian woman's child whimpered; the mother clapped her hand over its mouth. Femi said nothing, but her jiggling leg creaked the straw in her pallet, broadcasting her anxieties to the entire room.

Somehow, I slept.

Later I would learn that at midnight, in one fatal moment, Yʜwʜ slaughtered every firstborn male in the land of Mizraim, from the firstborn son of Pharaoh to the firstborn of the captive in the king's prison pit. The firstborn of every surviving beast died, too, from the new calves in their sheltered pens to the cats in the temple of Bastet.

Sorrow reigned in every house, for Egyptians married and divorced freely. One family woke to find three boys dead, for each had been the firstborn of a different mother. Many children awoke to find their fathers and grandfathers cold and lifeless, for both had been the openers of their mothers' wombs.

But no house bore greater sorrow than Pharaoh's. For the second to call himself Seti had more than thirty wives and concubines. Though the king himself had only one firstborn son, Seti-Merneptah, twelve of his sons had been the firstborn of his women.

Such a wailing issued from the king's house! They say the walls themselves wept with heartbreak. Twosre, the Great Royal Wife, smashed her idols and tore the hair from her head, while a lovely concubine from Syria threw herself into the ink-black Nile and drowned in her grief.

Pharaoh rose in the dark and listened to the terrible cry that shattered the night silence. For throughout all the Beautiful Land, not a single house had escaped the resolute hand of the Destroyer.

The king sent chariots to fetch Moshe and Aharon, but I knew nothing of it until Moshe gently shook my foot. "Let us see what YHWH hath wrought."

Moving silently so I would not disturb the others, I drew on my veil and followed the chariot-drivers.

As the walls of Pi-Ramesses rose into view, we began to hear wailing. The moon, a bloodred circle hovering near the horizon, now lent its light, so we could see dead animals on the side of the road. But I will never forget the sound of that journey—dreadful ululations of mourning rent the night, rising like ghostly howls from the distant villages and making my heart thump almost painfully in my chest.

Depositing us at the city gate, the three chariot-drivers made no move to escort us to the palace. Without being told, I knew why—they wanted nothing to do with those who spoke for the God of the Hebrews. We collected our thoughts beside the twin granite statues of Ramesses, then walked into the city, steeling ourselves as the terrible cries intensified.

As we moved toward the avenue of the temples, however, an eerie stillness prevailed, and the silence surrounding Pharaoh's palace was as thick as fog. The guards who usually stood at the gate had disappeared, either victims of the Destroyer or caught up in their own mourning.

"Tonight," Moshe murmured as we passed through the open gate, "the people whose lives centered on preparing for death have met the God who is more powerful than the keepers of the underworld."

The light of flickering torches revealed an empty vestibule. We slipped silently over the marble floors, then paused at the threshold of the king's audience chamber. The bronze doors yawned open, and a single torch glimmered within, casting shadows that seemed to animate the murals on the wall.

We found the king sitting cross-legged on the floor, staring up at the painting of himself, his wife, and his son offering sacrifices to Amon-Re. No courtiers lingered at his side; no priests waited in the shadows. The confident king who had taunted us before an audience of priests, nobles, and slaves sat with bent shoulders and red-rimmed eyes, staring at a picture of the treasure he had lost.

He heard us, for he trembled at the sound of our footsteps, but his gaze did not waver. "Go." In a voice fainter than air, he added, "Go out from among my people, you and the children of Israel. Go and serve YHWH according to your words, even your sheep, even your oxen. Take everything you have spoken of and go."

He looked at us, his eyes damp with pain; then the king of the world's mightiest nation gave utterance to one final plea: "And bring a blessing even on me."

ᏕᏍ

The sun had begun to brighten the sky by the time we returned to our village. Questioning faces peered at us through the open windows, and Moshe did not hesitate to trumpet the news: "Rejoice! For today YHWH has set his people free!"

"Take your belongings and move toward the river," Aharon called with rare exuberance. "And speak to the Egyptians you pass by. Let each man ask for objects of silver, each woman for objects of gold. And the Lord will cause them to give to you with gladness!"

Thus we came out of Mizraim, driving our herds before us. As the Lord had commanded, we stopped at the houses of the Egyptians we had served for generations, but we did not even have to ask for things—people gave us gold, silver, and garments; they pressed bowls and pottery into our hands and bid us take our leave of them in peace. The children of Israel walked out of Mizraim in a single day, more than six hundred thousand men, their wives, their little ones, and their livestock. Moreover, just as Moshe predicted, we women carried our kneading bowls upon our backs, for the dough we had mixed that morning had no time to rise. YHWH's deliverance had been swift and sudden.

But not unexpected, especially among the old ones. The most-beloved son of Yaakov, known to the Egyptians as Zaphenath-paneah, had brought our people into Mizraim during a time of famine. Upon his deathbed, the renowned Yosef had made his descendants swear that they would carry his body out of Mizraim: "When God takes account of you, bring my bones up from here!"

Finally, the day Yosef had predicted arrived. Eight unmarried men from the clans of Ephraim and Manasseh took an ox-drawn sledge to the stone tomb where Yosef's mummy rested, then broke the seal and dragged the sarcophagus onto the sledge. While the Egyptians watched in awed silence, the descendants of Yosef guided the sledge to a place of honor in our procession.

As we assembled at the river's edge outside Pi-Ramesses, the sky, which had been a faultless curve of blue, filled with floating blankets of clouds. While we tipped our heads back to stare in awe, the clouds congealed into a single pillar, suspended in the sky like a column from one of Pharaoh's temples.

Wearing that curious inward expression he adopted whenever he heard the voice of YHWH, Moshe called the cloud the *Shekinah,* the evidence of God's presence, and told us to follow.

The cloud moved ahead of us at a steady pace, drawing us behind it. I had begun to worry about how we would cross the Nile at Pi-Ramesses, but the pillar of cloud led us to a marshy place where the water scarcely came up to our ankles. The children squealed with delight, the animals paused to drink, and we women wet our veils in the cool water, for this was the season of drought and hot weather.

As we streamed across the river, the Shekinah moved again, leading our people in a joyous trek . . . southward.

Having journeyed into the wilderness with Aharon, I knew this was not the most direct route to the land YHWH had promised Avraham. Leaving Femi with Elisheba, I lifted my tunic and strode ahead to catch up with Moshe, who walked behind the pillar.

I tugged on his sleeve. "Why does the cloud lead us toward the wilderness? They say the King's Highway is a far shorter route to Canaan."

Moshe nodded as if he had anticipated my question. "The King's Highway leads through the land of the Philistines, and it is heavily fortified. Our people are not prepared to fight."

I could not argue with that observation, so I clamped off the protests that gurgled in my throat. And as we left the emerald valley that had experienced so much destruction, I felt my heart begin to lighten. YHWH had promised to deliver us, and he had kept his word. With such a powerful God to aid us, how could any of us doubt him?

I soon learned that the human heart is a very fickle thing.

⇜

We spent our first night as free people at a place called Succoth. Mass confusion reigned as we settled into a camp, but Moshe divided us by clan
into groups of fifty. I worried that we shouldn't take time to deal with
organizational tasks so close to Pharaoh's capital, but the Shekinah
remained above us, glowing with fiery brilliance throughout the night.
The pillar lit the darkness, an unexpected blessing, for we had left in such
haste that we had packed few lamps and even fewer pitchers of oil. We
had no tents, either, so our women scrambled to devise some sort of covering for their families.

Fortunately, the weather was warm and our spirits buoyant. We slept
that first night under the stars, and traveled the next day under a bright sun
that seemed less punishing than when it had baked us in Mizraim.

We spent our second night at a place called Etham; then Moshe called
us together. "In order that YHWH may be glorified through Pharaoh and
all his army," he warned, "YHWH will once again harden Pharaoh's heart,
and he will chase after us. God has planned this so he will receive great
glory at the expense of Pharaoh and his armies. After this, the Egyptians
will know that YHWH is the Lord."

Moshe dismissed us; the cloud moved forward and we followed. As
we progressed I breathed in the tang of salty sea air . . . and came to an
abrupt halt, my heart thudding in my chest. Moshe had said Pharaoh
would pursue us today . . . but we were moving toward the sea.

I hurried toward Moshe as quickly as my eighty-eight-year-old limbs
would allow. I was panting by the time I drew near enough to speak.
"Brother, is it wise to march beside the sea when we are expecting an attack?"

Moshe's dark eyes flashed a gentle but firm warning. "Are you questioning YHWH, Miryam?"

"I'm not questioning . . . just curious. And thinking it might be better
if we marched toward the west. If we change course, surely the Shekinah
will go with us—"

"No." He pointed at the pillar above his head, hovering like the finger
of God. "We have only to follow the Presence, and all will be well. Obey,
Miryam, and believe."

I halted in midstep, purposely falling behind as I drew a deep breath and reminded myself to be patient. Despite his strong presence, in many ways Moshe was as dependent as a child. I had been his nursemaid as a baby, Pharaoh's daughter had spoiled him as a youth, the Midianite woman had obviously coddled him in the wilderness, and now YHWH was directing his every step.

Surely God would honor Moshe if he demonstrated a little self-reliance!

Propping my hands on my hips, I turned to see if I could spy Elisheba and Aharon among the crowd. They would certainly understand my irritation. They had grown up in Goshen, where no one enjoyed a pampered childhood. The silver provided by Pharaoh's daughter had given my family an advantage in the marketplace, but we shared our bounty with the entire village. The trials of Mizraim had taught us to take the little we had been given and multiply it through hard work.

"Every jar must stand on its own bottom," my father always said. So I had to develop my own strength and wits, and those qualities had served me well through the years. I had lost both parents, a husband, and a child, yet I was still standing.

What would support Moshe if YHWH decided to depart as abruptly as he had come?

While I pondered Moshe's unfailing dependence, my brother's words were being fulfilled in Mizraim. Fueled by regret and a desire for revenge, Pharaoh called for his chariot teams and assembled his warriors. By the time we were settling into our camp by the sea, six hundred chariots were churning up the dust outside Pi-Ramesses, each carrying a team of three: a driver, an archer, and a spearman. Then all of Pharaoh's army set out in pursuit.

The sun had just begun to lower in the west when we saw the swirling dust heralding their approach. Despite Moshe's assurance, fear swept through the camp like a whirlwind. Dozens of elders ran to our tent, crying out for help. Many of them railed against Moshe: "Is it because there are no graves in Mizraim that you brought us out to die in the wilderness? Didn't we tell you to leave us alone? Being enslaved was better than dying in this wilderness!"

But Moshe did not waver. As the chariots of Egypt streamed over the dunes we had crossed hours before, Moshe lifted his hand. "Do not be afraid! Stand fast and see the deliverance YHWH will work for you today! Look at Pharaoh's warriors, watch them approach! For as you see Egypt now, you will never see it again! YHWH himself will make war for you—be still and behold!"

I watched in anxious fascination as the Shekinah cloud advanced toward the Egyptians, then settled over the empty space between us. As the sun hastened toward its setting in the west, the pillar of cloud filled with flame and unfurled like a curtain, becoming a wall of blazing protection between us and Pharaoh's army.

As Moshe turned and extended his shepherd's staff toward the sea, a strong easterly wind began to blow. The wind blew all that night, plastering our veils to our heads, ruffling the walls of our scanty tents, and scouring our skin with sand. We huddled in the fire-tinted darkness, trying to calm our hearts enough to sleep, but rest was impossible for all but the youngest children. Every so often I would turn on my blanket and look toward the north, where I could see the roiling shimmer of flames.

But when the sun began to rise, we stared seaward in stupefaction. The sea had not disappeared, but the wind had pushed its waters to the north and south, leaving a trail wide enough for twenty men and oxen to pass abreast.

Old men and little children alike gaped at the sight. The men who had grumbled against Moshe now looked at him with surprised respect in their eyes.

"See here!" Aharon called, striding down to the water's edge. "YHWH has given you dry land to walk upon!"

We did not delay. With the eager hearts of astounded children, we gathered our belongings, our flocks, and our little ones. We moved across the seabed clan by clan, company by company.

I stood on the western bank with my brothers, calling encouragement to the women and occasionally looking back at the Shekinah, which still blocked the Egyptian army. Moshe noticed my wayward glance. "YHWH is throwing them into confusion. They know the Lord is fighting for us."

"How much longer will they wait?"

Moshe looked toward the eastern bank. "When the last of our people are safe, the cloudbank will lift."

Moshe, Aharon, and I were among the last to cross the dry seabed. As befitting a leader, Moshe walked with a slow and stately tread. I kept pace with him, but struggled to keep from glancing over my shoulder to see if the Egyptians had burst through the cloud.

When we finally climbed the opposite bank, Moshe turned. As he did, the cloud on the opposite shore began to rise, then dissipated into the atmosphere.

A thrill of frightened anticipation touched my spine. Atop the hills of Pi-hahiroth we could see the mighty chariots of Egypt gleaming in the scorching rays of the sun. For an instant I thought they would not charge, for surely they now recognized the power of our God, but seeing us safely on the other side of the sea seemed to have no effect. Like a stampeding herd breaking through a fence, the front line of chariots advanced with hooves thundering. Shouting in triumph, the warriors of Egypt rolled over the sand where we had camped and approached the sea-path we had just crossed. There they halted, their horses whickering restlessly as the captains shouted orders and formed them into lines of ten abreast—narrow enough to fit between the walls of water.

My uneasiness swelled into alarm when I saw Pharaoh wearing the blue war crown. As regal and awe-inspiring in battle as he had been in his throne room, Seti rode in a golden conveyance drawn by two white horses. He pulled his vehicle into the front position, then lifted his arm, leading the chariots into the sea. Onward they came, row upon row, closing the distance between us. Ten chariots, twenty, thirty . . .

I held my breath, losing count as the opposite shore emptied. Pharaoh drew closer, near enough that I could see the determined arch of his brow and the vulture upon his war helmet. When he looked directly at the rock where Moshe, Aharon, and I stood, that proud mouth curled in derision. He reached for his bow, then lifted his hand for an arrow, which his servant placed in his palm. A cold panic prickled down my spine as Pharaoh notched the arrow against the string.

From the corner of my eye, I saw Moshe lift his staff, and something in that wordless gesture gave the walls of water permission to return to their

places. They roared in collapse, crashing down upon the Egyptians . . .
and YHWH crushed the Egyptians in the midst of the sea.

The waters churned, covering the chariots and the warriors of
Pharaoh's army until not one of them remained . . . not even the king.
Though we had crossed upon dry land, the pride, power, and Pharaoh of
Egypt drowned in the sea.

I don't know how long we stood there watching. Something in me
feared that Pharaoh would rise up out of the water, for his magicians and
priests had not been completely without power, but when we saw
Egyptian dead turning in the wavewash, we knew YHWH had defeated
Mizraim with a firm and final hand. In that moment, even the most skeptical of our people trusted in YHWH and in Moshe, his servant.

That night, we divided into groups for worship—Moshe and Aharon
with the men in one circle, the women and I in another. Then, in his still-
halting Hebrew, Moshe sang a song of praise unto the Lord:

> I will sing to YHWH,
> For he has triumphed, yes, triumphed, the horse and its
> charioteer he flung into the sea!
> My fierce might and strength is YAH,
> He has become deliverance for me.
> This is my God—I honor him,
> The God of my father—I exalt him.
> YHWH is a man of war,
> YHWH is his name!
> Pharaoh's chariots and his army
> He hurled into the sea,
> His choicest teams-of-three
> Sank in the Red Sea.
> Oceans covered them,
> They went down in the depths
> Like a stone.
> Your right hand, O YHWH,
> Majestic in power,
> Your right hand, O YHWH,

Shattered the enemy.
In your great triumph
You smashed your foes
You sent forth your fury,
Consumed them like chaff.
By the breath of your nostrils
The waters piled up,
The gushing streams stood up like a dam,
The oceans congealed in the heart of the sea.
Uttered the enemy:
I will pursue,
Overtake,
And apportion the plunder,
My greed will be filled on them,
My sword I will draw,
My hand—dispossess them!
You blew with your breath,
The sea covered them,
They plunged down like lead
In majestic waters.
Who is like you among the gods, O YHWH?
Who is like you, majestic among the holy ones,
Feared One of praises, Doer of Wonders!
You stretched out your right-hand,
The Underworld swallowed them.
You led in your faithfulness
Your people redeemed,
Guided them in your fierce might
To your holy pasture.
For Pharaoh's horses came with their chariots and riders
into the sea,
But YHWH turned back the sea's waters upon them,
And the children of Israel went upon the dry land
Through the midst of the sea.

As the men danced in celebration, I took up a tambourine and led the women in a song to echo the men's praises. "Sing to YHWH," I shouted to my sisters, "for he has triumphed, yes, triumphed. The horse and its charioteer he has flung into the sea!"

Later, as I reflected upon the incident that brought about our final and irrevocable salvation from Mizraim, I realized a nation had been born that day. As a child passes out of its mother's watery womb, a ragtag collection of clans descended from Avraham passed through the waters of the Red Sea and emerged as Israel, a nation without territory, allies, or a king.

But we had YHWH, our God; we had Moshe, his emissary; and we had the promise of land to call our own. And that, at least for a while, was enough.

After a night's sleep repaired the happy exhaustion ensuing from our celebration, we followed the divine Shekinah through the wilderness of Shur. During the journey we emptied our water bags, and three days later we were so parched I would have been happy to drown myself along with Pharaoh.

Our spirits lifted when we spied an oasis in the distance—a sweet spot ringed with fringed palm trees, acacias, junipers, and leafy green shrubs. Our phrase for oasis is *naot midbar*, or "beautiful place of desert," and the name fit this lovely spot. Delirious with the thought of water upon our dry tongues, we quickened our steps. When we reached the spring, however, we found the water clouded and white, undrinkable. We would later call this place Mara, a name meaning "bitter," but at the time the word also described our hearts.

I have been dreadfully hungry on occasion, but never in Goshen did I know true thirst. The marshes had provided us with all the fresh water we needed, and in the season of inundation the problem was always too much water, not too little.

At Mara I learned that hunger bears no resemblance to thirst. When the body lacks water, the tongue swells, the heart pounds, and the skin withers far beyond the ravages imposed by time. I pinched the age-spotted skin on the back of my hand and idly noted that the uplifted ridge remained in place, for my skin had completely lost its elasticity.

When they tasted the bitter water, the people began to grumble. Again they wailed that Moshe had brought them into the wilderness to die, and again I felt my heart breaking at the sound of insurrection. Had they not seen what YHWH could do? Did they not see the sign of his presence in the cloud overhead?

But a desperately thirsty man will not listen to reason . . . and neither will a doubtful heart. Distressed by thirst myself, I began to wonder why God was waiting. Surely he knew we were thirsty—he had demonstrated that he knew everything, even the heart of kings. He had led us to this dry place, and he had to know the water here was foul. So why was he making us suffer with thirst?

Had Moshe done something wrong? Had he been tricked by one of the gods worshiped by his pagan father-in-law? Had some deceptive god of Egypt led us out here to die in a malicious act of revenge? Moshe had not listened to me or the elders, but had relied completely on the voice only he could hear. What if that voice had led him astray?

Frustrated by the people's complaints, Moshe cried out to YHWH, who directed him to a shittah tree by the water's edge. Moshe threw a branch of shittimwood into the pool, and within moments the water sparkled with such clarity that we were able to see the bubbling mouth of the spring in the rocks below.

"Drink." A shadow of annoyance crossed Moshe's face as he turned to face the assembled elders. "Water your flocks. And then listen to the word of the Lord."

When we had satisfied our thirst, Moshe bade us sit around him in companies while he climbed onto a rock. "If you will hearken," his voice rang over the oasis, "to the voice of YHWH your God, and do what is right in his eyes, giving ear to his commandments and keeping all his laws, all the sicknesses he imposed upon Mizraim he will not impose upon you. For he is YHWH, your healer."

Indeed, he was. I closed my eyes and let the words of YHWH, like the branch, cure the bitter doubt that had crept into my soul.

∿

Led by the visible majesty of YHWH's divine presence, we moved on. We camped at beautiful Elim, a palm-fringed oasis rich with twelve springs of water (almost as if YHWH were blessing us with abundance after our complaints), then we moved to the wilderness of Syn, between Elim and the Mountain of God at Sinai.

There we ran out of bread. We had carried jars of grain and oil with us as we left Mizraim, and though we knew those containers would eventually be emptied, I suppose we had hoped for a more direct route to the land God had promised. We possessed meat in abundance, but we had already slaughtered a number of animals in order to obtain food and skins for our tents. We dared not slaughter more because a certain number of livestock had to be preserved for milking, breeding, and bartering.

The grumbling clans sent representatives to Moshe and Aharon, who stood outside our tent and listened to their protests.

"Would that we had died by the hand of YHWH in the land of Mizraim," a man from the clan of Manasseh grumbled. "At least there we sat by flesh pots and ate bread until we were satisfied! But you have brought us into this wilderness to bring death by starvation to this entire assembly!"

One by one they complained, some decrying the lack of meat, some the lack of bread, others the lack of herbs and spices. Finally, Moshe put up his hand and withdrew to commune with YHWH. The assembly waited in silence for the space of an hour; then Moshe returned. Because he had not yet mastered our tongue, he called upon Aharon to translate the words of YHWH.

"God will make bread rain down upon you from the heavens," Moshe told us through Aharon. "You shall go out and glean each day's amount in its day, but on the sixth day, you should pick up a double portion compared to what you glean day after day. At sunset today you will know that YHWH brought you out of the land of Mizraim, and at daybreak you will see the glory of YHWH, when he hearkens to your grumblings."

He couldn't help adding a personal rebuke: "And what are we, that you grumble against us? You are complaining against the Lord."

As Aharon spoke, we could see the Shekinah cloud hovering over the desert, and the awesome glory of the Lord glowing within it.

At sunset the wonder Moshe had predicted came to pass. Without warning, a flock of quail flew in from the north and blackened the sky with their beating wings. They settled on the ground like a thick blanket, delighting everyone who had hungered for meat. Coated in mud and set in coals, they would bake beautifully.

We had not seen the end of God's provision. The next morning, at daybreak, a layer of heavy dew covered the camp. When the moisture evaporated, we could see something as fine as hoar frost upon the land. Drawn by curiosity, we ventured out, and nearly every person had the same reaction: "What is it?" The question was pronounced *mahn hu* in our tongue, and that is what the white substance became: manna.

Speaking through Aharon, Moshe told us, "This is the bread YHWH has given you for eating. Glean it from the earth, each man according to what he can eat, an omer per person. Take enough for all those in your tent."

So we did. We gleaned according to our hunger, plucking the substance from the dew-damp sands, and each morning YHWH sent exactly the amount we needed. The desert sun melted the manna we did not pick up, so we had to gather in the morning, and Moshe warned us not to reserve the food. Some of our people discovered why—even when protected in a covered pot, day-old manna stank and writhed with maggots. But on the sixth day, when we obeyed the Lord's command and gathered a double portion, the manna stayed fresh.

"The seventh day," Moshe told us, "is a Sabbath for YHWH, and you shall not glean or work in it. Forget how you slaved in Egypt—now you will rest on the seventh day, for it is holy unto the Lord."

Femi and I experimented with the manna, discovering that we could bake it, boil it, or eat it raw. Almost pure white, it looked like a clump of coriander seeds and tasted like a honey-flavored wafer.

YHWH told Moshe to have Aharon take a container and put an omer of manna in it for safekeeping, so future generations would know how God provided for us in the wilderness. I took great comfort in that command, for it assured me our people would survive.

For there were occasions, especially in the savage wilds, when I wondered if our people would know a future at all.

⟳

After the wilderness of Syn, the glory of God led us to a place called

Refidim, a barren spot far from any spring-fed oasis. The mountains were higher here, and crowned with sharp, angular peaks. After the miracle at Mara and the bounty of Elim, I couldn't believe YHWH would direct us to another parched desert. Hadn't we learned the lesson of water?

Apparently not. While I struck out to look for hidden rivulets and streams in the surrounding rocks, the clans sent representatives to Moshe and Aharon. By the time I arrived back in camp, their complaints had escalated to quarrels.

Moshe fled to the foothills to avoid the angry crowd, and as I climbed the rocks to ask him a question, I overheard his impassioned debate with YHWH. "What shall I do with this people?" he shouted, apparently not caring who might hear. "A little more and they will stone me!"

I fell silent, not wanting to intrude. YHWH must have spoken, for a few moments later Moshe came down from the rocks. He touched my shoulder as he passed. "Come, Miryam. Let us show the doubters how YHWH will provide yet again."

Moving to a place where the infuriated crowd could see him, Moshe lifted his shepherd's staff and struck one of the red desert rocks. Instantly, the stone split. Water rushed out of it, spilling over the ledge, splashing onto the rocks below, and settling into a gully. The people cried out in awe and relief, then hurried to fetch their water skins. Later they would bring their flocks, and peace would prevail once more.

I went to my tent. That night I slept the sleep of a child, but perhaps I should have been more alert. For trouble stood beyond the horizon, and my brothers had kept the news of its approach from me.

We had been warned, Moshe later admitted, that the king called Amalek did not want us to cross through his territory. Long before we approached Refidim he had sent scouts to warn us away, but Moshe only pointed to the Shekinah overhead. "We go where YHWH leads us," he had told Amalek's men. "Even if it leads through the lands of Amalek."

"Amalek does not know YHWH," the scouts retorted.

Moshe had a two-word answer: "He will."

The sun rose hot and bloodred on our second day at Refidim, and within an hour of my waking the sentries came running to rouse Moshe and Aharon. One of them, a young fellow whose hands were more accustomed to molding bricks than wielding a sword, trembled as he bowed before my brother. "The warriors of King Amalek are assembling in the plain." His voice quavered. "They carry swords and shields and spears!"

Listening from behind the tent curtain as Aharon translated, I pressed my hand to my chest and drew a deep breath. What were we to do now? YHWH knew we were not warriors. He knew our frailty and our inexperience with arms. And I had heard stories about the fierceness of these desert tribes; they lopped off the heads and hands of their enemies for sport. Undoubtedly, they worried that our people and livestock would exhaust their wells and pasturelands, and those fears were justifiable. A company as large as ours could not move through any territory without leaving traces of our passage.

Another of the sentries, a young man I recognized, bowed before Moshe. I fished around for his name and came up with another one—Nun, his father, of the tribe of Ephraim. Nun and his handsome son had helped me find Aharon and Elisheba the day I left our clan to go speak with Moshe during a march.

I smiled as the name came to me—Hoshe'a, meaning "help." Unlike the first fellow, the appropriately named Hoshe'a did not tremble. "Tell me, Moshe, what we should do, and I will take men to do it."

Stepping out from behind the curtain, I chided him. "Hoshe'a, you are young. And what would you, a brickmaker, know of war? Let Moshe handle this."

I faced my brother, certain he would ask YHWH to strike the enemy with fire or water or a ripping blast of wind, but his reaction astounded me.

Turning to Hoshe'a, Moshe inclined his head in a grave nod. Through Aharon, he said, "Go, choose us capable men. On the morrow I will station myself on top of the hill, with the staff of God in my hand. Then you and your men will go out to make war upon this Amalek."

Without hesitation, the newly made commander turned and left the tent, eager to do my brother's bidding.

I stared at Moshe and Aharon, not certain I had heard correctly. Why would the God who had accomplished so many signs and miracles now expect us to resort to physical violence? Why would our young men have to face pagan warriors who were intent upon defending their homeland? Our men might be lucky to survive a battle with seasoned fighters. And though Moshe had been trained in the art of war while an Egyptian prince, he was now eighty years old, and no youth.

As Femi entered the tent and bowed, ready to serve the midday meal of manna and goat cheese, I scolded Moshe. "Brother, what are you doing? You will bring our old men and women to the grave with mourning! Why do you not ask YHWH to send the fire or hailstorm to destroy this enemy? Why must we risk our lives?"

Moshe thanked Femi with a slight nod, then took a bite of the boiled manna. Chewing thoughtfully for a moment, he swallowed and looked at me. "YHWH does not always work in miracles. And he knows we will never take the land of Canaan if we cannot defend ourselves with strength and skill. So on the morrow we will meet this enemy with determination and help from YHWH. And we will learn from the experience."

As usual, I could not argue with his wisdom, though something in me recoiled from the thought of sending our young men into battle. Allowing YHWH to deliver us in Mizraim had been a matter of endurance; trusting him to deliver us while bronze flashed and blood flowed would be far tougher.

The next morning Femi and I watched silently as Moshe, Aharon, and Hur, an elder from the tribe of Yehuda, climbed to a rocky point overlooking the plateau between our camp and the amassed Amalekites. At the edge of our encampment, Hoshe'a set out with his men, an unthreatening army of worn bricklayers and adolescent boys armed with fishing spears and bronze swords gathered in the plundering of Egypt. A few of the younger boys, I noticed, were armed only with flint knives, chipped and wrapped within wooden handles during the hours of darkness.

The two armies lined up, face-to-face, in the rays of the rising sun. From where I stood at a midpoint of the rocks, I saw Moshe lift his hand, then our line surged forward to attack. The Amalekites responded, matching our progress, and men set upon each other with the reckless fury they reserved for battle.

I do not think a woman has words to adequately describe a pitched struggle between desperate fighters. I had never witnessed an armed confrontation like this, and the horrifying sight pebbled my skin. Throughout the morning, a tide of nausea crashed in my belly, but our warriors steadily advanced . . . until Moshe's uplifted arm began to droop. The moment Moshe's hand fell, the Amalekites gained ground and our men bore the brunt of the attack. Then Moshe would gather his strength and elevate his arm again, enabling the army of Israel to prevail.

As the day wore on and the battle grew ever more grisly, Moshe's arms began to tire. I worried that he would collapse, but Aharon and Hur discovered a solution. While Moshe stood still and streamed with sweat, they rolled a rock toward him to serve as a chair. Once Moshe had been seated, they supported his arms, one man standing on his left, the other on his right. So Moshe's arms remained uplifted until sunset, and the Amalekites finally fled in confusion.

The next morning, Moshe went out to the bloody battlefield. As our people buried the corpses of the fallen, my brother built an altar and called it "YHWH, My Banner."

"Because the Amalekites have dared to raise their fist against the Lord's throne," he told us, "so the Lord will be at war with Amalek generation after generation."

He had one further bit of business to conduct before the assembly. Summoning Hoshe'a to his side, Moshe proclaimed that the son of Nun would henceforth be known as Yehoshua, meaning "YHWH is help."

That night we danced in celebration, the men spinning in one circle and the women in another. Afterward, as we slipped away to rest, I noticed Moshe speaking to Femi outside our tent. The Nubian woman who had joined us in Goshen had found a husband and moved on, but the Cushite remained with us, sleeping with me behind the modesty curtain in our goatskin shelter. Though she rarely spoke, still having no gift for our language, she watched everything with wide eyes, often irritating me with her hovering presence. I half-expected—perhaps I half-hoped—that she would run away, taking advantage of her freedom to find her way back to Cush and her own kind.

"Femi." My greeting made her start. "Moshe is weary. Let him rest."

She may not have understood my words, but my tone left no doubts as to my meaning. Bowing her head, she slunk away like a scolded dog.

Moshe gave me a look of rebuke. "You are too hard, Miryam." He stepped aside so I could enter the tent. "She is alone here. Would it be so difficult for you to offer her a cup of kindness in honor of my Egyptian mother?"

"Your mother was Yokheved, wife of Amram." I glared up at him. "And Femi is far from alone. Since you find the sand-crossers so appealing, why don't you find her a husband from among them?"

He did not respond, but in his eyes I saw surprise, disappointment, and a depth of hurt I had not known he could feel.

Nearly two months after leaving Egypt, the sentries brought news of an approaching caravan—a band from beyond the Sinai, they reported, bringing greetings from Reuel, priest of Midyan.

Grinning with an enthusiasm I had never seen him display, Moshe dismissed the elders with whom he'd been meeting and strode out to the edge of the camp to welcome the traveling party personally. The old man at the front of the train alighted from his stallion as nimbly as if he'd been born on horseback, then threw his arms around Moshe.

"Reuel!" Moshe kissed the man on both cheeks. "How I have missed your wise counsel!"

I stood silently in a knot of onlookers as Moshe's two sons, Gershom and Eliezer, alighted next. Both tall, strong, and handsome, they, too, embraced their father and Aharon.

Finally, the woman slid from her saddle and bowed low before Moshe. He strode confidently toward her, then took her hand and lifted her from the ground. "Zipporah." His voice was warm and caressing. "It is good to see you."

Her eyes searched his face, looking, no doubt, for changes in him. "Life and good health to you, husband."

What did she see when she looked at him now? Shifting my attention from her face to his, I studied my brother and tried to compare his present countenance to the face he'd worn when we met in the Sinai desert ten months ago. He had changed—a new confidence animated his features, and new lines had appeared around his mouth and eyes. Streaks of gray now colored his long beard, and in repose his skin bore fine white lines in the squint wrinkles that rarely saw the sun.

"Zipporah." Smiling, he repeated her name like a love-struck adolescent. Then he lifted his hand, and with a start I realized he was gesturing to me. "You remember Miryam. Go with her, and let her greet you properly in our tent. I'll be along soon."

While Moshe moved away to make arrangements for his sons and his father-in-law, I found myself face-to-face with the woman I had instinctively disliked on our first meeting. She looked at me, her eyes clear and cool, then arched her brows, waiting for me to respond.

"Come." My voice sounded flat in my own ears. "Our tent is this way."

I led her through the encampment, past dozens of pairs of eyes that demanded to know why Moshe's sister was playing the role of a servant before a pagan Midianite. Finally, we reached our tent—*her* tent, I suddenly realized, hers and Moshe's. As long as she remained, she would be the woman in charge, for Moshe's wife would hold more authority than Moshe's sister.

She bent to enter the cool shadows, but I hung back. I knew I ought to follow her, serve her a cup of water and offer bread and cheese, but I couldn't. Femi waited inside; I would leave the ritual of hospitality to her.

Gripped by a strong emotion I could not name, I turned and strode across the camp, ignoring the curious women who called out to me. I crossed to the edge of the camp, then climbed into the rocky foothills, finally stopping to rest in an alcove of red stone.

There, completely alone, I lowered my head into my hands and surrendered to the tears that had been stinging my eyes. I wept for the husband and child I had lost, for the opportunities I had never received, for the lack of children and grandchildren to comfort me in my aged years. The one treasure I did possess—a measure of respect as a prophetess and Moshe's sister—would fade as the pagan Midianite woman usurped my place at Moshe's side.

Our tent would become crowded, but I could not move to a dwelling of my own. A proper woman should live under the protection of a close male relative, and Moshe and I had grown comfortable with one another. Though I felt certain Aharon and Elisheba would welcome me, I did not want to test the relationship with my beloved sister-in-law. We had been equals for far too long; I did not want to become a subordinate in her household.

No, I could not move out of Moshe's tent. I would have to grit my teeth and tolerate the presence of another pagan woman in my quarters . . . and pray that no other ghosts from Moshe's past would rise to trouble me.

Through tear-blurred eyes I looked up at the red mountains in the distance. "Why, YHWH, have you despised me so? Why did no one ever lift me from the poverty of Goshen? Why have you worked no miracles in my life?"

YHWH did not speak to me as he spoke to Moshe—I heard no answering voice, neither in the wind nor in my heart.

ZIPPORAH

My husband had changed in the months of our separation, but I liked the alterations I observed in him. Moses looked stronger, and seemed completely sure of himself. The melancholy that had clung to him in Midian had vanished, replaced by an aura of responsibility.

In my father's camp Moses had held himself at arm's length, but among these people he was father, priest, and elder statesman. When we first arrived, I thought the people considered him a king, for he directed their movements, settled their disputes, and, like Pharaoh, intervened for them with their God, but no people ever treated their king with the disdain with which they approached Moses. Oh, how these children of Israel grumbled!

While we sat in the shade of Moses' dwelling, a pair of brothers came to complain because the younger had taken the better goatskins for his tent. A husband approached to complain because his wife could not seem to season manna as well as his neighbor's wife. A wife came to whine that she and her husband had no privacy in the camp, for goatskin walls were not as substantial as mud brick and their neighbors could hear every marital disagreement.

Like a dutiful wife, I remained on the fringes and took pleasure in observing my husband. Like a dutiful mother, I worried as I watched my sons observe their father. Gershom and Eliezer seemed proud of Moses and his new role, but they, too, were unaccustomed to seeing him in a position of responsibility. They had grown up with an aloof, quiet father who enjoyed the solitude of the desert wild; this father lived in the midst of a noisy rabble and, on that first day at least, seemed more dedicated to the rabble than to his flesh and blood.

My father probably understood the change in Moses best. As the priest of Midian and a true lover of people, he had always found joy in listening to problems and dispensing advice. For several hours after we arrived in the camp, he sat by Moses' side and listened as the children of Israel approached Moses with their irritating questions.

But in the hours before sunset, when the men reclined in the tent and we women set about serving dinner, Moses' thoughts turned from the present problems of his people to the miracles YHWH had performed in Egypt.

In a subdued voice brimming with wonder and awe, Moses spoke of the river of blood, the frogs, the biting gnats, the flies, the pestilence against the livestock, the boils, the hail and firestorm, the swarm of locusts, and the dense, tangible darkness. His voice brimmed with tears as he spoke of the night when YHWH passed over the children of Israel in order to strike the firstborn of all Egypt . . . and my heart contracted as I recalled how my stubborn unwillingness to circumcise my firstborn son had nearly cost my husband his life.

Unlike Athirat, my gentle goddess, this YHWH demanded blood . . . and obedience. Grateful that the men could not see me behind the woven curtain separating the men and women, I lowered my head as a fresh surge of old guilt rose within me. Athirat may not have streaked the skies with thunder and lightning to defend her followers, but neither did she demand that I cover my threshold with blood.

I made an effort to turn my thoughts away from the men's conversation. Miriam sat nearest the curtain, kneading manna in a bowl with one hand while steadfastly avoiding eye contact with me and the other woman. Recalling the way she treated me when we met months ago, I was not surprised she did not welcome me now. I *was* surprised to notice that she displayed no warmth toward the other woman who lived in her tent.

When Miriam abruptly departed soon after my arrival, I had entered Moses' tent and found the young woman weaving at a small loom. She rose and bowed as I waited for my eyes to adjust to the dim light, then smiled when I nearly ran into one of the supporting poles.

"It's not that this tent is dark," I said, blinking, "but the sun outside is so bright."

The woman laughed. Slim, willowy, and dark, she reminded me of a tender terebinth tree. I also think she was thrilled to discover that I spoke Akkadian—Miriam spoke the language, too, of course, but apparently she did not speak very often to Femi. Latching onto my arm with the tenacity of a terrier, the Cushite woman introduced herself, then bade me sit and talk.

I found her conversation pleasant and interesting. In a low, melodious voice that served as a lovely undercurrent to the rhythmic sound of her loom, the young woman explained that her ancestress had served Moses' royal mother in the palace. That confession touched a tender place of sympathy in my heart. Moses had suffered a tremendous blow when he parted from his mother, and I did not yet know if his wound had healed. Femi's presence, though, was a hopeful sign.

"Moses has mentioned his mother many times." I reached out to pat her hand. "And he spoke many times of his life in the palace. I am sure you must find the desert a strange place."

Femi's eyes glowed. "Strange, but wonderful. It is so vast! And so empty."

I laughed softly. "It is only empty when you first look at it. In time, you begin to see the hidden life among the rocks, in the sky, and under the sand. The wild is like a person—the more time you spend with it, the better you will know and appreciate it."

Femi had smiled at my words, and she was still smiling when we finished serving the men that afternoon. We three women drew apart to eat from a large bowl of boiled manna, seasoned with herbs brought from Midian, and I had never tasted anything more unique. The soft food from heaven seemed to pick up flavors from whatever food it touched.

I opened my mouth, about to say something to Femi, but she shook her head slightly and arched a brow toward Miriam. I glanced at my sister-in-law, then understood—her stony silence might as well have been an amulet worn to cast off evil spirits, for her dour expression certainly cast a pall over any pleasant conversation we might have enjoyed. Trusting Femi's intuition, I smiled and nodded, tacitly agreeing to remain silent and keep the peace while we ate.

On the other side of the woven wall, Moses was telling my father of how the children of Israel had escaped Pharaoh's chariots. When he described how the waves came crashing down upon the warriors of the Black Land, my father leaped up in unrestrained joy. "Blessed be YHWH," he cried, lifting his hands, "who has rescued you from the land of Egypt and from the hand of Pharaoh. Because he has rescued you from the proud and cruel Egyptians, I know YHWH, yes, YHWH is greater than all other gods."

Without waiting for Moses, my father went outside. Calling upon Gershom and Eliezer to help him build an altar, he proceeded to sacrifice one of our lambs in praise to YHWH. As he set the quartered meat upon the uncut stones, Moses, Aaron, and the elders of Israel came out of their tents to join him. The glistening, pillarlike cloud that had hovered above the camp all day moved toward the gathering, then altered, becoming a pillar of fire as the sun sank behind a rim of crimson rocks.

As the metallic scent of blood mingled with prayers of thanksgiving from my father and the elders of Israel, Aaron and Moses gathered portions from the sacrificial lamb, then brought them to me. I dressed and roasted them over a fire; then Femi and I served the men as together they ate a sacrificial meal in YHWH's fiery presence.

Later that night, as my father was about to enter the tent he and my sons had erected beside Moses', I drew near and asked, "Are you now forsaking all gods but YHWH?"

My father laughed softly. "A man would be a fool, little bird, to wager his life on any god but the highest. Yes, henceforth I will worship YHWH alone, and will bear witness to his power throughout the land of Midian lest others endure the suffering that has befallen the Black Land."

I patted his shoulder, wished him a good rest, then slowly crept toward my husband's tent. Looking toward the open flap, I felt as though I had swallowed some sharp, cold object that now pressed against my breast-bone.

Tonight I would sleep beside a man I had not seen in nearly a year. We had both changed in our months of separation, but I had spent the day observing him, listening to him, hearing about him.

He had not spent a single moment listening to me.

I had heard his stories, but he had not heard mine . . . and I feared he would not understand. For the midwives of my clan assured me that the bulge in my abdomen was neither a baby nor the evidence of a glutton-ous woman, but something malignant. Myriad sacrifices to my father's gods had not driven the bulge away, neither had Athirat heard my prayers. For healing, I had no god but YHWH to turn to . . . but would he hear the prayers of a doubter like me?

Ducking inside the tent, I ignored the darkness of the women's side. I knew without looking that Femi and Miriam lay within that curtained chamber, both of them discreetly trying to ignore my awkward approach to my husband.

Moses was already abed. I went in to him, lay down on the lambskin by his side, and felt the comforting pressure of his arm as he draped it over my waist. But we did not speak, nor did we kiss, and after a few moments I heard the deep and even sounds of his breathing.

We had come so far in the last months, each of us following a different path, and we did not yet know where to find common ground.

MIRYAM

~⊗~

The Midianites remained in our camp for several weeks. I tolerated their presence as best I could, skirting around the woman and avoiding the priest.

My heart leaped in relief when Moshe's father-in-law finally announced he was ready to depart. He left with his horses, his tents, and a new name—Jethro, meaning "excellence." No longer was he *a friend of the gods,* but *an excellent priest,* or so Moshe proclaimed. The pagan had offered the first sacrifice to YHWH since our departure from Egypt, Moshe said, so his name would be forever honored among us.

Before he packed his donkeys and departed, the Midianite priest committed one final misdeed. Moshe had established a habit of allowing people to approach him with their burdens and problems, and the line to seek his wise judgment usually stretched around our camp by the time the sun reached its zenith. By the end of the day, the procedure had exhausted my brother, the people who waited to hear from him, and me, for I took it upon myself to police the line and bring the most urgent situations to Moshe's attention first. The system was taxing, but Moshe was the man God had chosen to lead us.

But the night before he left, Jethro gave Moshe a cartful of unwanted and unwelcome advice. "This manner of hearing the people is no good," he told Moshe at dinner. "You will exhaust yourself, and these people with you. This job is too heavy for one man; you cannot handle it alone. So hearken to what I am about to tell you."

I paused outside the tent, a bowl of dried herbs in my arms. What did this pagan know of organization? Some of our men had been captains in Pharaoh's workforce, and Moshe had been a prince of the most civilized kingdom on earth.

But Moshe did not interrupt, and Jethro continued: "You, Moses, must stand between God and the people. You handle the matters pertaining to God and make YHWH's laws and instructions clear. Tell these people the way they should go and the deeds they should do. As for these other matters, choose men of high caliber, men who hold God in awe, truthful men who despise personal gain. Set these men over the people as chiefs of thousands, chiefs of hundreds, chiefs of fifties, and chiefs of tens. Let them judge the people. Small matters they shall judge themselves, but great matters they shall bring to you. Lighten your burden, and allow the people to share it with you. If you do this, when God commands you further, you will be able to hear him."

To my astonishment, Moshe listened to his father-in-law and obeyed his suggestion. The next morning he chose men of integrity from throughout the camp of Israel, and placed them as heads over the people as chiefs of thousands, hundreds, fifties, and tens. These men, he announced, would judge the people at all times, and only bring the difficult matters to him.

With unmerited graciousness, Moshe bid his father-in-law farewell, then Jethro went home to his land and his pagan people.

Watching him go, I wished he would carry all his family back to Midyan. The people he left behind festered like a splinter in my flesh for months to come. Moshe's sons were the least objectionable—though they were likable young men, they probably knew less than nothing about our people or our history. Moshe had not been available to teach them, of course, and who could expect a pagan woman to know anything of Avraham, Yitzhak, or Yaakov?

Jethro also left his son, a sun-wizened man called Hobab, and the woman we called Tzippora. Moshe's wife said little in my presence, confirming that the antipathy between us was mutual. Her mere presence in our tent was enough to destroy my personal peace. I didn't care that her father had claimed belief in YHWH. It didn't matter that she was Moshe's lawful wife and the mother of his sons. She was still pagan, and she had a narrow-eyed way of looking at me that made me wonder if she wanted to confront me in some sort of duel in which the winner would command Moshe's attention. Though I was certain she had ruled over the men in her father's compound, she would not rule here. Moshe and Aharon were YHWH's chosen, and all of us, men and women, submitted to their leadership . . . most of the time.

As I suspected, Moshe's wife was not even willing to follow YHWH. Though she did not worship other gods openly, I had seen her clay idol— the small figure of a nude woman in an Egyptian wig. Tzippora had not been so brazen as to display the pagan object, but she kept it hidden in a wooden chest within our tent.

We had established a shaky and unspoken truce, and its terms required that we rarely speak to one another. The younger woman from Midyan oversaw the cooking of the meals, the mending of the clothes, and the care of the tent. She looked after Moshe and her sons, who spent most of their day tending the livestock and usually slept beneath the stars. With Femi to assist her, she certainly didn't need my help.

Since our arrangement freed me from household duties, I spent most of my time sitting in the shaded porch of our tent, visiting with anyone who came by to seek Moshe. When the other women peered through the narrow opening and asked me what I thought of my sister-in-law, I would shrug as if I hadn't given the matter a great deal of thought. "Moshe married her before YHWH called him," I would explain, lifting my voice so Tzippora would be sure to hear. "And he is too honorable to put even a heathen wife away."

Still . . . in private, and at night, I would lie upon my straw pallet and listen as Moshe's deep grumble answered her soft tones. I was not so immature as to envy their passion, but found myself resenting the simple companionship that drew them together at day's end. From my narrow, joyless pallet I could hear his long sigh of weariness as he sank onto his bed, followed by her gentle laughter. Often the muted chorus of their voices continued long past the time when Femi began to snore, and I had to clap my hands over my ears and hum to drown out the sounds of their intimate conversation.

I could not deny that she met his needs. At the end of a long day Moses could look as weary as a parent with an overactive child, but after an hour with Tzippora, his weary eyes would again sparkle with life. He spoke to her in an Akkadian dialect I could not understand, and I felt more excluded from his life with every passing day.

What did Moshe see in her? And why did she remain where she was not wanted? She was not beautiful, delicate, or especially talented. Though she remained slender for a woman of her years, a decided belly had begun to protrude from the fullness of her tunic. At first I feared she was pregnant, but Femi assured me she was not. Tzippora was, I finally decided, merely developing a most unattractive potbelly.

Unable to comprehend my brother's unswerving loyalty, I tried to pretend that I lived in a household consisting of my brother, myself, and two foreign servants.

Exactly two lunar months after we left Mizraim, the pillar of cloud led us to the red and jagged mountain called Sinai. As we set up camp, Moshe strolled in the foothills of the mountain, then ascended and disappeared from our sight. A few hours later, however, he strode back into camp and summoned the elders. When all the leaders of the people had gathered around about him, Moshe told us what he had heard from YHWH.

"God says thus to the house of Yaakov," Moshe called in a booming voice, "'Yes, tell the children of Israel: "You yourselves have seen what I did to Egypt, how I bore you on eagles' wings and brought you to me. So now, if you will hearken to my voice and keep my covenant, you shall be to me a special treasure from among all peoples. All the earth is mine, but you shall be to me a kingdom of priests, a holy nation."'"

The words, which Moshe spoke in our own language, thrilled my soul. Finally, we were to receive our due! God was about to honor his covenant with our father Avraham and exalt the leadership of my brother Moshe.

With the others, I lifted my voice: "All that YHWH has spoken, we will do."

Then Moshe told us to make ourselves holy and pure. Today and tomorrow we were to scrub our clothes and wash ourselves, so on the third day we would be clean before YHWH, who would then come down from the mountain and meet with his people. As we purified ourselves, the clan leaders were to erect markers around the base of the mountain, lest anyone inadvertently encroach its boundaries and touch the holy place. Anyone who disobeyed would have to die through stoning or being shot with an arrow, for he could not live and we could not touch him. We were not to approach the mount until we heard the long sound of a ram's horn on the third day.

For two days we washed, scrubbed, and beat the sand from our clothing. During this time, men did not sleep with their wives and women did not apply cosmetics to their skin in the manner of the Egyptians. I took a woven cloth and scrubbed my neck, then took a branch and cleaned under my fingernails. The Cushite woman, I noticed, imitated me, and so did Tzippora, though I wasn't sure why she bothered.

On the third day, at daybreak, we heard sounds of storming thunder. Lightning lit the sky around the pinnacle of the mountain, and a heavy cloud roiled around its heights, but it did not rain. We waited in our dwellings, shivering in anticipation; then an exceedingly strong shofar began to sound in a long, unending blast.

We stepped out of our tents and walked to the mountain, casting looks of wonder and awe at one another as we moved toward the blood-colored rocks. No human could have sounded a shofar for so long, so had God himself summoned us?

Moshe did not stop to explain, but set out with a quick and confident step. Streaming from the camp, we followed him and gathered around the base of the mountain. The red rock smoked as YHWH came down upon it in fire, and the earth trembled beneath his presence. The sound of the shofar kept intensifying, and in the midst of it Moshe lifted his hands and began to speak to YHWH.

Then I heard YHWH—the voice was audible, but it was not like the utterance of any human. The sound of it streamed over us like a rushing river, and within it I heard snatches of Egyptian, Canaanite, and Akkadian, mixed with the tongues of Cush and Nubia and Hatti. Trembling beneath the engulfing flood of sound, I realized that YHWH must speak all the languages of men.

I cried out as a murky mist of dread churned across the sea of my soul. I was not the only one petrified by the voice of God, for one of the elders called to Moshe, "You speak with us and we will hearken, but let not God speak with us, lest we die!"

Shamelessly, I lifted my voice in agreement. Many times I had found myself wishing to speak with God as Moshe did, but this was not the voice I had yearned to hear. I had imagined that YHWH spoke in a soft whisper I had been too busy or too deaf to notice, yet if this roaring, crushing, soul-twisting flood of power was his voice, I wanted nothing to do with it.

Moshe turned to face us, surprise etched into his face. "Are you afraid?"

"Yes!" As one, we confessed our anxiety and discomfort. "Tell YHWH to retreat!"

Moshe's features hardened in a look of disapproval. "Do not fear! For God has come down to test you, to help you develop an awe of him so you do not sin."

And while we watched in fascinated horror, Moshe climbed to the top of the mountain and entered the dark cloud where God was.

We did not see Moshe for several hours. But as the sun tipped toward Egypt he climbed down from the mountain and stood upon a stone platform to give us commands from the Lord—instructions about how to worship, how to live in peace with our fellowmen, how to treat our animals and slaves. He gave us guidelines for property, social interaction, and details regarding annual festivals we were to hold in YHWH's honor.

So Moshe recounted to us all the words of YHWH and all the regulations of a holy people, and in one voice we answered, "All the words YHWH has spoken, we will do."

Early the next morning, Moshe wrote all the words of YHWH on a papyrus scroll, then built a slaughter site beneath the mountain. He placed twelve standing stones at the site, one for each of the twelve tribes of Israel; then he sent young men to offer sacrifices. He took half of the blood and put it in basins, and the other half he tossed against the stones of the altar. Then he took the scroll containing the regulations of YHWH, and read it again so everyone heard. And again we said, "All the words YHWH has spoken we will do!"

Then Moshe took the blood of the young bulls and sprinkled it upon us. "This blood confirms the covenant the Lord has made with you in giving you these laws."

Then Moshe and Aharon climbed the mountain, along with Aharon's two oldest sons, Nadav and Avihu, and seventy elders. There they saw the God of Israel, and beneath his feet something like the blue of sapphires, as pure and clear as the heavens. They knelt in the presence of God, then shared a covenantal meal.

Later, when I pressed Aharon for more details about what God looked like, I received only a trembling smile in answer. "I confess I do not recall much." Aharon smoothed the disheveled strands of hair at the back of his neck. "I was so overwhelmed that I cowered on the ground and glimpsed only the tiles beneath his feet."

"But you ate with him! You broke bread in his presence! Surely you were not lying on the ground then!"

Aharon smiled with a distracted, inward look, as though he were thinking of something beyond his power to describe. "No, I was sitting upright. But I was so astounded to be sitting in God's presence that I could only stare at my trembling hands."

He looked up, and for a moment his face went smooth with secrets.

I knew that look. I had seen it a hundred times in our childhoods, and always when spite or selfishness motivated Aharon to keep a secret from me.

I captured his eyes with mine and steeled my voice. "Tell me, Aharon."

He drew a deep breath. "I did catch a glimpse of him . . . but only a glimpse."

"So tell me!"

My brother pressed his lips together, then wiped sweat from his eyelids and squinted toward the horizon. "He wore many crowns upon his head. A name had been woven into a shawl around his neck, but I could not read it, and only he knew what it meant. He was clothed in a white tunic, but blood stained its edges. And his eyes . . ."

Ever impatient, I prodded him. "Yes?"

"His eyes were as bright as the sun, and should have been painful to gaze upon. Yet in the instant I looked at him, I felt no pain . . . only love and understanding. And though we were eating a meal of celebration, when I looked into his eyes I saw sadness there, as though he had suffered greatly . . . on my behalf."

"On your behalf?" I made a face. "Why? What have you done to displease him?"

"I don't know." Aharon's voice sounded uneasy. "But I must have done something."

I exhaled sharply and waved the matter away. "If you had displeased YHWH, do you think he would have invited you to celebrate the covenant meal? No. So stop torturing yourself. You are the brother of Moshe, and no one has done as much for these people as the children of Amram and Yokheved."

As I left Aharon's tent, I found myself wishing that I had been among those invited to the mountaintop. Perhaps if I had gone, I might have been able to stop the disaster that soon befell us.

For the next day Moshe told us he must go up on the mountain and remain long enough to receive tablets of stone engraved with the instructions and commands of God. He left Aharon and Hur in charge of the camp. I stood by, of course, ready to help when needed.

Then Moshe arose, with Yehoshua his attendant, and together they climbed the crimson Mountain of God. As they grew smaller and more distant in our sight, the Shekinah cloud withdrew from us and dwelt atop Mount Sinai, glowing like a consuming fire on the top of the peak.

Moshe stayed on the summit forty days and forty nights . . . long enough for us to get into dire trouble on the plain below.

～♡～

The murmuring began about a week after Moshe and Yehoshua went up the mountain. People peppered me with questions as I walked to the spring: "How long can they live up there? We didn't see them carrying food and water when they departed."

Though at first the questions were proffered in an attitude of compassionate concern, I gritted my teeth whenever I had to answer. "Doesn't YHWH provide food and water for us? Surely he will also provide for Moshe."

The people could not deny God's provision. Even though the Shekinah cloud had moved to the Sinai, manna appeared on the ground outside our camp every morning and water flowed freely from the spring. God had provided all we would need in order to wait upon Moshe.

Yet another week passed, and still we heard nothing from my brother or Yehoshua. The people began to grow restless, and certain of them whispered among themselves, occasionally casting furtive glances at Aharon and me. I warned Aharon that a spirit of mutiny had been born in the camp, but he told me I was imagining things.

By the time the third week had passed, the infant spirit of rebellion had matured. Though the Lord continued to provide, many of our people stopped seeing his provisions as miracles. Women went out to glean manna as casually as if it fell naturally from trees, and men regarded the Shekinah-covered Sinai as an ordinary cloud-covered peak.

Those who instigated the murmuring, of course, were the mixed multitude, or *erev rav*, that had come with us out of Egypt. While my own people restrained themselves out of respect, the outsiders openly taunted me at the spring. "Where is your brother, Miryam? Where is the man who promised to lead us to victory in the land of the Canaanites? We have not seen or heard from him in days, nor have we heard from his God."

One afternoon I snapped back. "Fools! Have you not seen the hand of God fresh every morning? What did you eat, if not his manna? What glows on yonder mountain, if not the glory of God's presence?"

"The gods of Midyan and Egypt are not powerless." Narmer, an Egyptian servant who had fled with us from the Black Land, tossed this challenge toward me. "Or were you lying when you said that Pharaoh's magicians were also able to change staves into snakes, and water into blood?"

I halted in my steps and felt my neck grow hot. "I was not lying. But their power is nothing compared to YHWH's."

Grinning at me, Narmer hopped up on a rock by the spring. "Did the waters of the sea fall back for us?" His voice rolled over the crowd with all the thunder and conviction of an Egyptian priest chanting before Pharaoh. "That could have been the work of Hapi, god of the river. Does manna cover the ground each morning? Such could be the work of Geb, god of the sky and father to Osiris. His tears formed the oceans and seas, so why shouldn't he give us his body to eat in this wilderness?"

I rose to my full height. "Narmer, you are an idiot." My rebuke spread a ripple of alarm among the people at the spring. Women did not upbraid men in public, not even ridiculous fools who deserved it.

Narmer did not back down. Grinning even wider, he leaned toward me. "I beg your pardon, Miryam, sister to Moshe. I had forgotten that you know so much of life in the Beautiful Land. Perhaps you would like to explain how you know Osiris and Geb are *not* protecting us in this wilderness?"

The Egyptian asked the question with a delicate ferocity that made it abundantly clear that he suspected I knew little about the Egyptians and their pagan gods. I drew a breath to answer, but how could I explain a religious system the average Egyptian could scarcely fathom?

Seizing upon my silence, he spread his hands and turned to face the growing crowd. "Who watches over us in this place? Look above your heads and witness! Re, the sun god, rises each morning and oversees our efforts through the day. In the sky above, who flies overhead to warn off our enemies? Nekhebet, the vulture goddess of Upper Egypt. In these past days I have seen no sign of YHWH or Moshe, but the gods of Egypt have never abandoned us! We need to return to the truth and give the gods of Egypt worship and sacrifice!"

Had Narmer begun to spout this blasphemy a week earlier, his cries might have been drowned in a wave of reproachful shushing. But in the light of Moshe's absence, the children of Israel stopped to listen. The crowd around the Egyptian grew as he continued cataloging the benefits and powers of the pagan gods, and soon other influential voices joined his.

The elders protested, of course, but as days passed and Moshe did not come down from the mountain, their protests dwindled in strength and number.

When Moshe had been gone thirty days, Aharon came to seek my counsel. Sitting in the doorway of our tent, he glanced back at Tzippora and Femi, who worked in the shadows; then he nodded to me.

"What shall I do?" he asked, once again the younger brother who could never make a decision without guidance. "The people are restless. Narmer's influence grows daily, and soon the people will not listen to me. If we are to save these people we must restore order, but how can we restore order when they want a god we cannot produce?"

In some dim recess of my heart not preoccupied with the immediate crisis, an inner voice speculated that it might be best to wait for Moshe . . . but hadn't we spent more than eighty *years* waiting for Moshe?

I shoved the thought aside. Moshe had left Aharon and Hur in charge, but Hur had retreated into his tent and Aharon had come to me for help. So the woman who had not been invited to YHWH's mountain banquet would help save his foolish people from themselves.

I drew a deep breath. "You should give them what they want, but do not give them the gods of Egypt. If they want to see YHWH, tell them you cannot make a representation of him in less than pure gold. By this you will test their mettle and their will, for unless they are willing to sacrifice their treasures, this desire for a visible god will come to nothing."

Aharon's brows lifted. "Indeed, they may not want a god enough to sacrifice gold for it. But what if they do?"

I shrugged. "If they persist in this folly, give them what they want. Design the image so that it looks a little like the gods the Egyptian spoke of, but be sure it is different enough that he cannot say we were influenced by his words."

Aharon's forehead knit in puzzlement. "The instructions YHWH gave Moshe clearly say we are not to make idols of any kind, neither in the shape of birds, or animals, or fish—"

"Every jar must stand on its own bottom, Aharon! *We* will not worship it, nor will we be responsible for the fools who do. But they are grown men, not children. Let them decide for themselves. Sometimes a leader must compromise in order to maintain the peace."

"No."

Tzippora's soft voice startled me, as did her objection. Aharon and I had been speaking Hebrew, and I had not realized that Moshe's wife had begun to understand our language. But she stood in the doorway of our tent, one hand upon the flap, her gray eyes wide with alarm.

Apparently not minding her intrusion, Aharon gave her a smile. "You disagree? Why shouldn't we let them worship as they choose? Of all people, you should understand that people will revere whatever they want to worship—"

Tzippora's eyes went soft, then she spoke in Akkadian, apparently not trusting her words to our language. "I have learned many things in my life, and one of them is this: Your YHWH is a stern god and does not suffer disobedience. You encourage these wicked rebels at great risk."

Perhaps Moshe's absence made me more brittle than I ordinarily would have been and harsher, perhaps, than I should have been. But Moshe was not with us, the people had brought us to a crisis point, and his potbellied wife was treading on my nerves.

Only with great difficulty did I manage to constrain a bitter laugh. I took her measure in a quick head-to-toe glance. "Mind your tongue. I know you cling to the old gods; I've seen the idol in your trunk. So you are not qualified to advise us."

Tzippora's brows lifted like the wings of a bird; then she cast a glance of well-mannered dislike in my direction and retreated to the black woman's side.

I looked to Aharon. "If you do this, you are not encouraging the people to worship idols. You will be acting to preserve the peace. If you don't, the camp will follow Narmer, and then what will happen? He'll have us killed, for leaders cannot allow a rival to stand."

Aharon's brow wrinkled, and something moved in his eyes. Finally, he nodded. "It is settled, then. Tomorrow I will give the people permission to worship the god of their choosing. And we will see how much they are willing to pay for this liberty."

I glanced over my shoulder, half-expecting to hear another outburst from Moshe's wife. Tzippora caught my gaze and held it, her eyes dark and shining with an unpleasant light, but she remained silent.

Convinced I had nothing to fear from within my tent, I stood and brushed the sand from my tunic, then followed Aharon.

∽

"Break off the gold rings in the ears of your wives, your sons, and your daughters," Aharon's voice rang over the assembly, "and bring them to me. Because you have asked me to make a god who will go before us, I will make you something you can behold with your eyes!"

Baskets began to move among the people. I crossed my arms and wandered among the tents, watching as the children of Israel eagerly filled them with the gold of Egypt—the earrings, bracelets, necklaces, chains, and pectorals we had been given as we left Mizraim, payment for years of service rendered to Pharaoh. Not everyone tossed gold into the baskets, but when representatives from each clan poured the offerings at Aharon's feet, I knew he had more than enough gold to fashion a god.

Aharon took the treasure, melted it down, and carved out a mold in the sand. For four days he and his sons worked in seclusion; then Aharon sent word through the compound—the god was ready to be unveiled and would travel throughout the camp to receive the praises of anyone who wished to worship him.

I stood frowning in the doorway of Moshe's tent as the procession approached. Music heralded the god's arrival, the sounds of reeds blending with the rhythmic chink of sistra and the strains of a harp. A mob of dancers preceded the idol, men and women leaping and somersaulting with athletic grace; then the idol itself came into view. Borne upon a wooden sledge and festooned with garlands of desert flowers, Aharon and his sons had created a golden calf vaguely reminiscent of the Apis bull worshiped by the Ptah-Sokar-Osiris cult in Egypt. The four-legged beast gazed out at us with painted eyes and a benign expression, but the resemblance was enough to satisfy those who yearned for Mizraim.

"Hail to thee, Apis," Narmer chanted as the procession moved by our tent. "Hail to thee who art the incarnation of Ptah and ready to guide our way in the wilderness. This, O Israel, is your god, who brought you up from the land of Egypt."

I felt the air stir beside me, and glanced down in time to see Tzippora and Femi step out of the tent. I steeled myself, certain they would join the procession and worship the golden monstrosity, but neither woman moved. They stood beside me, silent and, for the moment, united.

As the procession moved past us, Tzippora whispered something to Femi, then together they slipped back into the solitude of the tent, leaving me alone. I tilted my head to eavesdrop, then decided I didn't care what they were up to. Crossing my arms, I lifted my chin and proceeded along the fringe of the observers who were silently watching the jubilant worshipers.

The procession proceeded to the center of the camp, where the noise increased as others joined the festivities. Pressing my lips together, I turned to stare up at the cloud-covered mountain. What had happened up there? Had Moshe done something to displease YHWH? Had the God who destroyed so many Egyptians decided to destroy Moshe as well? If so, we might as well worship Apis, for YHWH would no longer want anything to do with us. Moreover, since I placed no more faith in Apis than I did in Tzippora's gods, we might as well return to Egypt. Without divine aid we would never cross the desert, defeat the Canaanite kings, and make a home for ourselves.

Sighing with defeat, I trudged back into our tent and dropped to my pallet, ignoring the burning pressure of Tzippora's eyes. I covered my head with my arms and slowly exhaled, considering that eighty-eight years was lifetime enough for one woman.

Since the people had enthusiastically approved of the golden calf, the next morning Aharon instructed men to build an altar before it. "I know Narmer and his followers are trying to convince people that the idol represents Apis," he told me, "but I will turn their thoughts to the truth. So I have declared that today shall be a festival to YHWH!"

I lowered my head into my hands. "This is not one of the festivals YHWH instructed us to hold. He gave Moshe specific instructions about the feasts of Passover, unleavened bread, harvest, sukkot, and final harvest, but he said nothing about this—"

"Don't quit on me now, Miryam." I thought I saw a smile flitting in Aharon's eyes, but it might have been anxiety. "You told me to give them what they wanted—I did, and now we have to see this through. We will hold a festival, and you and I must be present lest Narmer turn the people to the gods of Mizraim. You will help me keep the people focused on the God who truly brought us out of the Black Land."

Reluctantly, I agreed.

I knew the worshipers would begin the celebration early, bringing offerings of food and wine. Aharon and I went to the festival, where we sat under a canopy near the new altar and observed those who brought sacrifices to lay before the golden calf. After offering their gifts, they shared the food and drink. By the third hour, when the sun stood nearly at its zenith, most of the revelers were drunk.

I would have slipped away at midday, but Aharon caught my arm and held me. Now the worshipers were not only drinking, but dancing in foreign forms, with women whirling about in sheer fabrics that exposed their breasts and private regions.

I leaned back and closed my eyes, preferring to doze in the heat of the day rather than watch the foreign rabble lead the children of Israel astray. Our people had rarely witnessed such things, but I knew such behavior was common in Mizraim. One only had to look at the pictures of half-naked slaves on the walls of Pharaoh's palace to realize these entertainments were common in the Black Land.

I don't know how long I drowsed on the edge of sleep, but awareness hit me like a slap in the face when I next opened my eyes. My face burned with shame when I saw drunken men reaching for scantily clad women, couples moving to the rhythm of the drums, imitating, then enacting, scenes that should not be displayed before children—

Numb with rage and shock, I spun to face my brother. "Aharon! What have you done here?"

He glared at me with burning, reproachful eyes. "You told me to give them what they wanted."

"I told you to give them a choice."

"And they have chosen. Look, now, and see what they have chosen!"

I turned, but my eyes could not bear the obscene acts they beheld. I covered my face with my hands, then froze as the sounds of revelry sputtered to a halt. Above the dying music, a voice roared—Moshe's!

I leaped up, then leaned against Aharon's shoulder as the world spun dizzily. Moshe had returned . . . but he could not have come back at a worse moment.

Moving as rapidly as I dared, I threaded my way through the drunk and debauched, unclothed and unveiled, until I stood near the base of the altar supporting the golden calf. Beside the altar, on a lower rock, Moshe stood amid shattered shards of red granite.

His eyes met mine, but he seemed to look right through me. "YHWH told me what you were doing." His face purpled as he stared out at his wayward people. "Since this morning he has wanted to destroy you with his anger, but I convinced him to stay his hand. Yet now I see . . . *this!*"

Moshe drew a long, quivering breath, mastering the passion that shook him, then turned to Aharon, who stood beside the altar with a wreath of fragrant foliage upon his shoulders. "What did this people do to make you bring such a great sin upon them?"

Stuttering and fumbling, Aharon yanked the greenery from his neck. "Let not my lord's anger flare up! You yourself know this people, how set upon evil they are! They said to me, 'Make us a god who will go before us, for this Moshe, the man who brought us up from the land of Egypt, we do not know what has become of him!' So I asked for gold, and they gave it to me. I threw it into the fire, and out came this calf!"

Shaking his head in disgust, Moshe stepped off the rock and moved toward the gate of the camp. For a moment I thought he was abandoning us, but when he reached the gate he turned and lifted his shepherd's staff. Looking around at the unruly mob, he lifted his head. "Whoever is for YHWH—come to me!"

The camp swelled with silence as we struggled to make sense of what Moshe was saying. Come to him . . . physically? A ripple of confusion moved through the crowd, then the people began to divide. Those who had participated in the revels remained by the idol, insistent and defiant. Those who had not donated gold or participated in the debauchery surged toward Moshe. The people from my clan, all descended from Levi, were the first to move.

When the people had settled into two groups, Moshe looked at the men who stood closest to his side. His face had gone quite pale, with deep red patches over his angular cheekbones, as though someone had slapped him hard. "Thus says YHWH, the God of Israel," his voice rumbled with portent, "'Put every man his sword on his thigh, proceed and go back and forth from gate to gate in the camp, and kill every man his brother, every man his neighbor, every man his relative!'"

The intent was clear. No matter how closely related we were to those who stood by the idol, we were to put them away from us.

For once, I was glad I had been born a woman. The men silently went to fetch their blades, while we women hurried to hide our eyes.

The executions began a few minutes later. I did not witness the scene, but I could not help but hear the screams of those who begged for mercy and shrieked in horror. My stomach swayed as the men of Levi moved through the camp. Narmer and his sons died, as well as the women who had seduced men at the base of the altar. Before the sun set, more than three thousand of our people lay dead in the empty space where hours before they had been drinking and celebrating in false freedom.

Exhaustion lined Moshe's face when he entered our tent after dark. A few moments later Aharon knelt to enter. He did not speak, but sat silently, his head bowed in shame.

Moshe broke the silence. "Yes, Aharon?" His voice wavered with weariness.

"You should have killed me," Aharon murmured, not lifting his head. "For I gave them permission to make the calf."

Moshe brought his hand to his mouth, blinked slowly, then shook his head. "You have committed a terrible sin." He lowered his hand. "Tomorrow I will return to the mountain. Perhaps I will be able to obtain forgiveness for you . . . and these wretched people."

I hovered outside the circle of lamplight, terrified that Aharon would look up and include me in his guilt. I probably had been wrong to suggest that he make an idol, but I had never meant for things to get so out of hand. Surely Moshe—and YHWH—would understand.

Pressing my hand to my pounding temple, I retired to my pallet, leaving Femi and Tzippora to serve the evening meal. As I lay there, feigning sleep, I heard Tzippora ask Moshe if YHWH had provided food and water on the mountaintop.

"I neither ate nor drank," Moshe answered. "But I did not hunger. When one is eating the words of God, one does not miss food."

I huddled in the darkness as other sounds battered my ears. Outside my tent, mothers wailed for the daughters of friends; young men wept for the cousins they had struck with the sword. Finally, after the women had cleared away the remains of dinner, Moshe went outside and addressed our mourning kinsmen.

"Today," he told them, interrupting the sounds of their grief, "you have been ordained for the service of the Lord, for you obeyed him even though it meant killing your own sons and brothers. Because of this, he will now give you a great blessing. You, the descendants of Levi, will be called to the service of the Lord."

The next day Moshe took a tent he called the Tent of Appointment and erected it outside the camp, at the base of the mountain called Sinai. When he had finished, he went inside the Dwelling. The pillar of cloud came down and stood at the entrance, blocking our view of Moshe. All day he remained inside, and when he came out he ordered that the golden calf be melted and ground up. When the object of our disobedience resembled a pile of dust, he mixed the dust into water and made us drink from it, then cast the remaining dust into the stream that flowed down the mountainside.

When he had finished destroying the golden calf, Moshe caught Aharon's eye. "YHWH was so angry that he wanted to destroy you," he said simply. "But I prayed for you, and the Lord has spared your life."

Aharon looked at me, the muscles of his throat moving in a convulsive swallow. I knew he was thinking that I deserved some of that blame, yet YHWH had not spoken of destroying me.

I lifted my chin, sending Aharon a silent message: *Your sin was greater than mine.* We had both been wrong to even consider creating an idol, but I had protested the festival, the dancing, the immoral behavior.

God had not finished with us. A plague struck our camp, and many others died because they had yearned for another god to worship.

The next morning, Moshe rose and cut two new tablets of stone to replace those he had smashed at the base of the idol. When he had finished, he climbed Sinai again.

We settled down to wait for his return. Even after five weeks, no one suggested that we create a substitute god.

After forty days, Moshe returned with the two Tablets of Testimony in his hand. When we saw him, we shielded our eyes and turned away, for his countenance shone as bright as new silver.

Gathering us together by clans, Moshe told us all YHWH had said. He relayed the Instructions and the Ten Words, then yielded to my suggestion and draped a veil over his face.

From that time forward, Moshe would remove the veil whenever he entered the Tent of Appointment to talk with YHWH. He would come out and speak to us, allowing us to see his face radiating with the reflected glory of God; then he would drape the veil over his head and come home . . . where those of us who knew him best chafed under the constant reminder that we did not deserve to glow with glory.

ZIPPORAH

How do you share your heart with a husband who glows in the dark? The first time Moses came into the tent after encountering the glory of God on the mountain, I quavered in the corner of the tent for the better part of an hour. Even though he wore a covering of lightweight wool over his head and shoulders, a ring of luminescence surrounded him like the glowing circle around the moon.

"Zipporah." He reached out to me in the darkness. "I have not changed."

I gritted my teeth in an effort to keep them from chattering. "Yes, Moses, you have."

"But I need you. I need someone to talk to."

"Why would a man who talks to God need a woman? Surely you have no need of any counsel I could give."

"You underestimate yourself. You always have." The undertone of melancholy in his voice drew me to his side despite my fears. I lay down next to him, turning to face the inner curtain so I would not have to stare into that unearthly glow, but my heart contracted in pleasure when he wrapped a strong arm around me and drew closer to share my warmth.

When we were snuggled together like young lovers, Moses pulled the veil from his head. Instantly, our small chamber brightened, and I could see our shadows faintly outlined upon the woven wall.

"YHWH knew about the golden calf before I did," he confided, his breath warming my ear. "His anger was kindled. He said he would destroy the people and make a great nation out of me."

"Out of you?"

"Out of our children, Zipporah. And I do not doubt he could do it. If he could produce this people out of Abraham and Sarah through Isaac, he could certainly produce a nation out of Gershom and Eliezer."

I considered this—a holy nation from an Egyptian prince and the daughter of a pagan priest? The idea seemed ludicrous.

"But I soothed YHWH's anger," Moses continued, murmuring drowsily against the back of my neck. "'For what reason,' I asked him, 'would you want the Egyptians to mock us? For they would say YHWH brought us out into the wilderness to kill us, and the name of YHWH would be defamed.' So the Lord let himself relent of the evil he had spoken of doing to his people."

I remained quiet, listening to the susurrant whisper of the wind against the walls, then murmured, "I am glad."

"So am I."

My husband said nothing for a long moment, then his hold on me tightened. "Zipporah—do you remember when we were trying to discover the name of the Israelite God?"

"Of course."

"There is power, *real* power, in his name. YHWH passed before me when I called it out, and his name echoed off the stones of the mountain and echoed in the heavens. His name means showing-mercy, showing-favor, long-suffering in anger, abundant in loyalty and faithfulness, keeping loyalty to the thousandth generation, bearing iniquity, rebellion and sin, yet not clearing the guilty, calling to account the iniquity of the fathers upon the sons and upon sons' sons to the third and fourth generation . . . and when I had called out his name, Zipporah, I saw him."

The urgent note in his voice startled me. "But you have already seen him. You and the elders ate a meal with him upon the mountain."

"That was different, that day we saw God-in-flesh. What I saw upon the mountain was his Spirit essence, God-in-glory. I begged that I might find favor in his eyes and see his face, and he told me no mortal can see his face and live. Yet he put me in a cleft of a rock, and protected me with his hand as his glory passed by. What I saw was only the remnant of his passing glory, but it was enough, Zipporah, to change everything."

An involuntary shudder raced down my spine. Moses did not need to explain that the glow on his face was merely a shadow of the dazzling glory he had beheld, and the thought of such power was enough to make my mouth go dry. I had seen something of YHWH's power, for I had encountered it the night we camped before this mountain on our way to Egypt.

I needed a touch of that power in my own life, but I did not deserve it . . . and I feared it.

"Moses." I closed my eyes. "I am sick. And I have a favor to ask of you."

I felt him lift his head as his arm tightened around me. "Sick?"

"Something is growing in my belly and each day it saps my strength. The priests of Midian could not help me, and neither could the midwives. I fear I will not live long enough to enter the land promised to you and your people."

His hand squeezed my shoulder as his gentle breath blew against the back of my neck. "What would you like me to do? Pray for your healing?"

I smiled at the kindness in his voice. From the day I met him at the well, I had always trusted Moses' goodness.

"Your god has no reason to heal me. But the woman, Femi—she should have a husband, for her safety's sake. She is unattached in this camp, and Miriam does not care for her. If you hold any regard for Femi at all, you should make her your wife."

His hand tightened upon my shoulder. "I will protect and care for her, but I had never thought to take a second wife. You are the only wife I ever wanted."

I chuckled. "You did not want me. My father tricked you into marriage."

"Your father is not as clever as you think."

"He made you jealous! You would not have wanted to marry me if he had not mentioned all those other men—"

"You give me too little credit. Avoiding your father's eagerness to marry off five other daughters took a fair amount of skill, as I recall."

I bit my lip as a blush of pleasure warmed my cheeks. "You . . . you really waited for me?"

"Who else among Reuel's daughters had courage enough to speak her mind? Yes, Zipporah. I waited for you."

I lay quietly, a kernel of happiness warming the center of my being, then patted his hand. "I will not feel threatened if you take another woman, Moses. Moreover, I am not strong, and Femi will be able to help you if I fall ill. Miriam is . . . busy about other things."

My husband did not respond at first; then his strong arm turned me to face him. After studying my eyes for a long moment, he drew me into the silvery glow that bathed his features.

"I will consider it." Warmth and gratitude mingled in his voice. "Thank you, wife, for thinking of her."

MIRYAM

⌒◯⌒

With the institution of the Instructions and the Ten Words, order descended upon our camp. For the first time since leaving Mizraim, the children of Israel set to work on a project that would benefit something greater than our individual households and clans, and we rejoiced in the labor.

YHWH seemed in no hurry to lead us away from Sinai. The Shekinah continued to hover above the Tent of Appointment, so we remained in place, eager to do our work and learn about the laws that should govern a people directly ruled by God.

Moshe spent the first part of every day teaching the elders, who then dispersed and taught the captains, who taught the men under them. Through the instructions of YHWH's moral code we learned how to worship God and treat one another; through the spiritual code we learned how to observe the seven festivals and five offerings; through the social code we learned how to govern our diet, manage illnesses, and maintain cleanliness in the camp. YHWH gave us rules for soil conservation, taxation, military service, marriage, childbirth, divorce, and family authority. In fact, we soon discovered that our God had clear ideas about nearly every aspect of life.

We learned that YHWH expected his people to lead holy lives, so no sins of deliberate disobedience or perversion would be tolerated. We were, Moshe told us, to be holy, because YHWH was holy.

The teaching that stirred the most tangible excitement, however, was the instruction for building the Dwelling. Moshe explained that YHWH would no longer dwell apart from us, but would live among us. Anyone with a willing heart could bring contributions to build the Tabernacle of YHWH.

God had given strict and detailed instructions concerning its construction. Stirred by a willingness to make YHWH an appropriate habitation, our people responded with unexpected generosity, filling a storage tent with brooches, nose rings, signet rings, and necklaces. The Tabernacle would also require fabrics, so piles of blue-violet, purple, and worm-scarlet cloth appeared beside stacks of goats' hair, dyed rams' skins, and tanned leather. Women spun cloths of beautiful colors while families brought olive oil for the lamps, fragrant incense and spices for the anointing oil, onyx and other stones to be set in the ephod for the high priest, as well as silver, bronze, and stores of valuable acacia wood.

Then Moshe told us, "YHWH has chosen Betzalel, son of Uri, son of Hur, of the tribe of Yehuda, to create designs of gold, silver, and bronze. God has filled Betzalel and Oholiav, son of Ahisamakh, of the tribe of Dan, with wisdom to make all kinds of workmanship of the jewel-cutter, the designer, and the embroiderer. YHWH has given them special skills as jewelers, designers, weavers, and embroiderers in blue, purple, and scarlet yarn on fine linen cloth. They excel in all the crafts needed for the work."

So Betzalel and Oholiav and the other craftsmen took the materials and began to construct the Dwelling and all the things needed to fill it, including the Ark of the Covenant, a container designed to hold the inscribed stone tablets Moshe brought down from Mount Sinai. The people continued to bring offerings until Moshe told them to stop.

For months the craftsmen worked, and on the first day of the first new moon in the second year, the Dwelling began to rise in the center of our camp. As Aharon and his sons watched in reverent attention, Moshe put the Dwelling together by setting its frames into their bases, attaching the crossbars, and raising the posts. Then he spread the coverings over the framework and assembled the roof, exactly as YHWH had commanded him.

He placed inside the Ark the stone tablets inscribed with the terms of the Testimony given upon Mount Sinai; then he attached the Ark's carrying poles. He also set the Ark's cover—the place of atonement—on top of the gilded box. Then he brought the Ark of the Covenant into the Tabernacle and set up the inner curtain to shield it from view, just as YHWH had commanded.

Once each year, Moshe had explained, Aharon, our high priest, would enter the Most Holy Place and sprinkle blood upon the mercy seat, the top of the Ark. This blood offering would stand between us and the holy wrath of God.

Next Moshe placed the table in the Tabernacle, along the north side of the Holy Place, just outside the inner curtain. He arranged the Bread of the Presence, twelve cakes to represent each of the twelve tribes of Israel, on the table that stands before the Lord, just as YHWH had commanded.

Moshe then stood the gold lampstand in the Dwelling across from the table on the south side of the Holy Place. Then he set up the lamps in the Lord's presence and placed the incense altar in the Holy Place in front of the inner curtain. On it he burned the fragrant incense made from sweet spices, just as YHWH had commanded.

The lampstand, as tall as the average woman, held seven lamps, which were never to be extinguished at once. The priests would burn sweet spices on the altar of incense each evening to symbolize the prayers we lifted to God each night.

He attached the curtain at the entrance of the Dwelling, and placed the bronze altar of burnt offering near the Tabernacle entrance. On it he placed a burnt offering and a grain offering, just as YHWH had commanded.

Next he placed the large washbasin between the Tabernacle and the altar. He filled it with water so the priests could use it to purify themselves. Whenever Moshe, Aharon, or Aharon's sons walked past the altar to enter the Dwelling, they were to stop and wash their hands and feet.

Then Moshe hung the curtains forming the courtyard around the Dwelling and the altar. When he erected the curtain at the entrance of the courtyard, Moshe finally finished the work.

Then the Shekinah covered the Dwelling, and the glorious presence of YHWH filled the Most Holy Place. Standing back in reverent awe, Moshe explained that whenever the cloud rose up from the Dwelling, the children of Israel would follow. If the cloud did not move, neither would we.

Like the Egyptians, whose god lived among them in the person of Pharaoh, our God now lived in our midst. But we did not celebrate his presence with dancing or drinking or immoral excess.

Most of us sat reverently in the doors of our tents, our eyes wide and our hearts humbled by the knowledge that YHWH, who had made a covenant with Israel and humbled Egypt on our behalf, had descended from heaven to live among us.

On the twentieth day of the second month of the second year since we left Egypt, the cloud moved from its place . . . and we followed. When the Shekinah lifted from the Tabernacle, Moshe claimed YHWH's promise with a prayer: "Arise, O Lord, and let your enemies be scattered! Let them flee before you!"

During the eleven months we camped at the base of Mount Sinai, Moshe had organized us. In preparation for the coming conquest of Canaan, he had taken a census of all men twenty years and older. To my surprise, we former slaves now boasted of an army 603,550 strong. Moshe's vision of our triumphant entry into the land of YHWH's promise had never seemed more reliable.

After the establishment of the Tabernacle, we traveled and camped in clans, our formations centering on the Dwelling of God. The tribes of Yehuda, Yissakhar, and Zevulun led our procession, for they camped to the east of the Dwelling. The Gershonites and Herarites, divisions of the clan of Levi, followed, carrying the dismantled Tabernacle structure. After them came the tribes of Re'uven, Shim'on, and Gad, who camped toward the south. The Kehatites followed them, Levites who carried the Tabernacle furnishings; then came the clans of Efrayim, Menashe, and Binyamin, who camped toward the west of the Tabernacle. The clans of Dan, Asher, and Naftali brought up the rear, and at day's end they camped on the north side of the Dwelling.

After a full day of leading us through sand and wind, the cloud rested and Moshe ended our march with another prayer: "Return, O Lord, to the countless thousands of Israel!"

As much as my heart rejoiced to know we were moving northward toward the land of promise, I could not be completely happy as long as the *erev rav* remained within our camp. The incident of the golden calf had weeded out three thousand of the infidels, and the ensuing plague had taken others. God had purged less-than-committed Israelites from our company, too, at Taberah, where fire from the Lord immolated those who complained about our hardships, and at Kibroth-hattaavah, where many people died from a plague in the quail God sent to stop their complaining. I held the foreign rabble completely responsible for the difficulty at Kibroth-hattaavah, for this gathered riffraff enticed our people to yearn for the fish, cucumbers, watermelons, green leeks, onions, and garlic of Mizraim.

Though God had cut through the rabble, still foreigners lived, ate, and worshiped with us . . . or pretended to. Though I never saw Tzippora setting food before an idol, I knew she carried one in her trunk; and only heaven knew what sort of dark deities Femi carried in her heart. Though she and Tzippora outwardly obeyed the instructions from YHWH, what fellowship could they have with us? We were the children of Israel, heirs of the covenant God had established with Avraham, Yitzhak, and Yaakov. While Tzippora was fond of mentioning that the children of Midyan had sprung from Avraham, too, her words had no effect upon anyone who knew the complete history of our people. In truth, our father Avraham had sent the children of Keturah away so they would not infringe upon the children of Yitzhak, but here they were, insinuating themselves among us, hoping for a few crumbs from God's table.

I might have learned to tolerate a small number of pagans in the camp, but I could not escape those living in my vicinity. Not only did I have to deal with Tzippora and Femi living under my roof, but Tzippora's sons, Gershom and Eliezer, and her brother, Hobab, staked their tent directly behind ours. I had hoped Hobab would leave when we packed up and left the wilderness near Midianite lands, but Moshe invited him to continue with us on the journey.

At Hazeroth, my irritation reached a boiling point. One night after dinner I returned to the tent to find Tzippora reclining on a lambskin in the corner where Femi usually slept. Too stunned for words, I could only gape at her.

Something sly moved in her eyes when she beheld my shocked expression. "Don't worry, this arrangement is not permanent." She pulled a blanket over her shoulder as she rolled onto her side. "I thought Moses and his new bride should have an opportunity to be alone."

I drew a wincing breath. "His *what?*"

She smiled, an expression of satisfaction creeping over her features. "Moses has taken a second wife."

I opened my mouth, but the question would not come. I could not imagine why, who, or how Moshe would marry again, but I could think of only one woman Tzippora might allow near her husband—

"Yes." A small smile hovered at the corner of her mouth. "Moses has married Femi. Now she will be respected in this camp."

I clutched at the pole supporting our tent as the blood rushed from my head. I think I made a noise that sounded like every Hebrew consonant being spoken at once, then I whirled so the Midianite could not see my face.

She'd done this on purpose. She had not been content to sully Moshe's purity with her own marriage; she had been determined to debase him further by marrying him to a pagan woman with skin as black as the night sky.

I clapped my hand over my mouth and heard myself breathing hard through my nose. I would be sick in a moment, spewing my dinner all over the floor, giving the Midianite woman another reason to gloat.

Wordlessly, I pushed my way out into the night and staggered toward the tent where Aharon and Elisheba lived. They were doubtless tired after a long day, but a strong dose of indignation might rouse them enough to join me in confronting Moshe.

"Aharon!" My voice sounded hoarse and strangled in my own ears. "Aharon, come out!"

I heard rustling sounds; then my brother thrust his head through the opening. His eyes showed white all around, like a panicked beast. "Miryam? What's wrong?"

I jerked my thumb toward my tent, where the unspeakable had occurred. "It's Moshe. He has taken another wife."

The alarm on Aharon's face faded to weariness. "I know, Miryam. I blessed their union myself."

"You *what?*"

"Come inside, lest we wake the camp."

I entered Aharon's tent, but not even Elisheba's sweet smile could cool my burning temper. Rancor sharpened my voice as I shook my finger in Aharon's sleepy face. "Did YHWH not tell us to refuse wives from other kingdoms? Yet Moshe has taken a woman from Cush, and now she will walk behind him as if she is one of us!"

Aharon glanced at Elisheba, who shrank back, clearly not wanting any part of the argument.

"YHWH told us not to take wives from the land of Canaan," Aharon said, his voice thoughtful. "He said nothing against Cush."

"Does he have to list every kingdom in order to make his point? YHWH wants us to remain pure and devoted to him! Besides, if Moshe wanted to protect this woman, he could have made her his concubine or his slave. She was already a servant in the household—so why did he have to marry her?"

Aharon lifted his hand in a silent shrug, then looked at his wife. "I blessed them because Moshe asked me to. But one wife is enough for any man."

Shaking my head, I released a bitter laugh. "How many wives does an eighty-two-year-old man need? Surely he does not want to father children at his age! Moreover, the Cushite is not so young. He did not marry her for his pleasure."

Elisheba wrapped her shawl closer about her shoulders as a cold wind blew through the tent opening. "Perhaps your brother wanted to give the woman a home."

I snorted. "Have I not given her a home? She has been sleeping in our tents, eating our food, and marching with our clan since we left Mizraim. She is neither a child nor an invalid, that we should feel sorry for her!"

"Moshe has the gift of persuasion." Pressing his lips together, Aharon stared at the swaying flap of the tent. "And he does what he wants. No man tells him what to do."

"Yet he is our *younger* brother." I let the words hang in the silence for a moment, giving Aharon a chance to remember that he'd spent a lifetime coming to me for advice, then turned to my bewildered sister-in-law. "Tell me, Elisheba, have you ever heard of such a thing? Since when does the younger son rule over the elder?"

My sister-in-law's eyes widened for a moment, then her narrow lips curved in a smile. "Yaakov received the blessing meant for Esau. And Yaakov blessed Efrayim over Menashe."

I glowered at her—the woman had never been helpful in an argument.

Aharon lifted his hand, and it was clear from his expression that he hadn't heard his wife's comment. "Has YHWH not spoken through us? In Mizraim, did he not use me to speak to the children of Israel? Moshe could not have addressed them without me."

"And has YHWH not used me among the women? Who else could carry Moshe's words to the mothers and daughters of Israel?"

Aharon tapped his fingertips together in a meditative rhythm. "It is not right for Moshe to take a second wife. This thing was ill-advised."

"Particularly a woman from Cush, and not of our people. We should bring this matter before the elders. We should let them judge the matter according to the law, then let Moshe stand under the judgment as one of us."

"Tomorrow," Aharon agreed. "We will see to it tomorrow." He stood and shuffled toward his pallet at the corner of the room, and I suddenly realized I had nowhere to sleep. I couldn't go back to my own tent after leaving in such a huff, but Aharon had not extended his hospitality—

"Please, Miryam, stay here tonight." Elisheba's soft voice broke into my thoughts. "Put this thing far from your heart. The matter may seem less troublesome in the morning."

I thanked her for her hospitality and pulled a sheepskin from a pile by the door, but I doubted my feelings would change before sunrise.

My intuition proved correct. My irritation continued boiling through the night, and by the time Aharon emerged from his chamber I had girded my heart with righteous determination. The elders would hear of Moshe's marriage, and we would let them decide the matter. If they would not disallow this union, perhaps Aharon could take it before YHWH in the Tent of Meeting.

I had no sooner nodded good morning to Aharon than I heard a commanding sound unlike anything I had ever heard—and knew it was the voice of YHWH. This voice did not ripple with power like the overpowering voices I had heard at Sinai, but sliced through Aharon's dwelling like a spear, sharp and pointed.

"Come out! Moshe, Aharon, and Miryam, come now to the Tent of Appointment!"

I looked at Aharon, and knew from the fixed look on his face that he had heard the voice, too. A glance at Elisheba convinced me that she had heard *something,* for she had gone as pale as death and stood trembling in the center of the tent. "What is that?" Her hand rose to her lips. "Aharon? Did you hear it?"

I squeezed her shoulder. "God calls Aharon and me by name, Elisheba. Wait here while we meet with YHWH about Moshe."

Convinced that God had heard and heeded our concerns, Aharon and I walked to the Dwelling. Once we stood before the entrance, we turned and saw Moshe step out of his tent, a question on his face. The new bridegroom nodded in our direction, then began to walk toward us, his eyes wide with curiosity and alarm.

I chewed on the inside of my lip, hoping the Cushite and Midianite would come out as well. I wanted them to see this.

Before we could hail him, YHWH descended in a column of cloud and filled the empty space at the entrance to the Dwelling, blocking our entry. Though I remained motionless, something inside me began to tremble, and again I wondered how Moshe could stand in the presence of God without wanting to scream, flee, laugh, or weep hysterically.

I had yearned to speak with God as he did, and today, finally, YHWH had called me to meet with him. If I could only make it through the encounter with my sensibilities intact. . . .

"Aharon and Miryam, come forward!" The voice drew me like a rod of iron, compelling a prompt response. I had been thinking it would be best if YHWH held this discourse with us inside the Dwelling, for though it would be appropriate for the entire camp to witness YHWH's address to Aharon and me, it might be better to handle the matter of Moshe's unsuitable marriage within the privacy of the Tabernacle's curtained walls.

The concerns that had been lapping at my subconscious crested and crashed as YHWH's words rolled over us like a wall of pure energy: "Hear me! If there should be among you a prophet of YHWH, I make myself known to him in a vision, in a dream I will speak with him. Not so my servant Moshe—in all my house, he is trusted. Mouth to mouth I speak with him, in plain words and not in riddles, and the form of YHWH is what he beholds. So why were you not too awestruck to speak against Moshe?"

The powers of speech and thought fled away from me. The self-assurance that had supported me only moments before vanished like the dew beneath the scalding sun, leaving me gasping in a pool of terror, shame, and regret.

The pillar of cloud whirled, and my eyes burned as I felt the singeing fury of YHWH within it. Though my garments flapped against my flesh and bones, in that instant I felt naked and exposed. For a dizzying moment the color ran out of the world and the rushing sound of the cloud faded, but just as I thought I would pitch forward in a faint, the Shekinah rose and returned to the Holy Place.

After the roar of the voice and the whirlwind, the resulting silence seemed as heavy as the waves that had covered Pharaoh and his army at the bottom of the sea. I turned in the thickened quiet and through blurred eyes saw Aharon, who had buried his face in his hands, and a curious crowd staring at us in openmouthed astonishment.

I lowered my head, absently noting the patterns of the swirled sand in front of me; then the stillness shivered into bits as a woman screamed.

I looked up; the woman was pointing at me. Behind her, people were whispering, their voices like the rustle of leaves in the wind.

"Tzaraat!" I heard someone say. "She has tzaraat!"

She? I looked around, but saw no woman with the dread disease. Then I looked at my hands and felt ghost spiders crawl up the staircase of my spine—my hands, my arms, even my toes were white with the leprous skin condition that meant immediate exile for anyone unfortunate enough to encounter it.

Beside me, Aharon was frantically begging Moshe to spare me. "Please, my lord, do not punish us for mere foolishness! Do not let her be like a stillborn child who comes out of its mother's womb already half-decayed!"

I could not look at Moshe. I had not spoken to him about his marriage, so he had no idea why I had approached Aharon, or why the Lord had acted against us. He would be hurt or angry if he knew the entire story, and he might find it difficult to forgive.

Without pausing to ask what we had done to merit such punishment, Moshe lifted his hands toward the cloud over the Tabernacle: "Oh God, heal her, please!"

In a voice filled with quiet emphasis, YHWH answered: "If her father spat in her face, would she not be put to shame for at least seven days? Let her be shut up for seven days outside the camp. . . . Afterward she may be gathered back to her people."

No one had to tell me what must happen next, for I had learned the sanitation codes with everyone else in the camp of Israel. Since my hands, my feet, and my face bore evidence of YHWH's judgment, I could not stop for a kiss, an embrace, or provisions to take with me in my exile. I was unclean, and must depart the camp immediately.

As Aharon fell to his knees and continued to beg YHWH for mercy, Moshe looked at me, and in his eyes I saw the glimmer of tears. "Seven days." His voice broke with huskiness. "Then we will welcome you back."

Without speaking or turning to seek pity of anyone, I walked through a crowd that parted like the Red Sea at my approach. I paused at the boundaries of the camp, wondering if I might ask for a goatskin or jar in which to carry water, then remembered that an unclean person was not to touch anything.

"Wait!" I recognized Tzippora's voice, followed by the soft popping sounds of her sandals as she hurried toward me. I threw up my hands and took a step back, but she did not stop until she stood an arm's distance away.

She pulled an object from the girdle at her waist, then held out a sliver of red granite as wide as my hand and as long as my finger. Two sides of it were perfectly smooth, the others rough and striated. A Sabbath stillness reigned over the crowd as she offered it to me.

"I don't know if this will help you, but it might."

I stared at her. "What do you think you are doing?"

"It is a piece of the Ten Words—the tablets Moses broke when he came down from the mountain. It is holy, is it not?"

The pagan thought I would have some use for a protective talisman. I wanted to ignore her and walk away, but how could I spurn the offer of a rock engraved by Yhwh's hand when the eyes of Israel were upon me?

I held out my cupped palm, allowed her to drop the stone into it, then tucked the rock into the folds of my girdle. Apparently satisfied, Tzippora stepped back, leaving me to my fate.

From outside the camp, forlorn as the cry of a restless spirit, came the sorrowful call of a jackal. Lifting my chin, I stared straight ahead and passed through the gate, alone.

If public humiliation is not the bitterest cup in the world, it is certainly one of the most foul tasting. I stalked out of our camp determined, defeated . . . and angry.

What I felt went far beyond mere embarrassment—that emotion is reserved for thoughts that slip into words better left unsaid, belches that rise into your throat at inopportune moments, or one of those occasions when the body betrays your control in an inappropriate manner.

That first day I felt nothing but intense mortification. The emotion might have broken my spirit if I had been responsible for the act that brought it about, but as angry tears blurred my view of the orange-tinted rocks outside our camp, I realized I had never been given an opportunity to present my case to Yhwh or even to Moshe. What sort of God judged petitioners before allowing them to speak? What kind of deity overlooked the sins of his favored spokesman while punishing the good intentions of the spokesman's elder sister? Not even the gods of Mizraim were so capricious.

Resisting the surge of fury that murmured in my ear, I stumbled across the plain, seeking shelter in a ridge of rocks that rimmed our camp. Yhwh's sentence had been unjust, and he had chastised me before the entire camp, my brothers, and two foreign women I had come to despise. This punishment—turning my skin white because I had complained about

Moshe marrying a woman whose skin was black—felt more like a cruel joke than a proper judgment. Back at the camp, Femi and Tzippora had to be laughing.

Moshe wouldn't notice their attitudes, of course. He was foolishly, blindly loyal to those he loved. He lived on a different plane from the rest of us; the heartbreaks of life had not scarred his soul. While the rest of us were enduring slavery, beatings, starvation, and murder, he had been pampered by a foreign mother, loved by a foreign woman, and sheltered by a foreign people. What did he know of us, his true kinsmen? Virtually nothing! He still struggled to speak our language!

In many ways he was like a gently spoiled child—he was not demanding, yet he expected things and he always got them. He asked of YHWH and God delivered, just as Moshe had once asked for things from his doting Egyptian mother.

It wasn't fair! Moshe had never lost a spouse or a child, and he had not been around when Aharon and I lost our mother and father. Our parents were only idealistic figments of Moshe's imagination, but he had not seen them in their declining years. He had never nursed them in illness, changed their soiled bedding, or wiped spittle from their chins. He had never rubbed ointment into the bruises on our father's beaten back, nor did he have to comfort our brokenhearted mother after she surrendered her favorite child to another woman.

Those thoughts brought another in their wake, with a chill that struck deep in the pit of my stomach. Moshe had always lived in a dream world . . . and apparently YHWH had charged me with the task of keeping him safe in it.

I filled my first night outside the camp with bitter weeping. My stomach knotted with hunger pains, my throat ached with thirst, yet I had not been allowed to prepare for this sudden exile. What if I died out here? Would anyone care? Perhaps it would be best if I did, for my death would bring Moshe and Aharon to their senses . . . and might even color my memory in sympathy instead of shame. How can YHWH be just, people would murmur, if he killed righteous Miryam and tolerated Moshe's pagan wives?

The question of survival hammered at me. If I did last the week, how could I go back to camp after suffering this humiliation? I had been *Miryam*, sister to Moshe and Aharon, and eyewitness to all that transpired in Mizraim. People respectfully bowed their heads when I passed by, for I had walked with Moshe and Aharon into Pharaoh's audience chamber; my eyes had recorded the breaking of the earth's mightiest king. Pharaoh had trembled in my presence; and years before, another pharaoh's daughter had trusted me to find a nurse for her son. I had watched over Moshe in the bulrushes, keeping him safe from serpents and the hippopotamuses. He owed his life to me; he owed his knowledge, his skills, and his influence to my work in his life.

The desert lay silver under the moon by the time I found shelter in the rocks. Settling into a small crevice, I wrapped myself in my shawl and shivered. I wept until exhaustion claimed me, then drifted into a shallow doze in which the emotions of the day mingled with inchoate splinters of dreams.

I did not stir until the morning light touched my face. For a moment confusion clouded my senses, but as I reached up to brush my veil from my eyes, a thumbnail-sized piece of white skin flaked from the back of my hand and fell upon my dark tunic. Then I remembered.

I passed the second day in torment, my body suffering along with my heart. My scabrous flesh itched with disease, but scratching caused the skin to flake and fall off. Anything more than a few swipes uncovered raw flesh, which stung and bled when my fingernails brushed across it. The exposed flesh oozed without the protective white scabs, and the scorching sun dried the ooze to a crust that dried to my tunic, then broke away every time I moved.

The weather did not help. Blowing sand scoured the skin from my peeling face and seeped into every crevice of my tunic and every pore of my tortured skin. And while I scratched and winced and groaned and wept, images of life in the camp pushed and jostled with each other for space inside my heart. Just beyond the ridge, Femi and Tzippora were preparing a manna meal for Moshe, who would no doubt enjoy it. The women filling their water jars at the spring were sure to be talking about me, and a few of them would stop by Elisheba's tent, pretending to offer consolation while they eagerly sought snippets of gossip.

A weed of jealousy sprang up in my heart, stinging like nettles. Why should Aharon and Elisheba enjoy the comforts of friends and food while I suffered alone? Why had I been exiled when Aharon shared fully in my sin? He had doubted Moshe, too, and he had agreed with my stand on the Cushite wife. Though I *had* instigated the discussion, Aharon had done far worse things—he, after all, had created the golden calf. He had sacrificed to an idol and called it YHWH, while I had recoiled in horror and waited for Moshe. So why was I suffering alone?

I did not deserve this. I had always been a leader among the women and both my brothers looked to me for guidance. Aharon could not choose a new tunic without advice from me or Elisheba, and a few months ago Moshe could not even wish a fellow Israelite good morning without my whispering the proper word in his ear.

I did not deserve to be abandoned!

After wandering miserably through the heat of the day, I spied a juniper tree, and beside it a small spring bubbling up beside a rock. Falling to my knees before the spring, I beheld my disease-ravaged face for the first time. Aharon had not been speaking metaphorically when he mentioned the half-rotted stillborn child. My face, which before yesterday had still borne traces of beauty, had nothing to recommend it now. My high cheekbones were scabbed with oozing skin, my wide forehead a red-and-white expanse of mottled tissue. Red-rimmed eyes stared out at me above a cracked and bleeding nose. My lips, which had once kissed a husband and crooned to a newborn, were puffed and scaly with disease.

I lay down by the edge of the spring and wailed aloud, begging YHWH to take my life. A merciful God would not allow me to suffer so. As I huddled upon the packed sand, I felt something jabbing at my side, then removed the shard of granite Tzippora had given me. How apt, that a part of YHWH's broken law was causing me pain. I clenched the rock in my palm, testing its sharpness against my decaying skin, and debated using the jagged edge to open my veins.

That night, however, weariness defeated despair. I slept by the spring, and on the third day of my exile I struggled to summon energy enough to sit up. I had not eaten since my banishment, but my appetite had fled with my desire to live.

Gnats of pain buzzed along my arm, swarming in my fist. With an effort I opened my gnarled hand, finger by finger, and saw the shard of granite still against my palm. At some point during the night, my fingers had spasmed around the rock, and now my blood blended with the colors of the crimson stone.

Staring at the broken Law of God, I sat quite still and heard my pride break. The sound was sudden and savage, like the shattering of a pottery jar.

Why had God delivered me from Mizraim? I was an old woman, stubborn and set in my ways. I should have died with my parents, husband, and child in Egypt and been buried in the soft mud of the marshlands. I had no heart for conquest and no patience for new ideas, for I had witnessed too many painful scenes.

My heart was too set, too solid, to change. Since childhood I had been taught to watch out for members of our clan, to safeguard our uniqueness, and I was too old to abandon those lessons now. If God wanted to include foreigners in our covenant, I would not argue, but he could not expect me to understand.

Why hadn't he let me die in Egypt? I had lived ninety years, a full life, and could have died content to know that Moshe and Aharon would lead my people out of Mizraim. Knowing we were no longer slaves . . . surely that was enough. I did not want to learn new rules, face new battles, open my heart to new possibilities. My father had prayed to a quiet God, and I preferred YHWH's silence to his voice.

"God of Avraham, Yitzhak, and Yaakov," I whispered, my voice as flat and dry as the desert. "If you are at all merciful, you will let me die by this spring."

I did not die. Hunger pangs came nudging in among my dreams, waking me on the fourth day. I opened my eyes to see the horizon shimmering with heat-haze beneath a cloudless sky.

I drank from the spring, then stood and hunched forward to search for food among the desert grasses. I found myself wishing I had Tzippora's skills, for as a sand-crosser she knew how to find edible plants. She could have survived months in this rocky savannah, while I would be fortunate if I survived the week of exile YHWH had decreed for me.

I had always been proud of my self-reliance . . . but the jar that had always managed to stand on its own bottom had landed upon sinking sand.

I fell to my knees beside a thick stand of grass interwoven with artemisia, a white wormwood plant with tiny yellow flowers. "Get me out of here, God. And I will never mock the desert woman again."

On the fifth day, I broke my fast on a clutch of quail eggs hidden in a stand of weeds, then washed them down with the water from my small pool. Weary and sore, I huddled on the rocky ledge and stared at my ghastly reflection, wondering if the image I saw in the water was what YHWH saw when he looked at my heart.

Cold, clear reality swept over me in a terrible wave, one so powerful it stole my breath. YHWH knew the thoughts of men; we had seen that truth demonstrated when God predicted Pharaoh's reaction to each plague. So YHWH knew what resided in every human heart, and he knew mine. Over the past two years he had seen my resentment, anger, and jealousy . . . and how, like tzaraat, those emotions had devoured my happiness and peace.

YHWH was both a deliverer and a destroyer—the God who delivered me from Egypt was also determined to destroy the unholy things within me.

I took a deep breath and felt a dozen different emotions collide. Why had I been so hard-hearted against Moshe's wives? I had never yearned for him as a woman yearns for her husband; I only wanted my brother to love me as a sister, to appreciate how I had saved his life as a child. But how could I expect him to feel grateful for an act beyond his memory?

Swallowing the lump that had risen in my throat, I ran my disintegrating fingertips through the water, rippling the pitiful image reflected there. Perhaps I had been jealous that Moshe, who had been adored as a child, would be loved even in his exile from us. I had not known such love. After my husband died, the few men who approached my father only wanted caretakers for their children. I had enjoyed a mere two years of loving marriage, and before that, my parents had always given me more responsibility than affection. Few people knew that my father had married his aunt, an older woman, and Mother had treated me more as a servant than a beloved daughter. Yokheved cherished sons, so she had doted upon Aharon, then upon Moshe.

I watched the shadows lengthen across the plain, the feeling of an unformed thought teasing my heart. Our people would always remember Moshe-the-much-loved for his greatness, but few would be able to recall the private nature he revealed only to family. I had begun to know him in the months he lived in my small house in Goshen, but then we left Egypt and Tzippora arrived to assume her place by his side. At that point, his quiet conversations with me ceased, for he spoke with Tzippora in the Midianite dialect, a language I could neither speak nor understand. Later, after he descended from Sinai, the veil over his face prevented me from even reading his expressions.

My thoughts came to an abrupt halt. I had envied Tzippora because she cut me out of a life worth knowing. I had resented YHWH for the same reason.

And as much as I loved Moshe, I envied him, too, for he had been blessed with two fine sons while my baby died in the Black Land.

The truth dawned, not as a dazzling sunburst upon a horizon, but as a tiny pinhole of light. Slowly it widened, joining a crack of comprehension and a sliver of realization, until I understood: Aharon had joined me in complaining against Moshe, but he had not shared in my spirit of pride. Aharon was malleable; he had always bent to the will of a stronger influence. But I was strong, stubborn, and jealous, and YHWH, who knew my heart, had to show me that I could not rule the camp, that I could not rule Moshe, that I could not even rule my own heart.

"YHWH?" I lifted my eyes in the direction of the camp, which lay beyond my sheltering rock ridge. "I know you can hear me. I don't know if you will accept me now, but to you I confess my willfulness. I have twisted your words to suit my purposes; I have used Moshe's kindness as a weapon against him. What he meant for good, I saw as evil . . . but my eyes, not his, need correction."

I lay down beside the spring, then wrapped my cloak about my shoulders and rested my head upon a flat rock. The sun had disappeared behind a livid purple cloudbank piled deep on the western horizon, and above my head, an already star-thick sky swirled in silence.

On the sixth day a solitary figure approached from the camp. If I had been stronger I might have run away, for no one should approach a woman with tzaraat, but when the figure moved from shadow into sunlight I recognized the ebony skin. Femi, the one I had despised, had come to comfort me.

She stepped over the rocks on the path, her slender figure tall and erect, and did not turn away in revulsion when she drew close enough to see the degradation of my condition. Instead, she gave me a lingering smile more brilliant than the blazing desert sun.

"Shalom, Miryam." She lowered a basket to the rocks by my side. "We wait for you."

Since she did not speak much Hebrew, I did not know how to reply. But as I looked up, stricken dumb with guilt and repentance, she gave me another smile, then turned to retrace her steps.

Strengthened and fortified by the manna cakes and cheese Femi had brought, on the seventh day I knelt by the spring and slowly pulled the veil from my head. Large patches of dried skin broke away in the wind, and when I pressed my hands to my face, my palms came away streaked with blood. Fresh tears stung my eyes, for this should have been the day of my restoration.

As I wept, other shadows fell across the water.

I turned to see Tzippora and Femi standing behind me. Daring the intimacy of touch, together they lifted me to my feet, then removed my filthy garments and urged me into the spring. As I shivered in the water, Tzippora dipped a soft cloth in the pool and gently washed my back, my arms, my belly. Femi scrubbed my garments upon a rock; then, when I came out of the water, she dressed me in a fresh tunic and gestured for me to sit. While she pressed bread into my hand, Tzippora ran a comb through my tangled hair, then covered my head with a clean white veil.

When they had finished, Tzippora held out her hand. Femi had not stopped smiling at me, but Tzippora seemed to wear her calm expression like a mask. We had known each other too long.

She gestured toward the camp. "Come."

"Wait." I walked back to the spring, then lifted the edges of my veil as I peered into the water. Again, my eyes filled with tears when I beheld my image—I had been restored. My face was lined but healthy, my eyes bright, my hands strong and tanned.

Turning, I rested those hands upon Tzippora's slender shoulders and kissed her on both cheeks. "Thank you."

My words fell on the stony ground of her silence. Recoiling from my eager eyes, Tzippora stared at me a moment, then tried on a smile that seemed a size too small.

"I have wronged you," I continued, my voice crusty with age and disuse. "And I must beg your forgiveness."

Uncertainty crept into her expression; then she extended her hand.

With tears of gratitude streaming from my eyes, I placed my hands into those of my sisters-in-law and let them lead me back into the bosom of my people.

ZIPPORAH

Though my years with Moses had resulted in several supernatural encounters, Miriam was the one Yнwн used to bring me to himself. Drawn by his voice, I journeyed over bloodred stones that scalded my feet and seared my soul. In the wilderness of solitude I saw a diseased woman restored by a cleansing touch. And there I was healed by love.

With a malevolent mass growing in my belly, I fully expected to die not long after Moses' marriage to Femi. Then Yнwн struck Miriam with tzaraat, and a few nights later I awakened in the dark and knew what I had to do.

Moses' God did not thunder in my heart, or speak in the silvery sound of the trumpets that called us to congregate near the Tabernacle. His voice was part of the warp and woof of a midnight dream, yet still unmistakable. In a vital voice unlike anything I'd ever heard, he told me to minister to Miriam, to wash her, soothe her, and bring her food and fresh clothing. By doing so, I would heal her . . . and in obeying, I would find healing for myself.

I resisted, of course. Miriam and I shared a mutual antipathy that had grown stronger over time. Her very name meant "bitterness," and I could not believe that she would ever change her disposition toward me.

But YHWH had worked in her heart during her week of exile. And by the time we three women returned to the camp, my belly was as flat as a young girl's. My strength had returned, and so had my joy.

I could have persisted in doubt, ascribing my healing to Athirat or some other god, but what had any other god ever done for me? A benign god had no power to harm . . . but neither had it power to heal. So that day I strode into our tent, pulled the statue of Athirat from my trunk, then dashed it into pieces against a stone.

When in the privacy of our chamber I spoke to Moses of these things, he drew me close and breathed words of thankfulness into my hair. "There is more faith in honest doubt than in all the temples of Egypt, Zipporah. Do not feel guilty because you doubted, but rejoice that you have chosen to believe."

"Still, I feel unworthy." I locked my arms about his waist. "So many of your people act as though doubt is the greatest possible sin—"

"YHWH is not afraid of your questions. He wants you to test him . . . so he may prove himself faithful. The person who fears to doubt, in that fear doubts God."

I rested my head against my husband's chest, comforted and at peace. For though I had decided to embrace a God whose power awed and alarmed me, I could not resist his love.

MIRYAM

I could fill ten scrolls with the rest of my story—or Tzippora could, for she is writing this account for me—but that week in the desert was the pinnacle of my life. In solitude and suffering I learned that YHWH is merciful, but sometimes he must wound us in order to heal us. I also learned that solitude—even exile in the wilderness—is not abandonment. It is an intimate invitation from the One who knows us best and loves us most.

In the wilds at Hazeroth I realized the God for which I yearned bore no resemblance to the God who yearned for me. I had to be broken, but then I discovered a treasure amid the rocks and ravages of the wilderness.

I learned that the only true self-reliance is reliance upon God. Only when we find our worth in him are we free.

I was not the only one to learn this lesson.

After I had been welcomed home, the Shekinah led us to Kadesh-barnea. From that location we sent one man from each tribe to spy out the land of Canaan. Forty days later they returned with incredible tales, samples of sweet figs and pomegranates, and a cluster of grapes so large two men staggered beneath its weight.

All twelve scouts agreed that the land beyond was rich, flowing with milk and honey, and inhabited by warriors as impressive as the bounteous crops. Though Yehoshua and Calev urged the elders to go forward and possess the land, the other spies insisted that such an advance would fail.

Divided by conflicting opinions, the community of Israel wailed throughout the night. By sunrise the weeping had subsided to discontented grumbling against Moshe and Aharon. When I went outside, a group of loudmouthed, fainthearted men stood outside the Tent of Meeting and proclaimed that it would have been better for us to die in Egypt than in the land of promise.

"Why is YHWH bringing us to a place where we will certainly fall by the sword?" one elder asked. "Our wives and our little ones will become plunder for the enemy! Would it not be better for us to return to Egypt?"

When Yehoshua and Calev protested that YHWH had power enough to deliver the land into our hands, members of the outraged community began to pick up stones. As they advanced upon the two faithful scouts, terror snaked down my backbone and coiled in my gut. I glanced uneasily over my shoulder, searching for Moshe, and exhaled in relief when I saw him approaching with Aharon.

YHWH was watching, too. Above the Dwelling, the pillar of cloud began to whirl and spark. Startled, the men dropped their rocks as Moshe and Aharon went into the tent to hear the word of the Lord.

When my brothers returned, their message sent a chill through my spine. "As the glory of YHWH fills all the earth," Moshe said, a firmness in his voice that verged on threatening, "so says YHWH to you now: 'Indeed, all the men who have seen my Glory and the signs I did in Egypt and in the wilderness, and have tested me by not hearkening to my voice— all those who have scorned me will not see the land I swore to give their ancestors! As I live, in this wilderness shall your corpses fall, all of you from the age of twenty and upward, you who have grumbled against me! Except for Calev and Yehoshua, none of you shall enter! Your little ones, whom you said would become plunder—I will let them enter; they shall come to know the land you have spurned. But your corpses shall fall in this wilderness, and your children shall graze animals in the wilds for forty years. Thus shall they pay for your faithlessness, until the last of you lies dead. According to the number of days you scouted out the land, a year for each day, you are to bear your iniquities. I am YHWH, I have spoken!'"

When Moshe relayed these words to our people, they recognized their sin and mourned. The ten faithless spies died in the night, struck by a plague from the hand of YHWH.

I thought these events had settled the matter, but the next morning our men-at-arms rose, strapped on their swords, and went out to attack the Canaanites. Moshe tried to stop them, but they did not listen. Leaving the Ark of the Covenant and Moshe behind, they marched recklessly to the heights of the hill-country. As I feared, the Amalekites and the Canaanites swept down from their cities and crushed our army near Horma.

The following years brought many more unassailable proofs of YHWH's power. I saw the earth open and swallow three foolish men who challenged Moshe's leadership; I watched as fire struck another two hundred fifty who participated in that rebellion. A swift plague struck those who railed against Moshe for YHWH's fiery judgment; before Aharon could make atonement, more than fourteen thousand of our people died.

Yet I witnessed blessed events, too: I saw blossoms sprout from Aharon's staff to prove he was God's choice to minister as chief priest. I ate manna from the hand of God each morning and drank cool waters he provided in the heat of a desert afternoon. I also celebrated the beginnings of new life, for children were born in our tents, and they grew to maturity during our time of waiting.

Because I knew I would not enter the Promised Land, I was surprised to be still living when the fortieth year of our sojourn began. By the time I lay upon my deathbed, I understood that my generation had not been ready for the Promised Land. As people born into bondage, we had been tainted by the influences of Egypt and unknowingly dependent upon the system of slavery. More familiar with a chain of command than liberty, we were unaccustomed to taking individual responsibility for our actions. YHWH yearned to speak directly to us, but we had insisted that Moshe act as our intermediary.

Accustomed to fearing Pharaoh from a distance, we had acknowledged YHWH's dreadful aspect and blinded ourselves to his loving-kindness and compassion. We wanted to see him, but not face-to-face. We wanted to hear from him, but only in faint, distant whispers. We wanted to be his people, but we didn't want him to hold us too tightly.

Yet in forty years of wilderness wandering, God taught us and we taught our little ones. Because most of our people were illiterate, Tzippora and Femi established schools for our children. As the young ones learned to read and copy the Ten Words and the Instructions Moshe had written down, my heart filled with hope for their future.

I will not enter the Promised Land—as a woman of one hundred and twenty-eight, I have been blessed with a longer than average life, two loving brothers, and three sweet sisters-in-law. My eyes have beheld the Lord's power, glory, and salvation, and YHWH has personally drawn me out in order to teach me.

I cannot imagine asking for more.

Sometimes God speaks to us face-to-face, and sometimes he speaks in the shadows. But always he speaks . . . when we are ready to listen.

ZIPPORAH

We buried Miriam at Kadesh, then for thirty days we mourned Moses' sister and Israel's first prophetess. Moses, Femi, and I missed her terribly, for our tent seemed empty without her. I had learned to think of her as a sister and mentor, for in her later years she showed me how to walk with God in quiet, unremarkable humility.

The people had no sooner completed the days of mourning than they began to complain about another water shortage. The children of the wilderness picked up the familiar refrain of their parents, demanding to know why Moses had brought them out of Egypt to a barren place, without seeds and figs, vines and pomegranates . . . like fabled Egypt.

I closed my eyes as I heard their complaints. Why were these people so quick to yearn for the Black Land? Had they forgotten the pain and suffering of slavery?

Moses and Aaron met with YHWH in the Tent of Appointment, then set out to obey his command in order to supply water for the thirsty people. Assembling the community near a large boulder outside the camp, Moses stepped onto a smaller rock. His expression clouded in anger as he lifted his staff. "Now hear, you rebels! Must we bring you water from this rock?"

While the community watched, Moses struck the boulder with his staff—and nothing happened. I caught my breath, for never had YHWH failed my husband, then Moses struck the rock a second time. This time liquid flowed, an abundant stream that would provide more than enough water for the people and their livestock.

But one look at Moses' face convinced me that something had gone very wrong. "YHWH told me to *speak* to the rock," he whispered as he stepped down and took my arm. "And in my anger, I *struck* it."

I repressed the words of consolation that bubbled at my lips, for I could give no comfort in this situation. YHWH had proved himself an exacting God, full of mercy, but unequivocal in his commands. Even for Moses, with whom YHWH had a deep and abiding friendship, God would not tolerate disobedience.

Though Canaan opened before us and the forty years of wandering were drawing to an end, something of the old Midianite melancholy settled upon my husband in those last months.

It was a time of farewells. Soon after God gathered Miriam to her people, YHWH told Moses that Aaron's time had come. The next day Moses, Aaron, and Aaron's son Eleazar climbed Mount Hor. At the summit, Moses removed Aaron's priestly garments and placed them upon Eleazar, symbolically transferring the office of high priest from father to son. Supported by his brother, his son, and his God, Aaron died. Moses and Eleazar covered his body with stones, then returned to camp and announced Aaron's death. We mourned him for thirty days.

The children of Israel endured other tests during that time—battles from anxious kings, temptations from the pagan women of Moab (related, I'm sorry to say, to my own people in Midian), and strife from within the camp. Moses handled these challenges as he had handled the previous trials—by consulting with YHWH and obeying God's commands.

As that final year ended, YHWH told Moses that Joshua would succeed him as Israel's leader. Joshua, however, would not speak to YHWH as Moses had, friend-to-friend, but would instead seek YHWH's will before Eleazar the priest through the Urim and Tummim—two stones the priest would wear over his heart in order to know God's will.

Moses grew restless in his final days, and neither Femi nor I could distract him from the heavy thoughts that pulled him into depths we could not plumb. In quiet afternoons I would often find him sitting outside the tent and staring toward cloud-covered Canaan, the home for which he had desperately yearned. Because I had spent my lifetime loving him, I could see that Moses had never felt at home in Egypt, Midian, or the wilderness . . . but soon his yearning would end. He would not take his rest in Canaan, but in the presence of God.

One afternoon I lifted his hand and pressed it to my cheek. "Moses," I whispered, for his sight and hearing had not diminished with the passing of time, "you have been a faithful servant. No one else could give YHWH more than you have."

"YHWH will ask more of another." There was a note of regret that went beyond nostalgia in his voice, as though he had missed a rare opportunity. "For YHWH has told me that he will raise up for us another prophet from among this people. YHWH will put his words in his mouth, and he will speak whatever YHWH commands. And it shall be that any man who does not hearken to the words this prophet speaks, YHWH himself will require a reckoning from him."

"Is Joshua this prophet?"

Shaking his head, Moses' gaze remained focused on some interior field of vision I could not see. "His time has not yet come. But when he comes, he will lead his flocks like a shepherd. He will do no wrong, and deceive none. Then like a lamb to the slaughter he will be led, and as a sheep is silent before the shearers, he will not open his mouth. From prison and trial they will lead him away to his death, and who among the people will realize he is dying for their sins?"

As tears gleamed beneath the thin veil over his face, Moses continued in an aching, husky voice I scarcely recognized. "But it is God's good plan to crush him and fill him with grief. For when his life is made an offering for sin, he will have a multitude of children, many heirs. When he sees all that his anguish has accomplished, he will be satisfied. And YHWH will honor him as one who is mighty and great, because he exposed himself to death and interceded for sinners."

The silence of the hot afternoon flowed back into the space our conversation had made, filling in the gap as though Moses had never spoken. But he had, and I knew YHWH had given him a glimpse of the future for our people and all mankind.

No more would we have to visit the Dwelling to offer the blood of animals to atone for our sins. The prophet who would come, the prophet like my Moses, would offer his perfect life instead.

Turning, I trailed my fingertips along the edge of the fabric covering Moses' face. "May the daughter of a pagan priest look upon a man who has beheld the future?"

Beneath the veil, I saw the glimmer of a smile. "The wife of Moses may certainly look upon her husband . . . one last time."

As I lifted the veil my tear-blurred eyes did not see the shining face of a man who speaks with God, but the calm visage of one who walks with God and knows his soul is secure.

I kissed my husband, then accompanied him to the base of Mount Nebo, the mountain that faces the land God had promised to the heirs of Abraham, Isaac, and Jacob. Something in the fixed look on Moses' face drew the people after us—women came from the spring, men stopped training for battle, the shepherds left their flocks. Children interrupted their games and found their parents in the crowd assembling before Moses.

Once the people had settled, Moses reminded them of all the duties and instructions YHWH had given. As the priests of Egypt had taught him through song, he taught the congregation of Israel to sing the lessons of the Lord. Then he challenged them with a choice—obedience and life or disobedience and destruction. The children of Israel responded with an enthusiastic cry in support of life and YHWH.

"How blessed you are, O Israel!" he called from the foothills of the mountain. "Who else is like you, a people delivered by YHWH? He is your helping shield, your majestic sword! Your enemies will come cringing before you, and you will trample on their backs!"

Moses' voice simmered with barely checked passion. "So Israel will dwell in security, prosperous Jacob in safety, in a land of grain and wine where the heavens drop down dew."

A jubilant cry echoed back from the mountain as the young warriors' blood surged in eager readiness. While a sea of young men waved their swords, their fathers, women, and children looked upon them with shining faces. In that moment, even the most skeptical of outsiders would have believed that this band of former slaves held the promise of a great nation.

"Indeed," Moses added in a low voice only Joshua and I could hear. "How blessed you are!"

Did he wish in that moment to be young again? Did he regret the frustrated, angry act that had resulted in his banishment from the land of promise? I do not know. I only know that Moses trusted YHWH as a man trusts his best friend, and he was ready to follow the will of God.

I watched silently, pain squeezing my heart, as Moses and Joshua began to climb the mountain. Femi and Elisheba stood with me, supporting my arms as Aaron and Hur had once supported Moses'.

Later, Joshua told me that he and Moses said their farewells at a midpoint; then Moses left him to climb alone to the summit. Years later I heard a priest theorize that in Moses' final moment, God bestowed a single tender kiss upon his lips, gently drawing out his vibrant soul.

I think Moses simply sat down and waited for YHWH to honor his final promise. I also think the man who had yearned to see God's glory was finally granted the opportunity to behold the One who first sought him in a burning thornbush. In that moment, Moses' yearnings were fulfilled.

We mourned Moses for thirty days, then advanced to take Canaan. After a series of battles, Femi and I entered the Promised Land with the children of Israel and settled with my sons and their families in the area allotted to the tribe of Judah. My brother, Hobab, had taken a wife from that tribe, so I looked forward to spending many days with my grandchildren, nieces, and nephews.

From time to time, whenever a hot wind blew from the south and carried in it the faint sting of sand, I sat in my flowering garden and smiled at the memory of how I was convinced Moses was suffering from sunstroke when he told me about meeting YHWH at Sinai.

Would the prophet yet to come meet with the same sort of resistance? I, who should have been my husband's strongest ally, had been among the last to recognize the holy call upon his life. Likewise, the future prophet might face resistance from family and friends.

I had resisted the Israelites . . . but now I could not imagine dwelling with any other people or serving any god but YHWH. I lived with skepticism for many years, yet when I tested the God of Abraham, I found him to be everything his name meant: merciful, long-suffering, faithful, holy, and just.

YHWH is not benign, but a benign god never goads us to our knees or sends us free to conquer our enemies. A benign god never leads us onto holy ground . . . and now I cannot imagine living anywhere else.

Q & A

From my previous experience in writing historical fiction, I know readers are often curious about how much of the story is fact. If you're interested, I've tried to address some of these issues and explain some choices I made.

Q: Why are there so many spelling variations between this book and others?
A: The Egyptian language did not use vowels, and neither did the ancient Hebrew, so for that reason you will find many spelling variants in books about this era. You'll discover variations within this novel because I used the Hebrew spellings of Israelite names in order to singularize Miryam's viewpoint.

Q: Is Merytamon a historical character?
A: Yes. She really did accompany her mother, Nefertari, and her father, Ramesses II, to Abu Simbel. She is pictured on a monument there, offering sacrifices with her royal parents. In 1981 a statue of Ramesses' daughter-queen was discovered at Akhmin, and the inscription

describes Merytamon as "fair of face, beautiful in the palace, the beloved of the Lord of Two Lands."

While history does not definitively record the name of Moses' Egyptian mother, Josephus calls her Thermuthis, Eusebius calls her Merris, and the ancient rabbis identified her as Bithiah (see 1 Chron. 4:18) or Merris.

Q: *How likely is it that the daughter of Pharaoh mentioned in Scripture also became his wife?*

A: Extremely likely. As described in the text, all property and titles descended in the female line, especially in the royal family. Though the marriage laws of Egypt were never formulated and at a quick glance it seems that eldest sons often inherited the throne, those titles were actually granted when the heir apparent married the Great Royal Wife. So a king safeguarded himself from abdication by marrying every heiress, no matter if she was mother, daughter, or sister. If a titled lady was or was likely to be the heiress, she was married to the king. When he died, his successor also married all the heiresses.

Q: *Did the Egyptians really perform brain surgery?*

A: Yes. The procedure described in this novel is called trepanning, and it had been around thousands of years by the time of Egypt's nineteenth dynasty. Often the surgery was successful—at least the patients survived. Out of 400 trepanned ancient skulls examined by one researcher, 250 indicated patient recovery. Interestingly enough, Egyptian physician-priests did not fully appreciate the brain's role in human physiology. During mummification, brain material was always scraped out through the nose and discarded. Consequently, the Egyptians considered the *heart* the seat of emotion, intellect, and will. That's why the Bible does not speak of Pharaoh "changing his mind," but rather "hardening his heart."

Q: *The story of Pharaoh's dream of a suckling lamb—true or not?*

A: The story is not biblical, but contained in rabbinical literature. I adapted it slightly.

Q: *About that Egyptian love poetry and those songs . . .*

A: They're authentic. Translated, of course, but actual ancient Egyptian poetry.

Q: *Doesn't the Bible say Moses stuttered?*

A: Not exactly. In the encounter with YHWH at the burning bush, Moses says he is "not a good speaker" and "clumsy with words" (Ex. 4:10). But he's had no difficulty speaking with God until this point, and Acts 7:22 assures us that "Moses was taught all the wisdom of the Egyptians, and he became mighty in both speech and action." For a man who stuttered, he made some terrifically long and involved speeches during his time of leadership.

I chose to consider the aspect from the practical matter of language. Moses, reared in Egypt, would not have spoken Hebrew, but he would have been schooled in Egyptian and Akkadian, the courtly language of the day. He would not have feared speaking before Pharaoh, but he would have been helpless to address the Hebrews, his own people. Thus, God promises that Aaron will give him all the help he needs.

Incidentally, the story of the toddling Moses and the bowls of gold and coals comes from the Jewish Midrash, and is an attempt to explain why Moses might have stuttered. According to the Midrash, the infant Moses touched the burning coals, then placed his hands in his mouth, burning his lips and tongue.

Q: *If the Midianites were descended from Abraham, why was Zipporah horrified by the thought of infant circumcision? Didn't God establish circumcision as a sign of his covenant with Abraham?*

A: Yes. When Abraham was ninety-nine years old, and his son Ishmael thirteen, both were circumcised as a symbol of their covenant with God. (Isaac had not yet been born, and neither had the sons of Keturah.) God instructed Abraham to circumcise male children on the eighth day after birth, and there's no reason to think Abraham did not obey this command with the sons of Keturah (whom he married—or took to be his concubine—after Sarah died). But the six sons of Keturah were sent away, and did not inherit Abraham's estate or the covenant promise. Therefore we have no reason to believe they incorporated this ritual into their practices. Adolescent circumcision in preparation for marriage, however, was practiced in Egypt and neighboring countries (see Gen. 17:9–14, 26–27; 25:1–6.).

Scripture tells us that the Hebrews continued circumcising their children in Egypt (which could explain how Pharaoh's daughter knew she had found a Hebrew baby), though they stopped the practice during the wilderness sojourn. But before they could cross into the Promised Land, all males who had been born after the Exodus had to be circumcised (see Josh. 5:2–8).

Q: *I've never heard about the night when God attempted to kill Moses! Could that be true?*

A: In what may be the least-mentioned story in Scripture, the Lord confronts Moses and is "about to kill him" until Zipporah circumcises her son (see Ex. 4:24–26). Some say Moses was stricken with an illness and near death; others believe an angel actually attacked Moses. Because the Hebrew passage never contains Moses' name—only a masculine pronoun—we're not certain if it was Moses or his son who stood in danger of losing his life. But Zipporah obviously understood the purpose and intent of the night visit, and she did what she had to do. One note, however: If God had *wanted* to kill Moses, he would have. It's far more likely he wanted Zipporah to understand that his commands were not frivolous.

Q: *In the biblical account of the night visitor (Ex. 4:24–26), my Bible says Zipporah threw her son's foreskin at Moses' feet, yet you have her touching it to the intruder's thighs. Care to explain?*

A: We're not really sure what happened that night. Translators working from the original Hebrew have translated that passage as "touched it to his legs," and it is generally assumed that "legs" is a biblical euphemism for genitals.

Q: *I saw a time line that listed the pharaoh after Merneptah as Amenmesse, but you have placed Seti II in that position.*

A: Seti II, Amenmesse, and Siptah reigned briefly, left few monuments, and ruled in a time of great upheaval (which would have been logical if this were the time of the Exodus). Most time lines have Seti II following Merneptah, and his position being usurped by Amenmesse, another son of Ramesses II. Incidentally, historians believe that Twosre, Seti II's wife (who would have married the next pharaoh) seized the throne during the reign of his successor, probably Amenmesse.

Q: *Did Pharaoh's magicians have real power, or were they only practicing legerdemain?*
A: I believe Pharaoh's priests and magicians turned staves into snakes and water into blood by demonic power. Notice, however, that the magicians could not match the power of YHWH, and they recognized the almighty God when they encountered him.

Q: *Where, exactly, did the Israelites cross the Red Sea?*
A: Many have strong opinions, but no one knows. The Hebrew term *yam suf* is correctly translated "sea of reeds," and the Egyptians did not identify any body of water by that name, though one might expect that reeds surrounded all bodies of fresh water. But in Numbers 21, the Bible uses *yam suf* to refer to the Gulf of Aqaba, which was salt water.

I placed the crossing at the Red Sea, but it could have occurred at the Bitter Lakes. I do know this: The children of Israel crossed safely on dry land, and the subsequent crashing waterfall resulted in water deep enough to drown even the strongest swimmers of the Egyptian army.

Q: *Did the leaders of Israel really eat dinner with God? How is that possible?*
A: Yes, the story is recounted in Exodus 24:9–11. They saw God and ate a meal in his presence. (No word on who did the cooking.)

The Bible clearly teaches that God is a Spirit (John 4:24), and therefore invisible, so if they could see God, he had to be present in a physical manifestation. Physical manifestations of God are known as theophanies, and there are several recorded in the Old Testament.

Christians believe that these are Old Testament appearances of Jesus Christ, who is God revealed in physical flesh.

When Moses spoke to God "face-to-face, as a man speaks to his friend" (Ex. 33:11), I believe he may have been speaking with Jesus, God-in-flesh, who appeared to him—either that, or the phrase is a metaphor to describe the extremely close relationship between the Lord and Moses.

When Moses asked to see God—the entire glory of God the Spirit— he was refused, for no living man can behold things of a spiritual dimension. Yet God did allow Moses to see the parting remnants of his glory (see Ex. 33:18–23).

I don't claim to understand these mysteries. Even Paul, who was caught up to the third heaven and glimpsed visions of Paradise, admitted that such things were beyond his understanding (see 2 Cor. 12:2–4). But, as Paul wrote, even though we can't explain it, God knows.

Q: Did Moses really marry a black woman?

A: Probably—read the story in Numbers 12:1–16. Cush is another name for Ethiopia, and Zipporah was definitely from Midian, though some scholars believe "Cush" and "Midian" are interchangeable. Since Cush and Midian are two very different places on my maps, I think it's far more likely that Moses either took a second wife or married the woman from Cush after Zipporah died. The Bible never tells us that Zipporah died in the wilderness. After reuniting with Moses at Sinai (see Ex. 18:1–6), she is not mentioned in Scripture again.

Q: I thought Pharaoh lost just one son in the final plague.

A: You've seen *The Ten Commandments* one time too many! Scripture says that the "firstborn" died in the tenth plague, and it does not specify "firstborn of the father" or "firstborn of the mother." In fact, the Bible says, "And all the firstborn in the land of Egypt shall die, from the firstborn of Pharaoh that sitteth upon his throne, even unto the firstborn of the maidservant that is behind the mill; and all the firstborn of beasts" (Ex. 11:5). Exodus 4:21-23, in which God said Israel was his firstborn son, therefore he would smite Egypt's firstborn sons, seems to indicate only males were struck on that night, but the Hebrew definitely states that the firstborn of *women* as well as *men* died. So Pharaoh would have lost his firstborn son, as well as the firstborn sons of his wives and concubines.

Q: *How certain are you of this time line?*

A: Only a writer far more audacious than I would dare be emphatic about the timing of Moses' experiences in Egypt. Some theologians and scholars assert that Moses left Egypt before Egypt's nineteenth dynasty; others believe the Exodus occurred under the reign of Ramesses the Great. But Ramesses' mummy has been found, and it reveals that he died at age ninety-six of natural causes. (He was also bent and crippled in his latter years.) So it's highly unlikely he gave chase to the children of Israel and drowned in the Red Sea (see Ps. 136:15).

Because a novel must be set in a certain time and place, I studied many books and devised what I believe is a workable time table. Agree with me or not, but the following were among my guiding facts:

History tells us that Seti II reigned during a "troubled time." This, of course, could be said of many pharaohs of the New Kingdom, but Seti II had a young son, Seti-Merneptah, who died mysteriously.

Merneptah is famous for subduing a revolt in Palestine, and upon the stele commemorating this event we find the only mention of Israel in ancient Egyptian inscriptions. The quote: "Israel is laid waste and has no seed." To all appearances, Merneptah is boasting of having defeated Israel in Palestine. But given the fact that battlefield stele were often exaggerated to heap undeserved glory on a victorious king, might this be a reference to the dead babies of his father's reign? Given the vague language of the stele, in which he claims to have subdued national groups all over the map, it's certainly possible.

Biblical accounts indicate that Moses' audiences with Pharaoh took place near Goshen. Not until the nineteenth dynasty, when the Ramessids came to power, did Egyptian kings establish a northern capital within easy traveling distance of Goshen. (The ancient city of Avaris had been their clan home.) Earlier kings ruled from Thebes or

Memphis (except, of course, for Akhenaton's brief reign from el-Amarna). As further proof, Exodus 1:11 tells us that the Hebrews "built for Pharaoh treasure cities, Pithom and Ramesses." The latter city was the ancient Hyksos capital of Avaris, rebuilt and again made the capital by Seti I and Ramesses II, Seti's son. This rebuilding did not take place before the nineteenth dynasty.

In closing, let me say that this novel was difficult to write because I always work hard not to purposefully contradict the historical record. The trouble with ancient Egypt, however, is that interpretations of the ancient records don't always agree with one another.

In writing *The Shadow Women,* however, I did have a plumb line—the Bible. When experts bickered and dickered over the meanings and implications of ancient texts, I chose to follow the words of the first man in Israel's history to be skilled in the arts of reading, writing, poetry, and song.

Moses himself was my best and most reliable guide.

GLOSSARY

barque: sacred ceremonial boats used in ancient Egyptian religious ceremonies. Some were miniature, others full-sized and fully capable of transporting the idol and the pharaoh on the river.

catafalque: a decorated platform on which the coffin of a distinguished corpse lies before burial or during transport to the tomb.

felucca: a small boat with a triangular sail, still used to sail the river Nile.

Horus: the Greek name for the Egyptian Hor, one of the oldest gods and a solar deity, considered a manifestation of the living pharaoh. When the priests chant, "Make Horus green," they are, in effect, asking the gods to make Pharaoh prosper. When Pharaoh prospered, they believed, the land would prosper and become fertile and green.

ma'at: the spiritual ideal of ancient Egyptians. Ma'at was originally an ancient Egyptian goddess, but in time the term came to represent the ideals against which the goddess weighed the hearts and souls of the deceased in the Judgment Hall. Ma'at signified cosmic harmony, justice, order, and peace (Bunson, p. 152).

natron: a mixture of sodium bicarbonate and sodium carbonate—a sodium salt. Its chief property is the ability to absorb moisture, and it is slightly antiseptic. The ancient Egyptians used natron for many purposes, and it was the chief ingredient used in the embalming process (Bunson, p. 182).

Osiris: one of the oldest gods in ancient Egypt. The dead pharaohs of Egypt were considered embodiments of Osiris, having been equated with Horus, Osiris' son, while on the throne (Bunson, p. 197).

Re: the sun god, who was also known as Khepri (at dawn), Re (at noon), and Atum at night. He was also identified with Horus and often called Re-Horus, or the horizon-dweller. During the New Kingdom and the time of Ramesses II, Re and Amon were united to become Amon-Re, the most powerful deity in Egypt.

shaduf: a device consisting of a suspended pivoting pole with a bucket on one end and a weight on the other. With it workers lifted water from the Nile, swung it around, and dropped the water into trenches that irrigated the fields.

uraeus: the cobra worn on crowns and regal headdresses. The cobra represented the goddess Wadjet, the protector of Lower Egypt.

RESOURCES

Note: Though all of these books were useful, they don't necessarily agree with each other, nor do I support every idea held by the authors. Still, they provided background materials that were useful in drawing my conclusions.

Bianchi, Dr. Robert S. *Splendors of Ancient Egypt.* London: Booth-Clibborn Editions, 1996.

Brier, Bob, Ph.D. *The Murder of Tutankhamen.* New York: G.P. Putnam's Sons, 1998.

Buchanan, Mark. *Your God Is Too Safe.* Sisters, OR: Multnomah, 2001.

Budge, E. A. Wallis. *Egyptian Religion.* New York: Barnes & Noble Books, 1994.

———*The Mummy: A History of the Extraordinary Practices of Ancient Egypt.* New York: Wings Books, 1989.

Bunson, Margaret. *The Encyclopedia of Ancient Egypt.* New York: Facts on File, 1991.

Cahill, Thomas. *The Gifts of the Jews.* New York: Doubleday, 1998.

Coleman, William. *Today's Handbook of Bible Times and Customs.* Minneapolis, MN: Bethany House Publishers, 1984.

Comay, Joan. *Who's Who in the Old Testament.* Nashville, TN: Abingdon Press, 1971.

Coogan, Michael D., ed. *The Oxford History of the Biblical World.* New York: Oxford University Press, 1998.

David, Rosalie and Rick Archbold. *Conversations with Mummies.* New York: William Morrow, 2000.

Davis, J. D. *Illustrated Davis Dictionary of the Bible.* Nashville, TN: Royal Publishers, Inc., 1973.

Editors of Time-Life Books. *The Age of God-Kings.* Alexandria, VA: Time-Life Books, 1987.

———. *Egypt: Land of the Pharaohs.* Alexandria, VA: Time-Life Books, 1992.

———. *Ramesses II: Magnificence on the Nile.* Alexandria, VA: Time-Life Books, 1993.

———. *What Life Was Like on the Banks of the Nile.* Alexandria, VA: Time-Life Books, 1997.

Feiler, Bruce. *Walking the Bible: A Journey by Land Through the Five Books of Moses.* New York: William Morrow, 2001.

Fleg, Edmond. *The Life of Moses.* Pasadena, CA: Hope Publishing House, 1995.

Fox, Everett. *The Five Books of Moses.* New York: Schocken Books, 1995.

Grower, Ralph. *The New Manners and Customs of Bible Times.* Chicago: Moody Press, 1987.

Halley, Henry. *Halley's Bible Handbook.* Grand Rapids, MI: Zondervan Publishing House, 1927.

Hart, George. *Ancient Egypt.* New York: Alfred A. Knopf, 1990.

James, T.G.H.. *Ancient Egypt: The Land and Its Legacy.* Austin, TX: University of Texas Press, 1988.

Jenkins, Simon. *Nelson's 3-D Bible Mapbook.* Nashville, TN: Thomas Nelson Publishers, 1995.

Kaiser, Walter C., Peter H. Davids, F. F. Bruce, and Manfred T. Brauch. *Hard Sayings of the Bible.* Downers Grove, IL: InterVarsity Press, 1996.

Kaster, Joseph. *The Wisdom of Ancient Egypt.* New York: Barnes & Noble, 1993.

Kirsch, Jonathan. *The Harlot by the Side of the Road.* New York: Ballantine Books, 1997.

———. *Moses: A Life.* New York: Ballantine Books, 1998.

Manniche, Lise. *An Ancient Egyptian Herbal.* Austin, TX: University of Texas Press, 1989.

———. *Music and Musicians in Ancient Egypt.* London: British Museum Press, 1991.

Metzger, Bruce M., and Michael D. Coogan, eds. *The Oxford Companion to the Bible.* New York: Oxford University Press, 1993.

Menu, Bernadette. *Ramesses II, Greatest of the Pharaohs.* New York: Harry N. Abrams, Inc., 1998.

Montet, Pierre. *Everyday Life in Egypt in the Days of Ramesses the Great.* Philadelphia: University of Pennsylvania Press, 1981.

Murray, Margaret. *The Splendour That Was Egypt.* London: Sidgwick and Jackson, 1949.

Osman, Ahmed. *Stranger in the Valley of the Kings.* San Francisco, Harper & Row, 1987.

Potok, Chaim. *Wanderings: Chaim Potok's History of the Jews.* New York: Fawcett Crest, 1978.

Pritchard, James, ed. *HarperCollins Atlas of the Bible.* London: HarperCollins Publishers, 1997.

Romer, John. *Valley of the Kings.* New York: Henry Holt and Company, 1981.

Schaff, Philip. *Through Bible Lands.* New York: Arno Press, 1977.

Schulz, Regine and Matthias Seidel, eds. *Egypt: The World of the Pharaohs.* Cologne, Germany: Konemann, 1998.

Spencer, A. J. *Death in Ancient Egypt.* New York: Penguin Books, 1991.

Steindorff, George, and Keith C. Seele. *When Egypt Ruled the East.* Chicago: University of Chicago Press, 1957.

Swindoll, Charles R. *Moses.* Nashville, TN: Word Publishing, 1999.

Taylor, William M. *Moses, the Law-Giver.* Grand Rapids, MI: Baker Book House, 1961.

Unstead, F. J., editor. *See Inside an Egyptian Town*. London: Barnes and Noble, 1986.

Van Biema, David. *"In Search of Moses," Time Magazine*, December 14, 1998, 81–92.

Vercoutter, Jean. *The Search for Ancient Egypt*. New York: Harry N. Abrams, 1992.

Wilkinso␣␣␣␣␣␣␣␣␣␣␣␣␣␣␣␣␣␣␣␣␣␣␣␣␣␣␣␣mes and
Huds␣

Willmir␣␣␣␣␣␣␣␣␣␣␣␣␣␣␣␣␣␣␣␣␣␣␣␣␣ton, IL:
Tynd␣